Romantic Suspense

Danger. Passion. Drama.

Guarding His Secret Son
Laura Scott

Hunted By A Killer
Laurie Winter

MILLS & BOON

GUARDING HIS SECRET SON
© 2024 by Laura Iding
Philippine Copyright 2024
Australian Copyright 2024
New Zealand Copyright 2024

First Published 2023
First Australian Paperback Edition 2023
ISBN 978 1 038 91749 2

HUNTED BY A KILLER
© 2024 by Laurie Hoffman
Philippine Copyright 2024
Australian Copyright 2024
New Zealand Copyright 2024

First Published 2024
First Australian Paperback Edition 2024
ISBN 978 1 038 91749 2

MIX
Paper | Supporting
responsible forestry
FSC® C001695

Published by
Harlequin Mills & Boon
An imprint of Harlequin Enterprises (Australia) Pty Limited
(ABN 47 001 180 918), a subsidiary of HarperCollins
Publishers Australia Pty Limited
(ABN 36 009 913 517)
Level 19, 201 Elizabeth Street
SYDNEY NSW 2000 AUSTRALIA

Cover art used by arrangement with Harlequin Books S.A.. All rights reserved.

Printed and bound in Australia by McPherson's Printing Group

Guarding His Secret Son

Laura Scott

MILLS & BOON

Laura Scott has always loved romance and read faith-based books by Grace Livingston Hill in her teenage years. She's thrilled to have been given the opportunity to retire from thirty-eight years of nursing to become a full-time author. Laura has published over thirty books for Love Inspired Suspense. She has two adult children and lives in Milwaukee, Wisconsin, with her husband of thirty-five years. Please visit Laura at laurascottbooks.com, as she loves to hear from her readers.

But Jesus called them unto him, and said, Suffer
little children to come unto me, and forbid them not:
for of such is the kingdom of God. Verily I say unto
you, Whosoever shall not receive the kingdom of
God as a little child shall in no wise enter therein.
—*Luke* 18:16–17

DEDICATION

This book is dedicated to all the
wonderful midwives taking care of pregnant mums.
You are a blessing to so many.

Chapter One

"Please save my baby!"

Midwife Liz Templeton was doing her best to do just that. This stranger, Rebecca, had shown up at her clinic in Liberty, Wisconsin, with a bullet lodged in her chest and in full-blown labor. Liz had placed a pressure dressing over the bullet wound before turning her attention to the baby.

"Easy now, I see this little guy's head." Liz kept her tone reassuring. She'd had many unusual cases arrive on her doorstep, but a pregnant woman in labor suffering a gunshot wound was a first. "With the next contraction, you need to push."

"Okay." Rebecca panted, a layer of sweat over her brow. Her face was so pale because of the pain and the blood loss from her injury.

"It would be better if I could call 911," Liz repeated for the second time.

"No! Please don't. He'll find and kill me. Please!"

There wasn't time to ask questions about who "he" was and why he'd shot her. Not when the baby's birth was imminent.

"Push," Liz said. "Come on, Rebecca, push!"

Her wounded patient did her best, bearing down with the contraction. But Rebecca was weak, and the baby's head didn't breach the birth canal.

"Harder! Push harder!" Liz ordered.

With a low groan, Rebecca tried again, putting all her effort into the push. This time, Liz was able to gently guide the baby's head toward her. She quickly cleared the infant's nose and mouth with a bulb suction and towel.

"Good job. He's almost here. Come on, Rebecca, you can do it!"

Tears streaked down Rebecca's cheeks as she panted, waiting for the next contraction. Then she gave another push, and the baby was born.

"You did it!" Liz wrapped the baby in the towel, then clamped the umbilical cord. The little guy cried, showing off a nice set of lungs. Once she'd snipped the cord, she brought the crying baby up to Rebecca. "Isn't he beautiful? Meet your son."

"Yes. Micah. Beaut…" Rebecca's eyes drifted shut.

"Rebecca?" Panic seized Liz by the throat. She turned and placed the wrapped newborn in the warmer, then rushed to her patient. "Look at me, Rebecca. Open your eyes!"

The injured woman opened them just enough to look at her. "Take Micah to Deputy Garrett Nichols." Rebecca's tone was barely more than a whisper. "Tell him—keep his son safe."

Liz didn't understand. She peeked beneath the gauze over Rebecca's chest wound, horrified to see the right side of her chest blowing up like a balloon. The tension pneumothorax must have happened when she'd pushed to deliver the baby. "Who shot you, Rebecca. Garrett?"

"No!" Rebecca's eyes shot open, meeting her gaze. "Promise me. Take Micah to Garrett! He'll keep Micah safe…"

"I will." Ignoring the crying baby, Liz took a large needle and quickly inserted it between the fourth and fifth ribs along the right side of Rebecca's chest. If she didn't relieve the tension of the pneumothorax, the pressure would eventually stop Rebecca's heart. A whooshing sound indicated the air had been released, but then blood began pouring out of the opening.

No! Too much blood! Liz was losing her!

She needed to call 911. Unfortunately, her clinic was near the southernmost tip of the Oneida Native American reservation in the middle of nowhere. The closest hospital was eighteen miles away. She quickly made the call, requesting an ambulance, then turned toward the baby.

"Hey, Micah, it's okay." She gathered the baby close, knowing how important skin-to-skin contact was. She couldn't hold him for long, though, and quickly wrapped him in a soft blanket and set him in the warmer. She hurried back to her patient.

"Come on, Rebecca, stay with me." Liz attempted to start an IV, but her veins were already collapsed from blood loss. Desperate, she inserted an intraosseous needle to inject fluids directly into Rebecca's femur. It seemed barbaric, but it was her patient's only chance.

Liz opened the clamp so that the fluids ran wide open. Whispering words of comfort to the baby, she checked Rebecca's vital signs. The new mom's skin was pale and cold. Too cold.

Her muscles went slack beneath Liz's fingers; her head lolled to the side.

No, no, no! Liz checked for a pulse.

Nothing.

She pulled a stool over and jumped up to start CPR. She placed her hands on Rebecca's chest and began giving compressions. That's when she noticed that with every push downward, the pool of blood on the floor grew larger. The bullet must have nicked an artery. After one round of compressions, she felt for a pulse.

Still nothing.

Stifling a sob, she did another round, then another. But then she stepped off the stool. It was no use. CPR wouldn't help if there wasn't blood to circulate through Rebecca's body. She didn't have the luxury of packed red blood cells available in the clinic, and that was the only thing that would save Rebecca now. That, and surgery to repair the torn artery.

Bowing her head to offer a quick prayer, she mentally kicked herself for not calling 911 sooner. She should have anticipated the extensive internal bleeding. Her expertise was childbirth, not traumatic gunshot wounds! But the baby had already been crowning, so that was where she'd focused her efforts.

Now it was too late.

But not for Micah. Rebecca had been shot. Why, Liz had no idea. She hurried back to the warmer. She quickly checked Micah's height and weight, satisfied to note he was seven pounds, five ounces. She took a moment to wash Rebecca's blood from her hands, then used a soft washcloth to bathe Micah. After dressing him in a diaper and a blue onesie, she wrapped him in a clean blanket and carried him with her to her small living area adjacent to the clinic.

Thankfully, she kept a stock of supplies for her low-income mothers, including diapers, infant formula and bottles. Moving through the kitchen, she packed the items in a large diaper bag. As an afterthought, she tossed in the small stuffed bunny she'd bought all those years ago for her daughter. Then she crossed over to the computer she used for her notes. The reservation had internet access, although it wasn't great.

Shifting Micah to one arm, she single-handedly typed *Deputy Garrett Nichols* into the search engine. She got an instant hit. Chief Deputy Garrett Nichols worked for the Green Lake County Sheriff's Department. Discovering he was a cop was reassuring.

Green Lake was sixty miles from her clinic. What had Rebecca been doing here near the rez? Why hadn't she gone to Green Lake, if that's where Micah's father was? Liz hesitated, gazing down at Micah. He'd stopped crying now, having fallen asleep against her. Was she really going to do this? Normal protocol would be to call the Department of Health and Human Services, who would put the baby in foster care.

But Garrett Nichols was the baby's father. He deserved a chance to see his son. Leaving Rebecca behind didn't sit well. Maybe she should wait for the ambulance to arrive. Then she remembered the bullet in Rebecca's chest. No, she couldn't take the risk. If there was any remote possibility the baby was in danger, the best thing she could do was take him to Deputy Garrett Nichols, as his mother had asked—no, had *begged*.

Besides, dropping a baby off at a police station was allowed and protected under the Safe Haven Act. That might still be a stretch, though, because Liz wasn't Micah's mother.

For a moment, the memory of her stillborn daughter flashed in her mind. The ache was always there, a constant reminder of what she'd lost.

Willow was gone, but Micah needed her now.

She would not fail this innocent baby the way she'd failed her own daughter.

Garrett looked up from his desk when Sheriff Liam Harland rapped on the door. His boss's expression was full of concern. "Go home, Garrett."

"I will." He tried to smile, but it wasn't easy. The last ten months had been tough. The day he'd lost a fellow officer in a drug bust, he'd also lost his zest for life.

And his faith.

"I mean it, Garrett." Liam's scowl deepened. "You're not to blame for Jason's death."

He was, but Liam was too nice to say it. Avoiding the topic, Garrett gestured at the computer. "I'm almost finished. I'll be out of here soon."

Liam sighed, obviously not believing him. "If I hear that you slept here in the office again, I'm going to put you on a leave of absence. Understand?"

He winced and nodded. "Yeah, sure. I hear you."

Mumbling something about a bullheaded cop, Liam turned away. Garrett waited until he heard the door of the sheriff's department headquarters close before dropping his head in his hands.

The last thing he wanted was a leave of absence. Yet he also knew he was walking a very fine line. If he didn't pull himself together soon, he'd be no good to the other deputies they had working for them.

Their newest deputies on the team, Wyatt and Abby Kane, were doing great. As soon as they hired a replacement for Jason—no easy task these days, as rural cops were hard to find—he planned to submit his resignation.

Liam would try to talk him out of it, but he'd insist. The team would be better off without him. Wyatt had been an FBI agent and would be a great replacement as chief deputy. Besides, Garrett wasn't sure he had it in him to continue his career. If only he'd gotten to the scene soon enough to save Jason…

But he hadn't. The young officer, barely twenty-five years old, had died. Because he'd been too late.

Stop it, he told himself sternly. They were still short-staffed. That meant he had a job to do.

A loud banging on the front door made him frown. He rose from his desk and strode across the open desk area. Since it was summer, their peak season, he had all deputies out on patrol, leaving him to man the headquarters alone.

His eyebrows levered up in surprise when he saw a pretty woman with long, straight dark hair, pounding on the door. She wore blood-stained scrubs, which puzzled him. Then his gaze dropped to the baby carrier on the ground beside her.

"Deputy Nichols!" She pounded again. "I need to speak to Chief Deputy Garrett Nichols!"

Garrett unlocked and opened the door. He might have expected to see Rebecca, if not for the fact that she'd told him to leave her alone. Honoring her wishes, he'd stopped calling, but he had wondered if she'd just show up out of the blue again, the way she had ten months ago.

The woman standing there was a complete stranger. Someone he'd never seen before in his life.

"I'm Deputy Nichols." He gave her a stern look. "Who are you? Is there danger? Do you need police protection?"

"Oh, I'm so glad it's you!" The dark-haired woman turned and picked up the baby carrier.

"May I come inside? I— Yes, need police protection, but this may take a while to explain."

He had no idea what she was talking about, but he opened the door in a silent invitation. She hurried through, just as the baby began to wail.

"Oh, dear, Micah may need to be fed." She looked a bit flustered. "Is there a place we can talk while I give him a bottle?"

"My office." He'd heard of police departments finding babies on their doorstep, but in his ten-year tenure here in Green Lake, that had never happened. The way this woman attended to the baby, though, didn't give him the impression this was a Safe Haven situation.

"Thanks." The dark-haired woman set the baby carrier on his desk, then rummaged through the diaper bag. "I need this filled with warm water. Not too hot," she cautioned. "And only to the line, okay? The formula is in there, so you need to shake it to make sure it dissolves."

"Who are you?" he asked again, taking the bottle from her fingers.

"Liz Templeton." She glanced down at her bloodstained scrubs with a grimace. "Sorry to show up like this. I'm a midwife for the Oneida Native American reservation."

That explained her Native American looks. Straight black hair and light brown skin, but her bright green eyes indicated she had non–Native American blood in her veins, too.

Curious about why she was here, he took the bottle and filled it with warm water, knowing a bit about the process from watching Liam and Shanna take care of their daughter, Ciara.

When he returned to the office, Liz had the baby in her arms. "Thanks so much." She plucked the bottle from his fingers and gave it to the baby.

Watching her, he propped his hip on the edge of his desk, trying to put the puzzle pieces together. Had she delivered this baby? If so, where was the infant's mother? "Why are you here?"

"To find you." She looked up at him, her gaze intense. "Sorry, I should start at the beginning. Do you know a woman named Rebecca?"

Hearing the name of the woman he'd once loved was a sucker punch to the gut. "Yes."

"She gave birth to Micah in my clinic, then told me to bring him to you. His father. Because you would keep him safe."

Micah? *His* child? The realization hit him

like a ton of bricks. He'd spent the night of Jason's death with Rebecca, allowing their close friendship to go too far. He'd always cared for her, even loved her, but when he'd awoken the next day, she was gone. He'd called, and she assured him that as much as she cared for him, too, she didn't love him the way he deserved to be loved. He'd known then, she'd only come to stay in Green Lake as a temporary refuge. Not a permanent move. Especially when she informed him that she was heading back to Chicago, and that he needed to let her go to live his own life.

They'd always been close friends, having met as kids during summer vacations in Green Lake. He'd loved her but had known their relationship wouldn't go anywhere. Which only made his actions the night he'd lost Jason more despicable. He shouldn't have taken advantage of Rebecca's sweetness, her caring. And what he'd thought was her love.

But he had. And now?

"Are you saying Micah is mine?" He pushed the words through his tight throat. This couldn't be happening. Why hadn't Rebecca called him? Warned him? Told him they were going to have a child? "Where is Rebecca now? Why do you have the baby?"

Liz's expression filled with compassion. "I'm sorry, Deputy, but Rebecca died of a bullet wound to the chest minutes after I delivered Micah. I tried to save her, but she lost too much blood, and I don't store blood products in my clinic."

A bullet wound to the chest? He shook his head, grappling with the news. "I don't understand. Who shot her?"

"I don't know." Liz glanced back down at the baby in her arms. "She couldn't tell me much, other than to bring the baby to you so you would keep him safe."

"'Safe'? From the perp who shot her?"

"I assume so." Liz took the bottle from the baby's mouth and turned to rest him upright on her shoulder. She smoothed her hand in circles along the baby's back. "I was hoping you would know more."

"I don't." None of it made any sense. Rebecca knew he was a deputy; why wouldn't she have come to him sooner if she was in danger? He began to doubt this woman's story. "Why would Rebecca show up at your clinic with a gunshot wound?"

"Good question." She turned the baby back in her arms, gazing down at his sleeping face for a long moment before she looked up at him. "I wish I could tell you more, but honestly, her arrival was a complete shock. Most of my clients are poor, either from the reservation or referred to me because of the free services I provide. Rebecca was dressed in top-notch maternity clothes. She'd had her hair done and beautifully painted nails. Not like my usual clientele."

Yeah, that sounded like Rebecca.

"I've never had a pregnant woman suffering a gunshot wound show up like that," Liz continued. "But on my way here, I saw a Cadillac along the side of the road, about two miles from my clinic. I didn't stop to investigate because I was too scared to risk placing Micah in harm's way."

"We'll go there now." He stood. "I need you to show me the way."

"My clinic is sixty miles from here," she warned. "Although I do have to go home that way, I guess." She rose to her feet and offered the baby. "Don't you want to hold your son?"

His son. Garrett felt as if he'd been jettisoned into outer space. Was he dreaming? As Liz gently pressed the baby into his arms, he knew he wasn't.

"Micah," he whispered, his heart squeezing

in his chest. Ten minutes ago, he hadn't known about his son.

Now he found himself wondering what he was going to do with a new baby. This— He wasn't prepared for this!

"I can give you some of my supplies until you can shop for your own things," Liz said, as if reading his mind.

Her offer was another punch to the gut. He didn't have anything at his place for taking care of a baby. And he didn't have a clue what that all entailed.

"Please take him." He couldn't hide the desperation in his tone as he placed Micah back in her arms. "Let's go. I need to see Rebecca's car. There must be some explanation for what happened. A clue of some sort, to figure out what she meant by keeping Micah safe."

"Okay." She gave him an odd look but didn't argue. He took a moment to shut down his computer, then waited for her to secure Micah in his infant car seat. He noticed a small white stuffed bunny was tucked next to the baby. When she finished, she slung the diaper bag over her shoulder.

When he reached for the handle of the baby

carrier, she smiled in approval. He didn't have the heart to tell her that he'd only done that because he knew how heavy it was.

Not because Micah was his son.

His. Son.

There was no reason to believe Liz was lying to him. Why would she? But the entire situation sounded too bizarre to be real.

He was having trouble wrapping his head around the fact that the night Rebecca had comforted him after Jason's death had resulted in her giving birth to a son. *His* son. Without her telling him. That was the part he really struggled with.

"Are you sure Rebecca said the baby was mine?" He held the door open for Liz, then took a moment to lock it behind him. "Maybe she just wanted me to keep him safe."

"I'm positive she said you were Micah's father." There was no hesitation in her statement.

"What else did she say?" He led the way around the building to the parking lot. The hour was past eight, and despite the warm July breeze, the sun had dropped below the horizon.

"She begged me not to call 911 because 'he' would find her and kill her." Liz's voice dropped to a whisper. "She was deathly afraid, Deputy Nichols. And the baby was already crowning, so I placed a pressure dressing over the gunshot wound, then quickly attended to the delivery. But I underestimated how much damage the bullet had caused. There was far too much bleeding into her chest cavity." Her stricken gaze met his. "I— It was horrible. I'm so sorry. Maybe if I had called 911 right away, she'd still be alive."

"I don't blame you, Liz." He could only imagine what she'd been through. "I'm sure that was a very difficult situation to be in."

"One of the worst," she admitted softly.

They had crossed the parking lot and were heading toward a small blue sedan he assumed was Liz's car when the sound of a shoe scraping along the asphalt reached his ears.

Garrett whirled around, reaching for his gun. Holding on to the baby's carrier slowed him down, and he was a second too late.

The crack of gunfire echoed through the night.

"Down! Get down!" He awkwardly held the carrier behind his back with one hand as he aimed and fired toward the shadow of a man crouched near one of the parked cars.

He missed, the bullet pinging off the side of the vehicle. Garrett hoped the gunfire would bring backup, but the parking lot remained quiet.

Too quiet.

Had the gunman left? No, he didn't think so.

Another crack of gunfire confirmed his suspicion. Garrett placed himself between Liz and Micah as he returned fire.

The sound of running footsteps made him think backup had arrived. Then he saw the shadow of a man disappearing down the street. Every cell in his body wanted to give chase, but he didn't dare leave Liz and Micah unprotected.

Apparently, Rebecca was right: Micah was in danger.

Too bad he had no idea who had come after his son.

Chapter Two

Crouched behind Garrett, Liz had bent over Micah's carrier, protecting the baby with her body. Her heart thundered in her chest as gunfire reverberated around them.

What in the world was going on? How had the gunman who'd shot Rebecca known to come here, to Green Lake?

And why would anyone want to hurt an innocent baby?

"We're getting into my SUV, understand?" Garrett's voice was clipped.

She tentatively lifted her head to look around. "Is he gone?"

"I think so." Garrett's grave expression could have been carved from stone. "I'll need you to carry the baby so I can protect us if needed."

The baby? Not *his son*? She frowned but did as he asked since she appreciated the fact that

he'd needed his hands free. Seeing him holding the gun made her shiver.

Someone had shot at them! Being square in
the middle of gunfire was difficult to comprehend. She straightened and picked up the carrier. Garrett urged her to step in front of him,
guiding her to a black SUV not far from her
sedan.

He unlocked the vehicle, then stood behind
her as she secured the baby carrier, placing it in
the car seat so the baby was facing backward.
Then she set the diaper bag on the floor.

Garrett escorted her to the passenger seat,
again protecting her with his body. Only once
she was settled did he jog around to slide behind
the wheel. Moments later, he quickly drove out
of the parking lot.

"Where are we going?" She didn't like leaving her sedan behind. "I need my car to get
back to my clinic. I also use my vehicle to visit
patients on the rez." A horrible thought struck
her. "Deputy Nichols? Do you think the gunman followed me here to Green Lake?"

"Call me Garrett." He grimaced. "The perp
may have followed you, but I don't understand why he would wait to come after you
and Micah outside our headquarters. Shooting

at us near a police station wasn't smart. Especially when he could have taken you both out on some section of deserted highway, where you wouldn't be easily found."

A chill snaked down her spine. "Thanks for that image."

"Sorry." He patted her hand. "I didn't mean to sound callous, but I do think it's odd the gunman attempted to shoot you here, right next to the sheriff's department headquarters. And his aim was bad, too. The bullet only missed me by inches but didn't come anywhere close to you or Micah."

She frowned, not liking the idea of either of them being a target. Would the gunman kill her just because she'd delivered Micah? That didn't seem logical. Then again, nothing about this situation made sense. "Okay, so where are we going?"

"My place." He shot her a sideways glance. "Don't worry, you and the baby will be safe there."

Rubbing her temple, she strove to remain calm. Being targeted by gunfire had been terrifying. Garrett's place would be safe, but she couldn't just stay in Green Lake indefinitely. She had patients to care for.

Granted, not that many. The rez population had dwindled over the years, especially women of childbearing age. Young people didn't stay on the reservation; they went out to make their way in the world. Still, she was determined to offer her services to pregnant women in need. Pregnant women of any background—Native American, African American, Hispanic or Caucasian. She welcomed them all.

Thankfully, word of mouth—especially from the Green Bay and Appleton areas—had helped bring women to her clinic. Each time she assisted in bringing a new child into the world, her burden felt a little lighter.

Her clinic was partially subsidized by the government, and by the reservation, but she barely made enough money to pay her meager bills. Liz didn't mind. Tending to pregnant women was her calling. And it helped her deal with her own loss.

She was so encompassed with her thoughts that she hadn't realized Garrett had pulled into the driveway of a log home, one that blended nicely against a wooded backdrop. Glancing back at the baby, she wondered if Garrett planned to keep and raise his son. Or if the little boy would end up in foster care.

It bothered her to think Garrett wouldn't keep Micah. She pushed out of the passenger seat, then went around to unbuckle the baby carrier.

Garrett stood, sweeping his gaze around the area as she shouldered the diaper bag and then lifted the carrier out of the car. After a moment's hesitation, he took the heavy carrier from her hand.

The baby continued to sleep as he unlocked the door and pushed it open. Liz stepped over the threshold, greeted by the welcome scent of pine cleaner. The open-concept kitchen and living room were spotlessly clean. He was either a neat freak or had a cleaning service.

After setting the baby carrier on the kitchen table, he turned to look at her. "I have two guest rooms, but no crib or anything like that." He shifted from one foot to the other. "I wasn't expecting this. Rebecca never told me she was pregnant."

"I'm sorry to hear that." She couldn't help but wonder if Rebecca's secret had resulted in her being shot. "Micah can sleep in the carrier for now, although a cradle would be better." She sighed and crossed her arms over her chest. It was late, going on nine o'clock. Getting back to

Liberty would take an hour. "We're not going to be here that long, are we?"

"Depends on what the deputies find." He stared down at the sleeping baby for a long moment, then pulled out his cell phone. "Excuse me while I make a few calls. Please make yourself at home."

At home? She found the log cabin beautiful and cozy, but she wasn't comfortable in this level of luxury.

A cot and a small kitchen attached to the clinic was her home.

Micah woke up and began to cry, interrupting her thoughts. Garrett moved farther away from the baby while still on the phone. Liz quickly unbuckled the baby and lifted him into her arms.

"Shh, little one. It's okay. You're fine." She cradled the baby close, holding his head against the V in her neckline to enhance skin-to-skin contact.

He snuggled against her, melting her heart. She would do whatever was necessary to keep the child safe.

Should she take him to the closest hospital? Hand him over to a social worker who could take care of getting him placed in foster care? That may be the safest approach.

"Thanks, Wyatt." Having ended his call, Garrett returned to the kitchen as he pocketed his phone. He seemed confused as to why she was standing there. "Do you need something?"

She stared at him for a long moment. "Do you have any intention of keeping your son?"

His eyes widened as if she'd slapped him, and he took a step back. "I—uh, yeah. I just don't have much experience with babies."

"You won't learn if you refuse to hold him." She walked toward him, pinning him with a narrow gaze. "Take your son, Garrett. He needs to find comfort in your arms, too."

"I— Okay." He took the baby from her arms and cradled him to his chest, much the way she had. The infant rested against him, falling back to sleep within seconds.

"You need to bond with him," she said in a low voice. "He's already lost his mother. He can't lose his father, too."

A pained expression crossed his features. "How am I going to raise a baby? I can't stay home with him twenty-four seven."

She curled her fingers into fists, trying not to lash out at him. A baby wasn't a nuisance. She would have given anything to have Willow alive and in her arms. "Babies are a gift from

God, Garrett. If you don't keep him, he'll end up in foster care. Is that what you want?"

"No, but…" His voice trailed off.

She squelched a flash of annoyance. "I'm sure you can get a leave of absence from work until you can make childcare arrangements."

He nodded slowly. "Yes, I can do that." He sounded more sure of himself now. "But I still need to understand the source of the danger." He met her gaze head-on. "And for that, I need your help."

Her help? She wanted to flat-out refuse, but the way Micah slept against Garrett's shoulder gave her pause. He obviously couldn't fight a gunman with a baby in his arms.

Didn't she owe this much to Rebecca? The woman whose life she'd failed to save?

Yes. Because if something terrible happened to Micah, she would never forgive herself.

Garrett needed to get to work, try to figure out what Rebecca had gotten herself tangled up in—but he couldn't tear his gaze from his son.

At one time, he would have thought God was sending him a clear message, but he wasn't exactly on speaking terms with Him at the moment.

God should never have let Jason die. The

twenty-five-year-old officer had been on the force for just over three years.

He'd been so young. Too young to die. If only he hadn't sent Jason to the scene first. If only he'd gotten there sooner. If only...

Garrett gave himself a mental shake. He couldn't afford to wallow in a pool of self-pity. Not over Jason's death or the unexpected arrival of his son.

Liz was right about one thing: babies were a precious gift. He hadn't known about Micah—or why Rebecca had kept the news a secret—but as the baby slept with his face pressed into the side of his neck, he was struck by an unexpected wave of love.

"Rebecca named him Micah?"

"Yes." Liz gestured to the diaper bag. "I have birth certificate forms that need to be filled out. Rebecca didn't give me her last name, and I didn't see a purse or ID when she staggered into the clinic, either. Since she didn't give Micah a middle name, you can choose that one."

Birth certificate. He swallowed hard and nodded. "I'd like to name him Micah John Nichols. John is my middle name."

"That sounds perfect." She dug inside the bag and pulled out the paperwork.

Somehow, documenting the information on legal forms made it all the more real. There were so many things he'd need to do—to buy—but that would have to wait.

His phone rang. Holding Micah to his chest with one hand, he pulled out the device with the other. After seeing Wyatt's name on the screen, he answered quickly. "Wyatt? Please tell me you found the shooter."

"Sorry, boss, not yet. We have all deputies on alert, though. We scoured the parking lot and found a slug imbedded in the front of a blue sedan. We also found several shell casings. One looks to be from your gun."

"It probably is." He glanced at Liz. "What caliber is the other shell casing from?"

"A .45. We're getting it tested for possible fingerprints."

Garrett knew better than to count on the shooter making a rookie mistake. "Is the blue sedan drivable?"

Liz snapped her head up to look at him, her eyes wide. "My car?" she whispered.

He nodded.

"I'm afraid not. One bullet struck the radiator. There may be other engine damage, too. I'm no expert."

"Okay, do me a favor and call the garage. Have the sedan towed there to be repaired. I'll pay for the damage." He watched Liz sink into the closest kitchen chair as if devastated by the news. And really, he couldn't blame her. None of this was her fault. All she'd done was help deliver a baby.

"Will do. Anything else, boss?" Wyatt asked.

"Just keep an eye out for the shooter."

"We will—but keep in mind that finding someone who looks out of place among the crush of tourists roaming around will be impossible."

"I know." Their small department was over taxed during the peak tourist season, when those who came to visit their beautiful lakes often misbehaved. It was the main reason he'd intended to wait until fall to quit.

Now that he had Micah to consider, he realized that resigning from his position was no longer an option. How had his life gotten so complicated, so fast? "Just do your best."

"Sure thing, boss."

Garrett slipped the phone into his pocket and walked over to where Liz sat, her head bowed. "I'm sorry about your car, but I'm sure the repairs will be completed soon."

"I would offer to pay, but I honestly don't have the money for that." She lifted her head, her bright green eyes meeting his. "I should let my insurance company know. They'll cover the repairs above my thousand-dollar deductible."

"Don't worry about that now." He wanted to hand Micah over to her but feared she'd lecture him again. "I need to start investigating Rebecca's murder." He hesitated, then added, "Her father needs to know about her death, too."

"You want me to help take care of Micah while you do those things." She made it a statement, not a question.

"Give me at least twenty-four hours." It was a stretch to think he'd have the investigation completed that quickly. "Can we leave a message for your patients? Some way to let them know you won't be in?"

She nodded. "I left a note on my door saying I would be back in the morning. We'll need to go there sooner or later to check out Rebecca's car, right?" When he nodded, she added, "I'll update the note then."

"Thank you." He owed Liz a huge debt of gratitude. "I'm sorry to drag you into this."

She offered a wan smile. "Rebecca is the one who pulled me into this, not you." When Micah began to whimper, she held out her hands. "I'll take him. He may need to be changed, and I can try feeding him again. Newborns don't eat much, but every little bit is helpful."

He pressed a kiss on the top of Micah's head, then handed him over. "I have a lot to learn."

"Oh, trust me—" she stood and poked through the diaper bag for the supplies she needed "—all new parents feel the same way."

Leaving Liz to it, he crossed over to the small desk he used as a home office. After opening his laptop, he began a search on Rebecca Woodward's name.

Since she was the daughter of Robert Woodward, a real estate mogul in Chicago, Garrett wasn't surprised when dozens of links popped up. With a sigh, he realized going through the numerous articles would take time.

He could hear Liz cooing at Micah as she changed him. Diaper changes were another task he'd need to learn, but not right this minute.

Garrett took a minute to pull up a map of the Oneida Native American reservation. The town of Liberty was right on the border of the southernmost tip of the reservation.

Then he frowned, realizing Rebecca had gone much farther north than she needed to—

if she was, in fact, heading to Green Lake to seek his assistance. Not to mention, the many hospitals she'd passed along the way.

If she'd been in labor, the way Liz had described, why not go to the closest ER?

Liz's words echoed in his mind: *She begged me not to call 911 because he would find her and kill her.*

He, who? The gunman, obviously—but why?

Garrett clicked on the first article, from the online newspaper *Windy City Chicago*.

The headline was not what he'd expected: "Robert Woodward Diagnosed with Pancreatic Cancer."

With a frown, he quickly scanned the article. Rebecca was quoted as saying her father was receiving excellent medical care while fighting his stage four pancreatic cancer diagnosis.

Interesting, but not exactly a reason for Rebecca to have been shot and killed.

The baby cried louder now, causing him to glance over to see Liz making a bottle. He jumped up and went over to help.

"Take the baby," she said as she ran the water, waiting for it to warm up. "I'll be ready in a minute."

He picked up Micah, bemused by his loud crying. "Do all newborns have lungs like this?"

She froze, then nodded. "Most do, yes."

He sensed he'd hit a nerve, but he didn't push. He walked with the baby, pacing back and forth as she made the bottle. When she'd finished, she headed into the living room. He followed, giving her a moment to get settled on the sofa before handing Micah back to her.

"Forgive me for asking, but the name Templeton doesn't sound Native American."

She gave Micah the bottle, the baby instantly quieting in her arms. "No, it's not. My father wasn't from the reservation the way my mother was. Her last name was Blackhawk. Ava Blackhawk."

"Are your parents still alive?"

"No." She grimaced, then added, "My parents were killed in a motorcycle accident."

"I'm sorry to hear that." He felt bad for dragging out painful memories. As his gaze rested on Micah, a stunning realization hit hard.

Rebecca's son was likely the heir to the Woodward fortune.

Garrett's gut clenched in horror. What in the world had he gotten himself into? Was this the motive behind Rebecca's murder? Had she been shot to prevent her from inheriting her father's billion-dollar estate?

As much as he hated the idea, it made sense. Who stood to inherit if Rebecca and Micah were gone?

He had no idea, but he assumed it could be any of Rebecca's aunts, uncles or cousins. She was an only child, but there were likely other Woodward family members out there, just itching to get their hands on Robert Woodward's money.

Thinking about the family members helped steady his nerves. He didn't want anything to do with that much money. He sensed that would only bring trouble.

But he wasn't about to give Micah over to some of those same family members, either.

What a mess. He turned from Liz and the baby, and hurried back to the computer. A quick search on Robert and Rebecca Woodward brought up another article, with a picture. Robert had his arm around his daughter, claiming her to be the next CEO and owner of the company. The words on the screen only cemented what he'd already feared.

Whoever stood to inherit it if Rebecca and Micah were gone was now the top suspect in Rebecca's murder.

He began digging into Robert Woodward's

extended family. He needed a starting place before he approached Liam with a list of suspects.

"Garrett?" Liz's soft voice interrupted his thoughts. "I'm going to rest in one of the guest rooms. I'll keep Micah next to me in his car seat."

"Thank you." He felt guilty for taking advantage of her kindness. "Either room is fine."

"Thanks." She glanced down at her bloody scrubs. "I may need to borrow a T-shirt to wear."

"Of course." He jumped up from his seat, taking a moment to rummage through his things. He found a pair of athletic shorts with a drawstring and a navy blue T-shirt. Liz took the items gratefully and disappeared into the bathroom to change.

Micah was asleep again in his carrier just inside the bedroom door. It occurred to him that the baby slept a lot. Maybe that was the case with all newborns—what did he know?

Nothing, and wasn't that the understatement of the year.

He turned to head back to his desk. He'd already found mention of Robert's younger brother, Edward, and his two kids, Elaine and Jeremy.

The two kids weren't married, from what he

could tell, but they all stood to inherit now that Rebecca was gone.

Unless, of course, everything had been left to Micah.

His stomach knotted at the thought as he continued his search. His eyes began to blur from exhaustion, so he finally shut the computer down. Stretching his muscles, he turned off the kitchen light, plunging the house in darkness. When his eyes adjusted, he performed a quick check, going from window to window to look outside.

Did anyone in the Woodward family know that he was Micah's biological father? Was that part of the reason the baby was in danger?

A flash of movement from the shed in his backyard caught his eye. Garrett froze, keeping to the side of the window and hopefully out of sight.

Was someone out there? Or had it been one of the many white-tailed deer that roamed the woods around his property?

Moving with extreme caution, he slipped his service weapon from the holster and held the gun down at his side. Everything outside remained still for several long minutes.

His imagination? Maybe. Still, he continued to wait and watch.

There! The shadow moved again, going from one tree to the next.

Not a deer, but a man.

Garrett didn't dare use his phone, for fear the light from the screen would call attention to him. He waited until he saw the shadow move again, coming another few feet closer to the house.

This time, he saw the gun.

Easing back from the window, he moved quickly into the guest room, where Liz lay on the bed. "Liz? We need to get out of here."

"What?" She lifted her head, looking at him sleepily. "Why?"

"The gunman is outside." He needed backup; he would have gone after the guy himself if not for the need to keep Liz and Micah safe.

He grabbed the baby's carrier and hurried back into the kitchen. After stuffing the few baby supplies Liz had removed back into the diaper bag, he headed to the door. "You and Micah are going to slide into the back seat. You'll have to hold him until we're safe, understand?"

Liz's eyes were wide with fright as she nodded.

He eased open the door, hoping and praying

there wasn't another gunman waiting by his vehicle. He didn't see one, so he didn't hesitate. "Now," he whispered.

Liz sprinted toward the car, with Garrett hot on her heels. He thrust the baby carrier and diaper bag into the back seat, then quickly climbed behind the wheel.

The minute he started the engine, he saw movement. The gunman was running toward them.

He thrust the gearshift in Reverse and hit the gas, sending the SUV barreling backward down the driveway as the sound of gunfire rang out for the second time that evening.

Chapter Three

Please, Lord, keep us safe!

Liz held on to the baby carrier, fumbling with the seat belt as Garrett shot down the driveway. The sound of gunfire made her place her body between Micah's carrier and the back seat so she could shield him from any stray bullets.

The gunfire stopped, but she didn't move from her position.

Garrett hit the brake, shifted gears and then punched the gas. They jolted forward, speeding away from his log cabin. She couldn't see the road, but that was okay; her job was to keep Micah safe.

The baby cried, no doubt from the sound of gunfire. She placed the pacifier in his mouth, crooning to him.

"It's okay, Micah. You're safe. We love you. God loves you."

"Are either of you hurt?" Garrett asked in a clipped tone.

"No." She decided being scared to death didn't count as *hurt*. "I'd like to get Micah's carrier secured, though."

There was a long pause as Garrett turned the SUV in a different direction. Then he pulled over to the side of the road. "Make it quick."

She almost snapped at him, then took a deep breath and went to work. After a minute, she was able to get the seat belt secured, holding the carrier in place. Then she buckled her own seat belt. "Okay, we're ready."

Garrett's response was to pull away from the side of the road and to hit the gas again, reaching highway speeds in a span of five seconds. She understood his concern to stay well ahead of the gunman, but she found herself holding on to the door handle, anyway.

"How did they find us?" The wooded green scenery passed by in a blur.

"I don't know." He spoke through clenched teeth. "I made sure we weren't followed from headquarters to my place. It doesn't make sense that the gunman could know my name, much less my address."

She shivered despite the warm summer temps.

He was right about one thing: nothing about this scenario made sense. Glancing at Micah, she was glad to see he'd fallen back to sleep, the pacifier lying in the carrier next to the stuffed bunny she'd bought for Willow. The one she'd almost buried with her daughter.

That thought brought her back to the present. Who would want to hurt a baby? How could this little boy be a threat to anyone?

"Where are we going?" Liz tried not to sound as exhausted as she felt. Running from gunfire was wreaking havoc on her equilibrium.

"We'll have to find a motel." Garrett sounded less tense now that they were safe. "But I'd like to see Rebecca's car. There may be something to learn from the vehicle."

"What if a gunman is there?" As much as she liked the idea of being close to her clinic, a wave of apprehension hit hard.

"We left him at my place, remember? Which reminds me." He used his hands-free function to make a call. "Gloria? It's Garrett. Someone fired shots at my house. I need the area searched for the shooter, then combed for evidence."

"I'll send Wyatt, ASAP."

"Send Abby with him. I don't want them to walk into an ambush. And let them know it's likely the same shooter that was outside our headquarters two hours ago. If possible, I'd like the shell casings tested to see if they're a match."

"Roger that. Take care, Garrett." The woman's voice sounded brisk and businesslike, but the way she used his first name gave Liz the impression they didn't stand on formality here.

"Will do." Garrett disconnected from the call, then met her gaze in the rearview mirror. "Are there motels near your clinic?"

"There's one in Liberty, but it only has ten rooms and is nothing fancy. There are nicer ones closer to Green Bay."

"I don't need fancy. I can drop you and the baby at the motel before I head over to check the vehicle."

"I need to leave a new note for my patients on my clinic door, anyway, to let them know I'll be away for longer than planned." She frowned, then added, "Honestly, Garrett? I'd feel better if we stayed together."

"Then that's what we'll do." His easy acceptance of the plan helped her relax. He met her gaze in the rearview mirror again. "Try to get some sleep."

Sleep? He had to be kidding. On the heels of that thought, she yawned, finding the rhythmic sound of wheels on the road soothing. Micah must have liked it, too, as he continued to sleep.

Staring down at his adorable face, she thought of her daughter, Willow. Giving birth to a stillborn baby had been the most traumatic experience of her life. Her husband had blamed her for the loss because she'd been working long hours and hadn't noticed right away that the baby had stopped moving. And for years, she'd blamed herself, too. When her husband, Eric, had been diagnosed with a rare form of leukemia, he refused medical treatment. Less than a year later, he was gone.

Liz grieved Willow's loss more than Eric's, which seemed wrong. Yet her relationship with Eric had grown so contentious, she'd been relieved when he left her to move in with another woman on the reservation.

In the three years since losing her family, Liz had found God and accepted Jesus as her savior. With that, she'd dedicated her life to helping other Native American women and other low-income mothers avoid the same devastation. Even those who didn't much like Western medicine.

But deep down, she'd often wondered why

other babies were allowed to live, while Willow hadn't.

Liz must have dozed, because she jerked awake when the vehicle suddenly slowed. Blinking in the darkness, her gaze landed on the Cadillac sitting along the side of the road.

"That's the car I saw on my way to Green Lake." She craned her neck to see better. "I remember thinking that had to be Rebecca's car since no one out here drives anything that expensive."

"You're probably right." Garrett frowned. "I wonder if the caddy is new. She wasn't driving that when I saw her ten months ago."

"I could be wrong," she admitted. "It just looked out of place here."

"I believe it's hers." Garrett drove past the seemingly abandoned vehicle, his gaze raking the area. She couldn't help peering out her window, too, searching for any sign of danger.

After a short ride, he turned around to head back to the car. Then he made another turn so that he could park behind the caddy. She noticed the car was pointed in the direction of her clinic and wondered if this was where Rebecca had been shot.

Just thinking of her being shot and making

it two miles to her clinic gave her a new appreciation for the woman's sheer grit and determination. Looking at Micah, she understood Rebecca had done what was necessary to save her unborn child.

"Liz?"

She glanced up. "Yes?"

"I'd like you to get behind the wheel, just in case something goes awry."

"Okay." She pushed open her door, glancing at Micah. She was glad the baby was still sleeping, but she knew his peaceful slumber wouldn't last long. After closing the door as silently as possible, she slid in behind the wheel.

Flashlight in hand, Garrett stealthily approached the caddy. He took his time inspecting the outer portion of the vehicle before shining the light through the windows.

Liz gripped the steering wheel tightly and alternated between watching Garrett and scanning the wooded area around them.

She felt certain Garrett was right about how the gunman was likely in Green Lake rather than beating them out here in the middle of nowhere, just inside the rez.

But that didn't ease her apprehension.

After what seemed like eons—but was likely only ten minutes—Garrett opened the caddy's door. A minute later, he closed it again, then turned to head back to the SUV.

She pushed out from the vehicle so he could get in behind the wheel, then frowned when she saw he had a slip of paper in his hand. "What is it? What did you find?"

He looked at her for a long moment, then showed it to her. She gasped when she saw her name, cell number and clinic address on the slip of paper.

"Me?" she whispered. "Rebecca specifically came all this way to see me? Why?"

Garrett's intense gaze drilled into hers. "I was hoping you could tell me."

She shook her head, leaning weakly against the SUV. It didn't make sense. Sure, her services to low-income mothers were well-known among people living in the area, especially within the reservation. She also worked closely with an OB in Green Bay for cases outside her area of expertise.

But outside of this area, she doubted anyone knew her. There was no rational explanation why a woman like Rebecca, who had money and access to top-notch OB specialists, had come all this way to see her.

Or why she'd been followed and shot to death along the way.

Garrett watched Liz's reaction closely, believing she'd been thrown completely off-balance by seeing her name and contact information on the slip of paper he'd noticed halfway under the passenger seat of the caddy.

"I don't understand," she whispered.

Yeah, that was putting it mildly. He pocketed the slip of paper, then reached over to open her door. "Let's head over to your clinic."

She didn't move. "Did you find anything else in the car?"

"I didn't find what I'd expected." He gestured for her to get in. "We'll talk along the way."

Moving slowly, she slid in beside Micah's car seat. He closed the door, then climbed in behind the wheel. Shifting the car into gear, he pulled out onto the highway.

Micah began to squirm and cry. Liz did her best to soothe him. "My clinic isn't far. Take the second road to the right."

"Okay." He watched her bend over the baby. "Are you going to wait until then to feed him?"

"Yes." She met his gaze in the rearview mirror. "What did you find, Garrett?"

"What I didn't find was blood or a bullet hole inside the vehicle. I assumed she'd been shot while sitting behind the wheel. Did you notice the flat tire?" When she nodded, he said, "Makes me wonder if the bad guys shot out the tire, then gave chase. But you said she was shot in the chest, so that part doesn't make sense."

"Yes, that's correct—she was shot on the upper-left side of her chest." She frowned. "There was no exit wound, either."

He considered that for a moment. "Rebecca must have been far away when she was hit, then. A gunshot from close range would have likely gone all the way through."

Liz closed her eyes for a moment. "That's horrible. It's all so awful."

"Tell me about it," he muttered, half under his breath. The entire situation was difficult to comprehend. Rebecca hadn't gotten lost on her way to find him in Green Lake, like he'd assumed. No, Liz's clinic had been her destination all along. She'd come way out here to seek Liz's help in delivering her baby.

Their baby. Micah.

Why? Rebecca had money and access to exceptional obstetric care in Chicago. Why come all this way? And who had killed her? He felt certain the gunman had shot Rebecca to kill her and the baby.

If not for Liz's skill, he would have succeeded.

He was still getting accustomed to the idea of having a son, but the idea that someone intended to kill the infant made his blood boil. He made a silent promise to never let that happen.

Taking the second right-hand turn as Liz had directed, he saw the clinic up ahead, roughly fifty yards away. He frowned, not liking how the building was rather isolated. He didn't see any other houses or businesses nearby.

Did Liz work there alone? Or did she have help?

Scanning the area for threats, he pulled up next to the building. Then he took a moment to turn the vehicle around so they could get away quickly if needed.

Micah's wails grew louder now, so he shut down the car and jumped out. He opened Liz's door. "What can I do?"

"Take him for me. I'll make a bottle." She released the seat belt and handed the baby car-

rier to him. He tried to soothe the baby as Liz
opened the clinic door and stepped inside.

The clinic was spacious, with a room full of
supplies off to one side. The exam room was
in complete disarray; there were towels tossed
all over the floor, covering puddles of blood.

Rebecca's blood. Her body was gone, but the
scene of destruction had remained. He swallowed hard, grieving for the loss of his friend.

*What happened, Rebecca? Why didn't you call
me?*

There was nothing but silence for an answer.

Liz stared at the mess for a moment, then led
the way through another door, where a very
small and cramped living area was located.

Shaking himself out of his sorrow, he followed Liz, not surprised to see she'd sacrificed
her living area in favor of making sure the clinic
was functional. As she moved around the small
kitchen, he unbuckled Micah from the carrier
and gently cradled the crying baby in his arms.

As before, he was struck by how tiny he was.
His small face was beet red and scrunched up
in anger over being so hungry.

"Hang on, little man. Food is on the way."

"Have a seat on the sofa." Liz was shaking

the bottle to dissolve the formula. "I'd like you to feed him."

"Me?" He sat but stared up at her with wide eyes. "I don't know how."

"Time to learn, don't you think?" She adjusted the baby in his arms, then handed him the bottle. "He's your son. Practice makes perfect."

Thankfully, Micah took the bottle without difficulty. He found it hard to tear his gaze away from his son's peaceful expression—so different from the wailing just seconds earlier.

A wave of responsibility hit hard. This little baby was completely helpless, dependent on Garrett and Liz, at least for now, to provide for him.

He wanted to assure the little boy he wouldn't fail in his role as his protector, but considering how close the gunman had gotten to them—twice in as many hours—the words caught in his throat.

As soon as Liz finished up here and Micah had eaten his fill, they'd head to a motel for what was left of the night. And after that?

He sighed heavily. Other than checking in with Wyatt and Abby, he had no clue.

Liz used her computer to presumably send an

email to her patients and print out a new note to attach to her door. When those tasks were finished, she packed more items in the diaper bag and took a moment to change into fresh clothes: a soft forest green short-sleeved shirt and worn blue jeans.

"Micah fell asleep," he whispered, setting the bottle aside.

"Put him up on your shoulder and rub his back in soothing circles. He may need to burp."

"Ah, okay." He carefully moved the baby to his shoulder, half-afraid he'd drop him. "We should hit the road."

"We will, as soon as I change him." She flashed a smile. "Or rather, *you* change him. It's all part of learning how to take care of your son."

"I'm sure it's not that hard to change a diaper." Messy, but not difficult.

He'd underestimated just how messy and difficult, but he managed to get the job done. Liz took the baby as he washed up at the sink.

Through the window, a flash of light in the distance caught his attention. He stared at the area for a long moment, and when the light didn't reappear, he turned away, relieved to see Liz had buckled Micah in the carrier.

"How close is the next property?" He shouldered the diaper bag and reached for the car seat handle. "I saw a light outside, north of here."

Her dark eyes widened. "There's nothing close by. This was an abandoned property before I moved in. The building came with five acres of land."

That's what he was afraid of. "We need to go." He shut off the kitchen light, plunging the room into darkness. "Follow me."

Envisioning the clinic layout in his mind, Garrett carefully made his way through the building and toward the door, holding Micah's carrier at a level high enough to avoid the exam table.

Was he overreacting to the flash of light? He didn't think so. Maybe it was nothing more than a car coming down the highway, disappearing behind trees. Yet he couldn't ignore his instincts screaming at him to get Micah and Liz out of there.

Pausing at the door, he opened it a crack, listening intently. After a full minute of silence, he stepped outside, moving softly toward the vehicle.

Liz kept close, taking just a moment to lock the door behind them before crossing to the car. He hesitated, knowing that the SUV dome light would come on the moment he opened the car door.

It was a situation that couldn't be helped, although he wished he'd had the forethought to take the bulb out before going inside. Then again, he'd thought coming here would be safe since they'd left the gunman at his place.

Was anywhere safe?

"We need to move quickly," he said in a low voice. "Ready?"

She nodded.

He opened the door to the back seat. Liz slid in and reached for Micah's carrier. He handed it over, dropped the diaper bag on the floor and then closed the door. While she buckled Micah in, he opened the driver's-side door.

A twig snapped. Someone was in the woods!

He slid into the seat and started the SUV, thankful he'd parked it for a quick getaway. He hit the gas, moving down the driveway to the road.

In the rearview mirror, he saw a dark shadow burst from the woods. Another gunman!

He pushed his foot down on the gas pedal as the man behind them fired several rounds from his weapon. Garrett wanted to know how in the world this guy had found them. When he heard the ping of bullet against metal, he knew they'd been hit.

"Garrett?" Liz's voice trembled with fear.

"Hang on." He continued driving, silently praying the gunman's bullet hadn't damaged anything major. They made it all the way to the road before he glanced at the gas gauge. The needle dropped right before his eyes.

He didn't let up on the accelerator, praying they'd have enough fuel to get far enough away from the gunman.

But as the needle continued to fall and the engine slowed, he knew that wasn't going to happen. He wrenched the wheel, pulling off to the side of the road seconds before the engine died completely.

They would have to escape the gunman on foot.

Chapter Four

"Why are we stopping?" Liz tried to keep calm, but her voice trembled with fear. She couldn't believe the gunman had found them at her clinic!

Was he the same one who had been in Green Lake? Or a different one? Were there several gunmen after them? And if so, why were they all seemingly intent on killing an innocent baby?

"Gas tank has been hit." Garrett pushed open his door. "Get Micah's carrier unbuckled, then grab the diaper bag. Hurry."

She quickly did as he asked, praying for strength. Garrett opened the back passenger door and lifted Micah's carrier from the seat. Looping the strap of the diaper bag over her shoulder, she scrambled out of the vehicle to join him.

"Follow me." He didn't hesitate to break into a loping jog, heading toward a dense section of the woods. She managed to keep up but wasn't sure how long she'd be able to run so fast as Garrett's long legs ate up the yards. Good thing she'd changed into darker clothing.

Thankfully, he slowed his pace once they reached the shelter of the trees. But not by much. He moved swiftly, his head swiveling back and forth as he scanned their surroundings.

She had no doubt he expected the gunmen to show up at any moment. The mere idea of being stalked by these men made her shiver.

Liz did her best not to gasp for breath as she moved through the trees. Her Native American ancestors would know how to melt into the forest, but as much as she liked the rural surroundings of her clinic, she was no expert at hiding in the woods. Through the darkness, she could barely see the dark shape of Garrett's body up ahead.

Guide us to safety, Lord!

As if reading her mind, Garrett glanced over his shoulder. Slowing his pace, he waited for her to catch up. The diaper bag was navy blue, with a pattern of white giraffes on the outside, and she feared it would be a beacon to anyone searching for them.

Garrett didn't say anything but held her gaze

for a moment as if asking if she was okay. She nodded, deciding not to voice her fears. Especially related to Micah. The baby was sleeping for now, but what would happen when he awoke? Newborns cried and that, too, would lead the bad guys to them.

Her foot got tangled in a fallen tree branch. She sucked in a breath and held on to the tree trunk for support. Garrett continued moving, so she forced herself to do the same, understanding the importance of remaining silent and hidden.

Yet how long could they survive in the woods? Mentally reviewing the contents of the diaper bag, she remembered placing two cans of premade formula inside, along with the container of powdered mix. The cans would buy them a little time before they'd need water to make another bottle.

Her own stomach growled with hunger; she hadn't eaten much for dinner. Ignoring the sensation, she hoped the rumbles wouldn't be loud enough to draw unwanted attention.

After what seemed like an hour but was likely much less, Garrett stopped at the base of a large oak. He set Micah's carrier down, then gestured for her to sit, too.

"Rest." His low whisper tickled her ear.

She nodded and dropped to the ground beside the baby. While it felt good to rest her muscles, her body remained tense with fear. How long before the gunmen found them?

Imagining the worst wasn't helpful. Garrett was armed and would protect them, especially Micah. Thinking of the baby had her opening the diaper bag. She felt around inside until she found the can of formula.

Reassured, she held it up for Garrett to see. Thankfully, the can had a pop top, so she could easily open it.

"Do you need to feed him?" His voice was barely a whisper.

"Not yet," she said. "Hopefully, he'll sleep for a while."

"We need to keep moving."

She grimaced, tucking the can of formula into the bag. She rose, looping the strap over her shoulder. Garrett stood and lifted the baby carrier. Watching as the muscles in his arms bunched, she was grateful for his strength. She doubted she'd have been able to carry the baby carrier this far on her own.

Garrett stealthily moved through the woods. She understood silence was more important than speed, so she placed her feet in the same places he did. She might not be as quiet as he was, but the occasional snap of a twig could be attributed to wildlife moving through the area.

After another twenty minutes, Garrett stopped. She craned her neck to see what he'd found. A large tree branch was hanging down all the way to the ground, creating a small, sheltered area.

After placing Micah's carrier on the ground, he turned to her. "You should stay here with Micah. I'd like to walk the area to see if I can pick up any sign of the gunman."

Swallowing hard, she nodded. "Okay."

"Will you be okay for a short while?" He searched her gaze.

"Of course." She forced a reassuring smile. What choice did she have? She trusted Garrett's instincts in deeming it important to scout the area. His expertise, not hers.

His smile shot her pulse into high gear. It was the wrong time to be aware of how handsome he was. Grateful for the darkness that hid her flushed cheeks, she lowered herself down on the ground, using the tree branches around her as shelter. Garrett lightly touched her shoulder before moving away.

She shivered, but not from the cold. What

was wrong with her? Where had this weird attraction to Garrett come from? She hadn't been the least bit interested in anything remotely resembling a relationship since her husband, Eric, had left her for another woman—one, he'd claimed, who was more kind and caring than she was.

She let out a soundless sigh. No sense in reminiscing about the past. Especially since she knew Garrett only wanted her to help with caring for the baby. She couldn't turn her back on this father and newborn son.

Her feelings were irrelevant. The most important task looming before her was to keep Micah safe. And she would.

No matter what.

Feeling calmer, she listened intently to the sounds of the night. She was impressed at how quietly Garrett was able to move through the brush. Maybe it was his cop training, or he was an experienced hunter. Either way, she couldn't hear him at all.

The hum of insects, chirping crickets and belching tree frogs were oddly reassuring. Resting her hand on the sleeping baby, she relaxed against the branches behind her.

For the moment, they were safe. And she couldn't ask for more than that.

Garrett eased through the brush, every one of his senses on full alert. He didn't hear or see anything unusual but wasn't ready to let down his guard.

It was his fault they were in this mess. He shouldn't have come to investigate Rebecca's caddy without backup.

And worse, he'd brought Liz and Micah directly into the line of fire.

The fact that there were so many gunmen made him think they were hired killers. Nothing else made sense. No way had a single gunman take shots at them back at his place only to show up again here at Liz's clinic. How many of them were out there? He had no idea. But he suspected they'd been hired by someone in the Woodward family.

A man or woman determined to eliminate Micah as the heir to the family fortune.

The task of keeping his son and Liz safe loomed before him. When he'd completed a twenty-yard circle around the spot where he'd left them, he returned to the downed tree branch. When he stepped out from behind a tree trunk, Liz startled badly, placing her hand over her heart.

"Sorry," he murmured. "Didn't mean to scare you."

Liz nodded, then lifted a brow in a silent question.

"It's clear." He glanced at the sleeping baby. They couldn't hide out in the woods forever, so he needed to come up with a plan to get them out of here, safely. He dropped down beside her so they could speak quietly. "How much longer do you think he'll sleep?"

She grimaced. "You fed him at the clinic, so he should be fine for a while yet—although newborns can be unpredictable."

Since he had no personal experience with babies, predictable or not, he shrugged. "I'd like to wait here for a bit before we head back."

Her eyes widened. "Back where?"

"To the caddy." He held her gaze. "I can put the spare on to get us out of here."

"Are you sure that's a good idea?" She looked far from convinced. "Wouldn't the gunmen consider that as our only option, too?"

"It's possible." He gazed around their wooded sanctuary. "But what else can we do? If I call my deputies to pick us up, they'll draw attention, too." He couldn't knowingly put his deputies in danger. "It's better if we sneak up to the caddy on our own."

"I don't know." A frown puckered her brow, and she gnawed on her lower lip. "That seems risky. But I'll go along with whatever you think is best."

Her faith in his abilities only added to the weight of responsibility he carried. He forced himself to sit for a moment, thinking through their options. He could call Wyatt and Abby, but he feared the headlights of their vehicle would be act as a beacon for the gunmen. And he wasn't sure exactly where he and Liz were—just outside Liberty, but he couldn't remember the last mile marker they'd passed.

Maybe a combination of both ideas would work. He leaned toward Liz. "Can you tell me where the closest gas station or grocery store is in relation to your clinic?"

She thought for a moment. "I generally use the gas station we passed on the way. It's probably seven miles or so from the clinic."

He searched his memory. "The Gas and Go station?"

"Yes." She grimaced. "There's really nothing very close to me. Unless you want to head further into the Oneida reservation."

Bringing danger into the reservation didn't seem wise—not to mention, the local cops didn't have jurisdiction there. He shook his head. "No, we'll use the Gas and Go station. But we can't walk seven miles through the woods to get there. I'll stash you and Micah someplace nearby while I work on changing the tire."

"Okay." Her eyes were dark with apprehension. He understood her fear. It seemed the gunmen had been following their every move.

Was it possible that Rebecca had told someone Micah was his child? He wished he understood why she hadn't told him that he was to be a father.

"We'll stay here for a while." He tried to smile reassuringly. "Just pray Micah doesn't wake up crying."

"Maybe we should fill a bottle with premade formula, just in case."

"Good idea."

She rummaged around in the diaper bag and pulled out a can, setting it aside. Then she opened a small bottle, placing a plastic liner inside. When that was ready, she popped the top of the can and poured the contents into the bottle.

It occurred to him that without her generosity, they'd be sitting here with nothing for the baby.

She looked up at him. "The can is supposed to be refrigerated after opening."

"Fill another bottle. We may end up using it sooner than later, anyway. When we get to the gas station, we can buy a cold pack." He didn't want to leave anything behind that the gunmen could find.

"Okay."

While she did as he'd asked, he glanced at his watch, trying to estimate how much time it would take them to head back through the woods to where Rebecca's car was located. He knew the caddy was only two miles from Liz's clinic. They hadn't reached it before his SUV had run out of fuel, but the two vehicles were likely closer than he liked.

Pulling out his phone, he swallowed a groan when he saw there was only one bar of service. Being out in the woods often meant no internet access. Rather than risk making a call, he decided to text Wyatt, hoping he and Abby weren't still processing the crime scene. They'd pulled a double shift to help cover in Jason's absence. Since the trip to Liberty took almost an hour, he thought it likely they'd finished gathering evidence from his house by now.

Are you available? I need backup and a car.

For several minutes, there was no response. Then, finally, an answering text bloomed on the screen.

Yes. What's up?

He thought for a moment, then texted back. Gunfire outside Liberty. Bring two cars. Meet at the Gas and Go on highway 45 but no lights or sirens.

This time there was no delay in the response. Got it. We'll be there ASAP.

Even though he knew Wyatt and Abby wouldn't get there for at least fifty to sixty minutes, he felt better having them on the way.

Now all he needed to do was to get the caddy running enough to drive them seven miles down the highway—heading in the opposite direction of Liz's clinic, thankfully.

Then again, the gunmen could easily set up somewhere along the side of the road, assuming they'd go that way. Yet what other option did he have?

He turned toward Liz. "Do you have friends on the reservation?"

"No." She shook her head. "I have a few patients who live there, but I wouldn't feel comfortable showing up at their house in the middle of the night."

"Okay, then we'll stick with the original plan." Using his phone, he opened the compass app to make sure he was heading in the right direction. His dad had often taken him hunting and insisted he learn to read a compass. His dad had made sure to test his knowledge, too, purposefully leaving him alone to get back to their truck.

A test he'd passed with flying colors. His dad had claimed Garrett had an innate sense of direction.

A skill that would serve him well now.

After he'd mentally plotted their course, he pocketed his phone and gestured toward the diaper bag. "Grab that and we'll start heading back. Stay close behind me, okay?"

"Okay." She gamely did as he'd asked.

He lifted the carrier, his muscles taut. The baby wasn't that heavy, but carrying him in such a way as to prevent the carrier from striking anything was difficult. He was forced to carry it higher and farther away from his body than normal.

Pausing, he glanced back. "Oh, and I'll stop the minute Micah sounds like he's waking up, so get the bottle ready right away. Better to feed him a little early than let him cry."

Her dark gaze held his. "I understand."

He knew she was just as worried about giving away their location as he was. He moved forward, easing through the woods while doing his best to keep a sedate pace for her sake. He'd noticed that she was quieter when she was able to step where he had.

Still, he could hear Liz moving behind him. As they walked, Garrett found himself silently praying for God's strength and guidance as he moved through the woods. He still didn't understand why God had taken Jason from them, but he didn't hesitate to throw himself on His mercy now.

Please, Lord Jesus, grant me the strength and wisdom I need to keep my son and Liz safe from harm!

For the first time in months, praying filled him with a sense of peace. As if God might be there for him after all, despite his anger toward Him.

He continued walking, pausing every so often to listen for sounds that indicated they were not alone. But the night air remained quiet, except for the usual sounds of insects and tree frogs.

After they'd gone a hundred yards, he noticed Micah squirming in his sleep. He stopped and dropped to a crouch. Instantly, Liz came up beside him with a bottle in hand.

Without saying a word, she unbuckled the baby and lifted him into her arms. She quickly offered him the bottle. He latched on, thankfully not breaking into a wailing cry.

Garrett carefully scanned the area but didn't see anything suspicious. If he didn't know better, he'd think they were alone out here.

But he suspected the gunmen had set up somewhere close by.

Maybe they should try to walk the seven miles to the gas station. But as soon as the thought formed, he rejected it. They were vulnerable out here. At least the caddy offered some level of physical protection.

Micah must not have been all the way awake, because he fell back asleep within ten minutes. Liz shrugged and gently set the sleeping infant back in the carrier. He strapped him in as she tucked the bottle in the diaper bag.

Once the baby was settled, he continued walking. The sound of rustling leaves made him freeze, until he caught sight of a white-tailed deer moving away from them.

They must have gotten too close to the deer's bed.

After what seemed like eons but was only another twenty minutes, he caught a glimpse of the road through the trees. He went another ten yards, then veered to the right, heading toward a cluster of three skinny pine trees.

Liz followed close on his heels. When he reached the area, he could see several feet of the highway. And, just barely, the glint of the moon shining off the rear bumper.

Lowering to a crouch, he set Micah's carrier on a soft bed of pine needles. Liz's feet made no sound as she came up beside him. He gave her a reassuring smile. "I'll need you to wait here with Micah, okay?"

She frowned. "We're pretty far from the road. I can barely see it."

"It's only about another ten yards away. Move this way. Can you see the caddy now?"

She nodded. "Yes."

"Good." After slipping his hand in his pocket, he drew out his phone. "Take this. If anything happens, I want you to disappear farther into the woods with Micah and to call Wyatt and Abby. They're two of my best deputies."

Her eyes widened in alarm. "What about you?"

"I'm armed." He pressed the phone into her hand, then gave her the passcode. "Repeat it back to me."

She recited the month and year of his birth, backward.

He bent to press a quick kiss to Micah's head before rising to his feet. "Stay safe."

"You, too."

He nodded, then moved away, determined to execute this plan without failing. Getting through the woods to the highway wouldn't take long, but he knew that crossing the road meant being exposed to anyone watching nearby.

He stood near a large tree for several long moments, searching the foliage for anything out of place. Then he gazed up at the sky. There were a few clouds drifting toward the half-moon that illuminated the sky. The second the clouds moved over the moon, he darted out from his hiding spot and ran to the abandoned caddy, then ducked behind it.

Earlier, he'd noticed the keys lying on the driver's-side floor, so he'd picked them up. He used them now to open the trunk. As he lifted the spare and the jack out from the well, the clouds finished passing the moon, and the area around him brightened noticeably.

He went to work, using the jack to lift the rear of the sedan. Changing the tire didn't take long, although he felt exposed the entire time. When he finished, he didn't bother to replace the tire and jack in the trunk. Time was of the essence.

Still in a crouch, he rounded the rear of the vehicle to get into the driver's seat. The car was pointed toward the clinic, but he needed to go the other way. When he opened the car door, he heard the barest sound of a footstep behind him.

Whirling around with his weapon in hand, he dropped as gunfire rang out. Pain lanced his arm as he instinctively fired back, praying he wasn't surrounded and would be able to escape.

Chapter Five

More gunfire! Liz's heart lodged in her throat as she huddled over Micah in his carrier. Through a gap in the trees, she watched as Garrett exchanged gunfire with a man dressed in black. Garrett's bullet struck the guy in the chest, and he fell backward, hitting the pavement with a thud.

She stared at the downed gunman for a long moment, trying to ascertain if he was breathing. But she was too far away to be sure one way or the other.

A bullet to the chest didn't mean he was dead; Rebecca's injury proved that. Though Liz knew that Rebecca had had a reason to live—an important reason to make her way to the clinic.

She'd pushed herself to survive, for the sake of her baby.

Garrett rose and went to the injured gunman to check for a pulse. Then he checked the guy's pockets, pulling out a disposable phone and a bundle of cash. Only when he glanced in her direction did she stand, carrying Micah's carrier as she emerged from her hiding spot.

The nurse in her wanted to provide first aid to the injured man, but the baby's safety had to come first. Garrett opened the back door of the caddy so she could buckle Micah inside.

"He's dead. We need to get out of here."

She glanced over her shoulder to find him standing directly in front of her, scanning the woods for threats. She swallowed hard and whispered, "I know."

Within minutes, they were settled in the caddy, heading to the gas station. She couldn't relax, fearing more gunmen would pop out of the woods and start shooting at them.

After a few moments of silence, she asked, "Did you find an ID on him?"

"No." Garrett gestured to the cheap phone and cash he'd taken from the dead man's pockets, which he'd tucked into the center console. "I'll get my deputies to see if they can lift prints and get some information on the phone itself."

She stared at him through the darkness. "Don't you think it's strange he didn't have an ID on him?"

"Professionals don't carry IDs." Garrett's voice was grim. "He is obviously a hired hit man."

"Who would hire someone to kill a baby?" Liz had trouble comprehending what was happening to them. "What threat does Micah pose?"

Garrett arched his brow. "He's likely the heir to the Woodward fortune. With Rebecca and Micah out of the picture, Rebecca's cousins are set to inherit a billion dollars when her father dies. And it just so happens Robert was recently diagnosed with stage four pancreatic cancer."

A cold chill snaked down her spine. This was all about money. Killing an innocent baby to get their grubby hands on a fortune. "That's evil."

"Yes, it is." Garrett's gaze went from the rearview mirror to the highway ahead of them. He wasn't driving fast; the caddy lurched to one side, the spare tire smaller than the others. "The gas station is up ahead. We'll have to wait for my deputies, Wyatt and Abby, to get here. They're bringing a car for us to use but then will need to head back to where I left the dead gunman."

"I hope you don't get in trouble for shooting

him." She hated to think Garrett's career would suffer because of this. "I couldn't see everything clearly, but I heard multiple gunshots. I know you only fired in self-defense."

"Yeah. And I have the injury to prove it."

Injury? She gasped. "What happened? Where are you hit?"

"I'm fine. The bullet grazed my arm." He downplayed the wound, and she had to assume the injury was to his left arm because his right side looked fine. "We can get some stuff at the gas station to patch it up."

"I have gauze in the diaper bag, too." She wished she'd brought more supplies from her clinic. Unfortunately, there was no going back now.

In fact, she wasn't sure they'd be safe anywhere.

Lights from the gas station brightened the otherwise dark sky. Normally, she'd be thrilled to be near other people.

But instead, a cloud of apprehension hung over her. Bright lights meant being a clear target for the gunmen.

She put a hand on his arm. "Maybe we shouldn't go to the gas station yet. What if the gunmen are there?"

"I understand your concern. My plan is to drive past it and find a place to hide the caddy. You and Micah will wait for me to clear the place."

She shivered but didn't argue. So far, Garrett had succeeded in protecting them. She only wished he could be safe, too.

There were no cars parked in front of the fuel pumps as they drove past. The sign outside the building indicated the gas station was open twenty-four seven.

Soon, the lights were behind them as Garrett kept driving. He abruptly slowed the vehicle, then came to a stop. She glanced around curiously. "Why here?"

"Hang on." He put the car in Reverse and turned the wheel to back into a wooded area. Craning her neck, she realized he intended to hide the caddy between two large pine trees. He shut down the engine, then angled toward her. "You and Micah should be safe here. It won't take me long to head back to make sure the gas station is clear."

"I didn't see any cars there."

"I know. But the way things have been going, I want to be certain. Here are the keys." He tucked them into her hand, then wrapped his fingers around hers. "Give me your cell number, I'll call when it's okay for you to drive back to the gas station, okay?"

"That works." She gave him the number, watching as he entered it in his phone.

"Ready?" He glanced up at her.

She forced a smile, wishing she didn't have to let him go. He held her gaze for a long second before releasing her and pushing out of the car. She eased up over the center console to drop into the driver's seat, which held the warmth of his body.

As before, Garrett moved quietly through the trees, melting into the forest. She was the one with Native American blood in her veins, but he was much better at moving swiftly and quietly. She twisted around to see over the edge of Micah's carrier. Thankfully, the newborn slept peacefully.

She bent her head, closing her eyes for a moment to pray: *Lord Jesus, keep this innocent baby safe in Your loving arms. Amen.*

God had brought Rebecca to her clinic and had sent her to Garrett with the baby. If she hadn't have escaped, Liz knew she and Micah would both be dead.

Shaking off the horrible thought, she took heart in knowing that Garrett's deputies would be there soon. He'd mentioned they were bringing another vehicle for them to use, too. Hopefully, one the gunmen wouldn't recognize.

As the minutes ticked by slowly, her apprehension grew. What if Garrett had been caught and killed? She told herself not to imagine the worst, but it wasn't easy to let go of the fear that plagued her.

She frowned when she noticed the sky was lighter near the road. It took a second for her to realize the faint illumination she saw through the pine branches was from a car. Garrett had tucked her so far back, she couldn't see the vehicle until it passed directly across the highway in front of her.

Her heart thudded painfully against her ribs. Who was behind the wheel? Another gunman? The deputies? Someone else?

Seconds after the vehicle passed her line of sight, a second vehicle drove by. Two cars. She relaxed her deathlike grip on the key fob. The vehicles must belong to Garrett's deputies.

Yet her phone didn't ring.

Please, Lord, keep us all safe in Your care!

Garrett had taken his time scouting around the gas station, unwilling to make another mistake. The last gunman had gotten far too close. He inched his way through the woods, making a circle around the gas station. Once he'd cleared the building, he'd call Liz to let her know it was safe to drive over. Suddenly, he noticed lights approaching in the distance.

Out here, in the middle of nowhere, it was easy to see oncoming traffic. Glancing at his watch, he realized that if the car belonged to Wyatt and Abby, they'd made good time.

Then again, anyone could be driving along the highway, even at two in the morning. Could be another gunman, but he doubted it.

If the hired killer was behind the wheel, he wouldn't drive up with his headlights on. He'd be hiding in the woods, the way the gunman had back at the clinic.

Still, he remained hidden until he noticed the vehicle slow and pull into the gas station. On the heels of that SUV, another pulled in behind him.

Wyatt and Abby to the rescue.

Garrett emerged from the trees, crossing over to meet his deputies. Wyatt's gaze was somber as Garrett approached. "You're bleeding."

"It's fine. Thanks for coming."

"Where's the woman and the baby?" Abby

asked, joining them. She held out a set of keys for him. "Are they okay?"

"They are. I stashed them a little over a half mile from here." He sighed, then added, "I shot a man about seven miles back. He's the one who creased my arm. I took his disposable cell and cash from his pocket. They're in the caddy where Liz and Micah are hiding out. I need you to call the homicide in to whatever jurisdiction we're in. It didn't happen on the reservation. We're in Brown County. Their sheriff's department needs to know. Also, we need to get information on the dead guy's identity."

Wyatt let out a low whistle. "You've been busy."

"Yeah, well, Micah is in danger from members of his own family." Garrett still had trouble believing the infant was his son. "The short story is that Rebecca's father is dying, and our son is the heir to the Woodward fortune."

"You're joking." Abby looked shocked. He wasn't sure if it was from the news that he had a son or that the baby would inherit a fortune. Probably both.

"I'm not. And the numerous gunmen that have staked out various locations where Rebecca may have taken the boy is proof." Garrett pulled his phone from his pocket. "I'll call Liz, tell her it's okay to drive back here."

After he made the call, Wyatt asked, "Whoever hired these gunmen knows you're the baby's father."

He nodded slowly. "Yeah. Which is difficult to comprehend since I didn't know until Liz showed up with the baby on my doorstep."

"Rebecca must have confided in someone," Abby mused. "A best friend, maybe?"

He'd have thought *he* was her best friend. Then again, they'd gone beyond friendship, hadn't they? He winced at the memory. "I knew Rebecca from the summers she spent in Green Lake. Her father had a place there but sold it a few years ago. It's on one of those vacation-rental apps. Rebecca rented it last September, and that's when we reconnected."

He stared at the road, waiting for Liz and Micah. When he saw a vehicle come out onto the highway and head toward them, he turned back to his deputies. "I need your help. As soon as you learn anything about the gunman back there, please call me. I can only do so much investigating while keeping Liz and Micah safe."

"That reminds me, we brought you a computer, too." Abby gestured toward the SUV she'd driven. "It's in the front seat."

He nodded in admiration. "What made you think of that?"

She exchanged a knowing look with Wyatt, and the two shared a wry smile. "We know what it's like to be on the run from bad guys, like when the Mafia was after me and my father. Oh, and I tucked spare cash in the laptop bag." Her expression turned serious. "I think it's best for you and Liz to stay off-grid."

"Thank you." He was impressed with the extent of their support. Liz pulled up next to the SUV. First, he removed the cell phone and cash, handing it to Wyatt. Then he unhooked Micah from the back seat. He reached for the diaper bag, too, but Liz took it from his fingers.

"We need to go inside and get medical supplies for your arm," she said.

"Okay. Liz, these two deputies are Wyatt and Abby Kane." He made quick introductions. "Liz Templeton is a midwife. She delivered Micah before Rebecca died of a bullet wound to the chest."

"It's nice to meet you." Abby took Liz's hand, giving her a warm smile. "Wyatt and I have been praying for your safety—and Garrett's, too."

"Don't forget Micah," Liz said.

"We won't," Wyatt assured her. "But you'd better hurry. Grab your supplies and get as far away from here as possible."

Garrett had the same niggling feeling that they'd already lingered too long. He crossed over to strap Micah's car seat into the back of the SUV, then turned to give Liz some cash. "Go inside to buy what you need. Grab something to eat, too. I don't know where we'll end up staying."

"Okay." Liz handed him the diaper bag, then hurried inside.

"I wish there was more we could do for you," Wyatt said. "If not for the dead guy, we could escort you somewhere safe."

"We'll be okay." Garrett already felt better knowing they had cash, a computer and a different vehicle. "You've been a huge help already. Stay in touch."

"Will do." Wyatt clapped him on the back, then opened the driver's-side door of his vehicle. Abby surprised Garrett with a quick hug before joining her husband. They drove off, heading to where he'd left the dead gunman lying in the road.

He didn't like knowing he'd killed a man.

Even in self-defense. It would have been better if he'd been able to arrest the guy and question him.

Gazing at his son, he understood that he'd done what was necessary to save the baby's life. When Liz came out of the gas station with a large plastic bag, he didn't hesitate to jump up in the driver's seat.

"In addition to the gauze and tape, I bought us each power bars and several bottles of water." She set the bag on the floor at her feet next to the laptop bag, then latched the seat belt. "We should be set for a while."

"Good." He pulled out of the gas station, taking the highway in the opposite direction of where Wyatt and Abby were working on the gunman. "We'll head west on Highway 28."

"Okay." She unwrapped a power bar and handed it to him, then opened a bottle of water and set it in the cupholder at his elbow. "I'll need to take care of your arm soon."

"Once we find a safe place to stay." It wouldn't be soon, but that didn't matter. He wanted to get as far away from both Green Lake and Brown County as possible.

The power bar was just what he needed, and he washed it down with a healthy slug of water.

The nourishment helped keep him focused despite his fatigue. He needed to stay alert for any sign of danger.

If he were honest, he would admit to feeling as if they should head straight across the border to Minnesota. Yet they couldn't keep running like this forever. Micah wouldn't be safe until they uncovered the real culprit.

At the next intersection, he turned right and continued along the winding highway. When he saw a sign that indicated the small town of Viroqua was about twenty miles away, he decided that would be a good destination.

If he remembered correctly, there were some Amish farms along the north side of Viroqua. And the town itself was quaint, but there was a decent-sized medical center there, too. He wasn't hurt badly, but he was a little concerned about his son. At some point, the baby should be seen by a pediatrician. Not that he doubted Liz's medical expertise, but he knew from when Liam and Shauna gave birth to their daughter, Ciara, that the pediatrician had stopped in to examine her while she and Shauna were still in the hospital.

Liz was silent as they drove through the night. Micah slept the entire ride, too. Figured the little guy would sleep soundly now that they weren't hiding in the woods.

Thankfully, there was no traffic on the road, so they made good time. When he saw the welcome sign for Viroqua, he slowed and pulled into the driveway of a lower-budget motel. "Hope you don't mind."

She shrugged as she pushed open the car door. "You've seen where I live. I don't need anything fancy."

"Wait here," he suggested. "It's summer, but I'll try to get us connecting rooms."

She nodded. "Micah will need a bottle and a change soon."

As if on cue, the little boy began to cry. Garrett hurried inside, knowing Liz would take care of his son. Then he abruptly stopped, realizing that was his job.

It wasn't fair to take advantage of Liz's sweet nature.

Glancing back, he noticed she already had the baby in her arms. He forced himself to head inside to secure their rooms. From now on, he'd do his best to be Micah's caregiver.

Liz wouldn't be with him forever.

The twinge in the region of his heart made no sense, so he ignored it. Luckily, the sleepy clerk had two adjoining rooms, which she allowed him to pay for in cash. Grateful, he took the two keys and went back outside.

Liz sat in the front seat, giving Micah a bottle. But he was fussy, not wanting it and crying loud enough to wake others. She winced and shrugged. "I'll need to change him first."

"I'll do it." He gave her the room keys, then reached into the diaper bag. He opened the back hatch and set Micah down on the flat surface. When the task was done, he lifted the little boy and nuzzled his soft, downy hair. The baby quieted against him, filling his heart with love.

"Shall we go inside?" Liz asked in a whisper.

He nodded, leading the way across the small parking lot to where their rooms were located. She used the key to access her room, then unlocked the connecting doors between the two.

He still needed to bring in the items from the SUV, but he was hesitant to set Micah down. Finally, he handed the baby to Liz so he could grab the rest of their things.

Once that was completed, he double-checked both locks on their respective doors.

"Sit down. I need to look at your arm." She went to work, opening the gauze packs and getting towels and a washcloth from the bathroom.

He sat patiently while she cleaned his wound. It hurt when she used hydrogen peroxide on it, but he didn't complain.

He was keenly aware of her sweet scent. Her nearness was distracting, and he had to remind himself she was an innocent victim here, just like Micah.

When she looked down at him, it was all he could do not to pull her close for a warm embrace. His cell phone vibrated, breaking the moment.

His voice was rough when he answered Wyatt's call. "Do you have information already?"

"Yeah, although you're not going to like it." Wyatt sounded as tired as he must have felt.

"Why is that?"

"Because the guy you shot is gone. Someone—maybe even the person who hired him—must have come back and scooped him up."

Agitated, Garrett rose to his feet, pacing the length of the room. "Are you sure you're in the right spot?"

"Yep." Wyatt sounded grim. "I found the blood and the flat tire you left behind, so I know this is the location of the shooting. Abby and I spread out and searched the woods to see if he was dragged and dumped. There's no sign of him."

Garrett's mind whirled. This didn't make any sense. Who had taken the dead man away?

And if there had been another gunman there, why hadn't they been shot and killed?

Chapter Six

No dead body? Liz was close enough to Garrett to hear both sides of his conversation with Wyatt, but it was difficult to comprehend what he was saying.

"I checked for a pulse," Garrett said. "I know he was dead."

"I believe you. There's plenty of blood on the road." Wyatt's voice sounded strained. "You better be careful, boss. I don't like what's happening here."

"Yeah." Garrett caught her gaze. She offered a reassuring smile. "Thanks for checking in."

"Do you want us to contact the Brown County Sheriff's Department, anyway?" Wyatt asked.

Garrett considered this for a moment. "No. The report will only cause confusion. I need to think about what our next steps will be. I'm too tired to think clearly."

"Okay, we'll head back to Green Lake, then. But promise you'll call if you need us."

"Keep the county safe in my absence," Garrett said. "I'll call Liam in the morning to let him know I won't be in."

"We'll be okay. Abby and I can pull a double shift if needed," Wyatt offered.

She was impressed with how well the deputies supported Garrett. Their camaraderie made her realize how lonely her life had been since she'd buried herself in her clinic, caring for young mothers in need.

Maybe it was time to stop blaming herself for losing her daughter. Yet even as the thought flickered through her mind, she knew she couldn't.

Her husband had been right about the long hours impacting her pregnancy. She'd been too blind to notice. Until it was too late. Even though she'd lost Willow three years ago, she still remembered the moment she realized the baby had stopped moving.

Panic had gripped her by the throat, and by the time she'd gone in, it was too late.

"Take the deputy schedule up with Liam," Garrett said, interrupting her dark thoughts.

"Thanks again for coming with a clean vehicle for us to use."

"Anytime. Later, boss." Wyatt disconnected from the call.

Liz forced herself to stay back from Garrett. His warmth called to her in way she didn't understand. She glanced at Micah, noticing he was squirming a bit as if about to wake up. He hadn't taken much of the bottle before Garrett had put him in a new diaper.

Obviously, that was about to change.

"Hey there," she crooned, picking Micah up. "Are you awake?" His dark eyes blinked up at her, making her smile. "Oh, yes, you are. And hungry, too, hmm?"

"I can feed him," Garrett offered.

She hesitated, then handed the infant over to him. This was what she'd wanted—for Garrett to bond with his son. So why did she feel let down? She turned away and rummaged in the bag for the bottle she'd made just a few minutes ago.

Garrett lowered himself into the single chair in the corner of the room, giving Micah the bottle. She took the free time to slip into the bathroom to clean up.

Thanks to their trek through the woods, her

hair was tangled with leaves and other debris. Using her fingers, she combed through the long dark strands, dropping pine needles and bits of leaves and sticks in the garbage can. Then she splashed cold water on her face.

She reminded herself that it was a good sign that Garrett was taking over caring for his baby. She was happy for them, as the little guy needed his father now more than ever. Not only had he lost his mother, but there were multiple determined gunmen tracking them. Yet she had the utmost confidence that Garrett would do everything possible to keep his son safe.

Feeling better, she emerged from the bathroom. The chair in which Garrett had been sitting was empty, but she heard him murmuring to the baby through the connecting doorway of their rooms. He'd also taken the diaper bag with him, making her feel even more useless.

After crossing the room, she hovered in the doorway. "Everything okay?"

He glanced up in surprise. "Yes. I only moved to give you privacy. You must be exhausted, too. Besides, Micah is my responsibility, not yours."

It was on the tip of her tongue to remind him how he'd begged for her help when she first arrived, but she managed to hold back. She had to admire his determination to do his part. However, most young babies benefited from having two parents.

"I know Micah is your responsibility, but I also need you alert and focused on keeping us safe. Don't forget, I'm here to help."

His expression softened. "I appreciate that very much. And I promise I will wake you if needed. For now, try to get some rest."

"I will if you do the same." She smiled, then partially closed the door on her side. Not to shut him out, but to give him privacy, too.

After she'd crawled into bed, she found herself staring blindly up at the ceiling, wishing for something she could never have.

A family of her own.

Liz hadn't expected to fall asleep, but the sound of a baby crying jerked her from slumber. She bolted out of bed and hurried over the threshold to care for Micah. Garrett groaned and lifted his head. "I can get him."

"You need more sleep. I'll take a turn." Cradling the baby in her arms, she took the diaper bag into her room, using her hip to close the connecting door so that Garrett could fall back to sleep.

She truly didn't mind changing Micah and then making another bottle for him. The baby instantly quieted as she fed him, his dark gaze clinging to hers.

"You are so very precious," she whispered, her heart full of love for this tiny baby. "And I'm very glad you seem to be eating well." Up until now, it hadn't bothered her that she'd taken Micah directly to Garrett without having a doctor examine him. At the time, she'd been more concerned about his safety. Not to mention, women had been delivering children on their own for years without having a doctor in attendance.

But Micah should be seen by a pediatrician, and soon. Her expertise was delivering babies and caring for new mothers postdelivery. Her clinical practice didn't include follow-up appointments related to an infant's ongoing health.

Her thoughts turned to Rebecca. In reviewing her steps upon Rebecca's arrival, she couldn't come up with anything else she could have done to save the young woman's life. Especially not after she'd placed the needle to relieve her acute tension pneumothorax.

Still, the events of that night, followed by the subsequent gunfire, was troubling. She clutched

Micah close. Garrett would protect them, and he knew she'd do the same. Protect this innocent child with her own life, if necessary.

The way any mother would.

Garrett must have fallen back to sleep, because when he awoke, bright sunlight streamed in through the motel-room windows. He sat up, running his hand through his dark brown hair. He'd stayed up with Micah for too long, but he couldn't deny the sheer wonder at how he and Rebecca had created the beautiful baby.

He still felt guilty about spending the night with Rebecca, but having Micah softened the edges, making him realize how blessed he was to have a son.

After washing up in the bathroom, he took a minute to call Sheriff Liam Harland. His boss answered on the first ring.

"Harland."

"It's Garrett. I'm sorry to say I need a short leave of absence." He thought about how much to tell him, then decided it was best to come all the way clean. "I have a son, Liam. And his mother was shot right before she gave birth. She didn't make it, but the gunmen showed up at the sheriff's department and then again at my house. I need to keep Micah and the midwife who delivered him safe."

"A son? Congrats!" Trust Liam to look on the bright side first. "I'm sorry to hear about the gunmen, though. And the loss of the baby's mother. What can I do to help?"

He was humbled by Liam's willingness to pitch in. "We're safe now, so all I need is time off. To figure out what's going on and to bond with my son."

"Of course. That's a given. Take as much time as you need," Liam assured him. "And know this—we're here for you. It doesn't matter that this is our busy time. You're family. We'll do whatever we can to support you."

"Thanks." He was blessed to have Liam as his boss. "I'll be in touch soon."

"Okay, take care." Liam ended the call.

After pocketing his phone, he turned toward the connecting doorway. The power bar he'd eaten in the middle of the night was long gone, and his stomach rumbled with hunger. Peeking into Liz's room, he found her sleeping in the chair, Micah on the floor beside her.

She was so beautiful, he had to force himself to focus his attention on his son. Last night, he'd been determined not to take advantage of

Liz's kindness. But when she'd come to take Micah, he'd gratefully let her feed him so he could get more badly needed sleep.

How did single parents do it? These past twenty-four hours had made him realize how difficult some people had it.

It was humbling to know God had blessed him with this baby. He made a silent promise not to disappoint Him—and that meant letting go of his anger over Jason's untimely death.

And some of his own guilt, too.

"Good morning." Liz's husky voice drew his gaze from his son. Her smile sent his pulse into high gear.

"Good morning." He cleared his throat, hoping to sound normal. "I appreciate you letting me sleep in."

"Of course." She glanced at Micah, then stood. "How long can we stay here?"

"Checkout time is eleven. We have two hours." He frowned. "I would feel better if we moved on to a new location after we grab something to eat."

"Okay." She didn't argue his proposed plan. She stretched, then added, "I would love breakfast."

He grinned. "A woman after my own heart. Should we wait until Micah wakes up?"

"No need. He should sleep for at least another hour or so." She waved a hand. "We'll have his diaper bag with us if he wakes earlier."

He bowed to her expertise. "Okay, let's hit the road. There's a family-style restaurant across the street."

"Sounds perfect." She bent to grab the diaper bag. "First, though, I'd like to look at your arm."

He glanced at the gauze she'd wrapped around his injury. "It's fine. Trust me, I would let you know if it felt worse."

Scowling, she planted her hands on her hips. "I'd rather make sure there isn't an infection before it settles in your bloodstream."

Resigning himself to the inevitable, he gestured for her to come into his room, where they were less likely to disturb Micah. As before, she took a moment to spread out her supplies, including a washcloth and the hydrogen peroxide, then unwrapped the gauze. As she worked, he craned his neck to see the wound for himself.

To his inexpert eye, it looked fine. She pressed on his skin around the injury, then proceeded to wash and redress it.

"Told you it was fine," he grumbled.

"And I still think you could use a few doses

of antibiotics," she shot back. "Didn't we pass a sign for a medical center on the way in?"

"I'm not going," he said firmly. "Gunshot wounds are an automatic report to the police, and that will only open a can of worms." He frowned. "However, it might be smart to take Micah in to be checked out. Don't most babies see a doctor after they're born?"

"Yes. I had the same thought, but we can't just walk into the emergency department when there isn't anything wrong with him." She grimaced. "The emergency-department doctor would simply refer you to a pediatrician, anyway. They're not set up to perform well-baby visits."

"I guess that settles it." He stood and flexed his arm, glad it wasn't his shooting hand. The pain was negligible and wouldn't hold him back from keeping them safe. "No point in stopping in at the medical center."

She sighed but let it go. He thought about the computer, but he was too hungry to spend time searching for Rebecca's relatives now.

Food first; then he'd tackle their next steps. What he really wanted was to contact Rebecca's father. If the guy was still well enough to communicate, he hoped to convince him to take

Micah out of the line of succession for the inheritance. A college fund or something similar would be more than enough.

He could provide for his son. They didn't need the headache of fighting heirs over the Woodward fortune. That kind of money didn't buy happiness.

In fact, he felt certain it was just the opposite. Rebecca had claimed the summers she'd spent in Green Lake had been the best of her life. Nights spent sitting at the edge of the lake or stealing a kiss at the campfire...

No, that kind of money wasn't worth it.

Pushing those troublesome thoughts aside, he put the laptop strap over his shoulder. He peered through the window, scanning the parking lot, before carrying Micah outside. Liz followed close behind with the diaper bag.

The bright day without a cloud in the sky promised warm summer temperatures. Normally, he'd be concerned about tourists causing trouble out on Green Lake. But there wasn't anything he could do, now that he was on a leave of absence.

The family restaurant wasn't as busy as he'd anticipated. They were taken to a booth in the corner. He tucked Micah's carrier in beside him.

A server arrived with coffee. When their mugs were full, they perused the menu, then placed their orders.

"This seems like a nice town," Liz commented before sipping her coffee. "It feels as if nothing bad could happen here."

He'd once thought the same thing about Green Lake, until he'd gone into law enforcement. Liam's wife, Shauna, had been in danger; then some of the Amish members of the community had danger show up on their doorstep, too. Now this. He shook his head. "Unfortunately, bad things can happen anywhere."

"True." She lowered her mug. "Where are we going next?"

It was a good question. "We could push on through to La Cross. It's about thirty miles west of here. Or we could turn and head south to Madison." He shrugged. "La Cross is closer."

"I'd prefer La Cross—although I don't know how we're going to figure out who hired the gunmen."

He wasn't sure about that himself. He sat back as their server arrived with their food. When she left, Liz leaned forward to take his hand. "We should say grace."

Squeezing her hand, he bowed his head. It

had been a long time since he'd done this, but the prayer came easily. "Dear Lord, we thank You for this wonderful food and keeping us safe in Your care. Amen."

"Amen," Liz whispered.

He wanted to savor the moment, but Micah began wiggling in his carrier. He quickly dove into his meal, eating in record time so he could tend to his son.

"I'll make him a bottle in the restroom," Liz offered, scooting out of her seat.

Micah was awake but hadn't started crying yet. He blinked in the light as if wondering where he was, but Garrett knew it wouldn't take long for him to fuss. He lifted the boy from his carrier and held him with his injured arm while trying to finish his breakfast with the other.

Micah's tiny face crumpled just as Liz returned. Garrett flashed a smile as he quickly gave his son the bottle. "Just in time."

"I'll take him," she offered.

"He's fine. I'm just about finished, anyway." He ate the last slice of crispy bacon, then pushed his plate aside. "I'd like to call Rebecca's father sooner than later, though. Maybe we can stop by the motel long enough to use the internet so I can look up the best way to try to contact him."

"Okay, but I don't think billionaires list their personal phone numbers on the web," she said.

"I know. But there would be a phone number for his company, and I might be able to get through to someone by using Rebecca's name." It was the only idea he could come up with.

"Hang on." She pulled out her phone, then nodded. "There's internet here. Give me Micah, I'll hold him while you log on."

He did as she asked, passing the baby across the table. He couldn't help but smile at how Liz cooed over his son. Turning his attention to more important issues, he opened the laptop and connected to the free Wi-fi.

It was slow, but it worked well enough for him to find the corporate offices of Wood-ward Enterprises. He started with the general number, letting the assistant who answered the phone know that he had important information related to Rebecca and her baby that he needed to give to Robert Woodward.

"Hold on, please." Before he could agree, there was nothing but dead air. He waited three full minutes before another voice answered.

"This is Edward Woodward's assistant," a pleasant voice said. "How may I help you?"

Edward was Robert's younger brother—and a suspect, along with his children, Elaine and Jeremy. "I don't want to speak to Edward. I need to talk to Robert directly."

"I'm sorry, that's not an option. He's been moved into hospice care. Edward is in charge now, and he would be happy to help in any way he can."

Hospice care. The news shouldn't have been a shock. "I'm sorry. That won't work. Goodbye." He quickly disconnected, then powered down the phone in case they decided to try tracing the call.

"What is it?" Liz's expression reflected her concern.

"Edward Woodward is in charge," he said. "And Rebecca's father has been moved into hospice."

"Oh, no. That's so sad."

Did Robert even know about Rebecca's death? He thought it was interesting Edward's assistant hadn't asked more questions about Rebecca or her baby.

He decided to call the dispatcher to find out if either Wyatt or Abby were still on duty. A horrible thought had occurred to him, and he needed more information—fast.

"Wyatt is on his way home. Would you like me to connect you?"

"Please." There was a pause before Wyatt answered. "Hey. I need you to call the Brown County morgue to see if Rebecca's body has been taken there."

"Okay. I'll call you right back." Wyatt clicked off, presumably to make the call. He had a bad feeling about this.

It took almost ten minutes for Wyatt to call back. He put the call on speaker for Liz to hear, too. "No female Jane Doe or Rebecca Woodward has been taken to the Brown County Medical Examiner's office or to the local hospital."

That was exactly what he'd been afraid of. "These guys are getting rid of the bodies to eliminate any evidence."

"Yep," Wyatt agreed. "No body, no crime. At least, it's much harder to prove there was a crime. Are you guys okay? Do you need us to come back you up?"

"No thanks. Go home and get some sleep." He disconnected from the call, then powered down his phone. "Make sure to keep yours off from this point forward, too," he instructed.

Eyes wide, she nodded.

He stared out the window. Rebecca's body had been taken away, just like the gunman he'd shot in self-defense.

The situation had gone from bad to worse. And despite his years on the job, he wasn't sure what to do about it.

Chapter Seven

Liz swallowed hard, wishing she hadn't left Rebecca's body behind in her clinic. Yet she'd needed to keep Micah safe and had called the ambulance to respond to Rebecca's death. How had the gunmen found Rebecca's body prior to the ambulance arriving?

They must have been closer than she'd realized. And one had followed her to the sheriff's department.

Her distress must have been evident, because Garrett reached over to take her hand. "Please don't be upset. It's not your fault."

"I keep trying to tell myself that." She shook her head, feeling helpless. "I only left because of the potential danger to Micah. And that has been proven to be a bigger concern than I realized." She held his gaze. "It's all surreal."

"You have that right." He gently squeezed her hand. "We'll need to pick up disposable phones and continue staying off-grid as much as possible."

"I understand." She gazed at Micah's sleeping face, knowing just how lost she'd be without Garrett's support. Based on everything that had transpired, returning to her clinic wasn't an option.

What if she could never go back? A surge of panic tightened her chest. She couldn't abandon her patients. They needed her!

Then again, so did Micah—at least for now, while Garrett searched for the bad guys.

She struggled to breathe normally, letting go of her fears. Her future was in God's hands.

Their server returned with more coffee, smiling at Micah. "He's so precious. What's his name?"

"Micah," she and Garrett answered at the exact same time.

Their server laughed as she finished filling their mugs. "It's always nice to see a beautiful family."

Her gaze clashed with Garrett's, a flush creeping over her cheeks, but neither of them corrected her assumption. Garrett smiled softly, then turned his attention back to the laptop.

"If you don't mind, I'd like to stay here for

another few minutes." His fingers worked the keyboard. "I need to see if there are other possible heirs who should be considered suspects."

"Anything that helps us get to the bottom of this mess is fine with me." It still boggled her mind to think that anyone would kill an innocent baby over money.

She glanced around the restaurant, enjoying the cheerful atmosphere. The family-friendly place seemed safe, far away from the gunmen who stalked them.

"I need to make a list," Garrett muttered.

"A list about what?"

"Heirs to the Woodward fortune if Micah was out of the picture." He frowned. "Robert's brother, Edward, has two kids, Elaine and Jeremy. But now it looks like Robert has a sister, too—Connie. And her daughter, Anita."

"Edward, Elaine, Jeremy, Connie and Anita," she repeated, to memorize their names. "Would the inheritance be split between them evenly? Or would one sibling get more than the others?"

"That's a good question—although, from searching the website, it appears both Edward and Connie Malone, which is her married name, work in the business. They must report to Rebecca, who was named CEO a few months ago, which is when Robert declared her and her baby the heir to his company." He grimaced. "It's possible with her and Micah gone, they'd have equal shares, along with their children. If that's the case, Edward has the advantage."

She shifted her gaze to the sleeping infant. "Rebecca was CEO, huh? He must have given her that role right after he learned about his cancer. I'm not a cancer expert, but being diagnosed with stage four pancreatic cancer usually means a life expectancy of nine months to a year at the most."

"I think Rebecca was always slated to take over, but the timing may have been pushed up because of his diagnosis," Garrett agreed thoughtfully. "I wonder how her aunt and uncle feel about reporting to her. Although, that's not a problem any longer."

"Maybe that's part of the reason she was in danger." Remembering the fear in Rebecca's eyes made her shiver. "Are we sure Micah is the sole heir? That's a lot of pressure to put on one person. You mentioned an article, but maybe Robert's will names others, too."

"That gives me an idea." He went back to

the keyboard. "Maybe there's a way to speak to Robert's lawyer."

"It would be nice if he could put us in touch with Robert directly." She brightened at the possibility. "There's still time for him to change his will."

"It's possible." Garrett sighed. "Trust me, I'd love nothing more than to get the target off my son's back. However, I would think the rest of the family would have tried to convince him to change the will by now if that was possible."

She hated to admit he was right. "Rebecca sought help in my clinic for a reason," she murmured. "The note you found in her car indicates she came all this way to have her baby in a location no one would find her."

"Except they did find her." He raked his hand over his face. "I really wish she'd have called me beforehand. I could have been there for her. I could have kept her safe."

"I guess we shouldn't keep playing the what-if game." She sighed. "Rebecca must have had her reasons."

"Maybe." He scowled at the screen, not looking convinced. "There's nothing on the Woodward Enterprises website that mentions a lawyer."

Their server came over one more time to refill their mugs and leave their bill. Since the restaurant seemed to be filling up with people, Liz gestured to the receipt. "We should leave, let others have the table."

"Okay." Garrett closed the computer and stuffed it back in the case. He paid the tab, then waited as she strapped Micah into his seat. He carried the baby through the restaurant and headed outside.

As always, he scanned the area as they walked to the SUV. She was certain they were safe here, but she appreciated how he stayed alert.

It took a few minutes for them to get situated, and as Garrett drove out of the parking lot, pausing to turn right to head into town, she noticed a black SUV with tinted windows pull up to the motel.

"Garrett?" She reached out to grasp his arm as he made the turn. "Quick! Look at that SUV."

He glanced over, his expression turning grim as he continued driving down the road, away from the motel. "Did you get the license plate?"

"No, sorry." She twisted in her seat, trying to see better. Two men climbed out of the vehicle. "There's two of them," she whispered. "I can't see anything more."

"Two men?" he echoed.

She nodded, clasping her trembling fingers together. "It could be nothing, right? Just a couple of guys scouting the area, looking for a place to stay?"

"I doubt it." His gaze was glued to the rearview mirror. "We should have left the restaurant right away, rather than staying to use the internet."

She gaped at him. "You think they traced the internet connection?"

"No. They'd have come straight to the restaurant." She noticed he didn't speed or try to be conspicuous as he turned left at the intersection and drove through a suburban neighborhood. Her heart pounded with fear, but she tried to remain calm. The houses were quaint, and many had beautiful flower gardens out front. It would be a great place to stay, except for the black SUV with tinted windows back at the motel.

"How did they find us?"

He glanced at her. "They could have tracked our phones prior to our turning them off."

If that was true, she wished they'd shut them off earlier. As Garrett continued making his way through town, she thought about the two men who were determined to find them.

She and Garrett were the only thing standing between the gunmen and Micah. To hurt the baby, they'd have to kill them first.

She could only hope and pray it wouldn't come to that.

Kicking himself for being complacent, Garrett managed to wind his way through town to the other side of Viroqua. He took the highway south, deciding against going to La Cross. Since these guys had shown up here, he figured it was better to backtrack a bit, hoping they wouldn't anticipate that.

So much for finding a peaceful place to stay off-grid.

Tracking their phones was the only way they could have found them here. The gunmen seemed to have unlimited resources at their disposal. Far more than he did.

He told himself he was a cop with years of experience behind him. Surely he could outsmart these guys.

But not if he didn't keep his mind focused on their safety. Staying at the restaurant for so long had been a rookie mistake.

And he couldn't afford to make another.

"I thought we were going to La Cross?"

"Not anymore." He continued keeping a wary eye on the rearview mirror. The fact that they hadn't shown up at the restaurant was only slightly reassuring. He didn't believe they knew what car he was driving.

Keeping his speed near the speed limit as to not draw undue attention wasn't easy. He wanted to hit the gas and speed far away from the threat.

"Where are we going?" Liz asked, her voice low.

"I don't know yet." He tried to envision a map of Central Wisconsin in his mind. He didn't necessarily want to head to Madison, but Green Lake wasn't an option, either.

Should they drive all the way to Chicago? That would take the entire day, and even if he showed up at the office building that housed Woodward Enterprises, he doubted he'd get very far.

And the thought of taking Micah anywhere near the company his mother ran as CEO made him feel sick to his stomach. Rebecca had claimed to love working for her father; she'd thrived on the responsibility.

A decision that may have cost her life.

Not that it was her fault she had greedy relatives. He wondered what Joel had to say about that.

Wait a minute. He looked at the laptop computer he'd set on the floor of the front seat. "Joel," he said. "I should have thought about Joel."

"Who?" Liz looked confused.

"The last time I saw Rebecca, she mentioned a guy she'd hired as her chief financial officer. A man named Joel Abernathy." Had the guy been listed on the website? He had been so focused on identifying the potential heirs that he hadn't looked at the hierarchy of the company's leadership team.

"What about him?" Liz frowned. "I don't see how a CFO would be a possible heir to the estate."

He tried to put his feelings into words. "I was upset over losing a young cop in the line of duty during the time Rebecca came to visit. That night…" He flushed and forced himself to continue. "I let my emotions cloud my judgment. We spent the night together, and I have to assume that's when Micah was conceived."

"I'm sorry you lost a young officer." Liz

rested her hand on his arm. "I'm sure that was difficult for you—and you don't have to explain your personal life to me. I'm still not getting how Joel is a part of this, though."

He wasn't doing a good job of explaining. "I wanted Rebecca to stay in Green Lake, to give a relationship between us a try. She told me as much as she enjoyed spending time here, she couldn't give up her role with the company. She mentioned she'd been spending a lot of time with Joel, their new hire. At the time, I assumed she meant they were spending time together as professionals. But when I called a few weeks later, she told me she was seeing someone else."

"And you think that someone was Joel?" Her gaze was skeptical. "She could have been seeing anyone."

"True." He couldn't deny the possibility he was making a big deal out of nothing. "But what if she wasn't? What if she'd gotten close to Joel, then decided to date him?"

"After spending the night with you?" The way Liz said the words indicated she didn't think much of Rebecca's decision. "Why would she lead you on like that?"

"She didn't—not really." He glanced in the rearview mirror again, noticing there were a few cars on the highway behind him. They were too far away to make out whether they were SUVs with tinted windows, though. "We were friends for years. I cared for her, a lot. I thought she felt the same way, especially when we spent the night together. But maybe she ultimately regretted what we'd done."

Liz opened her mouth as if to argue, but she must have changed her mind. After a moment, she said, "Okay, so when we find a safe place and have the chance to get disposable phones, you should reach out to Joel. See what he has to say."

"I will." It felt good to have a goal. Now, if he could just come up with a destination... A sign loomed ahead, indicating the small town of Readsville was ten miles away. He pointed at it. "Keep your eyes open for any motel signs. I'm not sure if Readsville is big enough to have one or not. It looks pretty rustic out here."

"Okay." She flashed a wry smile. "I bet they have a library. *Reads*ville? Get it?"

He chuckled at her weak joke. "That would be nice, but I'd rather have a motel that takes cash and a place we can get carryout food." No more going to restaurants where they would be sitting ducks.

He looked at the cars behind him again. The closest vehicle was moving faster now, narrowing the gap between them. He tightened his grip on the steering wheel, trying to decide if the vehicle posed a threat or if he was letting his imagination run wild.

The car kept coming. Since they were on a narrow single-lane highway, he slowed and moved over onto the shoulder, hoping the driver would pass.

He didn't.

Highway Junction JJ loomed in his line of sight. He hit the brake and wrenched the wheel, taking the sharp right-hand turn. Then he punched the gas, desperate to put distance between them and the car following.

"What's going on?" Liz grabbed her armrest and twisted in her seat. "Did the tinted SUV find us?"

He didn't answer, mostly because he was desperately searching for a place where they could hide out. He hated the idea of risking Micah's safety during a high-speed car chase.

Although he would if he had no other choice.

"I don't understand. How did they catch up? We don't have our phones on!" Liz's voice rose in alarm.

"Hang on." The car tracking them had managed to make the turn, too, although the driver had lost some ground. Within seconds, the vehicle was out of view. This highway was even narrower than the one they'd left, and it was curvy, too. He seriously needed to figure out a way to lose their tail.

"Call 911. Let them know a black car is following us on Highway Double J." He went as fast as possible on the curvy road—which was no easy feat, since he couldn't see what was up ahead. He wished he had his phone so he could use the GPS. From what he could tell, there were no other intersections in sight, not even a driveway leading to a lone house.

He went several miles as Liz spoke to the dispatcher, explaining the danger and trying to give clues as to where they were located. Even as he heard her use the highway markers as identifiers, he feared any police response would be too late.

Please, Lord, guide us to safety!

When Liz glanced at him, he realized he'd whispered the prayer out loud.

There! He caught a glimpse of a small house partially hidden in the trees. He hit the brake hard, scanning the side of the road for a driveway.

There was a narrow opening between the trees, with gravel covering the ground. He hesitated, not wanting to put others in danger, but then he turned into the driveway, going up far enough for the trees on either side to give them cover—and hoping they weren't visible from the house, either.

"We're just going to sit here?" Liz asked.

"No, we're getting out. I'll take Micah. You grab the laptop case and diaper bag. Please, hurry. We need to be far away before the vehicle passes this driveway."

Liz jumped into action, grabbing the laptop and pushing her door open in one quick movement. By the time he'd unbuckled Micah's carrier, she had the diaper bag, too.

"Follow me." He'd noticed the small wooded area was slightly more dense to the right of the vehicle. He headed that way, hoping and praying the owner of the property wouldn't come down and demand to know what they were doing.

To his surprise, there was a small woodpile—cut logs that were neatly stacked between two trees offering some semblance of cover. They were a little too close to the open area leading up to the house for comfort, but it was the best protection they could ask for.

Liz didn't protest when he headed toward the woodpile. Rounding the tree at one end, he set Micah's carrier down, then gestured for her to crouch beside him.

"Stay down," he whispered. Then he pulled out his weapon and hunkered down beside her. He moved two of the logs so that he'd have a better view of the trail leading from their car.

The trees were thick enough that he could barely see the road. He alternated between looking at the road and the path ahead of them.

The area was so quiet, he could easily hear the car engine approaching. Liz huddled over Micah, using her body as a shield. It humbled him to know she'd risk her life for his son.

A car moved down the road before slowing to a stop. He held his breath, then forced himself to breathe as the vehicle backed up.

Keep going, he silently pleaded. *Keep going!*

The seconds passed with agonizing slowness. No doubt the driver of the vehicle was trying to decide if they'd turned off or not.

Keep going!

As if in answer to his silent plea, the car rolled past, gaining speed.

Still, he didn't move. This could be nothing more than a trap to draw them out of hiding. They were stuck here until he was convinced the gunmen were gone.

Chapter Eight

Silently praying, Liz covered Micah's body with her own. She trusted Garrett's cop instincts. If he thought the gunmen would return to find them, then she believed him.

For ten long minutes, she heard nothing. But then the barest rumble of a car engine reached her ears. Lifting her head, she reached out to touch Garrett's arm.

With a grim look, he nodded in understanding. He'd heard it, too.

The gunmen? Or someone else? Her heart thudded loudly in her ears as she strained to listen.

The sound of the car engine grew louder. From where she was positioned, huddling over Micah and tucked behind the wood stack, she couldn't see anything.

She felt Garrett tense beside her and knew something was going on. Then the car engine abruptly went silent. Garrett put a finger to his lips, indicating she shouldn't talk, then tucked the SUV key fob into her hands. His intense blue gaze implored her to get Micah to safety if anything should happen to him.

Please, Lord Jesus, keep us safe! Grant Garrett the strength and wisdom he needs to fight these men!

Taking a long, deep breath on the heels of her desperate prayer helped calm her racing heart. She couldn't hear anything else now but could easily imagine the gunmen spreading out to search for them.

A rustling sound almost made her gasp. She continued protecting Micah's body with hers, ignoring the urge to run from danger.

Then Micah began to cry. *No! Not now!*

A sharp retort of gunfire reverberated around them. Garrett must have been watching the guy approach, because he fired back a fraction of a second later. The sound of a man's cry, loud enough to be heard over Micah's fussing, indicated he'd hit his mark.

Another gunshot echoed through the trees. Had the second man come to back up the first? Garrett returned fire, only this time there was no sound of an injury. Or maybe she just

couldn't hear it, as Micah's cries were growing louder.

She glanced helplessly up at Garrett, but he
was focused on the scene beyond the woodpile.
Biting her lip, she considered her options. She
had the diaper bag, and there was still some premade formula in the can she'd used the previous
day—but it hadn't been refrigerated, and she
wouldn't dare offer that to a one-day old baby.
There was another can in the bag. She wasn't
sure there was time to make another bottle. Not
if they had to take off at a run.

Dragging the bag toward her, she found the
pacifier, hoping the baby would take it. Micah
accepted the rubber tip but then must have realized he wasn't getting any food, because he
spat it back out.

Garrett gave her a reassuring look, then eased
out from behind the woodpile. She wanted to
call him back, but she stayed where she was.
Had he injured both men? It seemed wrong
to pray that he had. Yet she wanted Micah to
be safe.

And men stalking them with guns was anything but.

She picked Micah up, holding him against
her shoulder to soothe him. He quieted a bit,

but it didn't last long. She wanted to look over the top of the logs, but she didn't dare expose herself or the baby to more gunfire.

After what seemed like an eternity, Garrett came back. "One man down. The other took off. I think I wounded him—there's a spot of blood where he'd been standing."

"We're safe?"

"For now." She should have known their safety was only temporary. "Get Micah into the SUV. I'm calling for backup. This time, the dead guy isn't going anywhere but to the closest morgue."

"Okay." She gently tucked the crying baby into the carrier and hauled him, the laptop and the diaper bag back to the SUV. She passed by a gunman lying face up on the ground between two trees.

She felt terrible for Garrett. This was the second time he'd been forced to kill to keep them safe. Granted, he'd only done so in self-defense, but she felt certain he didn't treat taking a life lightly.

She didn't, either. Why couldn't these gunmen just go away and leave them alone?

Upon reaching the car, she took the time to buckle Micah's carrier into place before crawl-

ing in beside him to make the bottle. She wasn't
sure if they'd have to hit the road again soon
but was determined to be prepared.

Micah's cries subsided when she offered him
a fresh bottle. She sighed in relief, realizing
they'd need to stock up on supplies very soon.
She'd used the last can of premade formula.
They needed more if they found themselves in
a similar situation.

Though she hoped they wouldn't have to
keep hiding from assailants for much longer.

Glancing out the window, she noticed an
older man standing several feet from Garrett,
his expression set in a deep scowl. The homeowner, no doubt. And she didn't blame the man
for being upset over what had taken place on
his property.

Garrett had his badge out and was gesturing
to the area behind him, likely explaining what
had happened. The guy kept his distance, as if
wary about Garrett's story.

The wail of police sirens was a welcome relief. She wondered if the cop was responding
to her initial call or to the homeowner, who'd
likely called in the shots fired.

Either way, she was glad they weren't in this
alone. Micah's gaze held hers, and her heart

squeezed with love and the realization of how close they'd been to getting hurt.

Or worse.

Two police cars pulled into the driveway behind the SUV. Garrett had his hands up where they could be seen, holding his badge in one of them as he jogged over.

The homeowner stayed back, watching from afar.

Micah was still drinking his bottle when the officers emerged from their squads with their guns drawn. She could hear Garrett through the closed windows.

"I'm Chief Deputy Garrett Nichols from the Green Lake County Sheriff's Department." He continued holding his hands palm forward, showing them the badge. "Two gunmen trailed us here. They initiated the shooting. I fired back in self-defense. One gunman is down. The other is wounded but took off."

"Who's in the SUV?" one of them shouted.

"Liz Templeton and my son, Micah. We're all in danger. The gunmen have been tracking us for the past twenty-four hours."

She watched as one of the officers used his radio to talk to someone. Both officers stayed alert until they'd received a response. Then they slowly lowered and holstered their weapons.

Garrett lowered his hands, too, but didn't put his badge away. Micah finished his bottle, so she held him up against her shoulder to burp him. Then she opened the door to step out of the car with the baby.

"You have to understand, we're in danger," she said.

"And you're Liz Templeton?" the taller of the two officers asked. "Lizbeth Templeton?"

The way he used her full name indicated he'd had her run through their system. Likely Garrett's, too. She nodded. "I'm a witness to the shooting incident. We tried to hide from the gunmen on this man's property, but they came back and began searching for us. When the baby started crying, the gunmen found us. That's when Garrett returned fire."

Maybe it was Micah's presence there, but the officers seemed to believe her.

The homeowner came down to discuss the situation, too. It took longer than she'd have liked to give their statements and to ensure the dead man was taken to the Volver County morgue.

A solid two hours later, she and Garrett were

allowed to leave. She found herself hesitant to part from the relative safety of the officers behind.

"Now what?" she asked, clicking her seat belt into place.

"We need to get to a motel and make arrangements with Liam to swap this for another vehicle." Garrett looked exhausted, as if the shooting had drained his energy.

"Another car?"

"The wounded man who got away could have this license plate." He raked his hand through his dark chestnut hair. "I wish we could head back to Green Lake, but I think we're better off in a different city—hopefully one that will enable us to go off-grid."

"That hasn't worked so far," she murmured.

"No, it hasn't." He looked completely dejected. She rested her hand on his arm.

"I knew you would keep us safe, Garrett. God is watching over us."

He glanced at her and nodded, though she didn't think he believed her.

But the cops who had arrived at the scene had. And she knew Liam probably did, too. All she could do was continue to pray for this nightmare to end.

Very soon.

★ ★ ★

Garrett was keenly aware of Liz's soft hand on his arm. As much as he felt bad about killing a man, he was glad they had a body for evidence. The officers who'd responded had agreed to keep him in the loop on the guy's identity.

They needed something to go on, some clue to link back to the person who'd hired these guys. The way the assailants had found them again was unnerving. Was it possible they'd chosen the same route he had by accident?

Or did they have more help and resources than he realized?

The thought of having access to cop-like resources was sobering. Either way, he needed a better plan. And maybe being out in the middle of nowhere was working against them. He'd originally intended to stay south, but now he embraced the idea of heading northeast toward Portage, the city that housed the state prison. It wasn't a large city like Milwaukee or Madison, but it was big enough for them to get lost in, or so he hoped. And there were plenty of transient people there, too.

They needed to buy replacement phones ASAP. The urge to call Liam was strong, but he wouldn't risk using their personal phones.

He turned north at the next highway, one that was even smaller than the one they had been on. Liz was unusually quiet. "You okay?"

"Yes. But I lost ten years off my life when Micah woke up crying when the gunmen were out there."

He grimaced. "I know, but it worked in our favor. The sound startled the guy who was closest to me. He lashed out, firing almost at random without looking." The exchange had been hairy, but in the end, they'd prevailed. "The good news is that we'll soon have an ID on this guy, if he's in the system."

"And if he's not?"

He sighed. "That's possible, but I don't think your average citizen accepts a job like this. It takes someone with a cold heart to kill a baby. It's more likely the perp has a criminal background already."

"That makes sense." She turned to look back at Micah sleeping in his seat. "That was a close one, Garrett. If something had happened to you, I don't think Micah would have survived."

"I know. We can't let them get that close again." At least they hadn't stayed in the car, where they would have easily been found.

They rode in silence for the next hour. He

was slightly reassured to see there were no vehicles on this deserted stretch of highway, but
he knew that would change once they came
closer to their destination. Despite their full
breakfast, his stomach rumbled with hunger, so
he searched for restaurant signs. There were several to pick from once they reached the town of
Portage. The large prison, surrounded by high
fences topped with barbed wire, could be seen
from the road as they approached. It made him
think about how many guys he and Liam and
the other deputies had arrested and ultimately
sent there to serve their sentences.

Not as many as those arrested in the bigger
cities, but they had seen an increase in crime
in their small town.

And that danger had returned tenfold.

Their first stop was at a store that sold phones
and other supplies. Liz looked relieved to have
the chance to stock up on items for Micah.

By the time they'd finished, his stomach
was growling in earnest. Checking his watch,
he figured they had time to eat before his son
awoke.

He considered ordering takeout, but he discovered the restaurant was on Main Street and
the parking lot for all the businesses was two

blocks away. Hoping they'd be safe enough for now, he requested a booth in the back of the restaurant that was closest to the kitchen so they'd have an escape route if needed.

"Everything looks good," Liz said as she perused the menu. "I don't know why I'm so hungry when all we did was sit in the car for hours."

"Being hit with an adrenaline rush works up an appetite." He'd experienced that before. "I noticed there were several hotels here, too. We'll see if we can get another set of connecting rooms after lunch."

"That would be nice."

When their meal arrived, he decided to take the lead on saying grace. God had watched over them today, and he knew how much he needed Him to get through this. Reaching across the table, he took Liz's hand. "Dear Lord Jesus, thank You for keeping us safe today. We ask for Your continued guidance and wisdom as we seek those who wish us harm. Amen."

"Amen." Liz lifted her gaze. "That was beautiful, Garrett."

He nodded, feeling self-conscious. "I know you said God was always there for me, and I believe that's true. I should not have turned my back on Him after Jason's death."

"We're all human, and we make mistakes." She munched on a french fry, then added, "When I lost my daughter as a stillborn, then found my husband in the arms of another woman, I went through the same anger toward God as you did. It wasn't easy to understand why God took my daughter." She glanced at Micah, a soft smile tugging at her lips. "Then I began helping low-income women living on and off the reservation and began to see how He wanted me to use my talents and my experience to help others."

"I didn't know about your daughter and husband. I'm so sorry." He marveled at her ability to put her anger aside.

"Thank you. It's been hard, especially after Eric's death, but I'm in a better place now."

Even with the gunmen on their tail? That was even more humbling. "I believe God sent Rebecca to you for Micah's sake. And I'm very glad you brought him to me."

"Me, too."

It wasn't fair that her life was in danger, and for a moment, he considered taking Micah far away, changing their names and dropping out of sight.

But he sensed the person behind this wouldn't rest until he or she knew the heir wasn't a threat.

Besides, he wouldn't walk away from Liz or force her to go away with him and Micah. No, the only way out of this was to find the person responsible and have them arrested.

With a renewed sense of determination, he dug into his burger. He needed to have a conversation with Liam about their next steps. And for that, they needed a motel room with electricity to charge and activate their new phones.

Feeling better with food in his belly, Garrett carried Micah back to the SUV with Liz walking beside him. Anyone looking in their direction would assume they were a family. And he found himself liking that image, more than he should.

Knowing now about Liz's loss and her dedication to serving low-income women, he doubted she was looking for anything like a relationship. Especially living as far away as she did.

Enough… There was no point in going down that road, even in his unspoken thoughts. He drove past all the motels, which were surprisingly located in a cluster—maybe because of the prison—and chose the one most likely to accept cash.

"Wait here, okay?" He pushed out of the car and strode inside. All three of the motels appeared fairly busy—probably due to the season—but thankfully, he was able to obtain two connecting rooms for cash.

Micah was awake and looking around when they entered their adjoining rooms. For a minute, Garrett simply gazed down at the curious baby, who looked up at him with dark eyes.

Rebecca had brown eyes, but he'd heard from Liam and Shauna that a baby's eye color could change in the first few months. It didn't matter to him one way or the other; he liked the idea of Micah sharing some of Rebecca's traits.

He wished again that she'd called him about the danger. When Micah's eyelids finally drifted shut, he went about charging and activating the phones.

When they were finally ready, he handed one to Liz, then used the other to call the Green Lake County Sheriff's Department.

"This is Deputy Nichols," he said when the dispatcher answered. "Is Liam around?"

"He's out on patrol but told me to patch you through if you called. Please hold."

Garrett winced at the thought of Liam being

forced out on patrol, likely due to his absence. And the fact that he'd asked Wyatt and Abby to help him late into the night. But the situation couldn't be helped. It was better for everyone if he kept the gunmen out of Green Lake.

No matter how much he wished he had his fellow deputies here to back him up.

"Garrett?" Liam's voice broke into his thoughts. "What in the world is going on?"

"I guess you heard from the Volver County Sheriff's Department."

"They asked me to vouch for you, which of course I did. But they mentioned you shot a man and wounded another. Are you okay? How is Micah?"

Garrett hastened to reassure him. "We're fine. I didn't have a choice, Liam. Micah's crying startled the perp into shooting. I had to stop him."

"I trust your judgment." Liam's support meant the world to him. "I just wish you were closer so we could help."

"It's better for you, Shauna and Ciara if I stay away. What I do need, though, is information. I've been doing some searching online and have a short list of suspects that I could use some help with." He gave Liam the names of Edward,

Elaine, Jeremy, Connie and Anita. "These are the possible heirs to the Woodward fortune, now that Rebecca is gone and once Robert succumbs to his cancer. I know you're busy, but when you or the others have time, see if you can find anything more about them."

"I still have that contact within the Chicago PD, too. I'll try him. Is this the number I can reach you at?"

"Yes. Thanks, Liam. I owe you for this."

"Stay tuned. Gotta go." Liam quickly disconnected. But it was only a minute later that his phone rang again. "Liam?"

"No, this is Aaron, the dispatcher. I have a call here from Deputy Jorge Rivera of the Volver County Sheriff's Department."

"Great, put him through." Garrett's pulse spiked. "Deputy Rivera? Do you have something for me?"

"Do you know a Tyler Richardson?" Rivera asked.

"No. Who is he?"

"The dead guy. His prints popped up in the system, as he has a long criminal record. Small time stuff, not attempted murder."

Tyler Richardson. Garrett jotted the name down on a small pad of paper on the desk. If they could connect Tyler Richardson to one of the Woodward heirs, they'd be one step closer to ending this nightmare.

Chapter Nine

Leaning forward, Liz read the name Garrett had written down. Tyler Richardson? She'd never heard of the guy, but she quickly understood this was the man he'd been forced to shoot when they were hiding behind the woodpile.

"Are you okay to watch Micah for a bit?" Garrett asked. "I'd like to dig into this guy's background, see if I can connect him to anyone within the Woodward family."

"Of course." She dropped her gaze to the baby sleeping in his carrier. Despite knowing this was a temporary arrangement, she'd fallen hard for this little boy.

He was a fighter, much like his mommy and daddy.

"Lizbeth." Hearing Garrett use her full name in his low, husky voice sent shivers of awareness through her. "You have a beautiful name."

"Thank you." Was that her squeaky voice? She managed a smile. "When I was young, I wished for a Native American–sounding name. But my mother didn't want anything to do with her heritage. Maybe she'd been discriminated against at some point. I know she loved my father." Her expression turned somber. "They died in a motorcycle crash near Green Bay."

"I'm sorry to hear that." He put his arm around her shoulder in a friendly hug. His earthy scent messed with her mind, and she had to remind herself again that this togetherness was temporary. "I lost my mom when I was young and was raised by my dad and grandparents. My dad and grandfather were all about hunting and fishing but tended to avoid emotional conversations."

"I wondered why you were so good at moving silently through the woods." She smiled teasingly. "You are much better than I am."

"Years of practice." He grinned, then stood. "I need to get searching on our dead guy. He must be connected in some way to the Woodward family."

She nodded, then drew the diaper bag toward her to get it organized with the new items she'd purchased at the store: a larger pack of diapers and wipes, along with more formula to replace the open cans that hadn't been refrigerated. She hated to waste them but refused to risk Micah getting sick.

When she'd finished, the baby began to cry. She changed him, then prepared a bottle. Garrett glanced over. "Do you want me to feed him?"

"I can do it." She nodded toward the laptop computer. "Have you found anything?"

"No, other than he's from the Chicago area. Did a short stint in jail for assault and robbery. I have to admit, he doesn't seem like the type to go from that to murder for hire."

Murder for hire. The words alone made her shiver. "Will Liam and your deputies investigate him, too?"

"I hope so. I texted Liam the guy's name and date of birth." He sighed, turning back to the screen. "Every time I put the Woodward name into the search engine, more articles pop up. It seems as if the business sector loves to feature articles on real estate moguls like Robert Woodward."

She crossed over to sit close beside him. When Micah needed to burp, she lifted him to her shoulder and rubbed his back. "Have you read any articles about Rebecca's death?"

"Not a single one." He grimaced. "And I would have expected it to be the highest-ranking post. It's obvious the gunmen who took her body are hiding the truth about her death until they've eliminated Micah as a threat."

She nodded slowly. That made sense. If a billionaire CEO had died of a gunshot wound, the news would make headlines across the country, not just here in the Midwest. "Maybe we should fake Micah's death."

Garrett spun around to face her. "That's an interesting idea. But we'd need documentation, wouldn't we?"

"Yes." She held his gaze. "It also means giving up Micah's inheritance."

He waved an impatient hand. "I don't care about that. That much money is the root of all evil. Too many people are desperate and greedy. It's not worth it. Besides, I have no interest in running a huge company like that."

She tipped her head, regarding him thoughtfully. She'd known from the beginning he was an honorable man, but he proved it again and again the more time they spent time together.

"You're one of the few people who would look at it that way."

"I'd do anything to get the target off my son's back." His blue eyes were resolute.

"I have death certificates in my clinic, so we could head back to fill one out and file it with the state. We could use a different name for him but list Rebecca Woodward as the mother." She hesitated, then added, "Then I'd need to create another birth certificate for him since I dropped the initial paperwork into the mailbox outside the police station. One that doesn't list Rebecca's name at all." On one hand, she didn't like to lie about something like this—yet, like Garrett, she was determined to do whatever was necessary to keep this little boy from being murdered.

"How do you feel about that?" She was touched by how he held her gaze. "I don't want to get you in trouble, Liz. And we'd be filing false paperwork, which is a crime."

"Yes, it's a crime." She forced a reassuring smile. "But if we don't figure out who is behind these murder attempts soon, I don't see that we have much choice."

He considered her offer, his expression serious. "I've asked so much of you already. I hate putting you in such a difficult position. Wouldn't doing that jeopardize your license?"

It would, so she looked away, hoping he wouldn't notice her hesitation. "I'm willing to do that to keep Micah safe. A baby doesn't deserve to be hunted and killed."

He sighed. "Let's give it a little more time. We have the name of the dead guy, which is more than we've had before."

"That's fine, if you want to wait." She frowned. "For all we know, there's still a gunman staked out at my clinic, waiting for us to show up."

"I'm sure there is. If we go back, you and Micah will have to stay somewhere else while I go in for the documentation."

Faking Micah's death had been her idea, but she didn't like this idea of returning to her clinic. Would the place ever be safe? Even after the person responsible for the murder scheme was put in prison?

For the first time since Willow's death, she wasn't eager to return to her clinic. Never had she been so tempted to walk away. Yet doing so was out of the question. She wouldn't leave her patients in limbo without a safety net.

She'd do her best for her patients up until

the moment she lost her nursing license. The thought of never practicing as a midwife was difficult to bear.

Still, this wasn't the time to ruminate over her future. Not when danger still dogged them. Garret had taken precautions, but that didn't mean they couldn't be found.

She cuddled Micah close, then reluctantly rose to place him back in his baby carrier.

"I've looked at all of Tyler Richardson's known associates, but there's nothing to link him to the Woodward family." He stared morosely at the computer screen, then abruptly straightened. "Wait a minute—what if one of the family members has spent time in jail?"

"Why would they?" She returned to sit beside him, close to the computer. "There's no reason to commit a crime if they're already rich."

"Not rich enough, if they've hired someone to kill Micah." He typed on the keyboard. "And I'm thinking more along the lines of drug or alcohol abuse."

"Start with the younger ones," she suggested. "They're more likely to have gotten in trouble with the law."

"You'd be surprised," he muttered, but he keyed in the name *Jeremy Woodward*. "One citation for driving under the influence, but no jail time, as it was a first offense."

"Who's his lawyer?"

He shot her a look of admiration. "Good idea. His lawyer is Jacob MacDonald of Mac-Donald & Associates." He reached over to add that name to the notepad. "Let me check the other family members."

They were on a roll. She had a good feeling that Garrett's investigative skills would provide them a clue. "Looks like Elaine was caught with a small bag of marijuana during a routine traffic stop, but she didn't do jail time, either. Her lawyer was also Jacob MacDonald."

"I'm sensing a theme," she murmured.

"No kidding," he said in a dry tone. He continued working for several minutes, then sat back in the chair. "Nothing on Connie or Anita, though. Edward came up clean, too, although there was one reckless-driving ticket on his record from almost ten years ago. That could have been an OWI—Operating While Intoxicated—that was pled down."

"Maybe Edward's side of the family is responsible for hiring the gunmen. At the very least, Elaine must have gotten her drugs from someone."

"Yeah, but Richardson wasn't busted for having drugs, so there's no way to know if they ever connected. And all of this isn't proof of murder for hire." His earlier excitement seemed to fade. "I hate to say it, but falsifying documents may be the only way out of this mess."

She leaned over to rest her hand on his knee. "Don't give up hope."

He covered her hand with his. His gaze went from her eyes to her mouth, and when he leaned forward, she did the same, meeting him halfway.

His kiss was tentative at first, then grew deeper as he tugged her close. Their positions were awkward, but she didn't care. Reveling in his kiss, the poignant moment was interrupted by the ringing of his disposable cell phone.

Garrett pulled back, fumbling for the device. The bit of confusion on his face made her wonder if he was already regretting their brief kiss.

Because she didn't regret their embrace one bit.

"Liam? Hang on, I'm going to put this on speaker so Liz can hear, too." He hoped his clumsy actions weren't too noticeable as he fought to recover from the emotional and physical impact of Liz's kiss. "Ah, okay. What's up?"

"I received an interesting call about a missing

woman by the name of Rebecca Woodward," Liam said, getting straight to the point. "Apparently, she didn't show up for work today, and her family is worried."

"They were forced into reporting her missing since others were aware of her absence," he mused.

"That's what I'm thinking. This guy who called it in mentioned that she may have been traveling and ended up at a local hospital, as she was pregnant and relatively close to her due date. He's calling all police jurisdictions to put us on notice."

"Isn't that kind of him." Garrett knew better than to assume someone was guilty without proof, but he felt certain this guy was involved. "Did he give you a name?"

"Joel Abernathy. Have you heard of him?"

He glanced at Liz as the name clicked. "Yeah, in fact, I have. Rebecca mentioned he was the company's new CFO. It's possible they were dating."

"Interesting. I'm still waiting to hear back from my Chicago PD contact," Liam said. "I'm hoping he has more information on the Woodward family in general."

"That would be nice. I'd like to talk to Joel

myself. He may know why she was in danger. Oh, and I discovered both Elaine and Jeremy Woodward were arrested for misdemeanor offenses related to an OWI and marijuana possession. They didn't do any jail time."

"They got the weed from someone," Liam said, echoing Liz's thought. "But low-level drug dealers are a dime a dozen."

"True. Connie and her daughter, Anita, are clean." He thought again about the lawyer for both kids. "I'm going to reach out to the law offices of MacDonald & Associates. If I hint at having information on Rebecca, I might get through."

"Can't hurt to try." Liam was silent for a moment, then said, "I'll text you Joel's contact information. I also think you should head back to Green Lake. We can protect you easier if you're close."

"We'd only bring trouble your way," he protested.

"Trouble that we can handle better with more resources at our disposal," Liam said. "We want to be there for you and your son."

"Thanks, I'll take that into consideration. By the way, I may need a different vehicle. The gunman that got away likely has the license plate of this one."

"Okay, let me work with Wyatt and Abby on that. Maybe you can meet up with them somewhere."

"That works. And I appreciate your help." He was grateful for Liam's support. "Anything else?"

"No, I just wanted you to know that Rebecca has been officially listed as a missing person."

But not a deceased one. "Thanks. Give Wyatt my new number and have him call me to set up a vehicle swap."

"Will do. Be careful out there."

Garrett ended the call, then turned to face Liz. "I have a bad feeling Rebecca's body will show up soon. I don't see how they can put a lid on her disappearance forever."

"Maybe we should head back to Green Lake." She bit her lower lip. "I like the idea of having your deputies close by."

"Maybe, but we also need the paperwork from your clinic." A trip he'd rather make with a replacement SUV than with the one they were currently using. "Let's wait until I hear from Wyatt."

"Okay."

He sensed her trepidation. From the way she'd reacted earlier, he knew she was putting her nursing license on the line for him.

For Micah, too.

Yet he wanted to have the death forms handy in case they were forced to go that route— something he'd only do as a last resort.

"Then it's probably best if we head to Liberty after we meet with Wyatt and Abby," she said.

"Yeah, I think so, too." Liam hadn't sent the contact information yet for Joel, so he glanced around their connecting rooms. If he had a choice, he'd rather go to the clinic under the cover of darkness, but without night-vision goggles, he was at the same disadvantage as the gunmen. If there was still someone there watching the place. "It's early enough that we should be able to get there and back without too much trouble. Hopefully, we can spend the night here."

"Are we running low on cash? These rooms can't be cheap."

"Abby stashed extra in the computer bag. Wyatt should be able to bring more." He had more than enough money saved in his bank account to repay the deputy. "It's better we continue spending cash to stay off-grid. Food, shelter and supplies for Micah are bare necessities."

"I agree. If I had any cash back at the clinic for you, I'd happily chip in."

"No need." His gaze dropped to Micah's face. "I'm more than capable of providing for my son."

"It's nice to see you bonding with him." She smiled gently. "He needs you, Garrett. Keep that in mind when you put your life on the line to head back to the clinic."

Her comment brought him up short. Who would raise Micah if something happened to him? The baby wouldn't survive being placed with the Woodward family. "Do you have any forms that I can fill out to make you Micah's guardian if something happens to me?"

"What?" Her eyes rounded in surprise. "No, a lawyer has to do that. And wouldn't you want Micah to go to your friends?"

"No, I'd want you to raise him." He paused, then added, "If you're willing."

"I—uh, of course. But nothing is going to happen to you, Garrett. Don't take any foolish risks, understand?"

"That's the plan." He didn't intend to get

shot, but he needed to have a way to make sure Micah would be raised with love and caring.

A woman like Liz could offer that and more.

Before he could turn back to his computer, his phone rang. He recognized Wyatt's number and quickly answered. "Hey, how are things going?"

"Busy, but it's under control," Wyatt assured him. "I hear you need a new vehicle."

"If you and Abby have time, I do." He quickly explained about the gunman he'd shot and the second guy who'd gotten away.

"We can make time. We're not scheduled until three o'clock. Can you meet us halfway?"

"Yes, we can meet at Montello. That's closer to you. Give me an hour or so, okay?"

"Sure thing. We'll rent a replacement, then meet you at the Montello park."

"Thanks again." He disconnected and rose. "I'll get Micah, if you could grab the diaper bag."

"Of course." Liz gestured to the table. "Are you going to leave the computer behind?"

"No, better not." He took a moment to shut it down and pack it away. "Coming back may not be possible."

"That's what I thought." He didn't like how easily she'd adapted to life on the run, being in danger just for delivering a baby. She took the computer case and the diaper bag. "Let's go."

He swept his gaze over their rooms, noticing how Liz had packed everything neatly in the diaper bag. Then he opened the door and peeked out, glancing around warily.

Seeing nothing alarming, he unlocked the SUV and quickly strode over to place Micah in the back seat. He deftly secured the carrier as Liz stored the bags on the floor in the back.

The trip to Montello took a solid hour, in part because he'd taken small highway roads to avoid a tail. Traffic was nonexistent, which helped. After they'd reached city limits, finding the park in the small town was easy enough.

When he pulled into the lot, two SUVs sat side by side in the far corner, away from other vehicles. Both had been backed in, for easy access out of there. He had to smile at Wyatt's and Abby's defensive tactics.

When he pulled up beside them, Wyatt emerged from behind the wheel. Abby quickly joined them, tossing Garrett the key to the second car.

"Thanks for coming." He genuinely appreciated their support. He handed over his service weapon, knowing Liam had promised it to the Volver County Sheriff's Department. Wyatt dropped it into an evidence bag.

"Brought you a replacement." His deputy handed him another gun. "Abby and I think you should come back to Green Lake, where we can back you up easier."

"I don't want to bring danger your way." He slid the gun in his holster, glad it was the same make and model as his own. Then he opened the back passenger door to remove Micah's carrier.

"He's adorable." Abby's smile faded as she glanced at him and Liz, then added, "Seriously, boss, you need to return to the Green Lake area. You know there's a few places you can use to hide out for a while."

The hopeful expression on Liz's face made him feel guilty. Being safe didn't seem like much to ask, yet he hadn't been able to deliver on his promise. "You're right, but there's something we need to do first."

Wyatt held his gaze, then nodded. "Just know we're here to help."

Movement caught his eye, and he turned in time to see a black SUV with tinted windows coming down the street toward the park.

"The gunman! Get the license plate!" He grabbed Liz and pulled her over to the SUV Abby had brought for them.

"I'll go." Wyatt jumped into the SUV he'd driven and peeled out of the parking spot, heading directly toward the approaching vehicle. The black SUV with tinted windows sped up, moving dangerously fast as they tried to escape.

"Get out of here, boss. I'll follow Wyatt." Abby jumped behind the wheel of the car he and Liz had come in. Thankfully, Wyatt was hot on the trail of the tinted-window SUV.

"Let's go." Garrett wished he could join the pursuit, but engaging in a high-speed car chase with Micah in the back seat didn't seem smart.

Yet as he left the park, heading in the opposite direction that Wyatt and the black SUV had taken, he couldn't help wondering how they'd been found.

The gunmen kept showing up, no matter what attempts they made to stay under the radar.

And he was very afraid they wouldn't be able to escape so easily the next time.

Chapter Ten

How was it possible the black SUV with tinted windows had shown up in Montello? A wave of desolation hit hard. What did they have to do to shake off these gunmen?

"Did they follow Abby and Wyatt?" The question popped out of her mouth before she could consider how it might sound.

"Maybe." Garrett's expression was hard as stone. "They are seasoned cops who would have watched for a tail, but it could be that the gunman managed to stay far enough back to escape their notice."

"You think these guys just assumed Wyatt and Abby were coming to meet with us?" She couldn't wrap her mind around it.

He shrugged, his gaze bouncing between the highway ahead and the rearview mirror. "Either that or they tracked our license plate."

"How? It's not like we have toll booths or anything."

"I don't know." His voice was low, and she realized he was beating himself up over this. The situation was hardly his fault.

"I'm sorry. I'm not blaming you." She put a hand on his arm. "It's just frustrating."

"For me, too."

More so for him, as his son was the true target. Despite the all-too-real possibility of losing her nursing license, forging death paperwork for Micah was looking like the best option.

Though she couldn't help wondering if it would work. It made sense that Micah not being an heir would mitigate the danger. Yet these guys seemed incredibly ruthless. So much so, that even with that paperwork filed with the state, they'd still seek to eliminate the possibility of Micah ever claiming his birthright.

When she noticed they were heading northeast, she voiced her concern. "Getting the forms from the clinic doesn't guarantee this will be over. We need to be prepared that simply filing Micah's death notice may not eliminate the threat."

"I know. I've considered that, too." He sighed. "I only intend to do that as a last resort."

"Okay, how long until we reach Liberty?" She wasn't as familiar with the state highways as he seemed to be. "I assume that's our destination."

"It is, and it's almost two hours from here. I'm hoping Wyatt and Abby will have information for us on the black SUV soon."

She nodded, a wave of exhaustion hitting hard. Her emotions were all over the place, making it difficult to concentrate. "I'm sure someone is keeping an eye on the clinic."

"Trust me, I'm taking that into consideration. My plan is to go in on foot. You'll take over behind the wheel, staying on the road with Micah. I'd like you to keep driving until I call with a location to be picked up."

She glanced back at the sleeping infant with trepidation. Being alone with him was a big responsibility. She wasn't armed and was limited as to what she could do to protect him. Yet she couldn't come up with an alternative solution, either. "Okay."

He must have sensed the reservation in her tone. "I'll program Wyatt's and Abby's numbers in your phone. You can call them if you need help."

"Sounds good." Green Lake was an hour

from Liberty, but she assumed they'd meet her halfway. If the gunmen didn't shoot out her tires, the way they had with Rebecca's caddy, she should be able to make it.

Best not to focus on the worst-case scenario. That was only asking for trouble. She'd pray for God's protection for Micah and Garrett. His role in this mission was far more dangerous.

"I keep the birth notices and the death notices in the bottom desk drawer on the right." She grimaced. "I haven't had time to submit the birth notice for Micah yet, which will work in our favor."

"I know." His expression remained grim. "I also understand that your career is at stake here."

"It will all work out." She forced all the confidence she could muster into her tone. "Micah's safety trumps everything."

He nodded but didn't say anything more. The rental SUV ate up the highway until she finally saw a sign that indicated Liberty was five miles ahead.

Being even this close to her clinic, the scene of Rebecca's death and the gunmen who'd shot at them made her shiver. She wasn't surprised when Garrett pulled off the highway just under three miles from their destination.

After he'd programed her phone with Wyatt's and Abby's numbers, and that of the dispatcher for Green Lake, he pushed open his door. "Keep your phone handy. I'll let you know when I'm clear."

"I'll be waiting." She slid out of her seat and walked around to the driver's side. Then she wrapped her arms around his waist and hugged him tight.

"Hey, don't worry." His low voice vibrated near her ear. "I'll be okay. Just keep far away from here for a while, okay?"

She nodded and forced herself to release him. "Be careful, Garrett. Micah needs you."

I *need you*.

She swallowed the words before they could tumble from her lips. How ridiculous, to be thinking about her needs when they were still in danger.

She climbed up behind the wheel and closed the door. Garrett flashed a quick smile before he headed into the woods. In a matter of seconds, he disappeared from view.

Shifting the gear into Drive, she pulled away from the edge of the road. After executing a

Y turn, she headed back in the direction from where they'd come.

Realistically, it would take Garrett at least thirty minutes to make the trip to her clinic. Maybe longer. And that same amount of time to return. In the meantime, she needed to stay far away from the area.

As she drove south, she whispered a silent prayer: *Lord Jesus, keep Garrett safe in Your care!*

Garrett melted into the woods, listening to the sounds around him. As he moved deeper into the dense forest, he searched for signs that the gunmen were hiding out there.

After covering a mile and a quarter, he caught the first sign likely left by the gunmen: a cigarette butt. He didn't have evidence bags, but he carefully picked up the remnant and dropped it into his pocket. If they made it back to Green Lake without incident, he'd ask Liam to check for prints and, more importantly, DNA.

Slowing his pace, he continued forward, making a large circle around the clinic. If anyone was hiding out here, he wanted to be able to sneak up behind them.

The trip through the woods took longer than he'd anticipated, but his patience was rewarded when he found another cigarette butt. This one still reeked of smoke, making him think it was fresh. He dropped that in his pocket, too, in case there was more than one gunman out here who smoked.

He was surprised the perp wasn't professional enough to have fieldstripped his cigarette butt—or better yet, refrained from smoking at all. Maybe this guy was lower on the totem pole, trusted only to keep watch on a location to which they were not likely to return.

If not for needing the forms, he wouldn't be here at all. He changed his route to get closer to the clinic. When he caught sight of movement about twenty yards ahead, he froze.

The gunman keeping watch moved restlessly from one foot to the other. The guy didn't have his weapon in hand, but a lethal-looking pistol was tucked in a belt holster.

With minute slowness, Garrett lowered to a crouch, watching and waiting. The gunman up ahead kept his gaze forward rather than scanning his surroundings.

A rookie mistake. One he'd use to his advantage.

Having a gunman in custody would help them uncover who was behind these relentless attacks. Granted, he suspected this guy wouldn't know much, but anything was better than what they currently had.

After a few minutes, it was clear this guy was bored. When he lit a cigarette, Garrett eased closer. The smoking gunman must have sensed someone coming up behind him, because he finally turned to look over his shoulder.

Garrett lunged forward, tackling the smoker to the ground. Thankfully, the lit cigarette flew from his fingers. The gunman tried to grab for his gun, but it was too late. Garrett wrenched the weapon free and tossed it into the brush behind him.

Holding the guy firmly on the ground, his hand over his mouth, he whispered, "How many others?"

The guy's eyes widened, then narrowed as if he recognized him as the target he was supposed to be looking for. Garrett suspected he wasn't going to cooperate, but he tried again.

"How many? If you don't want to talk, I'll shoot you and figure it out for myself." He was bluffing, as he would never shoot a man in cold blood, but this guy didn't know that.

The gunman made an attempt to talk, so Garrett loosened his grip. "One. On the other side."

He could be lying, but there was no mistaking the fear in his eyes. Garrett quickly shifted his weight so he could grab the guy's wrists. The perp began to struggle, but again, a second too late. He had a zip tie out and wrapped around his wrists before the guy could escape. Then he quickly patted him down, finding a knife in his pocket.

"Let me go!"

"Quiet." Garrett tugged him up into a sitting position, then used the perp's knife to cut a strip of cloth from the bottom of his shirt to gag him. When that had been accomplished, he zip-tied his ankles to keep him in place. "Behave, and I'll be back. Give me trouble, and I can easily leave you here to rot."

The guy watched him warily, as if ready to believe Garrett was capable of that and worse. Good. He needed this guy to be afraid of him.

Moving faster now, he made it to Liz's clinic without seeing anyone else. But that didn't mean someone else wasn't out there. Finding the forms was the easy part. He used duct tape to keep the envelope containing the documents adhered to his chest. Then he left the clinic as quickly as he'd entered.

He wasn't out of danger yet. He swiftly covered the distance to where he'd left the gunman. Trussed like a turkey, the perp glared at him. Interesting that his cry to be let go hadn't brought the other guy over.

Unless there wasn't another gunman hanging around nearby.

Garrett knelt beside him. "Where's your buddy?" he whispered.

The guy shrugged and looked away.

Hesitating, Garrett considered his options: head out to look for a possibly nonexistent perp or simply leave the area, dragging this guy with him. The problem with the second option was that he didn't believe the smoker was capable of moving quietly. If there was another bad guy lurking close, he'd likely hear them from a mile away.

Then again, why wasn't the second guy here already?

He slit the zip ties around the guy's ankles, then drew him upright. They'd barely gone ten yards when he heard a twig snap.

Garrett hit the ground, pulling the perp with him. Gunfire rang out but didn't come close to hitting them. He shoved the perp behind one tree, then took cover behind another.

Movement through the trees indicated there

was someone out there heading toward them. Apparently, the guy had been honest about the presence of a second perp.

Hopefully, there weren't more.

Garrett remained still, making the second gunman come to him. He hoped the bound perp wouldn't try to make a run for it. If he was smart, he'd stay put because the other gunman was likely to shoot the first thing that moved.

Unfortunately, the bound man didn't have the brains to figure that out for himself. He abruptly stood and began to run.

More gunfire rang out, this time pinpointing the shooter's location. Garrett returned fire as the bound guy fell face-first into the ground.

Had he been shot? Garrett's pulse spiked with horror, but he kept his gaze trained for more gunfire. Unfortunately, the shooter remained well hidden, too.

Garrett wanted to believe he'd wounded him, but without hard evidence, he couldn't assume the threat had been disabled. Ignoring the urge to check on the bound man who'd foolishly tried to run, he eased from one tree trunk to the next, carefully edging toward the spot where he'd last glimpsed the shooter.

It took an incredibly long time for him to

cover the distance. When he was finally close enough to see a man's body lying in a crumpled heap on the ground, he still didn't lower his guard.

Using another tree trunk for cover, he inched forward until he could see the blood on the man's dark shirt. Carefully, he leaned down to check for a pulse.

Nothing. The shooter was dead.

Frustrated, he rifled through his pockets, not surprised to find a disposable phone and cash. Then he turned to quickly make his way back to check the other assailant. What if he lost both these men? They'd have no hope in figuring out who'd hired them.

When he came closer, though, he heard the bound perp whimpering behind his gag. He was still alive! Garrett pulled him upright and quickly looked for evidence of an injury. Other than the scratches and soreness that had come from his wild dash through the woods, he was unharmed.

"You shouldn't have tried to run." He pushed him against the tree, then searched for the other guy's gun. He saw it lying nearby and stuck it in the back of his waistband for evidence.

Garrett took another minute to text Liz, letting her know he was fine and that he was on his way back to the highway. Almost seventy minutes had passed since she'd dropped him off, and they still had a lot of ground to cover.

Her response was almost immediate, saying she was ready to meet him anytime. Grateful to know she was okay, he turned his attention to the bound man.

"Let's go." He nudged him forward, refusing to remove the zip ties from his wrists or the stretch of cloth over his mouth. Another gunman might be hiding nearby.

Their trek through the woods was hardly as quiet as he would have liked. He tried to remain hidden in the trees, moving without drawing too much attention. It bothered him that the bound man stumbled often, brushing against branches and generally making more noise than an entire herd of deer.

Despite the possible danger from others, he didn't follow the same circular path he had to get here. Time was of the essence.

He wanted—*needed*—to get back to Liz and Micah.

After a mile, he took a break. The bound man seemed out of shape, as he leaned weakly against a tree. Maybe his stumbling around wasn't an act. It was the first crack in the armor of these hired hit men, and he needed to bust it open to his advantage.

But not until they were safely away from Liz's clinic. He waited another mile before texting Liz again.

Meet us at mile marker 23.

Again, her response was swift. Us?

Long story. Be there in 15 to 20.

I'll be waiting.

Liz's last message sent a wave of warmth through him. He knew better than to make a big deal out of their brief but poignant kiss. It was natural for them to become close while they were on the run and in danger. It didn't mean anything.

Still, it had been a long time since anyone had waited for him to come home.

He ruthlessly pushed the bound perp to go faster, letting him know they were almost at their destination. The guy was sweating profusely by the time they arrived at the mile marker.

Liz was parked along the side of the highway, the SUV as welcoming as anything he'd ever seen. She jumped out of the car when he emerged from the woods with his prisoner.

"Are you alright?" She raked her gaze over him, then glanced curiously at the perp. "Who's this?"

"Not sure. He was stationed in the woods, watching the front of your clinic." He removed the gag from the gunman's mouth, then opened the front passenger door. "Get in. Liz, you should sit in back with Micah." Even though the perp didn't have a weapon, he wasn't about to trust him to be near his son.

"I'm glad you're back." A frown furrowed her brow. "You didn't get the forms."

"I did." He gestured for her to climb in. "I'll explain later. We need to get out of here."

She looked confused but nodded and took the seat beside Micah's carrier. Then he slid in behind the wheel. "What's your name?" he asked as he pulled away from the highway marker.

"Lawyer."

"That's fine. You can lawyer up. After all, you have the right to remain silent. Anything you say can and will be used against you in a court of law. And you already know you have the right to an attorney. If you can't afford one, you will be appointed one at no cost to you." Garrett tried to sound casual as he recited the perp's Miranda rights, when he really wanted to shake the truth out of him. "But I don't know why you'd take the rap for attempted murder when it was someone else who hired you to do his dirty work. He'll hire a replacement for you quicker than you can blink."

The guy didn't respond; he turned to look out the window.

Garrett ground his teeth together in frustration but managed to remain calm. "Liz, call Deputy Wyatt Kane. Let him know we have a gunman in custody. They'll put him into the system, and we'll find out who he's associated with soon enough. His financial records will likely tell the tale."

"Happy to." She made the call while the perp beside him shifted nervously in his seat.

"Could you really kill a baby?" He cast a sideways glance at the guy. "Just because someone told you to?"

"I didn't kill anybody," the perp muttered.

"You tried to kill me. We found shell casings that will likely match the gun I took from you." Garrett smiled without humor. "Attempted murder of a cop holds a higher sentence."

For a long moment, there was nothing but silence. Then the guy blurted out, "I was hired by a guy named Joel Abernathy."

Joel Abernathy? Seriously? He caught Liz's gaze in the rearview mirror. She went to work on her phone, texting Wyatt.

A few minutes later, she gasped. "You were right, Garrett. Joel Abernathy is Rebecca's fiancé."

"What? Are you sure?" He felt as if he'd been kicked in the chest. Dating was one thing, but engaged to be married? While she was pregnant?

She lifted the phone. "According to Wyatt, they found an article announcing their engagement."

Stunned speechless, his mind reeled. Rebecca had never intended to tell him about his son.

She'd promised to marry a man who would have become Micah's father. A man who may have gone as far as hiring someone to kill his son!

Chapter Eleven

Liz thought back to those tense moments when Rebecca had arrived at her clinic in full-blown labor. The woman had never mentioned a man named Joel, much less that he was her fiancé. Liz's focus had been on delivering the baby and trying to save Rebecca's life. She'd remembered seeing her carefully manicured hands—but had Rebecca worn an engagement ring?

Yes, now that she thought about it, she *had* seen a large diamond ring.

"Why does Joel Abernathy want Micah dead?" Garrett's question interrupted her thoughts. "What difference does it make to him if there's a baby in the picture?"

The bound man hunched his shoulders. "Abernathy didn't ask me to kill the kid. He wanted the kid brought to him."

That was interesting news. "Then why keep

shooting at us when the baby was nearby?" she asked. "You could have killed him."

"I didn't try to kill the baby," the guy repeated. "And I'm not saying anything more until I talk to my lawyer."

"That's your right," Garrett said. "Just keep in mind we want the man behind these attempts. And try to remember that some rich people believe they're above the law. A guy like Joel only looks out for himself in these situations."

She was impressed with how Garrett seemed to know just what to say. The bound man remained silent, but she could tell he was considering Garrett's words. She felt certain this guy would eventually tell them what he knew once he'd lawyered up and could arrange to exchange information for a lighter sentence.

A text came through on her phone. "Wyatt is asking that we meet in Oshkosh."

"That works." Garrett met her eyes in the rearview mirror. "How is Micah?"

"He's sleeping." She texted Wyatt back, then glanced at her watch. Even though how they'd been on the run from one location to the next, Micah seemed to be on a regular schedule. Unusual for newborns, but something she was grateful for in this case. He'd likely wake up soon, needing to be fed. Thank goodness they'd purchased more canned formula for him.

When Garrett nodded and lapsed into a brooding silence, she wondered what was going through his mind. The news of Rebecca's engagement had seemed to rattle him. Not that she blamed him for being stunned.

Both Wisconsin and Illinois state laws deemed any baby born to a married couple provides parental rights to both spouses, regardless of who might be the real biological father. Was Joel's intent to get his hands on the baby so he could have access to the Woodward fortune? Wasn't it too late for that? He and Rebecca weren't married. And while he might claim the baby was his, a simple DNA test would prove otherwise.

If they had gotten married, pictures would be plastered all over social media and picked up by newspapers.

Right?

She texted Wyatt. Did Joel and Rebecca get married?

It took several long moments before she received an answer. Abby says no record of a marriage between them has been found on file.

Thanks.

"Let Wyatt know we're fifteen minutes from Oshkosh. I need to know exactly where he wants to meet."

She relayed the information. Wyatt responded, asking to meet at a popular restaurant located just off the interstate. The thought of food made her stomach growl, but they would hardly be able to enjoy a meal having the bound guy along as their passenger.

Micah began to squirm five minutes later. She wanted to take him out of his car seat, but she hesitated since they were still on the interstate. She quickly made a bottle, then gave it to him while he was still in the car seat. She cuddled as close as she could to provide skin-to-skin contact by pressing the top of his head into the curve of her neck. She worried he was spending too much time in the baby carrier and not enough being held and loved.

If only they could find a safe location to stay for a while. Not that she wasn't grateful for the protection they'd had so far. She firmly believed God was watching over them during this difficult time.

"Is he okay?" Garrett asked.

"Great." She forced a smile. "Babies are resilient."

Garrett's gaze clung to hers for a moment before his eyes shifted to examine the road ahead. She wanted to ask him what he was thinking but knew he didn't want to talk in front of their prisoner.

They arrived at their destination just as Micah finished his bottle. She quickly removed him from the car seat, then held him up to her shoulder so he could burp. She nuzzled the downy, dark hair on his head.

She prayed Joel Abernathy wouldn't get anywhere near this little baby. Not when she suspected he only wanted the infant for his own personal gain.

Unless he really did believe the baby was his. The thought brought her gaze to Garrett, but he was already pushing out of the car and going around to open their prisoner's door.

The more the idea circled around in her mind, the more she believed Joel may not be as much of a bad guy as they'd originally thought.

She opened her car door to hear better, but she stayed where she was, holding Micah close while Wyatt and Abby joined Garrett and the prisoner.

"I instructed him on his rights, and he says he

wants a lawyer," Garrett explained. "He mentioned being hired by Joel Abernathy. I'd like to follow you back to Green Lake so we can arrange a meeting with Abernathy. Liam was going to text me his contact info but hasn't. I'd like to talk to him one-on-one if possible."

"If Liam agrees, that's fine with me." Wyatt held the prisoner's arm in a firm grip. "This perp should ride in our vehicle in case you need to take a different route."

"Agreed. What happened with the black SUV?"

Wyatt shook his head, glancing at the prisoner as if he didn't want to say too much. "He escaped, but I sent the license plate to Dispatch. We haven't heard back yet. Things have been busy back there, between a series of robberies and a boating incident on Green Lake."

"That's understandable. By the way, there's a dead man in the woods near Liz's clinic." Garrett gestured to the prisoner. "His backup started shooting, so I was forced to return fire. I would suggest we let the local police know, but it's possible that the dead guy has been picked up by now, the way the others were."

"You've been busy, too," Abby said with a frown. "We'll reach out, mention a report of

gunfire in the area. Can't hurt to have someone go check the place out."

"Good. Better that way. I can't afford to turn
over my weapon again. Not until this is over."
Garrett glanced back at Liz, then gestured to the
restaurant. "We haven't eaten in a while. I'd like
to grab something here before heading back."

"Fine with us," Abby said. "But we should
talk about the proposed interview with Abernathy. We want to be sure to have plenty of
backup if you end up arranging a meeting."

"Okay, we can discuss that more later." Garrett smiled wearily. "Thanks for everything.
We'll be in touch when we hit city limits."

"Be careful." Wyatt nodded at Liz before
leading the prisoner to their SUV. Abby walked
along on the other side; then they took a moment to replace the zip ties with actual handcuffs.

Garrett came over to where Liz sat with
Micah. He reached for the baby, and she quickly
handed him over.

"I'm still in shock over Rebecca's engagement," he confided in a low tone. "But that ex-
plains why she didn't tell me she was pregnant."

Her heart ached for him. "It could be that
Joel believes the baby is his."

Garrett frowned. "Maybe, but sending gun-men after us to get him back is hardly the way to go."

"True. But he may have assumed we were keeping the baby for other reasons. Especially since he reported Rebecca's disappearance." She shrugged. "Maybe he doesn't deserve the bene-fit of the doubt, but you're right about the need to hear what he has to say."

"I know." Garrett kissed Micah's head, melt-ing her heart even more. "I guess going back to the clinic ended up working out. We know more information now than we did before."

Those hours spent waiting for him had not been easy. Her mind had conjured up all sorts of scenarios, none of them good. It was only after she'd received his text saying he was okay and would be meeting her that she'd been able to relax.

The idea of something bad happening to Garrett filled her with dread. She cared about him, far more than she should.

And not just because he was protecting her and Micah, too.

He was an honorable guy, one who was find-ing his way back to his faith. She admired his strength, his courage and his compassion.

Leaving him and Micah behind once this was over would be the second-hardest thing she'd have to do in her entire life.

Losing her daughter was still the most difficult. But leaving Garrett and his son would leave a similar gaping hole in her heart.

Pushing away his own disappointment and shock, Garrett focused on their next steps. He wanted to set up a meeting with Joel as soon as possible, but his stomach was rumbling with hunger, and he was sure Liz's was, too. They hadn't eaten since their early lunch, and it was going on five thirty in the afternoon by now.

Nourishment was important if they were going to get to the bottom of this. No matter what the prisoner claimed, there had been so much gunfire since this started that it was nothing short of amazing that Micah hadn't been hit.

No, he wasn't about to give Abernathy the benefit of the doubt. Not yet.

He caught Liz's gaze. "Are you hungry? We should grab a bite while we're here."

"Yes, that would be great. That way I can change Micah, too."

"I can do it. Would you unbuckle the car seat? And grab the diaper bag?" He couldn't explain his reluctance to set the baby down. Or hand him over to Liz. It wasn't that he didn't trust her—he did. He liked holding his son, feeling his small weight curled on his chest. It wasn't fair that they hadn't had much time to bond.

Hopefully soon, though. Once the danger was over, he would ask for Liz's advice on what he needed to buy, then formally submit the paperwork for his leave of absence from work. Liam had already approved some time off, but he wanted the full paternity leave.

He was looking forward to the days when he could concentrate solely on his son.

"Here you go." Liz handed him the diaper bag, hauling the empty carrier into the restaurant herself. He followed her inside and waited until they were seated in a booth before taking Micah to the restroom to change him.

The way his son gazed up at him filled him with love. How anyone could hire a gunman to take out a baby was beyond belief. And, in his opinion, anyone that heartless should be prosecuted to the fullest extent of the law.

When he returned to the table with Micah, Liz was studying the menu. They had fresh water, which he gladly gulped after he'd slid in across from her.

He kept Micah in the crook of his arm while he looked at the restaurant's offerings. He decided on a French dip sandwich, then pushed the plastic menu aside.

Liz set her menu aside, too, smiling at the sleeping baby. Then her expression turned serious. "It might be better to wait until tomorrow before meeting with Joel."

Before he could respond, their server came to take their order. Once they were alone, he shook his head. "It's time to put an end to this nightmare. It will still be light out by the time we get to Green Lake."

"But not for long," she protested. "You don't want to risk being ambushed in the dark."

He would take whatever risk was necessary to get Joel Abernathy in police custody. "We'll see what Liam thinks. Wyatt and Abby are working a second shift. It would be nice to have them as backup."

She grimaced and sighed. "You're right. I trust Abby and Wyatt to have our back."

When their food arrived, he reluctantly placed Micah back in his carrier. The sleeping baby didn't seem to mind, but his arms felt empty without his warm presence.

Liz reached out to take his hand. "Dear Lord, we are grateful for this food You've provided for us. Please continue to keep us all safe in Your care, especially Garrett, as he may face more danger tonight. Amen."

"Amen." He gently squeezed her hand. "I'll be fine. The good news is that this will all be over soon."

"I know." She dug into her roasted chicken while he enjoyed his roast beef. The simple meal helped rejuvenate his flagging energy. He was anxious to get back on the road to Green Lake.

When he pulled out some cash to pay their bill, he realized he'd forgotten to ask Abby and Wyatt to replenish his funds. They weren't going back to their previous motel room and would need to find another place to stay.

As if reading his thoughts, Liz asked, "Do you have enough?"

"Yes, we'll be fine." He could either get more from an ATM or maybe stop at his place. He wouldn't mind a change of clothes. The warm temps were nice in some respects, but he was sweaty after his long trek through the woods to Liz's clinic and back.

Remembering how he'd attached the envelope to his chest, he reached up to remove it, wincing at the amount of hair he pulled off with the tape.

"I wondered where you'd put that." Liz smiled ruefully as she took the envelope from him. "I'm glad you found the documents, but it appears we won't need them, after all."

He shrugged. "It was worth it to get one of the gunmen in custody. I have a feeling Abernathy's operation will come crumbling down once he realizes it's in his best interest to tell us what he knows."

"I agree." She tucked the envelope into the diaper bag. "I'm ready to go when you are."

He took a moment to make sure Micah was strapped in, then stood. He felt certain they hadn't been followed, but he swept his gaze over the area, anyway.

It was a little troublesome that they hadn't learned who the black SUV with tinted windows was registered to. Maybe the vehicle had been stolen or the license plates switched out—two common tactics used by criminals.

Once they were settled in their vehicle, he

headed back to the interstate. The black SUV bothered him. There had been no sign of the car used by either the dead man or the guy he'd captured outside Liz's clinic. How many hired gunmen were still out there? At least one: the driver of the black SUV.

Likely more.

"Let me know when you'd like me to text Wyatt and Abby." Liz's voice broke into his thoughts. "You said we'd let them know when we reached city limits."

"Right." He'd almost forgotten that. "I might swing by my place first. I desperately need a change of clothes."

She frowned. "Are you sure it's safe?"

He couldn't be sure of anything, but the way the gunmen had been following him and staking out her clinic indicated they may have someone at his place, too. He considered his options, then said, "We'll use the same approach as the clinic. I'll have you drop me off, then head to our headquarters. I know my property better than anyone else. I'm sure I can get in and out without being seen."

"Okay." She looked troubled by his decision, but his main concern was her safety—and Micah's, too.

When they were only five miles from Green Lake, he nodded at her. "Let Wyatt and Abby know we're close."

She used her phone to text them, then added, "I don't see why they can't meet us at your place."

It wasn't a bad idea. "You can ask, but they are working, and it's busy with tourists. Don't be upset if they can't take the time."

"I understand." She continued working on the phone, then grinned. "They're on their way to your house."

"Good." Maybe it was for the best. They could use the time to come up with a plan to run past Liam. If the three of them could agree, their boss likely would, too.

The sun was dipping low on the horizon by the time he pulled into his long driveway. He could see a pair of headlights near his log home and knew Wyatt and Abby had already arrived. Confident they'd have scouted the place for danger, he pulled up alongside them and quickly slid out from behind the wheel.

"The yard is clear," Wyatt informed him.

"Thanks. Why don't you all come inside?" He opened the back passenger door to remove Micah's infant seat. "We can talk after I change my clothes."

Abby shrugged. "Why not?"

Liz joined him as he lifted Micah's carrier and led the way up to his front door. He hesitated, realizing the door wasn't locked, but then remembered that they'd left in a hurry.

"Liz, take the baby. Abby, stand guard. Wyatt and I will clear the house, just to be safe."

Wyatt pulled his weapon. "Let's do it."

He pushed the door open, then stayed to one side, listening intently. A bad smell coming from inside made him wrinkle his nose. What in the world? Had an animal died in there?

Ignoring the stench, he went first, with Wyatt close behind. The moment they passed over the threshold, they spread out in different directions. He took the hallway leading to the bedrooms, where the putrid scent grew worse.

He pushed open the door to his master suite, freezing in place when he spied the source of the awful smell.

Rebecca's missing dead body had been found. She'd been left on his bed, likely in an attempt to implicate him in her murder.

Chapter Twelve

"Get back." Abby's tone was sharp.

"What's wrong?" The abrupt change in the female deputy's demeanor indicated something was amiss.

"I need you and Micah to return to the SUV." Abby gripped her arm and tugged her toward the vehicle.

"Wait." She dug in her heels. Abby hadn't pulled her weapon, so she didn't think there was a gunman nearby. "I want to know what happened."

Abby didn't answer, speaking instead into her radio as she continued pulling her toward the SUV. Reluctantly, Liz complied, for Micah's sake.

"Ten-four." Abby let go of her radio. "Liam will be here soon."

"Why? What did they find inside Garrett's house?" After having been shot at on several occasions, she was irritated they didn't deem it important enough to keep her in the loop.

Abby hesitated, then nodded. "I guess you deserve to know. Rebecca Woodward's body was in Garrett's master suite."

"What?" That was not one of the scenarios that had flitted through her mind.

"I know. It's not good." Abby stood almost directly in front of her, the same way Garrett always had. "Obviously, the bad guys were here at some point."

"You mean, other than the night they fired shots at us." Her mind spun. It was inconceivable to imagine a gunman—likely two—carrying Rebecca from the exam table in her clinic to their vehicle, then again inside Garrett's house. "Do you know how long she's been here?"

"No. Maybe the medical examiner will be able to determine a more detailed timeline."

"Poor Garrett." She could only imagine how horrifying it was for him to see the woman he'd once cared for dead in his bed.

"Yeah, but don't worry. No one will believe he had anything to do with her death."

She frowned and straightened. "Of course not. I was there when she died. I delivered Micah while she was still alive, then did my best to save her life. Garrett was miles away when that happened."

"I know, Liz. You don't have to convince me." Abby managed a grim smile. "But casting suspicion on Garrett was the reason she was left here."

The possibility made her shiver, especially if the gunmen had ended up succeeding in killing her and Garrett. Had Joel Abernathy orchestrated all of this? How far would he go to get Micah back?

Before she could say anything more, sirens wailed in the distance. She glanced over her shoulder, not surprised to see red and blue lights flashing in the darkness.

Garrett and Wyatt quickly joined them. The somber expression on Garrett's features tugged at her heart. Leaving Micah's baby carrier in the car, she closed the gap between them, reaching for his hand.

To her surprise, he pulled her close in a tight hug. She melted against him, offering her support. "I'm so sorry," she whispered.

He pressed a kiss to her temple without saying a word. She understood how the reality of seeing a loved one dead was worse than just hearing the news.

And it would be ten times worse to see that person stretched out like a victim in your own bed.

A police vehicle pulled up next to the SUV. The sirens had been silenced, but the red and blue lights continued to whirl, casting the area in an eerie glow.

Garrett loosened his embrace, taking a step back. She let him go, wishing there was more she could do for him.

"Thanks for coming, Liam." He gave the sheriff a nod. "We cleared the house while preserving evidence."

"You believe Abernathy is responsible?" Liam asked.

"It's the only thing that makes sense." Garrett gestured to his home. "According to our perp, he was hired by Abernathy to get Micah. Liz pointed out that he may believe the baby is his."

"Are you sure he's not?" Liam asked.

"Rebecca told me Garrett was the father and begged me to get Micah to Garrett so he would be safe," Liz told him. "I hardly think a woman who is dying would lie about something so important."

"Yet she hadn't told Garrett about the baby beforehand, either." Liam's reasonable tone was annoying. "Obviously, a DNA test will confirm which of you is the baby's father."

Garrett cleared his throat. "I understand what you're saying, but the timing works. I was with Rebecca the night after Jason was killed in the line of duty. No excuses, but I was a wreck that night. And Rebecca was there for me."

Liam nodded slowly. "Okay. Crime scene techs are on the way. They'll go over your place with a fine-tooth comb."

She remembered Garrett's plan to change out of his sweaty clothes. "Can Garrett get clean clothes without disturbing anything important?"

"No need. It's fine." Garrett frowned. "I don't want anything out of my room now."

She could certainly understand his reluctance.

"I have some things that should fit," Wyatt offered.

"Thanks." Garrett turned to Liam. "We need to set up a meeting with Abernathy ASAP."

"I'm open to suggestions," Liam agreed. "But first, we need to wait until your home has been processed and Rebecca is safely in the morgue."

"We need to keep her death a secret," Abby said. "If the newshounds realize she was found dead here in Green Lake, they'll descend on us like locusts."

"She's right," Garrett said. "That's a circus we don't need."

Liam grimaced. "Okay, I can keep it quiet for at least twenty-four hours—but sooner or later, the news is going to leak." He scowled. "It always does."

"Yeah, I hear you." Garrett raked a hand over his hair. "Once we draw Abernathy out of hiding, the danger will be over. From there, we can reach out to her father to give them the news before he hears it from the media."

"If he's still able to understand what's going on," Liz felt compelled to point out. She didn't like being the bearer of bad news, but they needed to keep their expectations realistic. "Cancer care isn't my area of expertise, but people generally lose their cognitive ability during the dying process. The brain simply shuts down, and the body soon follows."

There was a long pause as the group digested that information.

"We need to move quickly, then," Liam finally said, breaking the silence. "I'll put in a call to Abernathy myself since he reported Rebecca as a missing person. I'll let him know he needs to come make a positive ID."

"He'll know she's already dead," Wyatt said. "Why would he bother?"

Garrett spoke in a low voice. "Tell him we have her baby. That should convince him to come."

Liz stared at him. "But you're not giving him Micah."

"No, of course not." Garrett met her gaze. "We'll arrest him for attempted murder for hire."

"Yet if he knows we have his hired hand in custody, he'll stay far away," Abby pointed out.

"I'll make the call," Liam repeated. "If he doesn't answer, we'll think of something else."

She could tell by the despair in Garrett's eyes that he was thinking the same thing she was.

Abernathy wasn't stupid enough to walk into a trap.

Then she frowned. "Why would Joel kill Rebecca? Wasn't she his ticket to her fortune?"

Garrett shrugged. "Maybe she'd called it off. I have to assume he figured he was better off without her. All he needed to do was take custody of Rebecca's child, the next heir to Woodward Enterprises."

His logic made sense. And if that was what had happened, she could see why Rebecca may have driven all the way to her clinic to have her baby. Maybe she'd planned to take the baby to Garrett afterward.

Only she'd been hunted down and shot before she delivered her child.

Any hope of this ending soon withered away. Danger still lurked nearby, a killer's crosshairs centered on a small newborn baby.

Feeling sick at knowing that Rebecca had been left for him to find, Garrett tried to come up with an idea to coax Abernathy out of hiding.

He turned to Liam. "Let me call him. Greed understands greed. I'll let Abernathy know he can have Micah for a price."

Liz sucked in a harsh breath as if in protest, but he ignored it.

"I'll tell him I know he hired the gunmen who were outside Liz's clinic. I'll claim I shot both men and that I'm willing to make a deal. Wyatt and Abby, among others, can be hiding nearby to grab him."

Liam scowled, but Abby chimed in. "That could work."

"I like it," Wyatt agreed. "At the very least, Abernathy will try to take Micah by force without paying a dime, but we'll be there to stop him."

"I'll keep Micah safe," Liz said. "Garrett can use the carrier with a blanket stuffed inside as a decoy. In the dark, Abernathy won't realize it's empty."

"Fine. We'll give it a try." Liam glanced over to where more cars were coming in. The crime scene techs had arrived.

Garrett refocused on the plan. "I'll use one of the abandoned cabins." He turned to Wyatt and Abby. "Your father's old house would work."

"That's fine with me," Abby said. "Dad is staying in town, in the apartment over Rachel's former café, so he won't be in danger."

Liam was scrolling through his phone. Then he stopped and rattled off a number. Garrett quickly typed it into his phone as a contact.

"Let's head to our place," Wyatt suggested. "I'll get you a clean shirt and jeans, then you can make the call to Abernathy. We'll set up the meeting for later tonight."

"In the dark?" Liz asked. "Are you sure that's wise?"

"The darkness will hide Wyatt and Abby,

too." Garrett flashed a reassuring smile. "Trust me, this will work. You and Micah can stay at headquarters."

She hesitated, then nodded. "Okay. But promise me that you'll call as soon as you have him. I'll be on eggshells until I hear from you."

"I promise. You'll hear from us the minute we have him in custody or at the point we're convinced he isn't going to show." Garrett couldn't guarantee he'd make the call personally, but between the three of them, someone would contact her.

"What about having a deputy stationed at headquarters with her?" Abby asked. "Late at night, it's not as busy."

He glanced at Liam, who nodded. "I'll watch over them."

"Thanks, boss." He gestured to the SUVs. "Let's hit the road. I want to set this plan in motion ASAP."

Five minutes later, they were back on the road, Garrett following Wyatt's SUV. Their small house wasn't that far from his, although it wasn't nearly as rustic. They'd purchased a fixer-upper that still needed some work.

Abby and Wyatt quickly cleared the area before they all headed inside. Wyatt disappeared down the hallway, then returned with a clean black T-shirt and black jeans. He tossed the garments at Garrett.

"Thanks." He used the bathroom to change and then came back to the main room. Pulling out his phone, he glanced at Wyatt. "Should I set this up for midnight?"

"Yeah, that works." Wyatt grinned. "Maybe he'll try to move the time frame up."

"You should hurry," Liz said. "Micah is squirming around. He may need to be changed."

"Hearing a baby crying in the background could work in our favor." When Micah began to whimper, Garrett made the call. As expected, Abernathy didn't pick up, but he left a message with Micah's crying as a backdrop: "Abernathy, I have the kid. I know you hired those goons to grab him. I'm willing to trade him for cash. Call me at this number when you're ready to make a deal."

Liz picked up Micah and carried him over to the sofa with the diaper bag. She crooned to the baby as she changed him. Watching her made his chest ache with longing.

"Do you think he'll call back?" Wyatt asked.

He tore his gaze from Liz. "I hope so."

"He may have more gunmen stationed at

the meeting site," Abby said. She fiddled with her phone, then turned the screen toward him. "This is Abernathy and Rebecca's engagement photo."

The sight of Rebecca and Joel together didn't bother him anymore. He made a mental note of the guy's facial features, though. "We'll be prepared. You and Wyatt know that area better than they do. And I'm expecting him to bring backup. The most important thing is to make sure Liz and Micah are safe."

"Agreed," Wyatt said. "We'll be in place before they are."

"I trust you both." He was humbled by their willingness to jump into danger for him—and for his son, of course. "Thanks."

"Hey, we know what it's like, remember?" Wyatt clapped him on the shoulder.

It wasn't that long ago that they'd both been on the run from the Mob. And as awful as that had been, he was grateful he had two great deputies working for him now as a result.

His phone rang, startling him. He almost wished Micah was crying again as he lifted the phone to his ear. "Yeah?"

"How much?" Abernathy's voice was low and hoarse, as if he might be trying to mask it.

"A million." Garrett knew the Woodward fortune was worth a lot more. "I'm not greedy. I only need enough to retire early."

"When?" The guy was not much of a conversationalist.

"Tonight at midnight. I'm sure you can access the cash and transfer the funds electronically. I'll have my computer there and will make sure the cash transfers before you take the kid."

"Fine. Meet me—"

"No, you'll meet me at an old cabin near mile marker 260 off Highway Z. Come alone, or you won't get the kid."

"Midnight." The line went dead.

"Not sure you can really access banking information after hours," Abby said. "I mean, you can access the accounts, but the money won't show up until the next business day."

"Yeah, but he's planning on scamming me out of the money, anyway, just like we're planning to arrest him, so that doesn't matter." He glanced at his watch; it was a quarter past nine o'clock at night. "You and Wyatt need to get out there. I'll drop Liz and Micah off at headquarters, then head over."

"Got it." Wyatt glanced at Abby. "Still wearing your bullet-resistant vest?"

"Yes, but Garrett needs one, too."

When Liz glanced expectantly at him, holding Micah in the crook of her arm, he nodded. "I'll pick one up at the station when I get Liz and Micah inside."

"Sounds like a plan." Wyatt took his wife's hand. "Ready?"

Abby reached up to give him a quick kiss, then turned toward the door. "Let's go."

Garrett escorted Liz and Micah out to the rental. Liz placed Micah in his seat for the ride across town. When they reached headquarters, she put a hand on Garrett's arm, stopping him from getting out of the car.

"You'll be careful, right?"

"Yes. Now more than ever because I have a son to raise." He almost mentioned how much he wanted to see her again, but he held back. He didn't know how she would respond, and going into a dangerous situation with emotional baggage wasn't smart. "One of us will call you as soon as possible."

"I'd rather hear from you." She surprised him by leaning over to kiss his cheek. Then she quickly turned and pushed her door open. He followed suit, taking Micah's baby carrier.

Inside the sheriff's department headquarters, it was quiet. After making sure Liz was settled in his office, he took the empty baby carrier with a blanket stuffed inside and poked his head into Liam's office.

"I'm leaving."

"Be careful." Liam's gaze was solemn. "He's a desperate man."

"I know." He headed back to the car, taking the time to strap in the baby carrier the way he would if Micah was inside.

Finding the abandoned cabin wasn't difficult. He and the other deputies often drove past to make sure kids weren't using it as a party house. There was no sign of Wyatt or Abby when he pulled up the deeply rutted driveway, but he hadn't expected to see them.

Inside the cabin, he set the baby carrier on the wooden kitchen table, then went back for the computer and a flashlight. He opened the laptop and used his phone as a hot spot to get access to the internet. He turned off the flashlight to save the battery, then settled in to wait.

Watching the minutes tick past was agonizing. After a while, he stood and moved from one window to the other, with only the eerie glow of the computer as light.

He found himself trying to figure out where Abby and Wyatt had stationed themselves. Near enough to respond quickly but far enough to stay out of sight.

They had it harder than he did, crouching in the dark woods surrounding the place.

His phone rang, startling him. There was still an hour until their designated meeting time, but he answered Abernathy's call, anyway.

"Don't try to change the plan," Garrett said in lieu of a greeting. "It's my way or the highway. I can get someone else to pay me for the kid if you don't want to."

"Show me the kid." Abernathy's voice was still hoarse.

Garrett froze, glancing out the windows. Where was he? Did Wyatt and Abby have him in their sights? "I will when you get here."

"I can see you inside with the computer. Lift the brat up and show him to me."

"Hard for me to do that if I don't know where you are." He stalled for time, texting Wyatt on his disposable phone with one hand below the table. "I'm the one calling the shots. You don't want to play the game, I'll get someone else."

Wyatt's response vibrated his disposable phone: Found him. He has only one guy with him. We're moving in.

"Okay, fine," he quickly amended. "Hang on. I have to unbuckle the baby." Vying for time, Garrett tucked the phone between his ear and his shoulder and reached for the baby carrier. He figured Abernathy didn't have binoculars or else he'd already know Micah wasn't here.

He turned his back to the main window, hoping and praying Wyatt and Abby would apprehend them soon.

The sharp retort of gunfire reverberated through the night. Garrett abandoned the baby carrier and bolted outside, directly toward the spot where he thought Abernathy must be hiding. When he reached the area, though, Abernathy was on the ground, bleeding from a bullet wound.

"Take cover," Wyatt shouted. "Unknown shooters!"

Garrett dove to the side as more gunfire rang out. What in the world was going on? When the gunfire ceased, he belly crawled to the fallen man. Abernathy was still breathing, but blood seeped from a wound high in his upper chest.

It was clear someone else had wanted Abernathy dead, too.

Chapter Thirteen

Liam stood in the doorway of Garrett's office, his expression grim. "Garrett, Wyatt and Abby are safe and unharmed. But gunfire rang out prior to the planned exchange. Abernathy has been hit."

Liz appreciated that he'd led with the good news. "How bad?"

"He's alive but suffered an upper-chest wound. The ambulance is there now, picking him up. Abby will accompany him to the hospital. Garrett and Wyatt will stay to scour the scene."

The same sort of wound Rebecca had sustained. The difference here was that Abernathy could go straight into surgery without taking time to deliver a baby.

Then the reality of the situation struck hard. "Wait, how did Abernathy get shot? Did Wyatt or Abby hit him by mistake?"

"No, there was an unknown shooter that arrivcd on the scene." Liam's frown deepened. "Garrett believes Abernathy may have been followed there."

"It doesn't make sense. Who would do that?" As she uttered the words, she knew. "Someone from the Woodward family."

"That's the only thing that makes sense," Liam agreed.

She gazed down at the sleeping baby in her arms. Holding Micah was a joy, even though her arms were getting stiff from being in the same position for so long. A discomfort she gladly ignored. While waiting, she'd struggled with knowing her time with Garrett and Micah was ending soon.

But with this latest news, it was clear the danger wasn't over yet. Unknown gunmen had shown up on the scene, likely hired by one of the other potential Woodward heirs.

There were so many gunmen in the area, she was surprised they weren't tripping over them.

Her phone vibrated, and she shifted her position to read the text from Garrett.

J.A. is hurt but we are ok. Call soon.

With one hand, she awkwardly typed a response.

Thanks for info.

It wasn't easy, sitting here in Garrett's office. She carefully shifted Micah to her other arm, shaking the numbness from her dominant limb.

"Do you need me to take him?" Liam must have noticed her discomfort. He smiled. "I have a daughter of my own."

"Maybe just for a minute, to use the restroom." She handed the baby over, then stood, stretching out her back. "I wish I could go talk to Garrett and Wyatt."

"Not yet. They'll be updating me soon." Liam smiled down at Micah. "He's a cute kid."

After using the restroom and splashing cold water on her face to help keep her awake, she returned to the office. Liam looked extremely comfortable with a baby in his arms. For a moment, she wondered about his wife, how she felt knowing her husband and the father of her daughter put his life on the line every day to keep the community safe.

No, what she really wondered was how *she* might handle it, if she were in that position. A ridiculous thought because she wasn't in a relationship with a cop. Garrett had a life and career here in Green Lake.

And her mission was to serve pregnant

women in need, especially those who still lived on the Oneida reservation.

"Thanks." She took Micah from Liam. "Are you sure we can't head over there?"

He arched a brow. "I'm sure I'm not willing to take the risk. Micah is still in danger—now more than ever since we know Abernathy claimed to want him alive. And the new players may not feel the same way."

She sighed and dropped back into Garrett's chair. "Okay. You're right. It's just difficult to sit here, doing nothing."

"I understand." Liam's gaze was sympathetic.

Her phone vibrated again, this time with an incoming call. She quickly answered. "Garrett?"

"I'm okay," he assured her. "But Abernathy's sidekick was murdered, and he took a bullet to the upper chest. Thankfully, he was still alive when the ambulance carted him off."

"I heard from Liam." Although there had been no mention of Abernathy's dead cohort in crime. "Do you have any idea who is responsible?"

"Only theories at this point." Garrett sighed. "Once the medical examiner and crime scene techs get here, we'll head back. We found a vehicle nearby that we believe is Abernathy's. When the techs get here, we'll search the interior for additional information."

"Maybe Abernathy was staying in one of the local motels," she said. "He may have items in his room, too."

"Yes, Wyatt is working on that. It's late, though, so not sure we'll have that intel until morning."

"Understood." The crime scene techs were getting a workout: first, processing Garrett's log home and now this. She doubted they were used to this much crime, especially over a short time frame.

Hopefully, they were up to the task and wouldn't miss anything.

"I'll call when we're on our way back," Garrett said. "How's Micah?"

"He's great. Sleeping." She yawned. "I'm feeling the late hour myself."

"We'll find a place to spend the rest of the night. Hang in there." She heard the murmur of voices, then Garrett said, "I'll talk to you soon."

"Bye." She set the phone on the desk and rested her head back against the chair. No matter how tired she was, she didn't dare fall asleep, fearing she might accidentally drop Micah.

Being up like this gave her a new appreciation for what new mothers went through while tending their newborns. The chance she hadn't had with Willow.

Remembering her daughter didn't give her the same pang of grief as it had previously. Maybe she was too exhausted to feel anything.

Or maybe she was too preoccupied with Micah, the baby who needed her now.

Willow would always have a piece of her heart. But for the first time, it occurred to her that there was room in her heart to love more babies.

Maybe even another baby of her own.

Garrett had found an ID in the pocket of Abernathy's dead sidekick. His name was Kevin Carter, and the address listed on the driver's license was Chicago.

He showed it to Wyatt. "None of the other gunmen have had IDs in their pockets, but this guy does."

Wyatt scowled. "We know there are more players in the game, but the guy you caught claimed Abernathy hired him. And he didn't have an ID on him."

"Right." The contradiction nagged at him.

Garrett glanced around the clearing, lit up by the headlights of cars driven by the crime scene techs. "Maybe this Kevin Carter was a friend of Abernathy's. Rather than a hired gun."

"Or he was a bodyguard," Wyatt suggested.

"Could be. I was too far away to see what happened, but he may have tried to protect Abernathy."

Wyatt nodded, taking the ID and placing it in an evidence bag. "I'll ask Dispatch to run this guy, see if anything pops."

"A criminal record would be nice," Garrett agreed. "Then we'd know he was involved."

Wyatt made the call. When finished, he gestured behind them. "Let's go check on the vehicle they left down the road."

"I hope they left something useful behind." He was growing frustrated with the way every lead seemed to disintegrate before their eyes. Even learning the identity of Abernathy's sidekick wasn't helpful.

The vehicle was a black SUV but did not have tinted windows—more evidence that there were other gunmen involved. As if the shots fired at Abernathy and Carter weren't enough of a clue.

Using his flashlight, he peered in through

the windows, being careful not to touch anything. There was a laptop case on the floor in the front passenger seat, and he shined the flashlight beam on it. "What do you think? Would he really have gone through with giving me the cash?"

"Doubtful. But I'd like to check the bag," Wyatt said. "Let's see if we can free up a crime scene tech to get inside. As long as we don't disturb any fingerprints, it should be fine to check the bag."

The way things were going, Garrett didn't hold out much hope of finding anything useful. This case had been frustrating from the beginning, with no end in sight. Normally good, methodical police work paid off. The steady stream of gunmen was an aberration. Remembering what Liz had mentioned, he added, "We need to find which hotel they were using. It's more likely they left key documents there rather than in the car."

"Agreed, but that's no easy task in the height of tourist season," Wyatt drawled. "There's been more crime in the past few months than we've had all year."

"Tell me about it." Garrett sighed. "But now we have two names to question the hotels about. Abernathy likely secured the rooms under Kevin Carter's name rather than his."

"Good point." Wyatt gestured for a tech to join them. "We'd like to check inside that laptop case."

The tech sighed but didn't argue. Garrett had taken the key fob from Abernathy's pocket, and the tech used it now, through the evidence bag, to unlock the vehicle.

Using gloved hands, Wyatt carefully opened the door, trying not to smudge potential prints, then reached for the bag. He set it on the ground and unzipped it to look inside.

Garrett hunkered down beside him. There was a laptop inside. When they opened it, the screen was password protected, so Wyatt closed it again. Then he checked the inside pockets for any documents.

There was nothing inside. Not even a business card. Garrett swallowed a stab of disappointment. "Looks like finding their hotel is our priority."

"Right." Wyatt zipped up the laptop case, then set it back on the floor where he'd found it. "Thanks for letting us take a look. We'll need to get that laptop to the computer experts to see what they can find."

"We will." The tech closed the car door. "Anything else?"

"No, but thanks." It was useless to hang around here much longer. And since the hour was going on one o'clock in the morning, Garrett figured their time would be better spent searching for the hotel.

Or getting some badly needed sleep.

His mind rejected the latter, but his body was slowing down, thanks to the adrenaline crash that washed over him.

"Let's head back to headquarters," Wyatt suggested. "We'll update Liam and go from there."

"Okay." He turned to walk back to the cabin. "But I need to get the baby carrier. It's the only bed we have for Micah."

It didn't take long for him to pick up the carrier and follow Wyatt to the location where he'd left his vehicle. The rental SUV would need to stay put until it had been cleared by the crime scene techs.

He brooded over the way the events had unfolded, wondering if there was anything he could have done differently. Nothing came to mind, especially considering Abernathy's demand he lift the baby to prove he was there.

"Abernathy expected this to be a trap." He

glanced at Wyatt. "I'm surprised he didn't have more gunmen with him."

"Well, to be fair, you eliminated two of them," Wyatt said with a wry grin. The highway was deserted, so they were making good time. "Likely, he was low on resources."

"Maybe." Garrett yawned, then gave himself a mental shake. They needed answers, and waiting until morning didn't sit well. "I'll call hotels when we get to the station. Maybe you could take Liz and Micah to your place for the night."

"I think it's a good idea to have all three of you stay at our place. Abby's at the hospital with Abernathy, and I don't think Liz and Micah should be alone."

"Right." Garrett winced. "I should have thought of that."

A few minutes later, Wyatt pulled into the parking lot outside their headquarters. As Garrett removed the baby carrier from the back seat, he realized this was where it had all started at least for him. The crack of gunfire had nearly struck him, Liz and Micah.

Mostly him, if he remembered correctly. Had that been Abernathy's first attempt? Had the goal been to kill him, then get to Micah? They wouldn't be able to interview Rebecca's former fiancé until he'd recovered from his surgery.

If he survived at all.

When they headed inside, he belatedly realized he'd forgotten to text Liz. She came out of his office, holding Micah, her beautiful green eyes wide with hope. "Did you find anything helpful?"

"Not yet." He hated to disappoint her. After setting the baby carrier down on the closest desk, he reached for his son. "Thanks for watching over him."

"Of course." She managed a tired smile. "He's a content baby."

He bent to kiss Micah's head, then glanced up as Liam entered. Deciding it was time to give Liz a break from holding him, he gently set Micah in the baby carrier. "We pulled a laptop case from Abernathy's car, but there was nothing inside but a computer. We'll need the techs to get through the password protection for more intel."

Liam nodded. "You look beat. Get some sleep. There will be more work to be done in the morning."

"I just need to make a few calls first." He shot

a guilty glance at Liz. "Do you mind waiting a little longer?"

"No problem." Her fatigued expression belied her words. "Can I help?"

"Try to get some rest. I'm hoping this won't take long. There is a limited number of hotels in Green Lake." To be fair, there were literally dozens of rental properties, but he was hoping those had been booked well in advance for the peak summer months, leaving Abernathy to take whatever low-budget hotel rooms might be available.

"Okay." She took the closest chair and rested her head on the desk near Micah's baby carrier. Squelching a flash of guilt, Garrett took a seat at the next desk over and booted up the computer. He decided to call the hotels in alphabetical order, as they were displayed online.

"I'll work on the search warrant," Wyatt said as he picked up the phone. "Judge Henry won't give us too much trouble, based on the facts at hand."

"Thanks." He started with Apple Grove Inn, giving his name and badge number before requesting guest information on Joel Abernathy or Kevin Carter. When he struck out there, he moved on to the next.

And the next.

The screen in front of him began to blur. He blinked the exhaustion away, trying to remain focused. He slowly, painstakingly made his way down the list until he reached the last one.

Woodland Escape Motel.

It wasn't *Woodward*, but the similarity gave him a glimmer of hope. He called the number and waited for several long rings before a grouchy guy answered. "Woodland Escape."

He quickly introduced himself as Chief Deputy Nichols. "I'm looking for a guest by the name of Kevin Carter."

"Do you know what time it is?" Annoyance laced the guy's tone. "Hang on."

Garrett rubbed his eyes. If Carter wasn't there, he'd give up for the night. They could tackle the rental properties in the morning.

"Yeah, he's here in Room 8. Why?"

"He's there?" Garrett struggled to focus. "Right now?"

"I mean, he *rented* Room 8," the guy clarified. "I haven't seen him. He's not due to check out until the end of the weekend."

Garrett had to pinpoint the day of the week. Today was Wednesday. No—technically, early Thursday. "Okay, we'll be there in a few minutes with a search warrant. Do not go into the room, do you understand? I don't want anything touched."

"A search warrant? At this hour?" The grumpy guy seemed more upset over losing sleep. Not that Garrett could really blame him.

"Yes." He clicked on the map to pinpoint the exact location of the Woodland Escape Motel. "You're five miles outside town, right? We'll be there in seven minutes or so."

"Hurry up, then," the guy groused before hanging up.

"We got a hit. They're at the Woodland Escape." Garrett surged to his feet, renewed with energy. "Did you wake the judge for the warrant?"

"Yep. He sent it electronically." For being in his midsixties, Judge Henry had adapted well to current technology.

"Let's go." Garrett turned toward the door, but Liz's voice stopped him.

"Can we ride along?" She blinked the sleep

from her eyes and reached for Micah's baby carrier.

Liam had gone home, so he glanced at Wyatt, who shrugged. "Better we stick together."

"Sure, but you'll need to stay in the car." Garrett took the heavy carrier from her hand. "Try to get some sleep while you wait."

"I'm okay." She yawned, then smiled. "Well, I'm as okay as you are."

He couldn't help but chuckle as he secured Micah's carrier in Wyatt's SUV. Liz climbed into the back with the baby, leaving Garrett and Wyatt to sit up front.

When they reached the hotel, they drove around the building, checking things out before pulling into the small parking lot. There were several vehicles parked but a few open spaces, too. It occurred to him that other gunmen might be staying there, but you couldn't get a search warrant that would allow them to knock on every single motel-room door.

Still, the way Wyatt glanced at him indicated they were on the same page. They exited the vehicle, then headed inside.

An older gentleman with shock-white hair stood waiting for them. When Garrett flashed his badge and Wyatt showed him the warrant on his phone, he thrust the key card at them. "Take it and hurry up. I'd like to get back to bed."

"Thanks." Garrett took the key and turned to walk back outside. Wyatt stayed close beside him.

After knocking on the door without a response, Garrett used the key to get inside. The room was empty, as he'd expected. It was messy, as if there hadn't been room service lately.

"Here." Wyatt had opened the top dresser drawer with a gloved hand. "There's an envelope."

Garrett's pulse kicked up as he carefully opened the metal clasp. He was wearing gloves, too, but still tried to handle the contents carefully.

What he saw made him gasp. "It's a marriage certificate."

Wyatt leaned over his shoulder, then whistled. "No wonder he wanted the kid."

The document claimed Joel T. Abernathy was legally married to Rebecca M. Woodward as of one month ago.

A secret wedding? Or a fake marriage license?

As there was no record online about a marriage, his gut leaned toward the latter.

He could only pray the truth wouldn't die with Abernathy.

Chapter Fourteen

A noise woke Liz from her nap. She lifted her head, wincing at the pain in her neck. It took a moment for her to realize she'd fallen asleep in the SUV, with her head against the window at an awkward angle. No wonder her neck hurt. Glancing at Micah, she noticed he was squirming in his seat.

"Hey there, it's okay." She reached over to unbuckle the straps holding him in place, stifling a yawn. The short nap had not put much of a dent in her level of exhaustion.

She lifted Micah to her shoulder, nuzzling him for a moment before setting him down on her lap to change him. She quickly prepared a bottle, then offered it to Micah. Glancing outside, she watched as Garrett and Wyatt emerged from the motel room, their expressions grim.

There was a large tan envelope in Garrett's hand. A surge of adrenaline jolted her fully awake.

They'd found something!

Garrett must have sensed she was looking at him, because he quickly strode toward her. He opened the car door, his expression softening when he saw his son.

"What is that?" She nodded at the envelope.

"A marriage certificate."

"What?" Had she heard that correctly? "Whose marriage certificate?"

He turned so she could read both Rebecca's and Joel's names on the document.

She gasped. "No way."

"Yeah, that was my first thought, too. I hope it's fake, but what if it isn't?" He shrugged. "Then it looks like I'll have to fight Abernathy for custody of Micah. Hopefully, once he's arrested, the judge will grant me custody as Micah's biological father, considering Abernathy is facing charges. But I'm not familiar with family law to know if that will be enough. And I know DNA testing to prove Rebecca's deathbed statement that I'm his father will take some time." He shrugged wearily. "My biggest concern is being able to keep Micah with me while this issue works its way through the court system."

Fatigue made it difficult to think clearly. "When Rebecca came to my clinic, she didn't say anything about being recently married. And I saw an engagement ring, not a wedding ring."

Garrett frowned. "You know, now that I think back, I don't remember seeing an engagement ring when we found her body in my bedroom. Not that that fact alone means much. Abernathy will claim both rings were stolen. Who knows? Maybe that was why he scooped up her body from your clinic in the first place. Well, that and using it to try to frame me for her murder."

The lengths Abernathy had taken were staggering. "All because he wanted control over the Woodward fortune." She shook her head, looking down at Micah's innocent features. His dark eyes were open and looking up at her. She smiled and bent to kiss his forehead. What was it about babies that made them so kissable?

"Yeah, and he clearly planned to do whatever was necessary to get it." Garrett sighed. "Time for us to drive back to headquarters. I want to get this evidence locked up. Then we'll find a place to sleep for what's left of the night."

Wyatt came over to join them. "I sent another officer to the hospital to relieve Abby. We agreed that we'd like the three of you to stay with us. At least for tonight. She'll meet us at home soon."

Garrett frowned. "I don't want to put you both in danger."

Wyatt arched a brow. "Pretty sure with three deputies in the house, we can handle anything that comes up. Besides, this way, we can head over to the hospital first thing tomorrow to interview Abernathy."

"Yeah, but I can guarantee he'll claim the marriage was real," Garrett groused. "He has nothing to lose and everything to gain."

"He'll end up spending the rest of his life in jail," Wyatt said confidently. "And the DNA will prove you're Micah's father. Don't borrow trouble. Let's take this one day at a time."

"I agree with Wyatt." Liz held Micah up against her shoulder so he could burp. "Abernathy claimed he'd pay you for Micah. It's doubtful he planned on following through." She abruptly scowled. "I'd like to know exactly who shot him."

"I vote that it's someone from the Woodward family," Wyatt said. "Unless one of his gunmen decided to turn against him for some reason."

The brief spurt of adrenaline had faded, leaving her feeling shaky and more tired than ever before. "Can we talk about this tomorrow?"

"Yeah, that's for the best. We'll drop off this evidence, then take Wyatt and Abby up on their offer." Garrett stepped back and closed the door.

As the two men climbed into the front seat, she settled Micah back in his baby carrier. The trip back wouldn't take long, but she didn't want to risk more bad guys popping up out of nowhere, forcing them into another car chase.

Better to keep Micah safe in his car seat.

She'd almost nodded off again but jerked awake when they arrived. Wyatt slid out of the passenger seat and ran inside with the tan envelope. He returned a few minutes later, then proceeded to give Garrett instructions on how to get to his home.

Abby and Wyatt's house was smaller than Garrett's log cabin, but they had two guest rooms, which worked perfectly.

"I can keep Micah in my room," she offered.

"He's my son. I'll take care of him." There was a hint of testiness in his tone. They were all tired and crabby, so she didn't take offense.

"Just remember, this isn't over yet," Wyatt cautioned. "We still don't know who shot Abernathy. We need you at your best if we run across more danger."

Garrett frowned. "Micah is my responsibility."

"He should sleep for a few hours now," she said, gently taking the carrier from him. "Why not keep him with me? If he wakes up again, I'll take care of him, then leave him with you for a bit."

Garrett reluctantly nodded. "Okay, thank you."

"Anytime." She carried Micah into her room and set him on the floor beside the bed. Then she gratefully crawled in and closed her eyes.

As she drifted off to sleep, a surge of sadness washed over her, knowing this was probably the last night she'd have with Garrett and Micah before heading back to her lonely life.

One that didn't seem as noble as it had when she'd initially opened her clinic.

Selfishly, she wanted more.

Garrett awoke at eight o'clock in the morning, feeling refreshed after a solid five hours of sleep. He glanced around but didn't see Micah.

He quickly showered and changed into clothes Wyatt had provided, then went to find his son. The soft cries coming from Liz's room made him open the door quickly.

Liz was awake, though, blinking the sleep from her eyes. She glanced at him, then at Micah. "He slept this whole time!"

"He did? That's wonderful!" He was glad she'd been able to get some rest, too. "I'll take him."

"Thanks." She gazed at Micah for a moment before he grabbed the baby and the diaper bag. He gave her some privacy, following the enticing scent of coffee to the kitchen.

Abby was up, drinking coffee at the table. "I didn't hear him cry once last night."

"Me, either. I think five hours is a record," he joked.

"Wyatt is in the shower. He'll join us soon. We can make a plan over breakfast."

He liked the sound of that. He changed Micah, then fed him while sipping coffee. He tried not to stress over the idea of the court not granting him custody.

One step at a time, he reminded himself.

When Liz joined them, his heart thudded against his ribs. It wasn't just her beauty that got to him but also the way she bravely faced the danger stalking them while keeping Micah safe from harm.

She was an amazing woman, and despite how much he'd cared for Rebecca, he found himself wishing for a chance to spend more time with Liz once this was over.

Yet the distance between them, not to mention their unpredictable schedules, would make any sort of relationship nearly impossible.

And not a priority, he told himself sternly. Not now. Not until they got to the bottom of this.

"I can help with breakfast," Liz said when Abby began pulling food from the fridge.

"Sit." Abby waved her back. "After everything you've been through, you deserve to relax a bit."

"I can help." Wyatt came into the kitchen, pausing to give his wife a quick kiss before joining her at the sink.

Cherishing this time with his son, he couldn't seem to tear his gaze from his sweet, innocent face.

It was inconceivable that anyone could look at this baby and see dollar signs rather than the blessed beginning of a new life. He silently prayed they would uncover the truth today so that this innocent baby would no longer be in the center of danger.

Liz, too, deserved to have her life back. He felt guilty over knowing her patients couldn't get the care they needed until this was over.

The scent of bacon and eggs filled the kitchen. The way Wyatt and Abby worked as a team made him all the more aware of Liz sitting beside him. She'd been a rock through all this. He wouldn't have made it through these early days with his son without her.

When the meal was ready, he put Micah back in his baby carrier so they could eat. Wyatt took the lead in saying grace.

"Dear Lord, we thank You for this food we are about to eat. We are grateful for everything You've done for us and continue to seek Your care and guidance as we uncover the truth. Amen."

"Amen," the three of them added in unison.

"What's the plan?" Abby asked. "Other than interviewing Abernathy once he's able to talk?"

"I called Deputy Owens at the hospital. He informed me that Abernathy is out of surgery and is considered medically stable. He's heavily medicated, so not sure how much we'll get out of him," Wyatt informed them.

"I was afraid of that." Garrett sighed. "And if he is medicated, we can't question him while he's under the influence of pain meds."

"We can still ask if he saw who shot him," Abby pointed out. "That's different than asking him to incriminate himself in his plot to buy Micah."

"Maybe." Garrett wasn't a lawyer, but he'd been involved in enough cases to know they were treading on dangerous ground. "As long as we make it clear we're only trying to find the man who shot him and his bodyguard."

"Why don't you let me and Abby take the lead on that?" Wyatt suggested. "You should probably track down information on the marriage certificate we found in Abernathy's motel room."

"Okay." Letting them take the interview was going against the grain. Normally, he didn't have trouble delegating duties; that was a big part of his role as chief deputy. But it was his son who was in danger, and he preferred to be involved in each step of the investigation.

Yet he also doubted Abernathy would give them much of anything to go on. Even if their intent was to find out who shot him, the guy may still refuse to cooperate.

Maybe his time would be better spent here.

"I'll take Liz and Micah to headquarters to work. I need to fill Liam in on what happened."

"Sounds good," Abby agreed.

Liz nodded but didn't say much. She seemed more quiet than usual.

When they'd finished eating, Liz jumped up to help with the dishes. He joined her, shooing Wyatt and Abby away. "We've got this. You should hit the road."

They exchanged a look, then Wyatt nodded. "Okay. The sooner we get out there, the better."

"We'll lock up when we leave," Garrett added.

"That's fine." Abby waved her hand. "You could stay here to work, too, if that's more comfortable for taking care of the baby."

She had a point. "We'll see how it goes." He kept his response noncommittal. While he could easily talk to Liam over the phone, he didn't feel comfortable staying here without Abby and Wyatt. Hanging around their personal space felt like an invasion of their privacy.

Not that they would take it that way. He'd been leaning on the couple as friends when he was really their boss. Normally, he wouldn't cross the line like this.

But these were exigent circumstances. He would do that and more to protect Liz and his son.

"Do you really think you can prove the marriage certificate is fake?" Liz glanced at him, washing the dishes while he dried them.

"I honestly don't know. Wyatt said there was nothing on file with the state. But that could take time, too. I still think he faked Rebecca's signature with the intent on filing it later." He paused, then added, "The same way we were going to fake Micah's death."

"Yeah, I've been thinking of that, too." She sighed. "It won't be easy to prove her signature is fake. Especially if he somehow convinced her to sign under duress."

"I know." The more he thought about the document, the more concerned he was about how he'd fight to keep Micah.

"We have to trust that God has a plan," Liz murmured.

"You're right." He felt a flash of shame. "I won't lose faith. God sent Rebecca to you for a reason. She must have found your clinic online and thought you were her best option for delivering Micah in secret."

"Exactly," she agreed.

"I have to believe God won't fail to protect and guide us now."

A smile tugged at the corner of her mouth. "I wish there was something I could do to help. Maybe we should find a handwriting expert. He might be able to figure out if the signature is fake or was written under duress."

"It's possible." He had enough experience with court cases to know that for every expert to testify on one end of the spectrum, there was another expert who could annihilate that same theory.

"Are you planning to stay here?" she asked.

He dried the last dish, then turned to face her. "No. I'd rather go to headquarters to work. I know it would be more comfortable for you to take care of Micah here, but I don't want to abuse Abby and Wyatt's hospitality." He hesitated before adding, "We may need to stay here again tonight."

"I understand. Don't worry about me and Micah." She turned to glance at the baby. "We're fine sticking around the sheriff's department for as long as you need to work."

"Thanks. I appreciate that." He draped the damp dish towel over the handle of the dishwasher. "Give me a few minutes, then we'll head out."

"Sounds good." She crossed over to the table and began packing Micah's diaper bag.

He quickly made the bed in his room. When he paused outside the door to glance inside the guest room Liz had used, he found she'd already taken care of it.

Returning to the kitchen, he picked up Micah's baby carrier. "Ready to go?"

She nodded but stopped short when his phone rang. He fished it out from his pocket, then set Micah back on the table. "It's Liam," he explained before answering.

"Garrett?" Liam's voice sounded curt. "Where are you?"

His muscles tensed. "At Wyatt and Abby's place. Why? What's going on?"

"Wyatt thinks he may have picked up a tail. He wanted me to warn the two of you to be careful."

Goose bumps rippled along his skin as he met Liz's gaze. If the gunmen knew enough about Wyatt and Abby, they weren't safe here. "Okay, thanks for letting us know about the tail. We're getting out of here now. We planned to come to headquarters."

"Stay put, I'll have two deputies come out to meet you," Liam said.

"Okay, that's fine." He'd no sooner disconnected from the call when he heard the crack of gunfire. "Down!"

Instead of ducking down, Liz placed her body over Micah's baby carrier. As much as he was touched by her attempt to protect him, he pulled on her arm and quickly grabbed the handle of his son's carrier. He placed it beneath the oak table, then pulled Liz down to join him.

Another crack of gunfire shattered a second window. How many shooters were there? More than one, since a window on either side of the house had been broken.

And they were stuck in the middle.

"We need to move," he told Liz. "Follow me."

Her green eyes were wide with fear and determination as she nodded.

The center island had a granite-stone top, and there was a slight overhang on all sides. He wanted to be on the inside of the island, sandwiched between the two sets of cabinets.

He grabbed Micah's carrier, then crawled with the baby out from the table and darted around the island. Liz followed close behind.

Another round of gunfire reverberated through the room. He tucked Liz and Micah as far beneath the granite overhang as possible, then pulled his weapon.

Lifting his head, he tried to pinpoint the location of the shooters. No easy task, since he didn't want to leave Liz or Micah unattended.

Liz pulled out her phone and called 911. He listened to her explain the situation as he watched through the now broken window for signs of the gunmen.

A flash of movement caught his eye. He instinctively fired at the spot, grateful when he saw the guy hit the ground. He wasn't sure he'd hit him, but he'd pinned him down, which was almost as good.

A gunshot from the other side of the house echoed loudly. He didn't hear a window shatter, so he hoped the perp had missed. But at this rate, it wouldn't take long for these guys to force their way inside.

Come on, Liam, get our deputies out here!

Micah began to cry, a sound that ripped at his heart. Liz tried to soothe the infant as he continued keeping watch.

A thumping sound drew his attention. One of the gunmen had gotten inside the house!

Garrett edged toward the corner of the island. When he saw the shadow of the guy on the wall, he jumped out from the corner and fired two quick shots in a row.

The perp fired back, the bullet imbedding into the wall beside him, missing his head by an inch. Then the perp he'd struck slid to the floor.

One down, one to go.

The wail of sirens indicated his backup was close. He could hear Liz whispering the Lord's Prayer as he inched forward to kick the perp's weapon out of the way and check for a pulse.

He was alive, but based on the chest wound, he wasn't sure the perp would make it.

"Who sent you?" He lifted the guy's head. "Come on, tell me who sent you!"

"Ebber…" The guy slumped sideways. And this time, when Garrett felt for a pulse, there was nothing.

A wave of frustration took over. What had the guy said? Edward? Elaine? Or someone else?

Chapter Fifteen

Curling her body over Micah's carrier, Liz silently prayed for safety. She couldn't believe more gunmen had shown up at Wyatt and Abby's house. Their quest to kill Micah was relentless.

She couldn't help but wonder if the innocent baby would ever be safe again. Right now, she held out little hope that they'd make it out of this nightmare unscathed.

"Garrett?" The deep male voice held an authoritative tone. "Is everyone okay?"

"Yes, thanks for getting here so quickly, Liam." Garrett came over to help her up from her crouched position under the granite slab of Wyatt's kitchen island. "One dead in here, but there's at least one other outside."

"The perp out here is down but alive. Stay put while we clear the area."

Liz's entire body was trembling, so staying

put wasn't a hardship. She should be used to bullets flying by now.

But she wasn't. This was so outside her normal life of offering pre and postnatal care to her patients.

"Here, let me take Micah." Garrett gently eased her aside to lift the carrier from the floor and onto the table. Then he gathered the crying infant into his arms, holding him close. She sank into one of the kitchen chairs, trying to control her rapid pulse. No wonder stress was often a precursor to a heart attack. "What did the gunman say? Who hired him?"

Garrett frowned. "I'm not sure. He may have said *Edward* or *Elaine* or something else. I don't think we can put much stock in his mumbled attempt to answer my question."

She wanted to scream in frustration. They were no closer to figuring out who had masterminded these attacks—someone other than Abernathy, who was in the hospital.

After several long moments as Garrett soothed his son, she heard Liam's voice outside shouting, "All clear!"

A quick glance around Wyatt and Abby's home revealed several broken windows. She felt certain bullets would be found imbedded in the walls or furniture. It wasn't their fault, but she still felt guilty for the damage that had been done to their property.

"We shouldn't have come here." Garrett's low voice held regret.

She waved a hand at the mess. "You couldn't have anticipated this. Wyatt and Abby didn't, either."

"We should have." His expression hardened. "Whoever is behind this must know more about me than I realized."

She nodded slowly, understanding his concern. "Or they followed us here somehow. Maybe waited until they saw Wyatt and Abby leave before striking out."

"That's a reasonable assumption, too." Garrett gently set Micah back in his carrier as Liam entered the house. "How many were out there?"

"Just the one. He's still alive but has fallen unconscious. An ambulance is on the way." Liam scowled. "We couldn't get any information out of him."

"I didn't get anything from this guy, either." Garrett gestured to the dead gunman. "I know I'm supposed to hand you my badge and gun after shooting a man, but I can't do that until we find the mastermind behind this."

"I wasn't going to ask you for your shield or your weapon," Liam said mildly. "Our small community hasn't had this much violence in a long time. I need the help of every deputy in the department."

Garrett winced. "I know my leave of absence is causing you to be shorthanded."

"Since you're smack in the middle of this mess, it's almost like having you on duty." Liam's gaze softened when he looked at Micah. "You're doing a fine job of protecting your son."

"Am I?" Garrett looked somber. "It doesn't feel that way."

"We'll get to the bottom of this," Liam assured him. "We're eliminating the gunmen, which is a step in the right direction."

Liz wanted to believe Liam and his deputies would uncover the truth, but so far, it seemed as if they were still stumbling around in the dark. She struggled to remain calm and positive. "How are Wyatt and Abby? I heard you mention a tail. Was someone following them?"

Liam glanced at her. "Good question. I'll check in with them now."

She and Garrett listened as the sheriff used

his radio to connect with Abby. "What's your twenty?"

"Still en route to the hospital," Abby responded. "We had to take a detour to lose our tail."

"I'm afraid two armed perps showed up at your place and shot out a few of your windows," Liam informed her.

"How are Garrett, Liz and the baby?" Abby quickly asked. "Anyone hurt?"

"Just the gunmen. One dead, the other on his way to the hospital." Liam frowned. "You better watch your six. Those guys following you may try to beat you to the hospital."

"We've put Owens and the hospital security staff on notice for that," Abby said.

Liz understood they were concerned about another attempt to silence Joel Abernathy—permanently.

Garrett spoke up. "We'll board up the windows, and I'll pay for the repairs."

"Don't worry, it's part of the job. We're just glad no one was hurt." Abby didn't sound the least bit upset about the property damage. "We'll take care of it. You have your own house cleanup to deal with."

From the determination in Garrett's eyes, Liz

knew he'd insist. Not that the property damage was their biggest concern.

Their sole mission was to stay alive.

Garrett must have read her thoughts. He glanced between her and the baby, then turned to Liam. "We need a safe house. And I'm running out of options."

"Let's drive to headquarters for now." Liam ran his hand through his dark hair. "I need to create a formal report about this. And you'll be safe inside the brick building."

Would they really? She forced the lingering doubt aside since it was likely their best option.

She turned when Micah began to fuss. No child should be in this tenuous position. She lifted the baby to her shoulder and bowed her head, resting her cheek on his downy, soft dark hair.

Garrett came up beside her, encircling her waist with his arm and squeezing her in a hug. Then he lifted his hand to stroke his son's back while pressing a kiss to her temple. In that brief moment, she felt as if they were a family.

As soon as the thought entered her mind, she thrust it away. No matter how much she wanted this, she knew better than to read into Garrett's gratitude.

At some point, the danger would be over and their lives would go back to normal.

Her patients needed her. More than Garrett did.

Garrett wanted to kiss Liz, but Liam's presence held him back. Besides, he wasn't sure she'd welcome a kiss from him. Not after the way they'd constantly been in danger ever since meeting. His promise to keep her safe was failing miserably.

It was only through God's grace that they'd survived this latest attack. That, and the warning from Wyatt and Abby about being followed.

Too bad he didn't know of any bomb shelters in town. It felt as if that was about the only place he'd be able to keep Liz and Micah safe.

He forced himself to step back from Liz and Micah. "Does he need to eat before we go?"

"Yes, I think we need a few minutes." She cooed to Micah, swaying back and forth until the baby quieted. Then she gently placed him in the baby carrier, tucking the small white bunny close. "I think the gunfire hurt his ears. I'll make a bottle. Shouldn't take too long before we're ready to go."

"Take your time." He wanted to feed Micah

himself, but he was determined to stay alert for more danger. He crossed over to the dead gunman. After donning gloves, he went through his pockets.

"Hey, Liam?" He drew out a wallet. "This guy has an ID."

"Let's see." Liam joined him. "Jacob Burns—and no surprise, his address is listed as Chicago, Illinois. Does that name ring a bell?"

"No." He wished it did. "Interesting this gunman had his ID when most of the others hadn't."

"Maybe he's not a professional. They could be running low on resources." Liam clicked on his radio. "Dispatch, run the name Jacob Burns through the system." He rattled off the guy's date of birth and address as listed on the driver's license.

"Ten-four."

A surge of excitement hit hard. This could be the break they were looking for.

He glanced over to where Liz was finishing Micah's bottle. She lifted the baby and sat with him in the crook of her arm. It was humbling how she'd set aside her grief over losing her daughter to care for his son.

The urge to pull her close was strong, but he

forced himself to turn away. This was hardly the time to be thinking about how beautiful she was and how much he'd come to care for her.

Far more than he should.

He needed to stay focused on the threat lurking outside and the never-ending stream of armed perps stalking them, who were obviously determined to kill his son.

"Garrett?" Liz's voice broke into his thoughts.

"Do you need something?" He crossed over to rest his hand on his son's head.

"I was just thinking about that marriage certificate you found in Abernathy's motel room." She frowned. "Don't you think there would have been an announcement in the newspapers about the wedding? Even a small wedding in the courthouse would be big news."

"Good point. Abernathy might claim they wanted to keep things quiet, but that will look suspicious if he shows up with a baby and a marriage certificate that the rest of the family knew nothing about." Yet it occurred to him that the couple may have gotten married in a private ceremony because of Rebecca's father's cancer diagnosis. And if the marriage was real, his life was about to get complicated.

Still, Abernathy would be arrested for the

role he'd played in hiring a man to shoot him. Could a good defense lawyer convince a jury that Abernathy was only desperate to get his own son?

Maybe. The problem with juries was that anything was possible.

His gut tightened at the thought of fighting for custody of his son. "As soon as Micah is finished, we'll go back to headquarters so I can dig into it further."

Liam's radio crackled. "Sheriff? We ran a check on Jacob Burns, but he doesn't have a criminal record."

"Thanks. See if you can broaden the search to family members. He's been killed, so we'll need to make a death notification."

"Will do."

"I pray he has family somewhere," Garrett said. "We need to know who hired him."

"Agreed." Liam glanced at Liz and Micah with a soft smile. "Reminds me of the early days with our daughter, Ciara. All she did was eat and sleep, but now she's more alert and smiling. Every day with her is a blessing."

"I hope I'm blessed the same way." He did his best to shake off the sense of doom. "It's hard to plan a future when I can't find a safe place to stay."

"We'll get to the bottom of this." Liam lightly clapped him on the shoulder. "Having an ID on the dead gunman is a good clue. I believe we'll find family that may be able to give us intel on what he was up to."

Garrett hoped his boss was right about that. He was anxious to get to headquarters to search for information.

While waiting for Micah to finish his bottle, he made good on his promise to board up the windows with plywood he found in the basement.

"Good boy," Liz murmured, holding Micah up to her shoulder. She glanced at Garrett. "We should be able to leave soon."

"Great." He tried to hide his impatience. It wasn't like they weren't well protected here, with deputies outside and Liam nearby. Yet there was a deep sense of urgency pushing at him to get out of there as soon as possible.

He glanced at Liam, who stood off to the side, working on his phone. "Liam? Do you have something?"

His boss turned to face him. "Wyatt and

Abby are at the hospital. Abernathy is refusing to speak to them without his attorney present."

That figured. "Does he realize how much danger he's in?"

A smile tugged at the corner of Liam's mouth. "They're doing their best to convince him to cooperate. Sounds like he's afraid of being hurt again but doesn't want to incriminate himself too much."

Garrett swallowed a wave of frustration. Time was of the essence, considering the recent attack. "I hope he gets his lawyer there ASAP."

"He will." Liam sounded confident. "He's upset they have one ankle cuffed to the bed."

"'Cuffed to the bed'?" Liz echoed. "Even when he's in the hospital?"

"Yes, that's what happens when you're under arrest." Garrett didn't have any sympathy to spare for Abernathy. Not after everything they'd been through.

Before Garrett could suggest heading out, Liam's radio crackled once more. Then he heard the dispatcher's voice say, "Sheriff? I have information on your perp, Jacob Burns."

"Go ahead, tell me what you have," Liam said.

"He has a wife, Alicia, and a ten-year-old

daughter, Amelia. Looks like there are serious money issues there. I see there are some debt collections on file, with legal action pending, and it appears their house has very recently gone into foreclosure." The dispatcher paused, then added, "Do you want to interview her about this? It would make sense for you to handle the death notification at the same time."

"Yeah, I'll take care of it. Thanks for the additional information." Liam lowered his hand from the radio and turned to face Garrett. "Financial issues may explain why Burns took this job. Could be someone from Woodward Enterprises promised to pay off his loans, even going as far as to get his house out of the foreclosure process in exchange for eliminating Micah as the Woodward heir."

"Yeah, especially since Robert Woodward's company specializes in real estate. They could easily buy the mortgage out without breaking a sweat." It wasn't proof, but it was a link back to the Woodward family.

A very weak link.

His feelings must have shown on his face. "Yeah, I know, it's not much. But once Abernathy's lawyer gets there, we should learn more,"

Liam assured him. "He has every reason to co-operate with us."

Since it was about the only break they'd gotten, Garrett nodded. "I pray you're right about that."

He glanced over to see that Liz had finished feeding and changing Micah. "Are you ready to go?" he asked.

"Yes." Her smile was strained. "I can't deny I'll be glad to get out of here."

"I'll escort you, Liz and Micah to headquarters," Liam offered.

"Thanks, we're ready." He watched as Liz placed Micah in his carrier. He crossed over to clean the bottle and put the formula back in the diaper bag, then looped the strap over his shoulder. He lifted Micah's carrier from the table. "Lead the way, Liam."

"You got it." His boss reached for his radio. "Make sure there's a clear path to the SUVs."

"Roger that," came the response.

Liam led the way outside. Garrett urged Liz to follow, holding Micah's carrier high in front of him to protect the baby with his body. Thankfully, covering the short distance to the SUV was uneventful.

"I'll follow you," Liam said. "My goal will be

to prevent you from picking up a tail the way Abby and Wyatt did."

"I appreciate that." As he belted Micah's carrier in the rear passenger seat, the back of his neck prickled. Almost as if someone was out there, watching.

Waiting for the opportunity to strike.

Reminding himself the deputies had cleared the area, he ignored the sensation. Liz was already tucked up front, and Liam stood a few paces back, covering them.

He stepped back and shut the door. As he rounded the back of the SUV, he swept another glance around the area but saw nothing alarming.

Once he was seated behind the wheel, Liam hustled over to the other SUV. Garrett started the engine, then headed out of Wyatt and Abby's driveway.

Liam followed close behind.

Five miles wasn't that far, but the winding highway roads made it difficult to go any faster than thirty miles per hour. He also didn't want to lose Liam or create too much of a gap between them.

As he took one corner, he heard a loud popping sound.

"What was that?" Liz asked fearfully.

"I don't know." He glanced in the rearview mirror, expecting to see Liam coming up behind him, but the stretch of highway behind him was empty.

Then he heard another sharp crack. The wheel beneath his hands jerked, the SUV swerving back and forth, then listing to one side.

They'd been hit!

His right rear tire had been struck by a bullet—no easy task, even for a professional. The realization that this was exactly how these guys had gotten to Rebecca flashed in his mind. Garrett managed to get the SUV off the road. He pulled his weapon but then froze as two men dressed in black came rushing toward them. They split up so they were positioned on either side of his vehicle—one outside his driver's-side window and the other on Liz's side. And each man had their weapon trained directly at them.

From this distance, they couldn't miss.

"Drop the gun and get out, now!" one of them shouted.

Garrett knew that he could probably take out one of the gunmen but not both.

They were trapped!

Chapter Sixteen

A strange sense of calm washed over Liz as she stared at the muzzle of the gunman's weapon mere inches from the passenger-side window. She, Garrett and Micah were about to die. And as awful as that was, she was at peace with her relationship with Jesus.

Oh, she didn't want to die. Especially knowing Micah would leave this earth, too, before he'd even had a chance to live. But it seemed as if God was calling them home, regardless of her wishes.

She couldn't tear her gaze from the lethal weapon. As if staring at it would somehow keep the gunman from shooting her in the face.

Garrett sat rigidly tense beside her. She almost blurted out how much she loved him when she heard a shout.

"Police! Drop your weapons!"

Fueled by a sudden burst of anger, she abruptly

threw her door open, catching the gunman off guard as the frame slammed into his weapon. As if they'd choreographed the move, Garrett did the same on his side.

More gunfire rang out, along with the shatter of glass, causing Micah to cry. The poor baby had been in far too many dangerous situations in his short life.

She ducked behind the now open door, using it as a shield. Then the gunfire abruptly stopped.

Tentatively lifting her head, she searched the area. The man who'd been standing on her side of the vehicle was lying on the ground.

Turning, she looked at Garrett. He still had his weapon trained toward his broken window. There was no sign of the gunman, but that didn't mean he was dead.

"Two perps down," Liam shouted. "Stay where you are."

Liz lowered her chin to her chest, reverently thanking God for saving them again.

Especially for protecting Micah. An innocent child who had been targeted for elimination because of greed.

"This one's wounded," Liam said, coming up on her side. "Garrett, your guy is down. Check him out."

Garrett slid out from behind the wheel. "This guy is dead. I took him out with a head shot."

"I can help the wounded man." She stood on shaky legs, then rounded the open door to kneel behind the man she believed had been seconds from killing her. He was young, his features vaguely familiar.

Liam had shot him high along the left side of his chest, an injury that reminded her of the way Rebecca had been wounded. She balled up his shirt and applied pressure to the opening. "Call an ambulance," she said. Then she added, "Garrett, does this guy look familiar to you?"

Garrett came around the front of the vehicle and kneeled on the injured man's other side. "Yeah. He's Jeremy Woodward."

Jeremy? It took a moment for her to place him as Edward's son. "Do you think his father sent him?"

"I do." Garrett scowled. "Edward isn't the type to get his hands dirty."

"Ambulance is on the way," Liam assured her. "Is there anything I can do to help?"

"Not yet." She prayed Jeremy wouldn't die, fearing they'd never know the truth about whether he was working alone or was in cahoots with his family. Leaning her weight on one hand covering the wound, she used the other to check for a pulse. "He's still with us."

"Good." She could tell Garrett wanted this guy to live as much as she did. The sound of vehicles arriving made her glance over her shoulder. Several deputy squads had arrived, likely coming from the scene at Wyatt and Abby's house.

She wanted to believe the danger was over. But the relentless attacks indicated Edward could keep hiring men to come after them if they didn't come up with some proof of his culpability soon.

As deputies swarmed the area, Garrett pulled Micah from his carrier and comforted the crying baby. Her heart swelled with love at the sight of them. He'd come a long way from their initial meeting, when he'd avoided holding his son.

In the moments she'd believed they would all die at the hands of the assailants, she'd realized just how much she loved Garrett. Especially his strength, kindness and integrity. Not that she expected him to feel the same way. She would miss him—and Micah, too—once it was safe enough to return to seeing patients in her clinic.

The ambulance arrived a few minutes later.

She didn't let up on the pressure until they'd started an IV and began infusing fluids. Finally, she moved back, giving the EMTs room to work.

"Here." Garrett handed her a few baby wipes from Micah's diaper bag to clean Jeremy's blood from her hands. "Are you okay? You're not hurt?"

"Fine." She managed a smile. "I couldn't believe you opened your door into the gunman at the exact same time I did."

"I was surprised, too," he admitted. "I didn't dare take the time to tell you to do the same. My hope was that Liam would take care of your gunman, leaving me to handle the guy on my side of the car."

"It worked." She took a step toward him, as if drawn by an invisible wire. "I fully expected us to die here today."

"The possibility flashed through my mind." To her surprise, he reached out and drew her closer. "I prayed Liam would get here in time to help."

She leaned against him, burrowing her face into the hollow of his shoulder. Micah was awake and looking up at his father with an intense gaze.

Tears pricked her eyes. She silently acknowledged she had no desire to go back to her former life. Granted, she liked helping mothers in need, but leaving Garrett and Micah would be incredibly difficult.

"Hey, I just heard from Wyatt and Abby." Liam's voice broke into her thoughts. "We need to join them at the hospital ASAP. One of the perps is ready to talk."

"Abernathy?" Garrett asked.

"No, the other guy you wounded, the one who left the scene of the shooting in Volver County. Was that yesterday? I'm losing track." Liam sighed. "We'll take one of these vehicles, leaving the deputies on scene to take care of our damaged SUVs."

"Are you okay to leave?" Garrett asked her.

"Of course." It was ironic how accustomed she'd come to being under fire. "I'm all for finding out if this guy can give us answers."

Garrett surprised her by pulling her close and giving her a kiss. The embrace was all too brief, but she felt the impact of his kiss all the way down to the tips of her toes.

Then he stepped back to address Liam. "Let's go."

She took the diaper bag as Garrett grabbed

Micah's carrier. This wasn't the time or the place to tell him how she felt. How much she loved him.

Not until the danger was over for good.

Those tense moments of being trapped by two gunmen had aged Garrett ten years. Yet a surge of adrenaline hit with the thought of getting information from one of the hired thugs who'd come after him and Micah.

He rode up front with Liam, leaving Liz and Micah in the back. He watched as she leaned over, gently caressing Micah's head as she tucked the stuffed bunny closer to the baby.

Liz was the only mother Micah had ever known. When they'd faced what seemed to be certain death, his biggest regret was not telling her how much he loved her.

Soon, though, he silently promised. He wasn't sure how they'd make a relationship work with the distance between them, but he was determined to try.

Even if that meant applying for a job with the Green Bay Police Department, since that would bring him much closer to where her clinic was located.

Liam used his flashing red lights to get them

to the hospital as quickly as possible. No sirens—probably in deference to Micah.

"Did we get a name on this perp?" Garrett asked.

"Sam Lawrence." Liam glanced at him. "He showed up with the gunshot wound, very weak from blood loss. I'm convinced he's the one who got away in Volver County."

"Oh, yeah." He was amazed the guy had come in for care. Then again, nearly dying tends to put things in perspective. "I hope he knows more that will point the finger at Edward Woodward. I can't shake the feeling he's the one responsible."

"If Jeremy makes it, we can work on convincing him to cooperate, too." Liam's expression turned thoughtful. "In fact, maybe I should call Edward to let him know his son has been shot."

"Don't you need to validate his ID first?" Liz asked.

Liam shrugged. "I could. But even if we don't know for sure, I might ask him to come verify the guy's ID. That gets Edward here in Wisconsin."

"I like that idea." Garrett wondered if Robert had been informed of Rebecca's death or if the rest of the family was keeping him in the dark on purpose.

He leaned toward the latter.

"We also need to find a way to speak to Robert directly." He glanced back at his son. "At the very least, he should know about Micah before he dies."

"Right after we hear what Sam Lawrence has to say." Liam grinned. "The hospital is up ahead."

"I see it." Liam had gotten them there in record time without being reckless. Garrett sat forward, eager to jump out of the vehicle the moment Liam had parked near the front entrance.

He grabbed the baby carrier, glancing at Liz. "I may need you to stay in the hallway with Micah."

Her brow furrowed, but she nodded. "If you think it's safe."

She had a point. He'd never taken a baby into a perp interview, but he wasn't willing to let anything happen to either Liz or Micah. Besides, it might be better for Liam to conduct the interview. "Okay, let's go."

Liam flashed his badge to the hospital staff.

They were soon escorted to Sam Lawrence's room, where Abby stood on guard.

"Abernathy's lawyer just arrived," she said. "When you're done here, you should come down the hall to his room. I suspect he'll be ready to talk, too."

"I can't wait," Liam drawled. He entered the room and quickly introduced himself. Then he read Sam Lawrence his rights. "Do you understand your rights as I've described them to you?" Liam asked. "Are you willing to speak with me?"

"Yes." The man grimaced, putting a hand to his abdominal wound. "I'm not going down for this alone. You gotta give me less jail time, though."

"That can be arranged if we can verify your story." Liam got straight to the point. "Who hired you?"

"Edward Woodward."

"And who was your target?"

"I was hired to eliminate the cop, the nurse and the kid." He grimaced and shifted in the bed. "But I know there were other guys who were hired to take out Joel Abernathy."

The information clarified why Abernathy

had been shot outside the meeting spot where he was to exchange Micah for cash.

"Who shot Rebecca Woodward?" Liam asked.

"Not me," the guy claimed.

"Who?" Liam pressed. His phone dinged with an incoming text, but he barely glanced at it. "You need to give us more if you expect to do less jail time."

"My partner. Kyle Gall." Sam's voice turned whiny. "I was there, but he shot her. Then we followed the nurse and the baby to Green Lake to try to finish the job."

Since Kyle Gall was likely dead, the only evidence they'd have were the shell casings found at the parking lot outside their headquarters. "How did Rebecca's dead body end up at my place?" he asked.

Sam's eyes widened. "What? That's creepy! I had nothing to do with moving a dead body."

Oddly, Garrett believed him. They had what they needed to prove Edward was behind the shootings, but they still had to talk to Abernathy.

"You'll need to testify against Edward if you want less jail time," Liam said. "And we need proof that money exchanged hands."

"He paid me twenty grand, with another

twenty once they were dead," Sam said. "And I secretly recorded the conversation as extra insurance in case he decided not to pay."

Garrett hated to admit he was impressed with the perp's cunning. One down, one more to talk to. He left the room, still carrying Micah. Liam fell into step beside him as Abby led the way to Abernathy's room. When Micah started to fuss, Liz quickly took the baby into her arms.

"I'll feed him." She offered a wan smile. "But I want to listen in."

He nodded and pulled a chair from the nurses' station so she could sit outside the door. Again, he let Liam take the lead. His boss scrolled through his phone for a moment, then nodded in satisfaction.

Liam approached Abernathy's bed. "I'm Sheriff Harland. I heard you're willing to make a statement?"

"Uh, yes." The way Abernathy's gaze darted to his lawyer made Garrett suspicious. "I believe my wife's uncle killed her, then tried to kill me and our son. I only approached Garrett because I wanted to keep my son safe."

"You'll take a DNA test?" Liam asked.

"I don't need to. Rebecca and I are—*were* legally married."

"No, see, I don't think so." Liam stepped closer. "Do you have proof?"

"Yes. I have my—*our* marriage certificate." Abernathy's gaze darted to his lawyer again. "I was desperate to get my son back. I acted out of extreme emotional distress."

His answers had been well coached. Too bad Garrett didn't believe him. Liam pressed on. "Do you have anything else? Like pictures of the happy occasion?"

"No. I—uh, Rebecca had them on her phone camera." Abernathy tilted his chin. "That's my statement. As soon as I'm medically cleared, I'll be taking my son home."

"No, you won't." Liam smiled without humor. He lifted up his phone. "My deputy just received Rebecca's phone records, and there are no photos of a wedding. In fact, there are plenty of text messages between the two of you that indicate she'd broken things off." Liam took another step forward, lowering his voice. "We'll prove the marriage certificate is fake, and a DNA test will prove Garrett Nichols is Micah's father. You're done, Abernathy. You might want to chat with your lawyer again, because as far as I'm concerned, forgery, attempted murder and attempted child abduction are just the initial charges on the table. Once we finish our investigation, more will follow."

For a long moment, Abernathy simply stared at him. Then his bravado collapsed like a popped balloon. "Okay, okay! I knew the kid wasn't mine."

"Stop talking!" his lawyer shouted. "Just stop!"

Abernathy fell silent, a sulky expression his face. Garrett knew it was over. There was no way he could talk himself out of this one. Turning, he joined Liz and Micah in the hallway.

"You got him," Liz murmured. "I'm so glad."

"Me, too. Those phone records sealed the deal." He stroked Micah's downy hair. "We have both of them. Abernathy and Edward Woodward."

"Thank the Lord," she whispered. "God was really watching over us today."

"He was." Garrett ached to kiss her again, but a woman pushing a large red cart full of emergency supplies rushed past them. "We need to get out of here."

"Wyatt and I can drive you back to headquarters," Abby offered.

"I'd rather stay and help Liam," Wyatt said. He tossed his wife a key fob. "You go."

"And what will you be doing?" Abby asked.

"Based on this new statement, we'll call the Chicago PD to arrest Edward. Then I'll give him the news about his son being shot." Wyatt grinned. "I can hardly wait."

Garrett was confident Liam and Wyatt could handle this without him. "When Micah is finished, we'll hit the road."

"When can I return to my clinic?" Liz asked.

Her words were like a punch to the gut. He wasn't ready for her to leave. Yet, obviously, there were pregnant women who needed her.

"Only once we know for sure the danger is over." He forced a smile. "Shouldn't be too long. Once the news of Edward's arrest goes out, any lingering gunmen will likely scatter like cockroaches in the sunlight."

"I hope so," she murmured. "I'm ready for this to be over."

The danger? Or their time together? He was afraid to ask.

Abby didn't use red lights on the ride home, so it took longer. Sitting in the passenger seat, Garrett mulled over the best way to approach his feelings for Liz.

When Abby's phone rang, she used the hands-free functionality to answer. "Hey, Liam."

"Edward Woodward is in custody, and the local cops are bringing him here to see his son." Liam's tone rang with satisfaction. "After you drop off Garrett and Liz, go to our headquarters. After his visit, I plan to question Edward. Not that I expect him to say much."

"Good," Abby responded with a grin. "Meet you there."

Normally, Garrett would want to be included. But not now, with his future happiness hanging in the balance.

What if Green Bay wasn't hiring? How close was Appleton or Oshkosh to Liz's clinic? He knew Cash Rawson had recently joined the Appleton Police Department, so he wasn't sure they were hiring.

By the time Abby pulled into the parking lot of their headquarters, he still wasn't sure what his future held.

He carried Micah to his office with Liz beside him. He set the baby carrier on his desk as Liz sank into the closest chair. He turned to face her. "I have something to tell you."

Liz tipped her head to the side, tucking a strand of her long dark hair behind her ear. "I'm listening."

Flowery words weren't his strong suit. He

pulled the second desk chair over so he could sit close enough to take her hand. "We haven't known each other long, and this may sound sudden, but I've fallen in love with you."

Her eyes widened in surprise, but then a hint of wariness filled them. "Are you sure you're not just saying that because you need a mother for Micah?"

"You have been like a mother to him, but that's not what this is about." He held her gaze, imploring her to believe him. "When those gunmen had us trapped in the SUV, I thought our time on this earth was over. My biggest regret was not telling you about my feelings. I can handle Micah on my own, but I can't face a life without you, Liz. I know you live far away, and I'm willing to relocate."

"Relocate?" She looked confused. "To where?"

"Anywhere that will hire me." He bent to kiss her hand. "Please, Liz, give me a chance. I don't want to lose you."

"You would give up your career here to take a position closer to me?" She looked shocked.

"Yes. My life is more than my job. It's about having a family." He managed a crooked smile. "With you."

She sat silent for a long moment. So long that he feared she was looking for a way to let him down gently. Then she said, "I'm glad to hear this because I love you, too, Garrett."

A wave of relief washed over him. He stood and pulled her into his arms. "You've made me a happy man, Liz."

She laughed softly, then lifted up on her tip-toes to kiss him.

When they both needed to breathe, he broke off the kiss but gazed down at her. "I'll start applying for new jobs right away."

"There's no need for that, Garrett. I'll see if I can shift my newer patients to another OB and finish up with those who are due in the next few months."

He frowned. "I want you to be happy, Liz. I admire your dedication to serving the women on the reservation. I will be happy no matter where I end up."

"Most of my patients come from outside the reservation—and don't worry. We'll find a way to make it work."

"Yes, all that matters is that we love each other enough to make the effort." He still planned to apply for other jobs, but since it may take time, they'd have to compromise a bit. "I love you."

"I love you, too." She kissed him again, but then Micah began to fuss. He picked up his son, then pulled Liz into a three-way embrace.

He was truly blessed by the family God had given to him. A blessing he would never take for granted.

Epilogue

One week later...

Liz only delivered one baby after she was able to return to her clinic, so she spent her time seeking midwife support in covering her clinic. One woman in particular had expressed keen interest in taking over.

It was a big relief. As much as she'd loved caring for these women, she wasn't interested in staying out here alone any longer, though she had agreed to back up the new midwife as needed.

She and Garrett had taken Micah to a pediatrician, who pronounced him healthy and fit. She was glad the traumatic incident hadn't seemed to impact him.

Garrett called when she'd crossed into Green Lake County. Her rental car offered the hands-free functionality, so she used it now. "Hey, where are you?"

"About five minutes out, why?" She imagined him holding his son.

"Robert Woodward wants to talk. I'm setting up a video chat with him, and I'd like you to be with me."

Rebecca's father was still alive? Edward Woodward was in custody, and Liam was working with the Chicago PD to arrange for transport back to Illinois, where the initial murder for hire interaction had taken place. Rebecca's uncle had refused to talk, but the rest of the men in custody—including his son, Jeremy— were happy to place the blame squarely on Edward's shoulders. "I'll be there soon."

"Sounds good. Love you."

As always, his low, husky words made her smile. "Love you, too."

Garrett had had professional cleaners scour his house from top to bottom and had insisted on paying for the same treatment to Abby and Wyatt's house. Rebecca's phone records had proven her intent to break things off with Joel Abernathy, which had sent him into desperation mode to get custody of Micah.

Since the day Edward's arrest hit the news, everything had been quiet. No more strange gunmen had shown up in Green Lake or at her clinic. Obviously, anyone still lurking out there knew the likelihood of being paid the balance of their fee was zero to none. That, and they were likely hiding to avoid being prosecuted.

A fact that suited her just fine.

She pulled into Garrett's driveway, then hurried inside. Holding Micah, he crossed over to greet her with a kiss. "We missed you," he whispered.

"Same," she agreed. "What time is the call?"

He led her to the kitchen table, where he had his computer set up. "Now. Take a seat beside me."

She did as he asked, waiting as Garrett made the call. Less than a minute later, a pale, thin older man's face filled the screen.

"Garrett Nichols?" the man asked in a weak voice.

"Yes, sir. And this is your grandson, Micah." Garrett held the baby close to the screen.

Tears glittered in the sick man's eyes. "He's beautiful."

"Yes, he is. And this is midwife Liz Templeton. She delivered Micah and tried to save Rebecca's life."

"Nice to meet you," Robert said. "Thank

you for being there for my daughter and for saving my grandson's life."

"You're welcome. But it was Garrett who kept him safe from Edward's gunmen," she added bluntly.

A pained expression crossed his features. "Yes, I know. I'm horrified about what transpired. But at least the Woodward fortune has an heir in Micah."

"No, sir, I don't want it." It was Garrett's turn to be blunt. "I'm sorry, but I respectfully ask that you change your will so that Micah is no longer a target."

A spark of anger flashed in Robert's eyes, but then he looked weary. "I understand your concern. It's not as if he can spend the money now, anyway. But Micah is a Woodward and deserves his inheritance."

"Please don't do this," she begged. "We barely escaped with our lives. If you truly love your grandson, you'll do as Garrett requested. Change your will to leave Micah out of it."

The older man was silent for a long moment. Then he said, "I do love my grandson. And I regret that I'll never get the chance to watch him grow up. Can I at least provide a college fund for him?"

When Garrett glanced at her, she gave a slight nod. "Yes, that would be nice," he said. "But set it up so that it covers other expenses, in case he decides not to attend a four-year university. I want Micah to do whatever he wants, even if that's a trade like being a plumber or an electrician." He smiled. "Even a cop."

Robert sighed. "I can do that. This puts me in a tough situation, though. The only people I can trust to take over the company is my sister, Connie, and her daughter, Anita."

Better them than Micah. But Liz held her tongue.

"There's one more thing," Garrett said. "Liz runs a clinic for low-income mothers. I would humbly request you provide a donation so that other pregnant women have the ability to get the care they need, just like Rebecca did."

"Done." Now there was a gleam in the older man's eyes. "I like that idea. I'll set aside ten million to start. I know that is what Rebecca would have wanted."

Ten million? She worked hard not to show the shock on her face. "Thank you, sir. That's very generous."

"I want to see my grandson in person," Robert said wistfully. "I'll get my lawyer here to change the will, but I would also like to send a private jet out to pick you up. I…don't know how much time I have left. I grow more and more weak each day."

"Of course," Garrett readily agreed. "But we can drive. No need for a private plane."

"I insist," Robert said. "Please? I want to hold him in my arms before I take my last breath."

Garrett glanced at her again, and she shrugged. Who was she to deny the wishes of a dying man?

"Okay," Garrett conceded. "That will be fine. Thank you, again."

"See you soon." Robert's voice trailed off and he looked away, his eyes drifting closed as if the brief interaction had sapped his strength.

When Garrett disconnected from the call, she asked, "Why didn't you warn me about the donation?"

He smiled. "I wanted to surprise you. I had a feeling he'd go along with the plan."

She leaned forward and kissed him. "You're a sneaky one. And I have news, too. I found another midwife to take over my clinic. With the additional funds from Robert's donation, I think I can get another midwife or two on staff, too. They can expand the clinic, maybe even relocate it so that they can provide care to a broader base of patients." She searched his gaze, then added, "I want to live here in Green Lake with you, Garrett."

"Are you asking me to marry you?" he teased.

"No!" Her cheeks burned with embarrassment. "I just realized I don't want to stay in the clinic anymore. It was exactly what I needed after losing Willow, but now?" She shook her head helplessly. "I loved meeting Wyatt, Abby and Liam. You have a wonderful community here. And I'd like to be a part of it."

"I'm thrilled to hear that." He smiled and pulled a ring box from his pocket. "I planned to wait for us to have a romantic dinner before asking you this, but this seems to be the perfect moment. Lizbeth, will you please marry me?"

She wrapped her arms around him and hugged him close. "Yes, Garrett. I'd be honored to be your wife."

"I love you." He kissed her, and she clung to him for a moment before breaking off to kiss Micah.

"I love both the men in my life." She rested a hand on Micah's back. She couldn't have loved the baby any more than if she'd given birth to him herself. She would always have a small hole in her heart for Willow, but now she couldn't wait to find out what God had in store for her, Garrett and Micah.

Her family.

* * * * *

Hunted By A Killer

Laurie Winter

MILLS & BOON

Multiple award-winning author **Laurie Winter** is a true warrior of the heart. Inspired by her dreams, she creates authentic characters who overcome the odds and find true love. She enjoys time with her family, who are scattered between Wisconsin and Michigan. Laurie has three kids and one fantastic husband, all who inspire her to chase her dreams.

Visit the Author Profile page
at millsandboon.com.au for more titles.

Forbearing one another, and forgiving one another,
if any man have a quarrel against any:
even as Christ forgave you, so also do ye.
—*Colossians* 3:13

DEDICATION

Dedicated to the CASA organisation and
the children I've been privileged to advocate for
during my years as a volunteer. You are greater
than your circumstances. You are a blessing to
everyone in your life. You are my inspiration.

Chapter One

He's back. Her blood ran ice-cold, producing a shiver. Detective Charlotte Reid glanced down at the crime scene photo before sliding it back across the table to Chief Gunther. The last time she'd seen a body like that—a body drained of life and stripped of all human dignity—it had been her sister's. "It's the same killer. I'm sure." They'd never caught him. A failure that haunted Charlotte.

Chief Gunther rubbed a hand down his stubble-covered face. "I thought we put the dark days of brutal killings behind us. Things have been quiet in Presque for six years."

She'd never shared the chief's optimism. Her hometown of Presque, Louisiana, had been a sleepy Southern town until a serial killer had turned it into his hunting and dumping grounds. Four murdered women had been tied to one killer, with her younger sister, Ruby, as his last victim. Until yesterday, when he'd added one more to the list. The evidence confirmed what she suspected.

Last night after dinner, Charlotte had been notified a body was discovered. She didn't mind working long hours with no breaks. She had no family at home. No significant other who needed attention. She *did* mind being called out to a homicide and viewing the body of an innocent woman who would never spend another day with the ones she loved. Anger brewed in her stomach. She would not allow the cases to grow cold again.

She continued her update to the police chief. "Our most recent victim has ligature marks on her neck. Red fibers were found embedded in her skin. She was left in a ditch outside of town." Charlotte's sister had been posed in an identical manner. "Most significantly, there's a crescent moon shape carved into her inner upper arm." The mark of a killer who wanted his murders linked. Did he believe he was too smart to be caught? To date, he *had* been.

"The crime lab needs to complete its testing. Could be a copycat." The chief pushed up to his feet. Collecting the crime scene photographs, he placed them into a large envelope.

"But I already alerted the FBI under the presumption we're dealing with the same perpetrator. They're sending an agent to assist. He should be here soon."

"Soon? The body was discovered last night. Surely the FBI won't send anyone down yet. And why not wait for assistance until we know what we're dealing with?" Having federal assistance meant she'd have access to resources outside her department's reach…but it also meant an FBI suit with a badge would take over her investigation. She checked her ego, refusing to let pride overpower good judgment. Last time, she'd waited too long to trust her federal partner and risked the quality of the investigation.

Charlotte had to remain on this case. The Presque Police Department wasn't large and lacked the resources of its big city counterparts. If she stepped aside, the Kingston Parish Sheriff's Department would likely take over the investigation. The department's prior work on the murder investigations left her uneasy about handing over a case of such great importance. It hadn't prioritized solving the killings of drug-addicted girls. Charlotte had to catch the sick person who killed vulnerable women—including her *sister*—and had gotten away with it for too long. That meant she needed the help federal law enforcement offered, and she couldn't allow her personal feelings to obstruct her work. Not like last time. Her former partnership with Special Agent Austin Walsh had been a distraction. Or should she say her emotional and physical attraction to the man had caused her to lose focus. A mistake that had contributed to the cases going cold. Her love for her late sister and drive to catch Ruby's killer surpassed any dreams of romance. Nothing could stand in her way.

Don't assume the FBI will send Austin again—even if his working knowledge of these cases makes him the most logical option.

"The feds deploy their resources rapidly. Detective, you know better than anyone that waiting to call in the feds could mean another murder." Chief Gunther placed the folder into her hands. The phone on his desk rang, and he glanced over to check the caller ID. "I need to take this. The FBI agent has your contact information and will reach out when he arrives."

She closed her eyes, willing the strength to see this case to the end. *Please God, don't let me falter.*

"Charlotte." The chief rested a hand on her

shoulder. "If you can't handle facing these murders again, speak up. I can assign…"

"I can handle it." She didn't let him finish. "I have to stop this madman and bring my sister's killer to justice." The note found on the ground near the latest victim left no doubt of his intentions.

"I've tried to be good but the urge to kill won't leave me. Can you find me before I find you?"

When she'd arrived at the scene last night to find the note left with the victim, she knew the Presque Killer had returned. If he sought attention, he had it. He would find no safe harbor in the town of Presque. She would flush him out before he hurt another soul.

Special Agent Austin Walsh had taken an early morning flight from Reagan National to Baton Rouge then headed straight to Presque, about a forty-five-minute drive.

He turned onto the main road, in the direction of the police station. The charm of the small town remained since his last visit. He passed a white clapboard-sided church topped by a tall steeple and wide front doors. A stain remained about three feet up the exterior wall, indicating where the water had stopped rising after the last hurricane swept through. A few stately homes lined the street like old sentinels, dripping with Southern architecture and history. He found the downtown area quiet, and the remaining stores still in business showed off attractive window displays. A colorful banner for the town's annual jazz festival draped high over the street. Unfortunately, a darkness stained the underbelly of the area. Five women had been brutally murdered, and their killer was still at large. Austin had failed last time to arrest the person responsible. He wouldn't make the same mistake again.

Six years ago, he'd worked in Presque and the surrounding area for six months with no answers. Three women had been murdered in similar manners in the year prior to his assignment to the case. Charlotte's sister had been the fourth, found murdered two months after he'd arrived in Presque. The trace DNA evidence collected on the first known victim's shirt offered no match to anyone in the system. Other than the drop of DNA, the killer had been clean in conducting his crimes. With no solid leads in four months after Charlotte's sister's murder, he was called back to his home office and forced to admit failure to his mentor—someone who understood losing a loved one to the hands of a serial killer.

His recollection of those events brought Charlotte's pretty face to mind. An attraction to the local detective had been one of those mistakes he planned to avoid during this visit.

He parked, then scanned the case briefing one more time. The truth was, he'd memorized the facts of the old cases. They never were far from his mind, despite the many other investigations he'd closed since. His background with this community and the victims was the reason he'd been brought back. But the prospect of going into the Presque Police Station and facing Detective Charlotte Reid after six years kept him glued to the seat of his rental.

You're stalling. Austin gathered up his nerve and exited the vehicle. Lifting his chin, he strode to the station's front door. He introduced himself to the man posted at the lobby window, then waited to be taken back to the police chief.

The door to the lobby opened and Chief Alan Gunther appeared. "Special Agent Walsh." He held out a hand in greeting. "Welcome back."

Austin was back, but for how long? Would he hit the same walls as before? He shook the offered hand and followed the chief down a brightly lit hallway and into his office. "Any leads?"

"None yet. Detective Reid is heading back to the scene to make sure nothing was overlooked." Chief Gunther leaned on the front of his desk. His left foot tapped on the tile floor.

Austin remained standing as well. A supercharged energy flowed through him. He was eager to get started. "I'll head over with her." He paused, considering his words. "In your opinion, can Detective Reid handle this investigation? If the killer we're chasing is the same person who murdered her sister, she could be too close to the case. Who else is available to take over if needed?"

He thought back to the last time he'd worked with Charlotte. She was the best local detective he'd ever teamed up with. A few years out of the FBI Academy, he'd been assigned to investigate a string of similar murders, starting with women disappearing in the Baton Rouge area then finally culminating in Presque. Detective Reid had led the latter investigation until her sister went missing. Then her sister had become a murder victim. They'd tried to convince Charlotte to step down but the woman dug in. She'd refused to give up the hunt. In the end, Austin had left town with an unfulfilled mission and a local law enforcement partner he'd let down.

He'd failed so many, including Charlotte. An outcome he wouldn't repeat. The Presque cases were dark spots on his career with the FBI, which had been filled with mostly captured murderers and accolades. Though Special Agent Caleb Boyce had died three months ago, Austin vowed to continue Caleb's important work of studying, hunting and catching serial killers. Austin wished to carry on the legacy of the man who'd been his instructor at the FBI Academy, an invaluable mentor and a trusted friend. Caleb had worked tirelessly to bring his daughter's murderer to justice. Austin could help bring peace to the families of the Presque Killer's victims.

Chief Gunther folded his arms and released a breath. "You know how I feel about our parish sheriff's department getting involved any more than they have to. Remember how badly they bungled the investigation the last time they got involved? Here's the thing." He paused and looked Austin straight in the eye. "I'm not placing Detective Reid on the sidelines without cause. She is the most committed detective I have to solve these murders."

That was what worried him. He'd witnessed fellow FBI agents grind themselves down to dust while working a case, including Caleb. Charlotte had been close to losing herself after her sister's murder. If she remained on the case, he'd keep a close eye on her. "I trust your judgment," he replied to the chief.

"Go see if you can catch Detective Reid before she leaves," Chief Gunther said. "I expect a report on the progress of the investigation by the end of the day."

He nodded, familiar with complying with orders from the local chief of police. Not that he was obligated to. He'd learned that to keep the peace, if the order didn't go against the direction of his own work, he'd cooperate. If the local law enforcement got in his way, he issued a reminder of who he answered to.

Austin stepped out of the chief's office and made his way to the section of the station where Charlotte's desk was located. Or at least had been. When he caught sight of her at her desk, head down in concentration, he paused. Besides longer hair, she looked the same.

The charge of fascination he felt proved he

hadn't gotten over her. He'd have to—immediately. Their relationship was strictly professional. Austin had come to do a job: put a killer behind bars.

Charlotte sat at her desk, gathering the files she needed before leaving for the crime scene. At the sound of footsteps, she raised her gaze. Her chest squeezed at the sight of Austin Walsh striding toward her. She hadn't wanted to see him again under these conditions.

Then again, under what other circumstances would their paths have crossed again? He was an FBI special agent who investigated serial homicides. She was a small-town detective. Working murder cases was not conducive to forming healthy relationships, even a friendship. And they hadn't been friends the last time she'd been this close to him. When he declared he'd been taken off the case and recalled to his home office, she'd taken out her frustration on him. She'd yelled and attempted to bully him into staying, and in the end she couldn't bring herself to say goodbye. Her shame at the way she'd conducted herself had recessed over time. But seeing him again brought all the feelings rushing back. Austin hadn't fought to remain on the Presque cases, which had grown cold. The two of them had failed to complete their job, and that knowledge haunted her every day since he'd left.

"Hello." She kept her greeting cool and professional. Standing, she offered a hand.

"Hi." He shook her hand. "It's been a while. How have you been?"

She quickly pulled her hand out of his grasp. "I'll be better when a murderer isn't walking the streets."

"I second that." He set the messenger bag he'd been carrying onto the empty office chair next to her desk. "I was told you're leading the recent investigation and believe the Presque Killer is responsible."

Austin's black dress slacks and button-down shirt advertised he wasn't local law enforcement. His styled hair, face perfectly made for a classic movie screen, and crisp attire suited his personality—all cool confidence and swagger. In her opinion, he deserved every ounce of ego he'd accumulated. Austin excelled at his job. He was precise and reserved. He'd brought down several high-profile serial killers and other criminals since they'd last worked together. According to the articles she'd read about some of his solved cases, Austin was a rising star—one of the top serial killer specialists in the Bureau. She'd seen him in action and been impressed by his sharp mind and accurate instincts.

She broke eye contact and returned to organizing the files of prior case notes. "Whoever murdered the woman we found last night is either the Presque Killer or a superior copycat. We're still waiting on lab test results but my gut tells me it's him."

"Okay, then, let's get to work." He rubbed his hands together. "Chief mentioned you're heading back to the crime scene for another look."

"I was preparing to leave right before you arrived. You're welcome to join me." The invitation had caught in her throat but her training overrode her awkward need to get far away from him.

"Sure. We can ride together."

"I have some other business to attend to afterward. We'll ride separately." A concocted excuse. She doubted she'd be able to avoid being in a car together forever.

"Understood. I'll follow you." He grabbed his bag.

"I'm parked out back. Watch for a silver

sedan. I'll swing around the building and drive past. The scene is approximately two miles west of the town limits." She waited for him to leave her desk area before taking a deep breath. *You can do this. No hard feelings. You're working together toward a common goal. That's all.*

With the folder of investigative materials in her hand, she strode around a barricade wall and across a long stretch of pavement to her car, which the vehicle maintenance staff had neglected to lock after bringing it back from the maintenance shop. She got in, then turned on the vehicle to start the AC. In this heat, she only needed seconds before her shirt began sticking to her sweat-covered skin. Could she trade Louisiana humidity for snow? Cold weather was preferable for preserving a crime scene.

The body had been found at dusk in a swampy ditch on the side of the gravel road outside of town. Charlotte had walked the scene soon after the call came in but wanted a chance to reexamine it with fresh eyes in the daylight. Like the previous times, the killer had left his victim near the roadside, as if he wanted them to be found before wild animals destroyed his work. A group of high school boys out cruising the country roads had discovered the body.

The preliminary report estimated she'd died approximately eighteen hours prior. The young woman hadn't been identified yet. Photographs and her basic information were uploaded into the federal missing persons system. No match yet. Perhaps she hadn't been missing long enough for someone to notice. Or perhaps she hadn't had anyone in her life who missed her. Like the other victims, another vulnerable girl stolen off the streets. The assumption brought tears to her eyes.

Charlotte hadn't reported Ruby missing until the day after she'd disappeared. She'd been wrapped up in work and when she learned her sister hadn't come home, she assumed Ruby had broken her vow of sobriety and stayed out partying. Looking back, as a detective investigating a serial killer, she should have known better. After searching every hole she'd known her sister to frequent, she'd feared for Ruby more than any other time in her life. Two days later, a local farmer had found Ruby's body. Her sister had been dumped like a bag of trash. A final indignity that Charlotte would never forgive. Ruby hadn't been perfect. She'd endured the trauma of parental abandonment, along with Charlotte. While Charlotte had been able to break free and build a successful life, Ruby had found comfort in bad relationships, drugs and alcohol.

Charlotte had to focus on the case before her. Dwelling on her sorrow over losing Ruby wouldn't help her catch the killer. She gripped the steering wheel, willing herself into the present, and took long, deep breaths. The Presque Killer would not slip away. Not again.

She took hold of the transmission lever to put the car into Reverse. The moment her finger touched the lever, she froze at the sensation of metal on the side of her neck. "Who's there?"

A quiet laugh answered.

She shifted forward in her seat and glanced in the rearview window to try to glimpse the person behind her. "Answer me."

The man's breathing grew louder. "I hear you're looking for me again. Will you stop me before I stop you?"

His voice sounded digital and strange. Charlotte's world narrowed to the interior of her car. The serial killer she'd been chasing for years could be seated only feet away. "I never stopped looking for you." With the end of her statement, a quick prick nipped her neck. Had he pierced her with a needle? *Get out of the car, now.* She pawed at the door handle but couldn't coordinate her fingers to take hold and pull. Her wild gaze traveled her surroundings, searching for anyone nearby who could come to her aid. The parking lot appeared empty of people. Black dots floated in her vision. She'd been drugged. Dizziness struck next. *I have to escape and find help.*

"Rest now," the voice whispered in her ear. "All I want is to talk, I promise."

Talk? She struggled to make sense of his words inside her slushy brain. A serial killer had drugged her and all he wanted to do was talk? Images of her sister floated into her mind. Death at the hands of this man wasn't an option. She flung herself toward the car door and desperately tried to get out. The space around her grew smaller and darker. Her battle was lost. At least for right now. If she awoke—no, when she awoke—she'd fight.

Detective Charlotte Reid would *not* become another victim of the Presque Killer.

Chapter Two

A uniformed police officer rapped her knuckles on the passenger-side window of Austin's car.

Startled, Austin jumped in his seat, then lowered the car window.

"Are you waiting for Detective Reid?" the officer asked.

"She asked I wait for her to drive by then follow her to the crime scene." Had he missed her? He glanced in the rearview mirror before checking the time. He'd been waiting for ten minutes. What was taking so long?

"I saw her car drive away not that long ago. It was going fast and heading east, in the opposite direction of where they found the body." She glanced back at the front door of the police station. "Chief Gunther noticed you were sitting out here and asked me to check in."

He turned off the car engine and exited the vehicle. "Has anyone tried contacting her?"

"No, but I'll call her cell now." The officer dialed and waited. "It went to voice mail." She attempted twice more to get through. "Detective Reid isn't answering."

"Something's not right." Probably nothing to panic over. Still, he carried an uncomfortable weight of worry in his gut. Detective Reid's negative feelings for him might remain, but Austin trusted her professionalism. He understood how seriously she took her work on this case.

He strode to the parking lot behind the station and walked the perimeter, then crisscrossed the area, searching for anything out of place. Austin still had Charlotte's cell phone number saved in his contacts. He dialed, and as ringing sounded, he prayed she'd answer.

The sound of a cell phone chime caught his attention. He followed the noise until it stopped, which coincided with his call going to voice mail. He dialed Charlotte again—and once again the chiming started. Lying in the mulch under a bush at the edge of the lot was a black cell phone. On the cracked screen, his name displayed as the caller. He pressed End on his call.

What had happened, and where was Charlotte?

A possibility left him cold. If a serial killer had resumed his hunt, had he just taken his next victim? Detective Reid might be perfectly safe but as a federal special agent trained to hunt serial criminals, specifically murderers, Austin didn't trust in optimism.

Pushing down fear, he steadied his emotions. He'd left his evidence collection kit in his messenger bag, which was in the car. Be Prepared for Anything—was a motto engrained in him since childhood. Both his parents had served in the army and taught him the values of service and hard work. He'd followed their example and selected West Point for college then served eight years in the army. Joining the FBI had become his objective after witnessing a murder on base. It haunted him that he hadn't been able to stop that death. So now his job was to remove killers from society and thereby save lives.

He stood and proceeded into the police station, straight to the chief's office. "Chief, I believe Detective Reid could be in danger. I found her phone on the ground outside with a broken screen. Both she and her car are gone. I was waiting for her to drive past so I could follow her to the crime scene. One of your officers saw her car head east."

Chief Gunther's face paled. "Let's not rush to conclusions. She may have dropped her phone getting into her car and gotten a lead she needed to check out in a hurry. Do you have her phone?"

"I didn't touch it in case it's evidence." The image of Charlotte as a prisoner of a psychotic murderer would not leave his head. "Had she received any threats lately? Any other cases she was working that would cause someone to hold a grudge and want to hurt her?"

"No recent case comes to mind." The chief scratched his chin. "I'll put out a notice over the police radio and have officers search the parking lot."

The action plan did little to ease Austin's worry. "The video footage from the surveillance camera outside will show what happened. Can you access that?"

"Will take a minute but I can." The chief put on his reading glasses and clicked around on the computer. After a minute, he picked up the phone. "My office...now," he said in a raised voice. "I need access to the video from the station's outdoor cameras. Detective Reid is missing."

Within seconds, a young man dressed in a

navy polo shirt and khaki pants arrived holding a laptop. He set it on the round table in the
chief's office and opened the recent video surveillance footage of the rear parking lot. "I'll
fast forward until we get to the time Detective
Reid left the building."

Austin watched the fast-moving images until
the video slowed. First, a black car pulled into
the parking lot, then moved past the sight line
of the camera. Fifteen minutes later, Charlotte
appeared. She walked off toward the rear of the
lot before disappearing from view. A few minutes later, her car drove toward the exit and out
of sight. The tech played that last section again.
Though the image wasn't clear, the driver of
the car didn't look like Charlotte.

"The black car is still there, parked in the
back corner where I found Charlotte's phone.
We need Forensics to go through it." Austin
rubbed his forehead, fighting the headache
squeezing his temples. A small-town department didn't have a large team of crime scene
techs. They relied mostly on the parish or state
resources. And those they did have were likely
busy on the murder investigation.

"I'll request a crime scene team from Kingston Parish," the chief said. "What kind of per-son kidnaps an officer in broad daylight?"

"Someone brazen and confident. This person is either taunting the police or eager enough to cause harm. Or both." Austin grew nauseous. One person fit the profile. A serial killer who got bolder each time he killed without being caught.

When arriving in Presque, Austin had been anxious about seeing Charlotte again. They'd ended their previous working partnership on not great terms. The fact he'd kissed her the week of Charlotte's sister being found murdered had soured any potential relationship. Austin should have kept his focus on the assignment. Instead, he'd fallen for the detective he'd been paired with. His professional integrity, which he held to the highest standard, had slipped. He hadn't solved the case and left town with a stinging heart. Getting emotionally involved in a case always ended badly.

Before meeting Charlotte six years ago, he'd ruled out romance and marriage. Witnessing multiple failed marriages of his coworkers at the Bureau had made him determined to stay far away from a committed relationship. The job was demanding and emotionally brutal. Agents

carried guilt, grief and anger as often as they
carried a badge and service weapon.

But for a brief time, Charlotte had begun to
alter his beliefs. He'd opened himself to the possibility of love but then reality had slammed the
door closed. Charlotte had blamed both Austin
and herself for not catching the killer in time
to save her sister. Remorse had driven a wedge
between them.

He studied the computer screen. Nothing
mattered more than finding Charlotte—safe
and alive.

"I'll review it again in slow motion and see if
I can spot anything we missed," the tech said.

"I can't wait." The perpetrator's awareness
of the police department surveillance cameras
didn't surprise Austin. He'd studied the Presque Killer going all the way back to the start
of the man's criminal life in Baton Rouge. In
the beginning, the perpetrator kidnapped and
strangled but did not kill his victims, who had
shown the same ligature strangle marks on their
necks. When the thrill of kidnapping and tor-
ture faded, the killer had escalated his choices.
Kidnap in Baton Rouge and dump the body in
Presque. Finally, he killed in Presque, where he
earned notoriety and his nickname.

Since Ruby's murder six years ago, the last known one until yesterday, Austin had studied this killer. A profile had been compiled by the FBI Behavior Science Unit. Austin had assumed he could read the killer's thoughts and intentions. Many serial killers, like the Presque Killer, snatched young women who had at-risk lifestyles. People who wouldn't be reported missing for a time or not at all. This killer liked the feeling of control and overpowering the weak. But the fact that he'd abducted a detective as physically fit as Charlotte, though, had Austin tossing all his theories out the window. Perhaps taking Charlotte was the start of a chess match the killer assumed he'd win. Austin needed to clear his mind of what he thought he knew and simply assess the facts before him.

"I'm heading out to search. Call me if you learn anything." He left the office, moving with speed to the front of the station and to his SUV. Where to start? Six years had passed since the last cluster of murders. Those murders had been spaced months apart. Had the killer resumed with an intensified instinct for murder? Or had he been active all this time in another part of the country? Murders that fit this killer's profile would have gotten Austin's attention, though.

Austin peeled away from the curb and headed in the direction the officer had earlier indicated. His gaze scanned the streets for any sign of Charlotte's car. Thirty minutes had passed since she'd been driven away. Chief Gunther mentioned that his police force didn't have the resources for GPS trackers on their vehicles. His hands tightened on the steering wheel. She could be so far out of town that they might never find her.

The first thing Charlotte noticed was the smell, reminiscent of a musty basement. A lethargic fog remained inside her brain. She was sleepy and fought the urge to descend back into the blackness. Snippets of her memory returned like looking through a stack of photographs. She'd been inside her car. Her current case and Ruby on her mind. A poke to her neck. The voice of a man behind her. A hidden face. A threat that terrified her.

The reality of her situation slapped her into an alert state. She'd been kidnapped by the Presque Killer. Had Ruby held the same terror Charlotte was feeling?

Her vision was obscured by a piece of fabric tied around her head, covering her eyes. The fabric brushed against her lashes as she blinked. Charlotte glanced down to take in a sliver of low light that the blindfold allowed in. She made out a small portion of her lap. Tugging on her hands, she couldn't free them from the binds that tied behind her. She was seated in a hard chair. The sound of a vehicle engine coming from outside grew louder then quieted. If she could free herself from the ties, she could escape before her captor reappeared.

She made small kicks with her feet, rubbing the soles of her shoes across a smooth floor. Her ankles were bound as well. Charlotte worked both her feet and hands to loosen the cords. After a few minutes, she regained her full awareness and her efforts increased. The cord around her ankles had loosened but not enough for her to move freely. The binds around her wrists remained tight, cutting into her skin. Her fingers tingled and started to go numb.

A door banged closed somewhere above, then footsteps thumped on nearby stairs. She stilled and dropped her chin. If he thought she was still knocked out, maybe he'd leave again. Charlotte slowed her breathing yet kept her body tense for a quick reaction in case of attack.

"You're much prettier than your sister." The

man's voice held the same digital quality as in the car. He must be using something to alter his voice. "Then again, you're not a junkie. I did you a favor, really. Isn't it a relief not to constantly worry about your troubled little sis?"

He'd connected Charlotte with Ruby, one of his victims. Ice shards of pain dug into Charlotte's skin. She didn't react. She had to keep calm and in control and not allow the killer to rattle her nerves.

"I only want to talk," he continued. "Then I'll let you go. It's not your death I'm after. At least not yet." He chuckled. "You get an advantage I've never given anyone else. You will know the rules of the game."

A game? Was that what he considered murder? "I'm not interested," she mumbled through the gag tied over her mouth. She'd engage him with caution. If he did let her go, she'd have information to use in the hunt to capture him.

"You don't have a choice." The sound of his footsteps grew closer. "I'm the game master. I make the rules. You get the opportunity to play."

An opportunity to play for what? The question burned her throat. For her life? She tilted her head in an attempt to glimpse the person taunting her, but the room was too dark to see much past her feet.

"You get the chance to be the hero, Charlotte. You get another chance to try and catch me." He let out a raspy laugh. "Not that you ever will."

His hot breath brushed the side of her face, and she recoiled.

"Listen closely." He coughed, then cleared his throat. "The game begins the moment I release you. The rules are simple. Starting today, I will take prisoners. Women I find pleasing to the eye. I haven't decided how many I'll take yet. Like fishing, I may get lucky one day and strike out the next. If you find and stop me in seven days, you win. The women go free and they can return to their miserable normal lives." The man's fingers loosened the knot of the gag covering her mouth.

When it fell, she sucked in air. "And if I don't?" Her heart pounded.

The man chuckled. "When the clock strikes midnight on next Thursday, seven days and twelve hours from now, they all die. And I come for you. Your life, Charlotte Reid, will be my reward for a job well done."

Her blood ran cold. "I'll catch you before

this day is done. You'll spend the rest of your life locked in a jail cell."

"Promises, promises." His voice sounded from behind her. "This was why I wanted you to play. You couldn't save your sister. How does that make you feel, Charlotte, that you didn't keep her safe?"

She tensed, anticipating another injection or a blow to the head. "You'll pay for what you did to Ruby and those other girls." Since she was young, Charlotte had felt a responsibility to protect her little sister. During their years in foster care and school, Charlotte had stood up to every bully. She'd been there to pick up the broken pieces each time Ruby shattered. They'd had a rough childhood, abandoned by their mother and sent into the system. Charlotte had managed to survive with a few emotional bruises, mostly due to her guarded heart. She'd sought a career in law enforcement to help her community. Ruby, on the other hand, the more sensitive one, had been buried under the pressure of trauma.

"Did you murder the poor girl we found last night in the ditch?" Would pride in his crime elicit a confession?

"That's for you to figure out, Detective.

Didn't you used to love puzzles? You won't put together the one I made for you in time."

Fury had Charlotte attempting to rise off the chair. With her feet bound and her arms tied behind her, she stumbled and almost fell forward. A combination of willpower and pure rage kept her balanced. She lowered the legs of the chair down to the floor. "Let me go and get on with it. Unless deep down you're afraid of what I will do to you."

His laughter didn't convey humor. Cruelty tinted the edges. "Your confidence is impressive. Remember, if you fail, people will die, including yourself." He relieved some of the tension in the cord around her wrist. "With a little effort, you should be able to work loose the ties and free your feet. You're in a basement in a house outside of town. I disabled your car. A long walk will get you back to the police station. I have no ties to this house and I won't return. You can have your techs comb the place for DNA evidence but you won't find any. You're good at your job. I'm better."

"We'll see about that," she ground out through clenched teeth. Charlotte went to work freeing her hands. The sound of footsteps fading as her captor went upstairs spurred her on. The cord fell onto the ground at the same moment a car engine roared to life. Had he parked a get-away vehicle ahead of time? *Hurry.* She untied the binding around her ankles and lowered the blindfold, stopping for a second to notice the color of the cord—red. The same type and color the Presque Killer used to bind and strangle.

His sick game pushed her off-balance. Kidnap women and if he was not stopped in seven days, the women would die. And so would Char-lotte. Why had he selected her? Was he exploit-ing the sore spot in her heart from the murder of her sister and her past failure to catch him? He'd mentioned her love of puzzles, something she'd enjoyed as a child. She'd found fitting to-gether hundreds of little pieces to be a way to gain control of her chaotic life.

She swallowed hard and took stock of her surroundings. The stairs and door to the base-ment room lay directly ahead. She charged through and up the stairs, ignoring the pins and needles tingling in her arms and legs. On the first floor, she halted in the kitchen. Every-thing appeared like the family living here had cleaned up before heading out of town. Perhaps they were on vacation and the killer had taken advantage of an empty house. Charlotte tried the landline phone and heard no dial tone. Either someone had tampered with the line or the homeowners had disconnected it in preference of cell phones.

She went outside and over by the driveway, which stretched about a quarter mile to the road. Nothing about this house or area seemed familiar. No neighbors were visible because of the trees surrounding the property.

Her car had been parked by the garage door. She went inside the car and searched for her keys and phone. The keys were in the cup holder. Her phone was nowhere to be found—probably tossed somewhere so it couldn't be traced to her location. She turned the key but the engine wouldn't turn over. True to his word, her kidnapper had disabled her car. The folder with her crime scene information had been moved to the back seat. Had the killer enjoyed reviewing the results of his labor? She grabbed the folder and tucked it under her arm.

Guess she was walking back to town. If she was lucky, she'd flag down a passing motorist for help.

Before leaving, she mentally noted the exterior of the house. When she got to the end of the driveway, she'd find the address listed on the mailbox.

Though her muscles trembled, her resolve firmed with every step. Charlotte didn't care about being a hero. No award would be as satisfying as seeing her sister's killer convicted of murder and sentenced to a life behind bars. God punished the wicked, and she offered her assistance to make sure the punishment fit the crimes. If the Presque Killer wanted a game, she'd play. She would win.

Chapter Three

Austin's cell phone rang. He pulled off on the side of the road and answered the call without looking at the caller ID. "Agent Walsh."

"It's Chief Gunther. Detective Reid has been recovered. A citizen found her walking on a road about five miles outside of the town limits. She's on her way to the station and should be here in ten minutes."

Austin exhaled a long breath. Relief flooded through him. But new worries popped into his head. "Is she hurt? Does she need medical attention?"

"She's spitting mad but otherwise fine. She said that the man who took her let her go. I requested a Kingston Parish forensics team go through the house and her car. The abductor's black car as well. The one left here at the station. It appears to be stolen."

Could it be the person who'd kidnapped

Charlotte wasn't the Presque Killer? A serial killer, as a general practice, did not regress in their tactics.

Austin ended the call, then returned to the station. He waited outside in the parking lot, in the heat, for Charlotte to arrive. When she exited the car of another officer, Austin couldn't suppress his smile. She did look mightily perturbed, but clearly ready to push her way through all the concerned officers waiting for her to get to her desk and back to work.

He stood against the brick building, taking advantage of the small amount of shade it offered, and studied her. The tragedy of her sister's death had hardened her, and he desired to smooth over those sharp edges of her facial features.

While accepting a pat on the back from a male officer, she glanced in his direction. Their gazes connected.

For a moment, the world stood still. He blinked, and events continued spinning. If he couldn't remain emotionally unattached from the case and the lead detective, he'd complicate their work. And complications on an already difficult investigation wouldn't be tolerated. Even the slightest error or missed clue meant a killer remained free.

As Charlotte walked toward him, Austin pushed off the building and into the sunlight. He took a few strides before meeting up with her. "I'm glad you're okay." *Keep it professional.* He sealed away the panic he'd felt while she was missing. "Can we talk about what happened? I need to know everything."

Her eyebrows arched. "Can I take a minute to gather my thoughts and get a drink?"

He mentally swatted himself. *You can be a professional and not be a jerk.* "Of course. I'm sorry. You've been through a lot today. Should you be checked out by a doctor first?"

"Not necessary. We made a quick stop at my doctor's office. They took blood and urine samples. They'll call if anything from the tests is concerning. Besides the shot that knocked me out, which has completely worn off, I wasn't harmed. Actually...he made an effort not to hurt me. My wrists have a few nylon rope burns from where he tied me but he wanted to release me in fighting shape. I will need to give a statement and have my wrists swabbed and photographed."

He should halt their conversation. Escort her inside to cool off, sit down and drink a tall glass of cold water. But his need for information was too urgent. "Do you have any idea who this guy is?"

"I didn't see him or recognize his voice but it was the Presque Killer. The man who murdered Ruby." She grimaced. "He's connected me to Ruby and taunted me with her death. This psychopath thinks this is all a game."

"What did he say he wants from you?" A weight settled in his chest. He'd studied cases with serial killers who fashioned themselves to be ring leaders in their own circus. They cracked the whip and made everyone perform to their tune.

"To be a player in his twisted world." Charlotte glanced over her shoulder—her face tense. "Let's go inside and talk somewhere private. It's bad, Walsh. What he plans to do is really bad."

Charlotte's gaze scanned her desk, searching to make sure she'd gathered all the files she wanted to bring along, before she glanced up at Austin. He'd stationed himself at the other side of her desk. His hawklike eyes watched everything going on around them.

Immediately when she'd arrived at the station, she'd sat down with the chief and Austin. Her tale of the events that transpired left them both at a loss for words. State police had been notified. All regional law enforcement stood on high alert.

She slipped a trembling hand into the front pocket of her pants. Her earlier adrenaline had left her body, resulting in the desire to take a long, deep nap. The abduction had taken a toll on her, but there was no way she'd admit it. She would charge on. The Presque Killer wouldn't deter her, despite his threat to her life. She couldn't dwell on the danger.

"I still want to revisit the crime scene in the daylight. You should have a look too before more time passes." She placed the stack of remaining files she'd removed from document boxes into a desk drawer and locked it. "We can come back afterward and go over all the files from the prior cases. It's been a while since you laid eyes on them." Charlotte, on the other hand, checked out the cold case files every couple of months to keep the details fresh. She refused to allow the victims to be forgotten. In all her examinations, she hadn't found anything substantial to provide a break in the case.

"I'll drive," Austin said while raising an eyebrow. "I want to make sure you don't take off on me again."

"I see you haven't lost your grim since of humor." A smile tugged at the corners of her lips. Her department-issued car, which had been towed back to the station, was under lockdown while they waited for the crime scene techs to arrive. She doubted they'd find anything useful. Same with the house where she'd been held captive. The Presque Killer was careful. But then he had revealed he was familiar enough with her to connect her to Ruby. That felt significant. Had he tipped his hand by selecting her to participate in his sick plan?

"Let's go, then." Austin halted in the hallway leading to the outside door and faced her. "When I get in work mode, I put on blinders. The person who took you also murdered your sister. I haven't forgotten how that tragedy affected you. Trust that I've got your back."

She knew he meant professionally. Personally, she couldn't help but remember that he'd abandoned her when she needed him the most. Despite her lingering lack of faith in his commitment to the Presque cases, her cheeks warmed under his intense gaze. "I'll worry about my emotional state when I know he's locked away and can't hurt anyone else." Not the healthiest way to deal with the situation but it was the best she could manage at the moment.

Austin pushed open the door and held it while she left the building. "My vehicle is the black SUV with tinted windows."

"Did the car rental company give you the FBI special?"

A small smile crept onto his face. The only way to stay sane during times like this was to allow humor to surface occasionally.

While he walked around the hood to get to the passenger side, she looked him over. Same dark hair with the same crisp haircut. Still smooth-shaven, showing off a dimple in the center of his chin. Austin was tall and athletically built—with more of a soccer player physique than football linebacker. He was classically handsome and carried the serious air that came with the weight of his job. He seemed more intense now than the last time they'd worked together, with his posture more erect and confident. A combination most women couldn't resist. She noticed the absence of a wedding ring on his left hand when he got into the SUV. Why was he still single?

"The Bureau rents cars for agents on field assignments, so I guess I do get the cliché special-agent-mobile." He slipped on a pair of aviator sunglasses. "Lead the way."

She provided directions as he drove to the crime scene.

Good thing her self-control had been reinforced with titanium bars. Austin signified a time in her life she could never return to. A moment when she'd forgotten her mission and let down her guard. Ruby had paid the price for her distraction. Charlotte vowed to never allow her feelings to take her focus away from her job. Not anger, fear, or frustration—or falling in love.

As he drove, Austin replayed Charlotte's account of her kidnapping and the killer's evil plan. The Presque Killer wanted more than a kill. He desired attention and to prove he could outsmart them all. Why involve Charlotte? Because she was the lead detective who'd been hunting him for years. Or was it for a more personal reason?

Austin pulled over to the side of the road where yellow crime scene tape marked off a large square. When he exited the car, his nose filled with the scents of fish and a faint sulfur produced from rotting vegetation. The scene would be released soon. With no breeze, the tape sagged, looking forlorn. The isolated area probably saw minimal traffic. "Were there any tire tracks of interest?"

"It hasn't rained much lately, so the dry gravel road didn't offer much. No footprints either. It appears the killer cleaned up where he'd stepped." She wiped something away from the corner of her eye. "Like before, the killer left little behind other than the body."

Mucky swamp bordered both sides, and appeared to go back at least a hundred feet from the road. The vegetation wasn't too thick, which was why the body had been spotted not long after it had been dumped.

Charlotte removed three large, glossy photographs from a protective sleeve. She handed him one of the photos. "Here's a wide view of what was found."

No matter how many years he did this job, the sight of a defiled corpse sickened him. He took his sensitivity as a good sign. The day he felt nothing at a crime scene was the day he left the FBI. "Was anything discovered in the area that tied back to the victim or possibly the killer?"

"Her purse was found hanging on the branch

of that tree." She indicated where. "No ID was inside. Only a small amount of cash."

He studied the photograph, then stepped closer to the area the victim had been placed. "This woman was posed in a similar manner to the prior victims. From what I recall, that information wasn't released to the public."

"No, it wasn't. Our victim matches the profile of the others… Caucasian, younger female in her twenties. They all had blond hair with the exception of Ruby. Propofol was used to sedated the other victims, and he likely used the same medication on the recent victim and myself." Shaking her head, she crouched and gazed at the matted grass.

"Do you have a close-up of her hands?" He noticed faint lines in the dirt where the victim's fingers would have been. They might have dragged in the ground when the body was placed. Austin took out his cell phone, zooming into the area on the ground, and took pictures at different angles.

"Here." She handed him another photo. "It's not a close-up but you get a good view of her hands. What are you thinking?"

He drew on the facts he knew about the cold cases. "Strangling someone is up close and personal. We didn't find anything under the prior victims' nails. I still believe the women fought back and the killer made sure anything that might identify him was wiped clean. I've assumed he cleansed trace evidence prior to moving the bodies."

"I know my sister did." Charlotte put on a pair of black-rimmed glasses and lowered to a crouch. "The killer taunted me with his knowledge of my love of puzzles as a child. I've a hard time believing I have a connection to the killer."

Austin considered the possibility. "He knows you, whether through researching you during your investigation or having some sort of a prior relationship with you. When we get back to the station, let's make a list of men you know who may fit the profile. See if any correspond to our suspect list from the older cases. Who knows, we may get a match."

She removed a pair of latex gloves from her pants pocket and slipped them on. Her fingers combed through the blades of grass as her eyes searched for anything left behind. "My sister and I spent time in foster care after my mom went to jail. She died prior to her release, so we aged out of the system. We came across a lot of people during those years, from the families who cared for us to fellow foster kids. It may be a stretch. We don't have time to chase dead ends."

"In this type of investigation we chase every lead." He lowered himself and searched the ground along with her. "Your history in foster care may not be connected but you considered the possibility, therefore it's worth digging into."

"Look, red fibers." She used a tweezer to lift up several. "They found more imbedded in her neck."

He opened the evidence bag he'd been keeping in his hand. After the fibers were inside, he sealed the bag. "I'll put in a request to contact the stores in the area. Let's find out if anyone's recently sold the brand of red cord we identified during our last investigation."

She stood, set her hands on her hips and sighed. "I wonder if the killer has been hiding in plain sight under my nose the entire time. Do serial killers take breaks before starting up again?"

"The human psyche is complicated." Austin swatted away the swarm of mosquitoes that had descended on him. "It's not often that a ritualistic killer stops cold turkey. He could have experienced a change in his life that made engaging in his prior activities more difficult. There's the possibility he moved and killed elsewhere but I believe his pattern would have been picked up by the FBI's CODIS database. In cases where a killer pauses, something triggers him to resume. An event occurs that reignites his urges."

"Whatever happened, it must have been big. Our killer hasn't returned simply to murder. He's issued a challenge with deadly consequences."

A threat to innocent women, including Charlotte. Another strong motivation to catch the killer. "I won't leave this time until our job is done. When I board a plane for home, the man who kidnapped you will be securely behind bars."

Chapter Four

Raindrops splattered on the windshield of Austin's SUV as they drove south to Baton Rouge. Charlotte stared out the window, wondering how a place so full of beauty and life could sustain such dark evil. She'd grown up in various towns in the area, including Presque, first with her mom and then through the foster care system. As an adult, Charlotte had found a home and a career in Presque. If only Ruby had felt the same. Instead of reaching for success, Ruby couldn't stay clean long enough to hold employment for more than a few months. For Charlotte, the most tragic piece of Ruby's murder was that Ruby had been clean and sober for almost two months leading up to her death. Her postmortem toxicology reports had indicated no drugs were found in her system. Ruby had been at the starting point of a new life, which had been stolen from her. But now there was a chance the killer had been connected to Charlotte. Had Charlotte somehow been the reason that a new life had been taken away from Ruby?

Austin parked in the lot of the medical examiner's office in Baton Rouge. The body of last night's victim had been brought here for assessment. Instead of speaking to the ME over the phone, they'd agreed viewing the body in person would provide more benefits to their investigation.

"How are you holding up?" Austin's brow furrowed with concern.

He's probably questioning whether I can emotionally handle working this investigation. She took in a deep breath. "These visits are never easy, but I'll be okay. I can't let my feelings cloud my vision." Her mind flashed back to six years ago, when she'd stepped into the same building on separate occasions to view the bodies of the initial four victims. After seeing her sister laying lifeless on a cold metal table, draped with a sheet, Charlotte had run outside to throw up in the hedges alongside the building.

"Let me know if you need a break or to step outside and get some air. I'll do the same." He exited the car and opened the door to the back seat to collect his messenger bag.

While he might be doubting her fortitude, Austin also was being considerate. He'd shown the same concern the last time they'd worked together. Her anger had blocked out the good she'd witnessed in his character. He'd often checked in on her emotional and physical state, even more so after Ruby's death. Until he left and all his care and concern no longer mattered. If Austin had really wanted to protect her, he would have attempted to stay.

She entered the building and introduced herself to the woman at the front desk.

Soon, an assistant greeted the two of them in the lobby, then waved them forward and down the hall. "Protective gear is located in the lockers by the doors to the room but I'm sure you already know that. This isn't your first trip to the medical examiner's office." He guided them to the area. "I need to collect the body and bring her into the room. Holler if you need anything." He hustled away to his next task.

"He's the friendliest person I've ever met at the ME's office." In her prior experience, the employees who worked here were somber and academic—expected traits for those whose job was to study the dead.

Charlotte and Austin dressed in protective gowns, gloves, booties and hats.

When she stepped inside, she sucked in a breath at the cold air. Despite being prepared for the change in temperature, it took her a few minutes to fight off the chill. Viewing the body of a murder victim always left her feeling like she'd never be warm again.

The medical examiner appeared through a door in the rear of the room, fully garbed in protective garments. He wasn't wearing eye protection or a face shield as they wouldn't be required for viewing the body. "Welcome." Dr. Connor held out a gloved hand to both Charlotte and Austin. "I've completed the initial examination. We're still waiting for some of the results of the lab tests." He flipped over the metal cover of a clipboard and scanned several pages. "The female victim was found to have opioids in her system at the time of death. She had some food in her stomach. Time of death is determined to be sixteen hours prior to the discovery of her body."

The rear door opened again and the same assistant who'd brought them back now wheeled a table inside. On the table lay the body of a female. Blond hair framed her lifeless face. Most

of her body was covered with a white sheet.
The assistant brought the table into the center
of the room and locked the wheels, leaving it
underneath a set of large lights secured to the
ceiling.

"Thank you, Robert," Dr. Connor said to
his assistant. "Alert the lab that the tissue samples we just collected are ready to be processed.
Make sure they know I need those results back
as soon as possible."

"I'm on it," Robert replied. "Anything else
you need from me right now?"

"Nothing in here." Dr. Connor turned his
attention to the body on the table, after which
his assistant exited the room.

Charlotte gazed down at the pale face of the
murdered woman. "Have you determined an
official cause of death?"

"Strangulation," Dr. Connor stated. "The
opioids in her system may have hastened her
death. But there's no doubt the ligature marks
on her neck indicate a rope or cord was used to
cut off her air supply." He pointed to the markings that circled her neck.

"I was told she had a crescent moon carved in
her arm." Charlotte's eyes stung with tears she

fought to hold back. She had to clear her mind of everything besides the data being presented.

Dr. Connor lifted the top of the sheet, exposing the woman's arm, creamy white except for a red mark.

At the sight of the design, an exact match to the one left on Ruby and the other victims, bile rose in Charlotte's throat.

"There are too many similarities to our group of victims six years ago." Austin leaned in to get a closer look at the symbol marked on the woman's arm. "We have to be dealing with the same killer." He moved his gaze down the woman's arm to her hands. "Did you swab under her fingernails?"

"I swabbed both under her nails and around each fingertip for evidence." Dr. Connor checked his paperwork, then logged into the nearby computer. "Those tests haven't been completed yet. I didn't see much from a visual inspection but most trace evidence isn't visible, even under a magnifying glass."

"Were her nails dirty?" Austin straightened, then glanced down at the victim's hands once again. "I noticed markings in the ground at the crime scene that may have been made by her fingertips dragging when her body was placed."

After a few clicks of the mouse, Dr. Connor pulled up color photographs taken during the examination and autopsy. "The fingers and nails look clean." He zoomed in to focus on the victim's left hand.

Charlotte studied the image. "Perhaps the markings you saw at the crime scene were from something else." The victim's nails appeared clean to Charlotte as well. Were they too clean? Surely the killer wouldn't have taken the time to scrub the body at the dump site.

"Perhaps." Austin had removed a notepad from his bag and was writing rapidly.

"Anything else of note?" Charlotte asked. The room had begun to feel tight, like the walls were closing in at small increments. The air tasted bitter and stung her lungs. As strongly as the urge struck her to race out the door, she held her feet firmly in place. This was not the time to run.

Austin listened closely to Dr. Connor's verbal autopsy report and jotted down significant information in his personal notebook. He'd receive the final report from the ME within the next few days, dependent on the return of test results. His hope that they'd found trace evidence, such as the killer's DNA underneath her nails, sank at the sight of her overly clean hands. The Presque Killer had only left one small DNA sample on the first victim, which hadn't matched to anyone in the system. A second sample might not bring them closer to identifying the killer but would tie together this new murder with the older ones. However, there was no doubt in anyone's mind that the same individual had killed and dumped all five women.

Austin and Charlotte's phones pinged with an incoming email. Charlotte had picked up a replacement phone on their way to Baton Rouge.

"They identified the victim," Austin said, reading the email. "Ginny Gerard. Twenty-two-year-old female. Last known address in Watson, Louisiana."

"That's not far from here." Charlotte's gaze was fixed on her phone screen, taking in the information provided in the email. "About half way between Baton Rouge and Presque."

"Ginny Gerard was last seen at a nightclub in Baton Rouge three days ago." No surprise that the killer hunted in more populated areas, where his actions could go unnoticed. All five victims had been dumped in the area around

Presque. Austin believed the killer was a local to Presque or someone who knew the community. Small towns had many observant eyes and chatty mouths. He doubted an outsider could have conducted his activity unnoticed.

"I'll call the Baton Rouge Police Department and request a detective canvas the area where Ms. Gerard was last known to be," Charlotte said. "A local cop will be better acquainted with the neighborhood and the people there."

"A city cop also may make the locals unwilling to talk." He'd witnessed the scene play out too many times. Residents grew suspicious of their police department. Fear led to sealed lips. If people had information, they refused to share it with anyone else but one another.

Charlotte nodded in agreement to Austin's concern. "Let's give them a chance and see what they come up with. First thing tomorrow morning, I want to get out the old case files and review everything."

He checked the time. How was it already seven o'clock? He hadn't eaten lunch or dinner. Then again, homicide damped a person's appetite. "Thank you for your time and the information." Austin shook Dr. Connor's hand. "Please send us your final report as soon as it's available."

"Absolutely." The medical examiner gazed at Charlotte. "How are you holding up? Reliving this can't be easy."

Dr. Connor had performed the autopsies on all the Presque Killer victims. He must remember Charlotte's struggle to view her sister's corpse in this same room. Austin would never forget that horrible day. He'd felt helpless watching Charlotte trying hard not to shatter.

"I won't lie and say it's easy coming here. If we had caught the murderer six years ago, this young woman wouldn't have ended up on your exam table." She quickly wiped the corner of her eye.

"He will be held accountable." Austin placed a protective hand low on Charlotte's back and guided her out of the room. This time, the Presque Killer had given an ultimatum. The investigation had been given a deadline. If they failed, Charlotte would pay with her life. An electric charge ran through Austin. He would not fail.

On the return trip to Presque, he listened to Charlotte's phone conversations with the Baton Rouge PD and Chief Gunther. Her professionalism and efficient work style continued to impress him. Nothing about Charlotte was ordinary. Her blonde hair, styled in its usual ponytail, reminded him of a ray of sunshine. She was fit and strong yet gentle when handling the families of victims. Her knowledge made her a good detective. Her empathy made her an extraordinary law enforcement officer.

Austin had struggled with the personal aspect of his job since joining the FBI. He loved reading and learning, which he found easy enough. What proved difficult was keeping in mind the fact that real people were affected by the crimes he studied. But working with Charlotte had provided him with lessons he hadn't learned at the training academy. How to talk to a witness without getting their guard up. What to say during conversations with victims' families and what not to share. When Austin had returned to his home office, he'd carried Charlotte's example going forward when working other cases. Like his last one in Oregon, during which he'd tracked and captured a killer who'd preyed on backpackers. His improved interpersonal skills helped him be a better special agent while retaining the aloofness he needed to avoid emotional burnout.

He glanced at Charlotte. Did she know how deeply he admired her?

When he parked in front of her house, a longing filled him. For what exactly, he couldn't tell. To return home at the end of the day to a family? That dream would never become a reality. His line of work demanded complete commitment. Nights, weeks, months spent traveling created fractures in even the best relationships. Marriages of fellow special agents that Austin considered strong had crumbled under the weight of a demanding profession. A woman as special as Charlotte deserved better. She was deeply rooted in this community while his job required constant travel.

She reached for the door handle, then paused. "Let's plan to meet at six tomorrow morning at the station. I'll ask for the evidence boxes to be brought up to the conference room."

"I'll bring coffee and doughnuts." He pushed back a yawn. His day had started before dawn. The travel, combined with the stress of Charlotte's kidnapping and the pressure to catch a serial killer, weighed heavy.

"I've come to accept that it was a good thing the FBI sent you back to Presque. I'd hate to have to bring up to speed a new agent." She appeared resigned. "I'm sorry for how we ended things last time. And for how I acted before you left," she added with a grin.

"I regret not pushing back on the orders to return to my home office." Although, even if he had, the likelihood of his supervisor granting his request would've been slim. Even Caleb would have had a tough time convincing FBI leadership that Austin's time was best served in Presque. After months of few leads, little evidence and no viable suspects, he wasn't surprised when the Bureau had directed its resources elsewhere. The cases he'd worked on since he left Presque six years ago had been important too. Each case had value. He'd witnessed numerous dangerous predators taken off the streets. Every solved case hardened his determination to keep fighting for justice. He couldn't allow his tender feelings for Charlotte to cause a special attachment to the Presque cases. Still, he had to see these cases closed. The victims' families deserved justice. "I never forgot about the Presque victims." *Or you*, he almost added.

"That's reassuring." She clutched her purse on her lap. "I need a partner who wants this killer caught as much as I do."

"Charlotte, the madman threatened your life along with countless others." The thought of her under the control of a vicious killer heated his blood. "Do you feel safe sleeping at home tonight?" She'd lived alone six years ago, but the idea she might be in a relationship knocked him off-balance.

She gazed at the cottage-style house with only the front porch light providing an illuminating glow. "I have seven days to find and stop him. If he wanted to harm me sooner, he would have earlier today."

Her logic didn't settle his anxiety. "I'm staying at the Magnolia Hotel. It's not far away, so if you need anything or hear a bump in the night, call me. I'll be over in a flash."

"Good to know my FBI partner is also a superhero." Charlotte opened the SUV door and stepped outside. "The FBI couldn't find you a better place to stay than the Magnolia?" Standing beside the vehicle, she leaned over to peer in and said after a pause, "On second thought, that is the nicest hotel in Presque. They spray for cockroaches, which is the best standard of quality around these parts. See you tomorrow."

At the mention of cockroaches, he shivered. Austin considered himself brave and had faced down many bad guys with guns, but creepy-crawlies sent him running in the other direction. After Charlotte closed the door, he waited for her to get safely inside her house. Instead of driving to his hotel, he got out and did a perimeter check of her property. Blame his time in the army for his hypervigilance. These circumstances warranted extra precaution, though.

While he searched for hidden danger, memories of his time in the service drifted into his mind. Mostly good recollections. Several he'd fought over the years to banish. Witnessing the murder on base was a bad memory he didn't want to forget because it stoked the fire he needed to do his job. He'd thought he could stop the men fighting as he raced toward them on the base's recreation field. Austin hadn't gotten there in time to stop the stabbing. There was nothing he could do to prevent a fellow soldier from dying. He had helped capture the soldier who'd murdered another and in doing so, stopped future violence. Sometimes, that was all a person could do.

When he decided all was quiet and clear, he returned to his car, then took a slow drive around the block. The sun had set. The streets were relatively quiet. Most houses had a few lights on inside. He passed Charlotte's house again and saw one light on in the front room.

He prayed she'd find restful sleep tonight. Austin knew sleep would elude him until the killer was taken off the streets.

Chapter Five

Charlotte managed to get a few hours' rest. Even before the first beams of sunlight breached her curtains, she rolled out of bed and started a pot of coffee. She had about an hour before meeting Austin at the station. With a little luck and guidance from God, they'd find a clue missed before, which would lead them to the Presque Killer's identity. He had to be stopped before he harmed anyone else.

Last night, she'd dreamed about Ruby and the sweet girl she'd once been. For so many years, they'd only had each other. The killer had not only snuffed out an innocent life but stolen Charlotte's best friend. No one would ever replace Ruby in her life. How could anyone fill the giant hole in Charlotte's heart? A hole the size of a sister whom she'd shared everything with. Every good and bad day. All the trauma of witnessing their mother arrested and then never seeing her again. Moving from foster home to foster home with only one another to cling to.

Thinking about all that the killer had stolen from her and the other victims' families filled her with rage. If her life was the cost of bringing him down, she'd pay without question. Charlotte could not live another year knowing the person responsible for five cruel deaths walked free.

She showered and dressed while mentally prepping herself for the day ahead. Her phone rang, and she assumed it was Austin checking in to make sure she'd made it safely through the night. After he'd dropped her off, Charlotte had noticed him walking around the property, searching for any danger that lay hidden in the shadows. His gesture warmed her heart and also set her on guard. What she needed from the dashing FBI agent was professional, not personal. He was here to save lives and catch a killer. Once the mission was accomplished, he'd get back on a plane and fly off to work on his next case. She, on the other hand, would resume her normal life and duties. "I can't wait for the day when my biggest challenge is catching some kid who robbed the corner convenience store."

She lifted her cell phone and noticed Presque PD on the caller ID. "Hello, this is Detective Reid."

"Reid, it's the chief. There's been a report of a kidnapping. A waitress working the late shift at the Pancake Café never came home after her shift."

Her stomach churned with dread. Some small part of her had hoped the Presque Killer had been bluffing about kidnapping women. She checked the calendar, where she'd circled next Thursday in red ink—their deadline. "Are we sure she's a missing person and didn't just go somewhere else after work?"

"Her husband called the station around three a.m. in a panic," Chief Gunther said. "The missing waitress, Karen Tremont, called him at midnight when she was getting ready to leave the café. Everyone is on edge due to the Presque Killer's return. A patrol officer went to the café, which is open twenty-four hours. He spoke with the staff there and was told Mrs. Tremont left around midnight, but her car is still parked in the lot. There's no sign of her in the building or surrounding area."

While the chief was talking, Charlotte slipped on her shoes and tied the laces. "I'm on my way."

"Notify Agent Walsh and have him meet you over there. If the waitress is the first kidnapping victim of the Presque Killer, we'll need to move fast."

"Agreed." She ended the call, heart racing. Even though she preferred not to work on assumptions, the Presque Killer would be the main suspect until Charlotte had facts that proved otherwise.

She made a quick call to Austin, filling him in on the few details known so far. After locking the door behind her, she raced to her car and headed to the Pancake Café.

When she arrived, Austin came out of the building to meet her. Two Presque Police Department squad cars were parked in the gravel-covered lot, both flanking a maroon minivan with Louisiana license plates.

"Is this the waitress's van?" She moved closer and used a flashlight to peer in the side windows. The van was confirmed to belong to the waitress. Beside a littering of children's toys and some trash, the van was empty. Glancing at the squad cars, she thought back to her own kidnapping yesterday. "Move your vehicles," she commanded the nearby patrol officers. "The kidnapper could have parked on the side of the van and snatched the victim as she approached to leave."

"How do we know this woman didn't leave with someone else?" one of the patrol officers, a young man who'd barely reached the drinking age, asked.

"Go interview the employees who were working with Karen Tremont before she left and find out." She pointed a finger in the direction of the café. "Let me know if anyone has knowledge of her whereabouts. But first, move your car."

She shook her head and prayed for calm. Normally, she didn't take out her frustration on other officers. This was not a normal situation.

Once the patrol cars were moved and their tire tracks marked, Austin studied the gravel ground. He turned to examine the building about twenty feet away. "No cameras."

"I asked," Officer Evans, the older of the officers, replied. He'd been on the force for eight years with his sights set on leadership. Charlotte respected his integrity and work ethic. "No video of the inside or outside of the building. Do you want me to tape off this area?"

"Yes." Charlotte said. "This is a potential crime scene."

Officer Kagan hurried out of the café, his fresh face alive with eagerness. "One of the cooks who worked overnight took a smoke break around eleven forty-five and noticed a box truck parked next to the waitress's van. It was over there." He indicated the parking spot next to the driver's side.

"Didn't anyone find it strange Karen Tremont's van didn't leave when she left after her shift ended?" Austin's intense gaze caused Officer Kagan to move back a few steps.

"I'll go ask the cook but he didn't mention it." Officer Kagan hustled back inside.

"A box truck." Charlotte examined the ground in the space beside the van. She saw two sets of tracks. One had been established as coming from the police car. The slightly larger set caught her interest. "We need to make molds of these tracks. It's a long shot and will take more time than we have but maybe we can match the make and model of tires to a specific vehicle."

"There's a lot of box trucks driving around," Austin said as a white box truck with the decal of a delivery company on the side rumbled by. "But…we'd be negligent not to work the lead."

She took out a pair of gloves and wore one on each hand. Starting her search with the van's exterior, she stepped with awareness. Several rusty dents dotted the body of the van. Some scratches on the back appeared like marks from a key. She studied the driver's-side door, particularly the door handle. Using her own kidnapping as a reference, she imagined the killer had entered Karen's car prior to her getting in. Every surface would be dusted for prints, although experience had taught the Presque Killer was too careful not to use gloves.

The corner of something white pressed against the windshield caught her attention. She looked closer and found a small note card secured under a windshield wiper. Had he left another calling card? "Austin, I found something."

Using her gloved hands, she removed the note, deep down hoping it was an innocent advertising flyer.

One

She recognized the handwriting, each letter formed with a linear style. It was similar to the note left by the murdered body of Ginny Gerard two days ago. No doubt remained in her mind—the Presque Killer's game had begun.

Charlotte made a call to the chief, requesting the crime scene processing team arrive as quickly as possible. She'd request Chief Gunther shake a few branches to bring in more resources. Lives were on the line.

Austin accepted a paper cup from Charlotte. "Thank you. I don't know how anyone can function without a cup of coffee in the morning." He removed the plastic lid, took a cautious sip and sighed, enjoying the rich flavor at the perfect temperature. The chill of the early morning had burned away with the rising sun. In the bright daylight, the café's parking lot appeared harmless. But not long ago a woman had been surprised on her way to her vehicle after a long shift, snatched before reaching the safety of the interior. Austin shuddered to imagine how terrified she must have been to encounter a killer.

No one who'd been in the restaurant at midnight had noticed any suspicious activity. From the interviews they'd conducted so far, they'd learned Mrs. Tremont left after serving her last table, one full of high school kids. She'd been tired but smiling when she'd walked out the door.

"The killer may have dined in the café. He could have used the opportunity to stalk his victim. I want to review all the sales tickets from ten o'clock until midnight. Another waitress could have noticed a man dining alone." He drew on his knowledge of criminals. A deep well he sometimes wished he could lock away and never peer into again. Witnessing a murder while in the army had left him feeling helpless. His training at the FBI Academy at Quantico and working under Caleb had solidified his mission to hunt the predators who hunted the innocent. Cutting off the wicked from harming others was his life's goal.

A while ago, Austin had confided in Caleb about his growing frustrations at his inability to stop evil from happening in the world. Leaving behind the murder cases in Presque had almost broken his will to continue in the FBI. Shortly after he returned, Caleb had sat him down and they'd spent time in prayer together. They studied God's messages in the Bible about good and evil, justice and mercy. Austin had come to accept that many events that took place were out of his control. He couldn't protect everyone.

Serving God meant fulfilling His purpose to the best of his ability. But only God was perfect, and ultimately He was in control.

"I don't believe he would risk being seen inside," Charlotte said before taking a drink of coffee. "Using my kidnapping as a model, the perp stealthily moves in, grabs his victim and gets out quick."

A Presque Police Department truck pulled into the parking lot and stopped next to the building. Chief Gunther exited, placed his Stetson on his silver-haired head, then came over to where Austin and Charlotte stood. "Do you have any leads?"

"No, sir." Charlotte stepped toward the area surrounded by crime scene tape. "Nothing was found in the van, at least nothing visible to the naked eye. We have no witnesses or anyone who noticed anything off last night. No one even noticed her van was still here until her husband called looking for her."

The chief scratched his chin. "What about the tire tracks? Do you believe the techs can cast a good enough mold to get a match on the type of tire?"

"They'll get a good cast but matching it to a specific tire and to a make and model of truck takes time." Austin's chest tightened as he counted down the days—six. An investigation this scale could take weeks if not longer. As a rule, missing person investigations had to move fast. The first forty-eight hours were critical. Unfortunately, many adults weren't reported missing for at least twenty-four hours after they were last seen, sometimes longer if they disappeared for days at a time.

"I'm setting up a task force." The command in Chief Gunther's voice couldn't be missed. "Detective Reid and Special Agent Walsh, you'll both lead the team. You're dealing with both a murder and kidnapping from a known serial killer. And the clock is ticking."

"Extra assistance is much appreciated," Charlotte said. "Have the task force members been notified?"

Austin's attention continued to be drawn by Charlotte and her fierce devotion to her work. He'd partnered with many other law enforcement professionals, but Charlotte felt like a true collaborator. What if he convinced her to join the FBI? He envisioned working alongside her on cases all over the country.

"Yes," Chief Gunther answered. "All members are meeting at the station at two this afternoon. I've tapped officers from state and parish departments. You'll have the best, but don't forget, you two are in charge. I don't trust anyone else to see this to the end."

Austin nodded. His job was easier with the full trust and empowerment of local law enforcement leadership. "I'd like to interview Mrs. Tremont's husband and friends to find out if there was anyone she could have gone with last night instead of going home. We need to make sure she's not somewhere unharmed."

"I'll let you get back to work." The chief patted Charlotte on the shoulder. "Say the word and I'll get you placed in protective custody. While I believe you to be the best detective ever to serve under my command, your safety is my priority. I couldn't live with myself if something happened to you."

Chief Gunther's statement mirrored Austin's feelings. Guarding Charlotte was as important to Austin as finding the Presque Killer. In reality, they were one and the same. But only if they arrested the killer before midnight on the seventh day.

"I appreciate your concern, Chief." Charlotte crushed her empty paper coffee cup in her fist. "I will see all these cases closed, both the cold and recent. My sister died at the hands of the Presque Killer. I have to be the one who brings him to justice."

And Austin would be with her every step of the way.

Leaving the Tremont house after speaking with Karen's husband, Charlotte held little hope the woman had decided to go out with a friend or secret lover. Karen appeared to be a devoted wife and mother who worked second shift at the café so her husband could care for their young son after he came home from his office job. The family lived in a modest house with a trimmed front yard and several colorful flower beds. Mr. Tremont's emotional state hadn't been an act, or at least Charlotte didn't believe so. He genuinely seemed distraught at his wife's disappearance.

Karen wasn't the Presque Killer's typical victim, as none of the others were either married or had children. Charlotte assumed the killer wasn't being picky while selecting his mark. He wanted a woman he could easily snatch without getting caught.

Interviewing Mr. Tremont had brought her backward in time to when Ruby went missing. Initially, Charlotte had assumed her sister had gone somewhere to get drugs and get high. Only when she couldn't find Ruby in all the usual spots had she begun to worry about Ruby's life and not just her sobriety. The panic she felt after acknowledging the possible connection of Ruby's disappearance to the Presque Killer still lingered to this day. She recognized the look in Mr. Tremont's eye—a fear so deep it pushed a person into dark places.

"Thoughts?" Austin asked as they walked to their vehicles parked on the street. Somehow, the FBI agent looked as perfect as ever. Each dark hair on his head in its place. His clothes spot-free and pressed. He'd found time to shave this morning. Must have been up even earlier than Charlotte, if he'd slept at all.

For her part, Charlotte's ponytail was in the process of falling out: frizzy blond tendrils of hair broke free like a well-orchestrated prison break. She glanced down to see a light yellow spot on the collar of her white button-down shirt. Why did she have white in her professional wardrobe when she was a magnet for everything and anything that stained clothes?

She considered Austin's question for her thoughts, and her head spun with information, not only regarding the Tremont kidnapping but the recent murder of Ginny Gerard. Police had notified Ms. Gerard's family last evening. They hadn't realized she'd been missing, since she had sometimes disappeared into the Baton Rouge party scene for weeks at a time.

"I believe the Presque Killer is true to his word. He's taken his first kidnapping victim." She removed her car keys from her pants pocket. "We need to get to the station and comb over all the old case files. I don't believe he will give us much in terms of leads but maybe there's something in the files we missed six years ago."

"Word is spreading around town." Austin unhooked his sunglasses from the front pocket of his shirt and set them on his nose. "Women around the area will be more vigilant."

"And their extra caution will make the killer more likely to make a mistake." Charlotte prayed for God's protection of everyone in the community, especially Karen Tremont. "All we need is one slipup, one witness, one clue to point us in the right direction."

"When he held you in the basement of the house, he provided you with a clue. The killer knows you, at least at some level. His current actions are personal and he's connected them to you." He stopped on the sidewalk by Char-

lotte's parked car. "The killer could have selected Ruby because she's your sister."

The ground underneath her feet swayed.
She'd always assumed Ruby had been selected
by the Presque Killer because she was an easy
target. But Austin was right. With the new
knowledge the killer had provided yesterday,
she had to consider the possibility that Ruby
had been chosen because she was Charlotte's sister. The thought made her sick to her stomach.

"I hate to admit it but you may be right." She
wrapped an arm around her midsection. The
increasing heat and humidity of the morning
only exacerbated her queasiness. "Let's hurry
back to the station. We have about four hours
until the task force meeting. Perhaps we'll have
some new piece of information to share after
we start digging into the old cases."

The sound of a clock ticking echoed in her
head. Six days. How many more lives would
the Presque Killer affect before she brought him
down? *Please God, no more.*

Chapter Six

Austin set out a fresh notepad, new pen and his cell phone in a neat row on the conference room table. He had a system, which often caused good-natured teasing. Order helped him process the facts of an investigation that usually were anything but neat and orderly.

Entering the room, Charlotte ended a call. "Officers have been dispatched to talk to friends of Karen Tremont. They've been directed to call me with pertinent information. Still no credible witnesses have come forward on Mrs. Tremont's disappearance, though the tip line that's been established is lighting up. Everyone in town has a theory."

"Have you received tips on any of the cold cases after the investigations were closed?" Austin asked with apprehension. The last thing he wanted to do was remind Charlotte that his departure had led to the murder investigations being closed.

"Sure." She lifted the lid off one of the dozen or so cardboard boxes that officers had brought up from the evidence storage locker. "Small towns are hotbeds for gossip and the behavior of one or two troublemakers always gets peoples' fingers pointed their way. I'd talk to people, ask questions, get alibis. Nothing ever rose to the level of a real lead."

He took another box and removed the lid. The smell of musty paper and years of heartbreak washed over him. With care, he took out each folder and stacked them in four piles, one for items relating to each of the four victims. Inside each folder were notes and documents not digitally filed. His laptop sat nearby. Austin logged in and pulled up his notes from their last investigation until he found the documents he wanted. "We had two main suspects six years ago, Pete Carter and Kevin DuPont. Both had weak connections to the young women, mostly due to drug sales." He read over the files they'd compiled on both men.

"May as well start there. Where are they now?" Charlotte powered up her laptop and after clicking and typing for several minutes, she moved her gaze from the computer screen. "Pete Carter is a resident of the East Baton Rouge Parish Penitentiary." She clicked and opened another webpage. "Kevin DuPont lives in Northern California. I'll place a call to the local police department to verify his where-abouts. But he was ticketed for drunk and dis-orderly two days ago in his home town, so I think it's safe to rule him out."

"Did you know either of them?" Although neither man had likely been in the area recently, he wanted to tie off any loose ends.

"Only on a professional level." Charlotte pushed aside her computer and pulled out files from a box, spreading the folders on the table. "I arrested both men on drug charges years ago. I don't have any personal connection to either."

He mentally crossed Pete Carter off his sus-pect list. Kevin DuPont would be cleared if he was located in Northern California. "While reviewing the documents and evidence related to each murder again, maybe something will point us in a new direction."

Opening the top folder on the first pile, he took out a glossy photograph of Mary Gury, the initial murder victim, and tacked it to the board on the wall. Mary's smiling face held no knowledge of the horror that would come. He posted photographs of the other victims from the old cases, and noticed Charlotte's face pale at the sight of her sister. "Let me know if this becomes too much." He worried about her. The last time they'd investigated Ruby's murder, Charlotte's strength couldn't be denied but no one could withstand the constant reminder of a loved one's suffering.

She took a shuddering breath and removed her gaze from the photo of Ruby. "I go through several of these boxes every other month in hopes I'll find something I missed. I hate that the man who killed my sister has been living free for all these years. And now he's stealing more lives. I face the pain of looking at the evidence because not bringing Ruby's killer to justice hurts more."

Austin registered grief along with a fierce determination in Charlotte's eyes. He wanted to touch her and absorb some of her heartache. Instead, he lowered his gaze and refocused on the task at head. Taking an evidence bag out of the box marked RUBY, he noticed its light weight. The contents listed a bracelet, earrings and nose ring. He emptied the contents on the table.

Charlotte froze at the sight of the jewelry. "We had matching bracelets." She held up her arm, and a delicate gold bracelet matching the one on the table hung from her wrist. "I'd thought about requesting it back but I felt it should stay with the rest of the evidence until her killer was caught and sentenced. Our mom gave them to us and we had them resized. It's one of the only things we had from our mom when we went into foster care." She picked up the bag with her sister's bracelet inside. "See? Matching moons— Wait, crescent moons! I didn't tie the crescent moon charm on the bracelets to the mark on each victim's arm... until now. Could the charms be related to the marks on the victims' arms?"

"It's possible." He took photos of Ruby's and Charlotte's bracelets on his phone. "The crescent moon symbol appears significant. Now let's start at the beginning and see what else we can link together."

"Mary Gury was discovered on a dirt road right on the Presque city limits." Charlotte unfolded a map of the town and outlying area then marked a red X where Mary's body had been found. "DNA not belonging to the victim was found on her sweater, which is believed to be the killer's sweat. The DNA did not match anyone in the system, and I have an alert set to notify me if a match is uploaded."

He reviewed the autopsy report completed on Mary. How had her killer not left any evidence behind except for a small dot of perspiration? "Cause of death, strangulation. Red nylon rope fibers were found in the ligature marks around her neck. A shallow laceration in the shape of a U on the inside of her arm was determined to be from her killer. Looking at the mark again, it could be a primitive attempt at a crescent moon."

"Witnesses described Ms. Gury as friendly and kind but as someone who struggled with drug addiction." Charlotte picked up a cluster of papers and fingered through them. "She was last seen leaving a party alone three nights before her body was discovered. No one knew what happened to her after she left or where she planned to go afterward."

"Was there any reason to believe the people with Ms. Gury at the party were afraid to talk?" If the perpetrator was a known violent offender in the community, fear of retribution created a cone of silence.

"I don't believe so." She scanned a few more

typed reports. "Mary's mother was well respected and those who were interviewed came off as motivated to help find her killer."

He nodded at her assessment. His focus turned to victim two. "Whitney Malone."

They talked through each of the four cold cases. In all the cases, nothing new jumped out. Mary Gury, Whitney Malone, Amy Casey and Ruby Reid had disappeared without a trace until their bodies were discovered. Cause of death was the same—strangulation. The instrument used—a red nylon rope. While the mark carved into Mary's arm was a U shape. Whitney, Amy and Ruby's marks looked more evolved, like a crescent moon. The recent victim's autopsy matched closely to the other known victims of the Presque Killer. He'd developed his signature. Though with the kidnapping of Karen, he was going slightly off course. Could someone have copied him, wishing for the notoriety of the Presque Killer? Possibly. Though many of the details of the killings were kept confidential. A copycat would need to have learned the killer's methods from the killer himself or been privy to classified information.

"How do we catch a ghost?" Charlotte tossed

a thick file folder onto the table, then rubbed her forehead. "We've arrived at the same dead ends that stopped us before."

Dead ends that resulted in his removal from the cases and then the cases growing cold. "Do any of the victims besides Ruby have a connection to you?"

"No, other than how they looked." She wrapped her arms around her body. "I didn't put the connection together before or maybe didn't want to but all of the first three victims were white females with blond hair, like myself. Each of them was approximately my height and weight. Of course, Ruby is my sister and we resemble each other. I don't want to believe the killer is targeting women who look like me."

The theory had come to his mind after Charlotte gave an account of her kidnapping. The killer had a strong association with Charlotte, and so far only the killer was acquainted with their shared history or why he chose her as his main competitor.

"Do you have the records of your time in foster care?" he asked. "There will be people listed who you may not remember being in your life at that time."

"I put a call into the parish family services

agency. They're working on getting my file over to me." She stepped closer to the photographs, map and timeline they'd posted on the board. "I asked they bring it by the end of the day. I don't remember everyone who was in and out of my life back then. Truth be told, I blocked out a lot of my childhood."

He checked the time. They'd blown through lunch and the task force would meet soon. On a narrow table pushed against the wall, two fast-food bags with two cups sat neglected. Someone must have brought them food at some point. Could have even mentioned it but he and Charlotte had been so hyper-focused that neither had noticed.

He unfolded the top of one of the bags, pulled out a wrapped burger and took it over to Charlotte along with a drink. "Take a break and eat something. You'll be leading the task force meeting in ten minutes."

She licked her lips. With a groan, she unwrapped the hamburger then took a bite. "I forgot what food tastes like."

Austin followed her example. But instead of Charlotte's controlled pace, he scarfed his burger down in a few bites. Once he was done eating, he took a moment to tidy the boxes, files and paperwork that had been scattered on the conference table.

"I forgot what a neat freak you are." She stood at the door, her laptop tucked underneath her arm. "Ready to go?"

Before following her out, Austin took a minute to look at the photographs of the four victims. He would put up one of Ginny Gerard as soon as they received the photo from her family. "You have not been forgotten." He spoke to the murdered women like they were standing in the room. In his mind and heart, they were. "Your killer will face justice for what he did." He turned his gaze to the picture of Ruby, whose resemblance to Charlotte was striking. "And I promise to keep Charlotte safe."

With notebook and pen in hand, he turned off the lights and left the room, locking the door behind him, securing the proof of stolen lives.

Charlotte left the first Presque Killer task force meeting more hopeful than she'd been before. The boost of personnel would keep the investigation moving at the fast pace required. For his part, Austin stayed in the background, his hands loosely clasped behind him. She'd learned from working with him years ago that he preferred to observe rather than talk. His quiet demeanor and relaxed expression hid a federal law enforcement professional who did not miss even the slightest detail. While the meeting was progressing and different personnel were sharing their opinions about the course of the investigation, Charlotte could almost hear the gears turning in Austin's head. Anticipation grew to hear his thoughts and gather his opinion on how best to use the resources the task force provided.

She unlocked the door to the conference room and stepped inside. Everything was how they'd left it. Not that she suspected a police officer of being the killer but the first thing that Austin had taught her when he'd arrived six years ago was that when hunting a serial killer, no one was ruled out automatically. No one got a free pass because of their job or who they were in the community.

A knock startled her out of her ruminations. "Detective Reid, a reporter from the newspaper is here to see you."

"Who?" Not that she had time for any of them but one local reporter in particular always raised her defenses.

"Ronald Rheault," Gladys, the woman who worked at the front desk, said. "He isn't taking no for an answer."

"He never does." At least when it came to stories involving the Presque Police Department and more specifically Charlotte Reid.

"What do you what me to tell him? Go away?" Gladys smiled. She had a motherly air about her that made Charlotte long for a mother who was still alive and had not been arrested and taken away.

"I'll talk to him," she said with resignation. "A few no comments and then send him on his way."

On her way to the front, she passed by Austin, who'd stayed behind after the meeting to talk with the state detective charged with investigating last night's kidnapping.

"Where are you headed?" he asked, pivoting to face her. "Not leaving without me?"

"Wouldn't dream of it." Warmth filled her chest. Normally, she pushed away any gesture of overprotection. Charlotte had a badge and a gun and a smart brain. She didn't need anyone, specially men, falling over themselves to keep her safe. But Austin's concern hit differently. Most likely due to the killer's direct threat to her.

She carried on down the hallway and exited into the lobby. Ronald had positioned himself at the front desk as if daring anyone to ask him to leave without getting what he came for. "Mr. Rheault, how may I help you?"

He jumped slightly at the sound of her voice in the otherwise quiet lobby. Turning to face her, he met her gaze.

A fleeting expression passed over his face that Charlotte couldn't identify but she sensed he'd concealed his true feelings.

"Detective." Ronald cleared his throat. "I'm writing a story on the reemergence of the Presque Killer. And since you haven't held a press conference yet, I'm here in person to get answers. How is the investigation going? Do you have any solid leads? What does the presence of an FBI agent mean in regards to the department's faith in your abilities?"

She ground her teeth and took another step toward him. "Those are a lot of questions."

"Only three." He flipped open a spiral notebook then took a pencil off its resting spot on his ear. "Let's start with suspects. Do you have any?"

"No comment." Keeping her facial expression neutral was difficult when she faced an annoying reporter. Actually, Ronald Rheault was more than annoying. He'd been downright intrusive during the last Presque Killer investigation. She didn't expect preferential treatment from the local media but he'd printed speculations and not facts after the murder of Ruby. Charlotte had never gotten over her irritation.

"Okay." Ronald made an act of writing in his notebook while wearing a smirk. "The FBI agent you're working with, is he the same one as last time?"

"Special Agent Walsh has returned to assist." Maybe a crumb would satisfy him.

"Has the FBI taken over the investigation?"

Her temper was rising by the question. *Stay calm. He wants to see a reaction.* "No comment."

"Is there anything you want to comment on for the story?" Ronald arched an eyebrow. "You've accused me of misrepresenting your work in previous stories."

"Don't write fiction and I won't have a problem." She turned her head in a signal her tolerance was almost gone.

Ronald jotted down some more notes before closing his notebook. "I'm covering this story, whether you talk to me or not. I have other sources in the department. I've lived in Presque

most of my life, which means I know most of
the people in the town. Went to school with
many, including you."

That comment captured her attention. She
studied him closely, not dismissing the reporter
anymore. "That's right, we were in the same
grade for a few years, until I changed schools.
I forgot."

"Of course you did." He snorted, shaking
his head. "Charlotte Reid, always keeping everyone at a distance. With your sister being
the only exception. Let me know if you want
to share any facts with the public. They have a
right to know."

She stood frozen in the lobby until Ronald
left the building. A scrawny news reporter was
not a serial killer. Half the town had known
her at some point during her youth.

But she couldn't rule anyone out. She'd ask
an officer to discreetly look into Ronald's recent whereabouts just in case. If anything, to
rule him out.

While she was still in the lobby, a social services worker entered. The worker had brought
over Charlotte's file from her years in the system. She'd been kind enough to print out the
documents. Charlotte found examining paper

documents easier than clicking around on a computer screen. Plus, she and Austin could share the task of looking over each one.

After thanking the worker for the quick delivery, Charlotte held the folder tight to her chest. *God, guide us to the person harming Your children. Use me for Your purposes.*

She strode down the hallway, back to the conference room and Austin. The time had come to take a looking glass to her history. The clues they'd been searching for might be buried in her past.

Chapter Seven

Charlotte rubbed her eyes and yawned. She and Austin had recorded the names and address of the six foster homes she and Ruby had resided in along with various foster children and families whom they'd shared a home with.

She was running criminal histories on everyone she'd listed. If she got a hit and their DNA had been logged into the system, she placed them on a "not likely" list. The one piece of trace evidence they had ruled out anyone who'd been arrested for a number of specific types of crimes. Each state's DNA collection laws varied, which made a broad search a little harder to use for eliminating suspects.

"We can rule out females, which removes about fifty percent of the people who touched your life during foster care." Austin glanced up from his laptop screen with his reading glasses perched on the tip of his nose. "You're confident the person who abducted you was a man, right?"

"Yes, even though he used something to alter his voice, it was male. Aren't most serial killers men?"

"Most but not all." He pushed his reading glasses back onto the bridge of his nose. "In these cases, a female suspect would be highly unlikely."

The fluttery feeling in her stomach produced by the intensity of his gaze was the reason she'd fallen for him. And his good looks were only magnified when he wore glasses. Why did her attraction to the dedicated FBI special agent resurface when all her concentration should be on catching a killer? She could not be distracted by the thick lashes framing Austin's eyes or the way the corners of his mouth turned down while absorbed in a task. Not again. The murdered women deserved every ounce of her attention. Meaning she'd reinforce their professional boundaries.

After enough time had passed, she could admit he'd broken her heart when he left six years ago. Why had Austin been the one man who'd smashed the protective walls around her heart? She'd known from the start he'd never be permanent.

Charlotte returned her attention to the list of names. One jumped out along with a couple of disturbing memories. Michael Duncan had struck her as strange on the first day she'd met him. Michael had a brief stay in the White household during the time Charlotte had lived there. She'd been about thirteen at the time. While Michael had lived with the foster family for only a short while, those months had been scary for the entire group living in the house.

"Michael Duncan," she said to Austin, "was a resident at a home I lived in with Ruby until he threatened to kill Mrs. White. He was sent to a group home after that."

"Where does he live now?" Austin stood behind her and gazed over her shoulder at the information Charlotte viewed.

She typed in Michael Duncan with his date of birth in the search fields of the database. Within seconds, pages of Michael's life history appeared on the screen. "No arrests and no criminal history. He's lived at the same address for ten years. His house is in Presque, on the south side of town. No wife or children listed."

"Have you had any interactions with him since

you lived together in foster care?" Austin scanned the computer screen, taking his own notes.

"I'd need to see how he looks to know for certain." She flipped through her memory. "I'm sure I've come across him given that we both live in the same town."

"We should pay him a visit." Austin checked his watch, and his eyes widened. "It's after ten already. I should send in a report to my supervisor."

The mention of contacting his supervisor produced a flash of fear. At any point, Austin could be pulled off the case for a second time for a higher priority case, and she had no doubt he'd follow orders. Charlotte glanced outside and for the first time noticed the darkness. "No wonder I'm so tired. I can't afford to sleep. At least not until the killer is off the street."

"You'll need to rest in order to function." He pulled back her chair and assisted her to stand. "Go home and sleep. We'll pay a visit to Mr. Duncan first thing tomorrow morning."

She arched her low back, stretching the tight muscles. "I can't stop yet. There are a few more people I need to check into." Especially if she might lose Austin's help at the word of someone hundreds of miles away.

The sound of footsteps preceded the entrance of Officer Kagan. A youthful eagerness shone on his face. "I spoke with Ronald Rheault about his whereabouts last night around the time the waitress was kidnapped."

Charlotte groaned. "I don't want him thinking he's a suspect."

"Who's Ronald Rheault?" Austin asked, glancing back and forth between Charlotte and Officer Kagan.

"He's a reporter for the local newspaper," she answered. "You may remember him from our last investigation. Tall, skinny guy with a way of showing up everywhere he's not wanted."

"Sounds vaguely familiar." Austin removed his reading glasses and set them on a stack of papers on the table. "Why are you checking on his alibi for when the kidnapping occurred?"

"He showed up at the station this afternoon, asking questions, which is his job," she answered. How to explain the sense of unease she'd experienced around him? Could be she was suspicious of everyone crossing her path who fit the killer's profile. A reporter's job was to chase a story, and one as big as the Presque Killer garnered national media attention. Charlotte didn't find it odd that the local news was desperate for an inside scoop. But something about Ronald in particular caused an extra dose of wariness. Even during the prior investigation, she'd gotten the impression he wasn't focused on the news story but instead some of his interest was directed on her. "I get a weird vibe with him," she continued. "And a job as a reporter could be a good cover for someone wanting to commit crimes then stay informed about the investigation."

"What did you find?" Austin asked the officer.

Office Kagan's posture straightened. "Don't worry, I made up a story of why I wanted to know where Ronald was last evening. I told him a strange man was seen lurking outside his house. I played it cool so he wouldn't tie my questions to the kidnapping."

She didn't want to burst the young officer's bubble by disagreeing. The news reporter had likely seen right through his story. Only ten years ago, she'd been filled with youthful ambition, striving to impress her superiors. Working for a small-town police department, she'd started out naive, much like Officer Kagan. She hoped the younger officer didn't make some of the same mistakes she had. Looking back, she wished she'd done some things differently. Falling in love with her FBI partner being top of the list.

"Did Ronald have an alibi?" she asked since Officer Kagan failed to provide the most crucial part of the story on his own.

"Not really. He said he was home asleep. He lives alone and parks his car in the garage."

"Would he have access to a box truck?" Austin took out photos of the scene by the café and pointed at the tire tracks found next to the victim's van.

"The newspaper has one," Charlotte replied. "Kagan, I'm sure your shift ended a while ago." Just as hers had. "Tomorrow morning go by the newspaper office and see if they can account for their truck and find out who has access to the keys. Who knows, it may morph into a lead."

Office Kagan gave a sharp nod. "Yes, ma'am. First thing in the morning."

Charlotte cringed at the use of *ma'am*. No matter how many times she asked to be addressed as detective instead of ma'am, she couldn't break the Southern habit that had been ingrained in generations of schoolboys and girls. "Thank you, Officer. Good night."

"Time to take your own advice." Austin organized the piles of reports, files and random papers, once again, then placed his belongings into his messenger bag. He checked his phone. "I have a missed call from my supervisor. He's likely looking for my report. I should call him back before I leave."

Her stomach clenched in speculation. *Please God, keep him here until I see this through.*

Austin followed Charlotte home after convincing her to halt their research for the day. Actually the day was almost over. Only fifteen more minutes until midnight. According to the killer's deadline, they had six more days to find him. Six days. Not nearly enough time but Austin prayed the killer would be identified and arrested well before the countdown ended.

The blinker on Charlotte's car flashed red and then she turned onto her street. She lived in a nice part of town, with well-kept homes and mature trees providing shade during these hot summer days.

When she pulled into her driveway, he parked on the street. Tonight, he would drop the act and get out of the car before she disappeared into the house. He was certain she'd seen him yesterday, walking around her property in a security sweep.

Charlotte left her car in the unattached garage, lowered the garage door, then waved at Austin, who stood in the driveway like a bouncer at a club. "See you tomorrow."

"Try to get some sleep and don't forget to eat." He didn't want her to think him a hovering mother but he understood too well the cumulative effects murder cases had on a person's body. An investigator who skipped meals and worked all hours of the day often crashed and burned, eventually being sidelined. The last time he'd teamed up with Charlotte, he'd seen the early signs of burnout. And then the murder of her sister had flipped a switch. Her drive had turned superhuman. Though no amount of hours worked or determination had resulted in a viable suspect and an arrest. *Work smarter not harder*, Caleb used to say. The man had been full of clever sayings. Austin needed his mentor's wisdom now more than ever.

"Austin," Charlotte called out as she approached the back door. "Someone broke in."

Hand resting on his gun, he rushed to where she stood, three feet back from the concrete steps to the door, which had been left ajar. "Are you sure you closed and locked it when you left? You were in a rush after you got the missing persons call."

"I'm positive." She removed her gun from the holster on her hip. "And if I had, my neighbor would call. She's eighty and her kitchen window overlooks this side of my house."

Austin crept forward, gun gripped in his hand. Pointing the tip of the gun forward, he pushed open the door with his foot.

"I'm right behind you," Charlotte whispered. "Calling for backup."

He entered a quiet house; only the light above the kitchen sink provided illumination. No movement caught his eye.

"I'll take the second story. You search down here." She waited for Austin's nod of confirmation before tiptoeing toward the staircase.

After exploring each room on the ground floor for signs of human disturbance, either past or present, he returned to the kitchen. All clear, at least on this level. The sound of a muffler backfiring from outside made him jump. He ran out and down the driveway. A half block down, a white pickup truck sped away and turned the corner, soon out of sight. The distance was too great for him to make out the license plate.

"What was that?" Charlotte asked in a breathless voice. "It sounded like a gunshot."

"A muffler backfired, and the truck raced off." He surveyed the neighborhood. Besides a dog barking nearby, all remained peaceful.

"Come back inside. Whoever was here left me a gift." Her face paled in the low light of the street lamps. The circles under her eyes seemed to have deepened to the shade of thunderclouds.

Austin returned into her house, keeping watch. "The first floor was clear."

"Same with the second." She waved him up the stairs, then guided him into her bedroom. "There's a note. I haven't touched it."

Dread spiraled. A note card lay on the center of her bed. Normally, a white card with a few words written on its surface wouldn't seem menacing. But by now he knew that script and whom it belonged to.

One hundred forty-four hours until you are mine

The Presque Killer had invaded Charlotte's home. Her bedroom. They were playing his sick game. Why the taunts? What purpose did it serve other than to boost the killer's ego? A lack of respect from others was a common propellant for men in particular to start killing. The man they were chasing possessed a strong need to validate his superiority. Austin considered how the killer's recent behavior modified the profile he'd created. An overexaggerated sense of self indicated a period in the killer's life when he'd suffered poor self-esteem. Childhood, perhaps. The killer had felt overlooked, or others had perhaps actively mocked him.

He planned to visit Michael Duncan, the man who'd once lived with Charlotte and her sister in foster care, and Austin would get a good opportunity to read him and learn if he fit the profile.

He checked out the window to find an empty street. "Backup response needs to be quicker."

"I know but the department only has two officers on duty most night shifts. They could be attending to another situation." She shivered. "It makes me sick that he was in my house, in my bedroom."

Austin called Chief Gunther, rousing him from sleep. As expected, the chief promised to come as soon as he changed.

"You should find somewhere else to stay." After Charlotte left the bedroom, he switched off the light. "Is there a friend you could live with until we catch this guy?"

"I can't put anyone in danger." She gripped the handrail and descended the stairs with care. "One hundred forty-four hours." Her feet touched the landing, then she halted. "Time is moving fast."

He took hold of her elbow and walked alongside her into the kitchen. After seating her on a chair at the table, he poured her a glass of water and handed it over. The stress was taking its toll. If they didn't stop the killer, women would die, including Charlotte.

"He's taking chances this time he didn't before. He's growing bold." Austin poured a glass of water for himself and took a long drink. The cool liquid quenched a thirst he wasn't aware he had. "He will slip up, if he hasn't already. Making the chase personal informs us that he knows you deeper than only as the detective assigned to find and arrest him, and coming here, into your house, tells me that success made him less cautious."

"The truck that sped away could have been him. Did you see the make and model or get a license plate number?"

He wished he'd gotten a better look. But

wishes didn't solve cases. He worked with the facts available and used logic to build from there. "A white pickup truck. An older model, judging from the muffler backfire."

"Of course, a white truck." She shook her head. "Half the population around here has a white truck, or at least that's what it seems."

"One of your neighbors may have seen something." With a good enough view to make an identification. If only they could get so lucky.

"A possibility." A knock at the back door jolted her.

Austin answered and found two police officers had arrived. He let them in. Soon, Chief Gunther marched in, appearing angry and concerned.

"Your house is a crime scene, Detective." The chief's tone of voice left no room for argument. "Pack what you'll need for a few days. On second thought, you're not coming home until this situation has ended."

"I don't have family left and even if I did, I wouldn't ask them to stay. My presence puts others in danger." She pushed to her feet and forcefully brushed her hand across the top of her head. "I can't stand that the killer is winning."

"Not for long." Austin stepped in front of

her to stop her from pacing. "You're coming to the Magnolia Hotel with me. You can get a room next to mine." At the sight of the scowl on her face, he pressed his lips together. "The hotel isn't that bad, really. The muffins in the lobby are tasty."

"Fine." She stomped off. The pounding of footsteps up above meant bags were being packed.

"I'll sleep better knowing you're close by." Chief Gunther tipped his chin to gaze at the ceiling. "Don't take her bluster personally. She's furious but not with you."

"The killer left her a note." Could he have been careless enough to leave fingerprints on the card stock? They'd know as soon as tomorrow morning. The task force included a dedicated team of forensic technicians to gather and process the growing collection of evidence left by the Presque Killer's actions.

"I'd love to send him a note." Chief Gunther pounded his fist on the counter. "Mine will be the first one he receives in jail."

The chief might have to fight Charlotte for that privilege.

But what if they failed again? The killer had promised to kill Charlotte. He believed he'd win the sick game he'd created and then disappear. Temporary doubt blinded Austin to all other outcomes.

No. He shook off the panic. This time was different. Good would prevail and evil would fall. He'd continue to lift up prayers to God, who promised to bring justice to the wicked.

Chapter Eight

The next morning, Charlotte startled awake. *Where am I?* She sat upright, and her groggy mind struggled to make sense of her surroundings.

The Magnolia Hotel. That was why it smelled of air freshener and stale air. She fell back and rested her head on the pillow. Austin was right, the hotel wasn't as bad as she'd expected. A relatively clean room and a comfortable bed. She'd need to remember to turn on the air conditioner before she left to drive away the humidity in the room. The best part, though—the reassurance that Austin was only steps away. Sleep had caught her fast after she'd checked in and gotten settled. Surprising, since her stress level had been as high as a rocket ready to burst through the earth's atmosphere.

She checked the time and wondered if Austin was up yet. Knowing the tireless FBI agent, he'd probably only slept a few hours and was drinking coffee while reviewing all the notes he'd scribbled down in his always-present notebook.

What would her life look like once the killer was locked away? Of course, she'd still be single, returning home every day after work to an empty house. Living until the age of eight with a mom who specialized in dysfunctional relationships then being tossed around in foster care did not provide a roadmap for a happy-ever-after. Charlotte had accepted long ago that trusting a man enough to love him with her whole heart and soul was too great a risk. The one time she'd let down her guard, believing God sent a man into her life worthy of her faith, had proven nothing good came from romantic love. Austin was a good man but his leaving had shown her that the pain she'd witnessed in her mom had been real. Charlotte had endured enough abandonment to last ten lifetimes. Only a fool would open herself to more. After Austin left, he'd moved on. She had not. Solving the Presque cases had become her life.

Her brain was struck by a jolt—a reminder why she was here at the hotel and not home. The Presque Killer had broken into her house.

She jumped out of bed. No time to lie around and mourn her failed romantic life.

Once showered and dressed, she holstered her gun then unlocked the door, checking for threats before fully opening it. The only threat she found was the one to her heart. Austin stood on the walkway outside her door with a small bag in one hand and a tray with two cups of coffee in the other.

"Breakfast." He said with a grin. "The hotel doesn't have real room service, so you'll have to make do with me."

She'd never consider Austin a *less than* option. He was the best there was, as an FBI special agent and at delivering breakfast. "Come in." Stepping aside, she waited for him to enter then shut the door. "I checked the vehicles registered to Michael Duncan last night," she said. "He owns a white truck."

"As you said yesterday, most of the men in Kingston Parish own white trucks. Eat first. Then we'll dig further into Mr. Duncan and pay him a visit." Austin pulled out two muffins and napkins from the bag.

Her appetite remained weak but she knew Austin would not let her leave without eating. She grabbed a muffin and took a bite. *"Mmm…"*

she hummed. "These are good. Orange cran-
berry, correct?"

"That's what the sign said." Austin downed
his muffin with only a few bites. "This hotel
really is the best place for you. I ran into about
a half dozen task force members from out of
town who are staying here as well. The killer'd
be crazy to attempt anything here."

"The killer is crazy, remember?" Even with
food inside, her stomach growled, asking for
more. She really should remember to eat on a
regular basis throughout the days ahead, even
if she didn't feel like it. Chasing criminals required strength. With her muffin devoured, she
opened the lid of her steaming coffee and took
a cautious first sip.

With her free hand, she powered up her laptop. "Here is the most recent driver's license
photo of Michael Duncan." A man with closely
cropped brown hair and pockmarked skin
glared back on the screen. "He has a sealed record as a minor. I'd need a warrant to read it."

"Right now, we don't have anything to show
a judge that supports a warrant request." He removed his reading glasses from the front pocket
of his crisp white dress shirt and put them on to
study the photograph. "What do you remember

about him from your time together? Did you see him after he left the foster home?"

"All I can recall are the feelings of panic whenever I was around him. He didn't have a nice bone in his body, and I believe he enjoyed the fear he saw in the other kids and our foster parents. He felt powerful making others feel weak."

"His childhood personality matches the path of a future serial killer but not all bullies grow up to kill people," he said. "What about after he was removed from the home? Did you ever run into him around town?" Austin tapped on the screen, indicating the face of the man.

"I'm not sure." She shook her head, frustrated with her lack of memory. "Presque isn't a big town and it's likely our paths have crossed. Any interaction doesn't stand out. Wait." She leaned closer to get a better look at the tattoo on Michael's neck—an inked image of a spider hanging down from a crescent moon. "I remember this tattoo. Years ago, I was at a restaurant with Ruby. He approached our table and acted offended we didn't know him. He even tried to sit at our booth next to Ruby. I'd wondered at the time if he was one of her druggie friends she didn't want to acknowledge in front of me.

He ended up leaving, never telling us how he knew us."

"Instead of one of Ruby's friends, he was someone who'd lived with you both in foster care for a short period of time." He removed his glasses, then took a long drink of coffee. "I'm ready to make a house call whenever you are."

"Let's roll." She put on her badge, which she hung from a chain around her neck, then checked her service weapon. "Do you think we'll need backup?"

"I don't want to spook him. I'll let the chief know where we're going. The task force is meeting at ten, so we have two hours to talk with Mr. Duncan."

Nerves fluttered in Charlotte's chest. The memories involving Michael Duncan still produced fear. Speaking with suspects was nothing new. Going to the home of the potential Presque Killer, a man who'd lingered as a dark storm over the area for six long years, couldn't be approached carelessly.

Austin drove, which allowed Charlotte time to write down questions and word each in a way to elicit the best response. He located the address, a run-down clapboard house set up on cement blocks, and parked on the street. No vehicle could be seen in the driveway. Once out of the SUV, Austin moved to get a better view down the long driveway. He saw no garage. Could be no one was home.

Charlotte took the lead, heading up the rickety stairs and onto the front porch. A worn-out lawn chair was surrounded by cigarette butts and empty beer cans scattered on the porch floor. She gave three sharp knocks on the frame of the screen door and stepped back. After no answer, she knocked again. "Either he's not home or he's hiding."

Austin's head turned toward the direction of the street to the sight of a white truck driving in their direction. The driver pulled into the driveway, stopping beside the house.

A man exited, with a cigarette dangling from his lips and a hard-sided cooler gripped in one hand. "What are you doing here?" The scowl on his face deepened the lines around his mouth and did not appear the least bit welcoming. However, he didn't act surprised to see them.

"FBI Special Agent Walsh." Austin showed his identification and badge. "This is Detective Reid with the Presque Police Department."

"I know who you are." He pointed a thick

finger at Charlotte. "I asked what you're doing on my front porch."

"We're investigating a recent murder and kidnapping," Charlotte said.

He stared at her with narrowed eyes, which were bloodshot. "That has nothing to do with me."

During the initial interaction, Austin made a quick study of Michael Duncan. His defensive demeanor produced suspicion. But that behavior was normal when FBI and police showed up unannounced at a person's home. He appeared like he was coming home from work, suggesting he worked third shift. A computer search of the property deed showed the house he resided in was owned by his birth mother. If she lived with her son, who had been removed from her care at some point, how was their relationship now?

Austin focused his gaze on the tattoo peeking out from underneath the collar of Michael's shirt. The spider, though it appeared menacing, didn't catch his interest. But the crescent moon, the shape that had been carved into the arms of the victims, held his gaze. What was the symbolism of a crescent moon, and how did it tie back to the Presque Killer?

"Where were you the last three evenings?" Charlotte inquired. Her body language suggested a simple question.

Austin knew the strain she was hiding on the inside.

Michael huffed and marched toward the front door. "I was at work. If you think I had anything to do with those girls, you're wrong."

"Mr. Duncan, we're looking into people with a shared connection to Detective Reid." Austin projected calm and confidence. Like Charlotte, he didn't want Michael to realize the depth of their interest. "Do you remember the detective from when you were in foster care?"

Michael's body froze with one foot on the bottom porch step. He swung around, still clutching the cooler. The cigarette in his mouth had been reduced to a small stub. He plucked it out and ground the remainder under the sole of his work boot. "I remember every day of that living hell." He clenched his jaw. "You were at the White home when I got there. Do-gooder family thought dragging us poor foster kids to church would save our souls. My soul was too long gone by that time." His gaze returned to Charlotte, intensifying. "You were there with your little sister. Both of you looked ready to

jump out of your skin at the slightest word."
He snickered. "But I never hurt nobody. Not
back then and not now."

Charlotte descended the stairs to stand on
the front lawn, which was covered in more dirt
than grass. Scattered litter added an extra layer
to the appearance of neglect. She stepped over
a rusted child's tricycle and moved closer to
where Michael stood by the stairs. "Where do
you work?"

"I don't have to answer your questions." He
jutted out his chin. "And I could tell you to get
off my property."

"Your mom's property," Austin corrected. He
scanned the ground to see if anything had writing that he could compare to the killer's handwriting. Nothing so far. "And yes, you could.
But that wouldn't help us clear you."

"You think I did those things?" Michael's
face reddened. "Except for some trouble I got
into as a kid, I've never been arrested for anything. Never in jail. Are you suspecting every
former foster kid or just me?" He hooked a
thumb at his chest.

"Not just you." Charlotte kept her voice
even, not giving in to the rising tension. "But
if you answer our questions, we'll be on our

way and you can get back to whatever you were going to do."

"Sleep," he spit out. "I work nights at Southern Healthcare Laundry Service. When I get home after a shift, all I want to do is have a beer and go to sleep."

Austin added the name of the business in his notes. "What do you do there?"

"Pickup and delivery. I pick up dirty linens from the area hospitals and bring them to the washing facility. Then I deliver carts of the clean linens back to the hospitals." He set the cooler on the step. "I'm a solid worker. Call my boss if you'd like. He'll tell you I've been working every night since Monday. They don't have enough drivers, so I'm on about sixty hours a week."

Michael was a driver, meaning he traveled the streets of Presque and the surrounding areas, alone in a work truck. Would he have been able to get his personal truck and visit Charlotte's house last night during his work shift? "Where is your work facility located?"

"Off Valor Road, by the old furniture manufacturer plant." Michael plucked out another cigarette from the packet stuffed in the front pocket of his T-shirt and lit up.

Austin had no idea how far that location was to Charlotte's house. A question for later. "Have you ever had any run-ins with Detective Reid recently? Any hard feelings?"

Michael's narrowed eyed gaze swung from Austin to Charlotte. The manner in which Michael looked at her, like he had secret knowledge about her, made Austin uneasy.

"I learned real quick that some people figure they're too good for you, even if y'all came from the same place." Michael directed his comment at Charlotte. "You and your sister didn't want nothing to do with any of us, even after we're all grown. After Ruby was killed, I felt sorry for you cause you had nobody."

Austin's instincts to protect Charlotte clashed with his professional obligation to let this interaction play out. Witnessing Michael's unguarded emotions could break open the case and help them find the killer. But seeing Charlotte's pale face and pain-filled large brown eyes hurt his heart. It wasn't fair that Charlotte had to relive her childhood trauma in an attempt to bring the killer to justice. The killer had pointed them down this path, and Austin asked God for the strength to finish the race.

Chapter Nine

You had nobody. With a sharp intake of breath, Charlotte took a small step backward, away from the words spoken with the intent to pierce her like a bullet. She steadied her emotions, fitted armor around her heart. This man would not catch her off-balance. "Did you know my sister, Ruby? As an adult, I mean."

He shrugged and shook his head, in contradiction. "Not really."

"Not really or no?" She pressed. "Ruby liked to party. I thought perhaps you both ran in the same circles."

"I'd see her from time to time." Michael drew a long pull of his cigarette. "Ruby knew how to have fun, unlike her big sister. Your enjoyment, Officer, only came from busting up a party."

A cough tickled in the back of her throat. The smoke from the cigarette aggravated her airways. It also brought flashbacks of Charlotte's time living with her mom, who'd chain-smoked since high school. The smell of cigarette smoke brought both good and painful memories. Her mom hadn't been all bad. She'd tried her best to provide love, food and a roof over their heads. Granted, most of her attempts at financial stability were illegal. A single mother with few resources. Finally, her crimes had earned her a jail sentence. Jail hadn't been kind to a child-like spirt like her mom, and the confinement had killed her.

Charlotte fixed her gaze on the tattoo on his neck, and a memory rattled loose. He'd stolen Charlotte's crescent moon bracelet while they'd lived together and then taunted her when she begged for its return. Only as Michael was being taken to the group home did she get it back. "When was the last time you saw Ruby?" she asked in a voice void of emotion. Charlotte could not let Michael know how much he'd disturbed her.

Austin's close proximity was the glue that kept her reactions in check. They made a great team. Too bad she didn't believe he'd stick around any longer than needed to get the job done. Next case. Next town. Next partner. And once again, she'd be a memory.

Michael remained silent, passively refusing to answer.

"Did you see Ruby around the time of her murder?" Austin asked again with a touch more force.

"I don't have to answer you." Michael scowled. "Girls like Ruby don't matter." He gestured to Austin. "The detective only cares because it's her sister who was killed. The poor and addicted get passed over by society all the time. A few go missing. A few are found dead. Who cares, right? Not the police."

"I care about every one of those women," Charlotte spit out, too enraged to fake control.

"Then good luck. You'll need it." Michael flicked the remainder of his second cigarette at the ground by Austin's feet, almost hitting the tip of his leather shoe. "You have any more questions, then call my lawyer." He chuckled. "I'm going inside to get some sleep." The slap of the screen door closing provided the final punctuation in his closing statement.

"What do you think?" She asked Austin.

His gaze was directed down at his feet. After going to his car and returning with gloves and an evidence collection bag, he slipped on the gloves and leaned over. Pinching the still smoldering cigarette butt in between his thumb and pointer finger, he studied it then motioned her to follow him to his vehicle. "I think we have a DNA sample," he said once they were a safe distance from the house. "Do you think the Presque Killer would be so careless with his DNA?"

She considered. "Sure, if he didn't know we have the killer's DNA on file from the first murder victim. That piece of information wasn't released to the public and only those in the tight circle of investigation know."

They stood on the sidewalk, waiting for the cigarette to cool in order to place it inside the plastic bag. While waiting, she scrutinized the house and what she'd learned about Michael Duncan. He still possessed the meanness she'd experienced from him as a child. A hard life would do that to a person. But not all those who experienced difficult childhoods killed for sport. No, something more sinister had taken root in a person's heart to compel him to snuff the life out of others. Did Michael Duncan's spiteful words mask something wicked and cruel? Or was he like so many other men she'd interacted with, especially in her line of work, who bullied and intimidated as a means of releasing their anger and frustration?

Austin dropped the cigarette butt into the evidence bag and sealed the top. "This will go to the state forensics lab with a rush order." He'd turned his back to the house, hiding the treasure he'd collected from anyone watching from inside.

"We'll either get a match or we can rule him out." She rubbed her temples. "The results will take too long to come back. I need them now."

They got into the car, and Austin started the engine. "My gut tells me Michael Duncan isn't our killer. His temper makes him quick to snap. In contrast, the Presque Killer is calculating and methodical."

"Could be an act." Charlotte turned to view the house as they drove away, catching a glimpse of a man standing at the window before the curtain dropped.

"It's a possibility. The killer we're hunting is cunning." He flipped the turn signal and directed the SUV back to the police station. "A smart person can wear a different personality while interacting with the public to hide who he really is. A sociopath has to learn from an early age to blend in."

She dwelled on what Michael had said about Ruby and herself. Did people in the town really believe law enforcement didn't care about women like Ruby? Did they speculate to one another that the murder cases had gone cold because no one cared enough to keep fighting for the truth? The idea brought tears to Charlotte's eyes. If only people understood how many hours she and other officers had dedicated to catching the killer even before her sister became a victim. She'd lived and breathed those cases. Even after her resources were pulled and the files were ordered into storage, she'd kept the fire of the investigation burning, unofficially.

"Hey." Austin reached over and rested a hand over Charlotte's hand, which was placed on her lap. "I can hear your thoughts. Don't let that guy convince you that people in the town don't know how deeply you care about solving these murders."

"Do they?" Her voice cracked while asking the question. "Some people blame me and the department for six years of no results. Women were murdered. They were sisters and daughters, and their families deserve answers. I can't bring back their loved ones but I should bring the person who murdered them to justice."

Alarm built at the realization of the truth. Having been blinded by her own grief and frustration, she'd failed to comprehend the feelings of the community. She heard their voices in her head, crashing into her all at once.

"I've worked enough of these types of cases to understand that no matter what you do or what happens, the people affected don't have a happy outcome." He squeezed her hand before returning his to the steering wheel. "How can they, with no sense of control other than to talk? Some families hire private investigators or start asking questions, but even if the killer is caught and convicted, it's a shallow victory. The death remains. They still no longer have their loved one."

Charlotte heard what Austin was saying and the intention behind his words. All she could think about was these murders in her community and that they remained unsolved for so many years. And if she failed to catch the killer by the end of his deadline, then more deaths would occur. More loved ones would grieve.

"I want to hold a press conference. The chief so far has only allowed press releases." The idea firmed in her head. "It's the only way to keep the public informed and maybe we'll get a lead. I want people to know we're not sitting on our hands."

"That's a good idea." Once they arrived at the police station, Austin found an open spot in the parking lot. He shut off the SUV and turned in his seat to face her. The corners of his mouth curved down with concern. "A press conference may shake loose some new information. Don't let anything Michael Duncan said get under your skin. If he is the Presque Killer, his intention was to further taunt you. And if he's innocent, then he's an example of a bitter man who's lived a hard life without love."

She took several deep breaths, in and out. Austin was right. The Presque Killer delighted in bringing her low, building fear and observing the destruction he created. Her mind needed to stop spinning and refocus on the investigation. The more emotion took over, the blurrier the facts appeared. *Be more like Austin. Use logic to gaze from a distance, and the pieces of the puzzle might come into focus.*

The conference room hummed with energy, which Charlotte used to feed her spirit. She stood at the head of the table and glanced at the men and women filling the room. All professionals in the investigative and law enforcement fields. A representative from the crime lab was present. Austin had entered the cigarette butt into evidence and handed it over to be processed. Could it really be that easy? Get a DNA match and arrest Michael Duncan as the Presque Killer?

She had an officer contacting the laundry where Mr. Duncan worked in order to verify he'd been on duty the nights Ginny Gerard and Karen Tremont went missing. Although, even if he had been working, if he'd driven the routes alone with no GPS tracker on his truck, any short side trips would go unnoticed. She also requested the make and model of the truck he drove in case it matched the tire tracks found beside Karen's van.

Charlotte cleared her throat, indicating it was time to start. "Thank you everyone for accepting the assignment to come to Presque and assist with the investigation. I realize most of you have left family at home to be here, and your sacrifice does not go unnoticed." She paused to take a drink of water. Nerves dried her mouth like pavement under a hot sun. "I'd like to start with each team reporting on their findings so far, bringing everyone up to date. Special Agent Walsh and I will cover what we've learned over the last few days and discuss the pertinent facts of the cold cases."

A rumble of agreement spurred her to continue. The sight of Austin boosted her confidence. She'd never led a group this large, with so many talented professionals. The killer's short time frame had sent the investigation into overdrive.

"Unfortunately no evidence has been recovered from my kidnapping a few days ago. Let's start with the kidnapping of Karen Tremont. Any new leads or pieces of information?" she asked the pair of Kingston Parish detectives seated nearby. During the last investigation, the parish investigators had shown no motivation to solve the murders of drug-addicted young women. Charlotte got a different vibe from the two from the parish today. They seemed eager to bring the killer to justice.

"A cast was made of the tire tracks found by Mrs. Tremont's van," a woman with auburn hair said. She wore a red short-sleeve shirt. "The imprint matches a brand of tires found on Freightliner medium duty box trucks. Axle to axle is eighteen feet. We searched trucks with tires matching the tracks and found several registered to different businesses in the area."

"Is Southern Healthcare Laundry Service on that list?" Austin asked.

The female investigator checked the sheet on the table, scanning it until she reached the bottom. "Yes, they own two of the same model. Why do you ask?"

"A potential suspect works there." Austin glanced at Charlotte, and his gaze locked on hers. "There's a chance he drives one of those trucks."

"I'll call the officers tasked with following up with the laundry as soon as we're done." She didn't want to interrupt the flow of information in the meeting to chase every new lead. "What else?"

"We've found no one who witnessed Karen walking out to her van," the female investigator reported. "There's only a few security cameras in the vicinity of the café and none work. Unfortunately, we've chased a lot of dead ends."

"Keep chasing." Charlotte understood the discouragement that crept in at small increments with each failure, until the negativity stalled the case. That was how they went cold.

Investigators grew tired of working hard for no results. Departments pulled resources due to lack of outcomes. People's attention moved to the next crime. The next crisis.

The Presque Killer and his victims, though, hadn't left the minds of those in the community.

"Next, I'd like an update from the team working the Ginny Gerard murder." Charlotte pulled her thoughts to the present. "Any new evidence come to light?"

"No," Sergeant Monroe, from the Louisiana State Police, answered. "Nothing new from the report provided of the initial investigation. Baton Rouge police canvassed the area Ginny was last seen. No one has come forward with any information as to who she came in contact with after she left the club on Tuesday, the night she disappeared."

More disappointing news. Although she'd expect to be notified immediately if a new piece of information came to light, hope remained that something positive would be presented at the task force meeting.

"Did you review the autopsy report?" Austin leaned forward in his chair, forearms resting on the glossy table surface. Other than a smooth pad of paper and pen, nothing else was on the table nearby. Austin was the neatest person Charlotte had ever met. He served as a balance to her inherent disorderliness.

"I did," Sergeant Monroe said. "The method of killing and other evidence, such as the red rope and skin carving, point to the same killer as six years ago. I agree that the victim was killed somewhere else and then dumped in the location she was discovered. Not enough ground was disturbed to indicate a struggle. Wood slivers were found in her clothes and back. My theory is she was lying on a plank floor when she was strangled. I've checked which local stores might have sold the killer's type of nylon red rope in the past six months. No reported sales, so I'll enlarge the search area. If he purchased it online, then the possibilities are endless. I followed the cold cases closely as an officer in the Baton Rouge Police Department. The killer always seemed one step ahead of the investigation back then. He still does. I'd love nothing more than to get a jump on him and haul the guy to jail."

A nod of agreement rippled through the meeting's attendees. Ten law enforcement professionals added their skills to Charlotte and Austin's efforts. Would it be enough to stop a killer?

She asked and received updates from the rest of the investigative teams. One was assigned to visit the local neighborhoods, gathering information and proactively convincing young women to stay off the streets at night. At any moment, the killer could take another victim.

Charlotte had booked a press conference to be held soon. She'd consulted with the chief and Austin about which facts should be provided to the public and which ones needed to stay confidential. If the killer wished to play a game, Charlotte would craft one of her own. Could she taunt him to come out of hiding and make a fatal mistake? Speaking live to the media and the public was a gamble as everyone needed to be tight with what they shared. But she was running out of time and could no longer play it safe.

Minutes before the press conference was scheduled to start, Austin's cell phone rang. His FBI supervisor's name appeared on the screen. He considered letting the call go to voice mail then calling him back after the press conference. But in the years he'd worked under Supervisory Special Agent Booth, the act of ignoring a call never ended well for the agent on the receiving end.

"Walsh here." Austin stepped into an empty room that seemed to be an interview area. His reflection showed on the mirrored glass window.

"Your update last night was lacking," Booth barked. "I have a decision to make and I need to know what's happening in Presque."

Decision? That caught Austin's attention. The only decision his supervisor would make at this point was one Austin didn't want to consider. "As I indicated last night, the investigation is moving slowly but we have a strong team. There was an incident late last night at Detective Reid's house. The man known as the Presque Killer broke in and left a note. Everyone here is fully committed to catching the killer."

"I know the killer you're searching for has given a tight deadline." Booth sighed. "I'm considering sending a different agent who'll have a fresh perspective. You could be too close to these cases and it's not prudent to leave you somewhere you're not effective."

What he'd feared from the moment he landed in Louisiana. His experience with the cold cases could be twisted to be a handicap. "I've had six years of distance from the first investigations. The serial killer is active and giving us a deadline. There's no time to bring another agent up to speed."

"I've already got Kolinski studying the old and new files." Supervisor Booth mumbled directions to someone inside his office before returning to his conversation with Austin. "There's an incident in New York that requires an expert in serial killers. You're my best option."

"I can't leave." Panic rose. He loosened his tie and heat rushed inside his body. Immediately, he thought of Charlotte. No hope remained of a romantic relationship but he cared deeply about her. Another abandonment, which was how she'd view it, would stick a sword through the heart of their delicately restored partnership. "I mean, I'm asking you not to reassign me."

"You don't get to make that choice. Expect another call soon. And you better answer it."

The call ended, and Austin lowered his phone from his ear. Following orders he disagreed with became more difficult the longer he was in the FBI.

He turned on his heel to leave and spotted Charlotte standing in the open doorway. *You should have closed the door.*

Her eyes conveyed betrayal. "They're pulling you from the Presque cases?" An accusation.

Moving forward, he reached for her arm, trying to convey loyalty with his touch.

She jerked away.

"It's an option my supervisor is considering. There's a situation developing in New York State. Another potential serial killer."

"He knows there's a serial killer in Presque, right?" Charlotte snorted. "We are in the middle of the fight of our lives, for my life and others, and the FBI wants to pull the only agent with working knowledge of the cold cases. And…who has been here, with the investigation, since I was kidnapped."

He held out his hands, palms up. "Nothing has been decided. And if Booth does order me to a different case, I won't go."

"You say that now, but when your job is on the line—" she bit her lower lip "—you'll follow orders."

His heart ached for the disappointment he'd caused when leaving before. He'd never blamed her for her hostility. Austin regretted his earlier lack of spine. He wouldn't make the same mistake twice. "I'd see this through. Your life is under threat. I'd rather be fired than abandon you."

She turned away and lifted her chin. A wall of emotional armor fell around her, as visible as if she were dressed for battle.

Was he prepared to leave his career so he could remain at Charlotte's side? He'd worked hard and dedicated many hours while advancing in the FBI. He'd studied and held knowledge not many others had.

His supervisor's call conveyed a reminder. They'd find the Presque killer, arrest him and complete the job. A new assignment would follow, chasing another criminal. His collaboration with Charlotte ended the moment their task was complete. He couldn't lull himself into believing he could find a forever happiness, not in Presque, not anywhere. As long as he worked for the FBI, and he loved his work, the possibility of a wife and family didn't exist. He chased evil into the shadows. Protecting others from experiencing the darkness, especially ones that he loved, compelled him to avoid serious relationships.

If his supervisor directed him away from the Presque cases, Austin planned to contest the command. He'd have the facts ready to support his continued assignment. At this moment, both his service in the FBI and Charlotte were important. He'd fight to stay. The victims deserved nothing less.

Chapter Ten

Charlotte stood inside the police station, taking deep, steadying breaths. A crowd of press and members of the public had gathered outside. People wanted answers. They were scared and worried. A serial killer was hunting in their midst. The questions sure to be asked echoed in her head. Why hadn't the police and FBI been able to stop him yet? Did they not care about the women murdered? How many more women needed to die before the killer was caught? Charlotte wouldn't be spared scrutiny because her own sister was a victim. She still represented and led the institution that had failed to catch a killer.

"Are you ready?" Austin looked over his typed statement before placing it inside a leather folio.

Ready for you to leave? Overhearing Austin's phone conversation with his supervisor had been a punch in the gut. Old feelings, ones she'd thought were buried, had come roaring back. Her attraction to him had been based on his good looks, kindness and competency on the job. Still was. She'd have to remember he wasn't staying, and bringing the killer to justice was her number one priority. If Austin didn't serve to help, then he was a liability. She couldn't allow herself to become emotionally entangled with him again.

"Ready as I'll ever be." She folded the piece of paper holding her handwritten notes. The rest of the task force was gathered behind them, ready to follow her and Austin outside to face the reporters and cameras. "It's time."

As she stepped outside into the sunlight and heat, the sight of the crowd left her dizzy. She scanned the faces of those gathered. Was the Presque Killer in attendance? It was very likely, as serial killers enjoyed watching the investigation into the crimes they committed. They loved attention. This killer wanted Charlotte's every thought to be directed to him. And a press conference to discuss him and his actions was the top prize.

The department's communications staff member along with the building maintenance team set up about thirty chairs in rows in a grassy section near the parking lot. For the comfort of the press conference attendees, most of the chairs had been placed in the shade of two ancient live oaks. The presenters weren't so lucky. The podium and area for law enforcement were located on the hot cement lot under a ten-foot canopy.

Austin quickly put on his trademark special agent sunglasses, causing Charlotte to almost smile. She wore a Presque PD baseball hat to protect her eyes. Not nearly as debonair a look.

She moved to the podium and checked with the sound engineer before speaking. After welcoming those in attendance, she introduced the task force set up to nab the Presque Killer and then provided a brief update on the investigation while omitting certain facts they didn't want known to the public. Like the fact that Charlotte herself was a target. If the killer were watching, either live or on TV, she wanted him to know that he hadn't frightened her. At least not enough to stop searching for him. She was still here in Presque, hunting him. He hadn't scared her away.

Once she read off her notes, she slid over to allow Austin to speak. He provided a high-level overview of the federal resources allocated for the investigation. During his speech, a hush grew over the gathering. FBI special agents were only sent to significant crime scenes meeting their threshold for violence of the crime or the number of victims. His return proved the FBI agreed with local and state law enforcement about the seriousness of the Presque cases.

Austin took a few questions and provided concise answers.

"Detective Reid," a reporter shouted out. "Residents of Presque and the surrounding communities are scared. One woman has been killed, another gone missing. All in less than a week. The killer hinted that he wouldn't stop until he was caught. What reassurances can you give the local residents that they or their loved ones won't be next?"

Every question that came from Ronald Rheault's mouth felt like a personal attack since the first time she'd encountered him professionally almost ten years ago. She'd been a new officer, fresh out of the academy. A fumbled arrest and an escaped criminal had made her a target of Ronald's scrutiny. He wrote a scathing article about the incompetence of new hires in the police force, using Charlotte as an example. Since that article, every time she made an error or the appearance of an error, the pesky reporter was right there to cover it. In contrast, if Charlotte experienced success, like her promotion to detective or her work on larger investigations, Ronald seemed more interested in other stories.

"I understand the concerns of the community." Charlotte made eye contact with Ronald and watched him stiffen in response. "The newly formed task force is working around the clock to locate the person responsible."

Another reporter stood in preparation to ask a question but Ronald spoke before she could get a word out.

"Why should the people who are living in danger trust the same group of people who failed to find the killer before?" Ronald asked through a smug smile.

Why are you getting pleasure out of this situation? she wanted to question him right back. His attitude had been strange since the day the first murder victim was found. Charlotte had believed he loved the thrill of chasing a big story in an uneventful small town. Could it be more?

"Only Special Agent Walsh and I are from the initial investigation six years ago." She glanced over her shoulder and caught Austin's puzzled gaze. Did he have the same concerns about the overzealous reporter? "The rest of the task force was brought in for their investigative skills and fresh perspectives."

The other reporter opened her mouth to try again to ask her question, but Ronald drowned her out. "A source told me that the Presque Killer has said you, Detective Reid, is his motivation this time around." Standing about ten feet away from the podium, Ronald leaned forward slightly. "Given that your sister was murdered during his first spree, the killer could have a personal vendetta against you. Do you feel your participation in the investigation may hinder its progress? He may view your attempt to bring him to justice as a challenge, one he needs to answer with more violence."

Her knees buckled, and she clutched the podium for support. Who had leaked the killer's connection to her? Someone on the task force? One of the officers who'd answered the emergency call when her home had been broken into and they found the killer's note? Whom could she trust? Did anyone have her back?

Austin placed a hand on her shoulder and gently moved her to the side. He raised the microphone to his mouth. "Whatever information you have is pure speculation. Of course, many details of our investigation are confidential, and believing everything you hear whispered on the street is not good journalism."

"I'm only attempting to validate my information." Twirling his pencil between his fingers, Ronald glanced around at the other press conference attendees as if attempting to gather support for his assertive tactics. "Provide a comment, Detective Reid, so I don't go making up stories, as you put it yesterday."

"We have no comment about Detective Reid and any possible motivation for a serial killer." The firm tone in Austin's voice quieted the mutterings of the crowd. "Why someone tortures and murders innocent women is something I don't fully understand and I've been studying serial killers for more than eight years. A serial killer might state a motivation but what it comes down to is that the person is sick and evil. That's it. There's no excuses or victim blaming. No trying to deflect blame on anyone else. Make sure to include that in your article." He pointed a finger at Ronald. "Does anyone *else* have questions?"

Even though Charlotte wanted to clap her

hands after Austin's short speech, she kept her expression and body language relaxed. Her mouth was neutral, in neither a smile nor a frown. She lowered her shoulders, which had been creeping up to her ears each time Ronald spoke.

Other reporters for local, state and national news peppered her and Austin with questions. Chief Gunther stepped forward to provide his assessment as the chief of police.

As Charlotte prepared to call the press conference to a close, an elderly woman stepped from her seat to the center aisle. "My granddaughter, Mary Gury, was the first to be found, murdered by a mystery man who nobody can seem to find. I often wondered if anyone cared about her afterward. Mary had her struggles but she was a good girl who loved her family and Jesus. I know y'all are doing y'all's best but you need to try harder." The woman gripped with both of her hands the handles of the purse positioned in front of her body. "If anyone knows anything about what happened to my Mary or those other poor girls, speak up. You can't blame the police for not doing their jobs when people are keeping their mouths shut."

"Amen," someone shouted in the back.

While the woman had been speaking, Charlotte watched Ronald. Instead of writing down the woman's moving speech, he'd already moved on, zipping up the folio that held his notebook, pen and recorder.

"I appreciate everyone's time and attention and we hope to provide another update soon." Charlotte took the paper with her notes off the podium. "The tip line is open. Anyone with information regarding the murders or kidnapping please call in." Sweat beaded on her brow, and a deep feeling of sorrow tightened her lungs, making it hard to breathe. She pictured the face of Mary Gury's grandmother. A face weathered by years of grief and unanswered questions.

She strode into the station. "I let them all down," she whispered to herself. The members of the task force were dispersing further into the building, returning to the tasks they'd abandoned to attend the press conference.

Soon, only Austin remained. "You okay?"

"No." Suppressed tears burned her eyes and throat, but she wouldn't set them free. She entered the station's kitchen and lowered herself into one of the plastic chairs that surrounded small, round, wobbly tables. With her feet placed wide, she rested her elbows on her knees, folded her hands and rested her forehead on her entwined fingers. She prayed for endurance and forgiveness.

"Hey." The scraping of chair legs across the vinyl floor announced Austin's presence. He scooted his chair closer and placed a hand on her shoulder.

They sat in silence for a minute, facing one another, until Charlotte finished speaking to God. She lifted her head to the sight of Austin's handsome face only a foot away. "I feel like I'm losing every battle. And hearing the woman whose granddaughter was the killer's first victim was a knife to the heart. I failed everyone in this town, including Ruby."

"Every person who's worked on investigations like this feels the same way at times. I do." Austin pulled his hand from her shoulder and straightened in his chair. "I struggle with the fact the killer, has eluded us for so many years. And now he's resurfaced with a vengeance and put you in his crosshairs."

"I can't dwell on his threat to me." She sucked in a breath. When Austin had pulled away slightly, he'd created more distance between them. She fought to maintain her professional demeanor when all she wanted to do was be wrapped tight in his arms. "I'd give anything to have my sister with me again. Ruby was the only one who really understood me. Growing up, we only had each other. It's so hard to deal with struggles in my life without her."

Austin stayed silent for a moment. When he spoke, his voice cracked. "You're not alone. I know I'm not your sister but lean on me as I'm leaning on you. We'll get through this. We may be losing ground in our current battle but we will win the war and the killer will face justice. Have faith in God and in me."

She had faith in God. It was Austin she doubted. Would he leave if directed to? How could he not? He was good at his job and held knowledge needed to find the bad guys. The world needed Austin, which meant she'd say goodbye to him at some point, likely soon.

When she glanced at him again through eyes blurred with tears, Austin's face drew close. His lips brushed her cheek then her mouth.

For a brief moment, her surprise caused her muscles to stiffen. But his warm touch melted her resolve. Another soft kiss reignited a longing she'd put away years ago.

He pulled away. "I'm sorry." His voice was husky.

Thank goodness they were seated in the corner of the station's kitchen, out of the view of anyone walking by the door. Their brief connection had brought back all the regret she'd felt after the last time she let her guard down and kissed him. Instead of focusing on solving the cases, her head had been filled with dreams of a future with Austin. Now she knew better. Grab a moment of happiness but don't expect more. She'd savor his kiss. Place the memory securely in the back of her heart. "When the going gets tough, we kiss."

Austin's sad smile almost cracked her resolve.

While fighting to not give in and kiss him again, she pushed up to her feet and locked away her emotions. The Presque Killer wouldn't turn himself in. She had work to do.

Chapter Eleven

The next morning was Sunday. The Lord's day. Even while traveling for work, Austin liked to attend church. Charlotte had invited him to accompany her to the early service at hers.

He'd barely slept. His mind had oscillated between the kiss with Charlotte and the prospect of his supervisor reassigning him.

That kiss. He knew better than to walk the path of heartbreak again. Their last kiss had ended in disaster. Charlotte blamed herself for not finding Ruby in time. And he blamed himself for letting his feelings for the detective in charge of the Presque Killer investigation cloud his vision. The personal connection between them served as a distraction, yet he struggled to keep their relationship strictly professional.

He believed God put people together for a reason. In Charlotte and Austin's case, the purpose wasn't to find love and a spouse. Instead, they made a great work team. His neatness balanced out her chaotic approach to a problem. Charlotte's broad way of observation enriched his logical point of view. She kept him balanced and grounded—and added a ray of sunshine that illuminated the darkness of their investigation.

He checked the date on his cell phone despite the countdown ticking inside his mind. Today was day three of seven. They had only four and a half more days to stop the killer. Time was running out.

Even so, he'd carve out an hour to honor God and ask Him for guidance. Time with God was never wasted.

He exited his motel room to find Charlotte waiting on the walkway. She'd traded her jeans for a blue dress and black heeled shoes. Her blond hair was twisted in a bun at the back of her head. A few strands framed her face. She looked beautiful, as always. What else did she enjoy doing other than chasing criminals? She held a deep faith in God, but when had her relationship with Him begun? He doubted she'd been brought to church by her mom, so who introduced her to the Lord? So many questions that might go unanswered.

"Good morning," he said as he approached. "You get any sleep?"

She shook her head. "Barely." A yawn escaped her lips. "I'll sleep for a year once the Presque Killer is behind bars."

He imagined once the case was over she'd turn into a maiden in a fairy tale who'd been placed under a sleeping spell. Would his kiss break the curse? *Get those crazy notions out of your head.* Especially now, when Charlotte's life was in danger. If anything, Austin had to slay the dragon hunting her.

"I'll drive." She dangled her car keys. "We're going to church and the black special-agent-mobile attracts too much attention."

"It's a regular SUV that's black." He went to her car, a silver sedan, and waited by the passenger side for her to unlock the doors.

"With tinted windows and an FBI special agent behind the steering wheel." After unlocking, she opened the door and seated herself. "You still look like a dashing secret agent but at least me and my boring car go unnoticed."

"I don't look like a dashing secret agent." Though he did like hearing she thought him dashing. His objection held an undercurrent of humor. He was more a workhorse than show pony. But her teasing created doubt. He took stock of his clothing, the same type of pants, shirt and tie he always wore. "Do I?"

Charlotte started the car, then pulled out of the hotel's lot. "I've never seen a real secret agent, so I can't say for sure." The car radio played classic country. She lowered the volume, quieting the soulful twang of Patsy Cline.

"I have. During a trip to London, I attended training with MI6. The experience was exhilarating and terrifying." His service in the army and FBI had gifted him with many exciting experiences. Some dangerous. Caleb had told him that someday Austin would find balance and start a family. In Austin's opinion, work was life. Work gave him purpose. If not for his position with the FBI, he wouldn't be with Charlotte at this moment, helping her catch a serial killer.

"I bet training with MI6 was awesome." She reached for her cup of coffee set in the cup holder while keeping the other hand on the steering wheel. "When I was little, I wanted to work for the CIA, go on undercover missions. Ruby would hide clues for me to follow. She was always such a good sport to play along with my fantasies."

"What you're doing now is just as important

as a CIA mission." He watched her sip her coffee while driving, anxious she'd spill on her silky dress. But unlike Austin, she could do more than one task at a time and returned the cup to its holder without spilling even a drop of coffee.

"Maybe someday I'll live my dream and become a spy." She turned into the church's parking lot. Most of the spaces were already full as Charlotte and Austin were arriving seconds before the bell tolled to announce the start of worship. She found one at the back of the lot and parked. "But for now, I will clear my mind and cast all my cares on God."

Walking up the front steps of the church, he regarded the wide double doors, flung open to invite all inside. He entered beside Charlotte, noticing her shoulders relax. The nave of the church wasn't large. Each wood pew held parishioners.

Charlotte found an empty spot in the back. They remained standing as the pastor positioned himself before the altar. He began to speak, welcoming members and guests. The piano played the opening notes of the first hymn. Austin sang along with the familiar verses, feeling some of the gloom from his spirit begin to lift.

"God is good," Austin said along with the congregation when the pastor motioned for them to be seated.

Making opportunity for worship was a struggle when working an active case. Thankfully, Charlotte believed in the value of church. A person took breaks from work for eating and sleeping. Wasn't praying even more necessary? No one offered more protection than the Almighty God.

When the service ended, Charlotte experienced peace she hadn't felt since she'd learned the Presque Killer had killed again. Perhaps it was Austin seated close beside her. Or the pastor's words of comfort during his sermon. When she invited Austin last night, he'd surprised her by eagerly accepting. While they spent hours working together, the subject of faith rarely came up. She knew he believed in God. How could he spend a career studying the worst of humanity and not question why God allowed evil to prosper? During dark, lonely nights, she'd lie in bed and engage in a one-sided debate with God. Why had He allowed Ruby to die? What was Charlotte's purpose once the Presque Killer was caught? Would he ever be caught? And more recently, would her life end by her sister's killer if she failed to stop him?

She left the sanctuary of the church, stepping into the humidity waiting outside.

"Hello." A man wearing a shirt and tie approached. A petite woman with long blond hair kept close to his side. "Don't know if you remember me. I work as the assistant to the medical examiner in Baton Rouge. I was there the other day when you visited Dr. Connor. My wife and I are thinking of joining the church. The one we've been going to hired a new pastor who's a little too fire-and-brimstone for our tastes."

Charlotte shook hands with both the man and his wife. "I'm sorry but I don't remember your name. When I'm at the medical examiner's office, I'm singular focused."

"No worries. Robert and Vanessa Sinclair." He glanced over at Austin. "Good to see you again, Special Agent. We live in Royal, about ten miles from Presque. My wife and I are nervous about what's been going on. Have you made any progress in finding who's responsible?"

Vanessa held tightly to her husband's hand.

"I won't go out by myself anymore and check in once I get to work."

"That's good," Austin remarked. "We're working hard to get this guy but for now, remain vigilant."

"If you need information from the medical examiner's office, ask for me when you call," Robert said. "Dr. Connor is busy, and I know you need answers fast. Here's my card with all my contact information."

"Thank you." She accepted the business card and slipped it into the front pocket of her purse. "Did you like the church service?" Charlotte asked despite the urge to rush back to the station. The task force was meeting again in a few hours.

"We did," Robert said with a smile. "I think we're ready to transfer our membership. My wife just found out she's expecting, so it's a good time to make a change." His smile faded. "Is that a news reporter?" He pointed to a man standing on the sidewalk, holding a camera in their direction. "He's shown up at the medical examiner's office too, looking for a statement. No one there would talk to him. The woman who works the front desk used to be a professional wrestler. The reporter didn't have a chance."

A scowl grew on Charlotte's face. Ronald Rheault. Could she not get a moment's peace from the man? Not even church saved her from the reporter's constant scrutiny. "He's everywhere these days."

"I saw the press conference yesterday at the police station," Vanessa said. "That reporter was rude and abrasive. Totally uncalled for, given the circumstances."

Ronald appeared to snap a few more photographs before blending into the crowd of parishioners leaving for their cars.

Filled with both anger and suspicion, Charlotte asked Austin to wait on the church stairs while she marched in the direction Ronald had taken. Why the interest in her? Did he believe she was hiding the key to solving the mystery of the killer or did he already know the killer's identity? "Ronald," she called out. "Stop."

He skidded to a halt about half a block away from the front steps of the church, then spun to face her. "Is that a police order?"

"A personal request." An image flashed in her head of this man overpowering a woman, taking her and killing her. Had he been the one who'd held her captive, tied to a chair in the basement of the house outside of town? Ronald was tall but thin. Was he strong enough to be the Presque Killer? "What are you doing here?"

"Following my story." He took out a voice recorder and pressed Play. "A killer is on the loose and the lead detective along with her FBI partner take time away to attend church. Don't you feel your time is better served protecting the community from the person killing local women?"

"Do you believe in God?" She took the measure of this man, who appeared to get some sort of weird pleasure from asking Charlotte passive-aggressive questions. A serial killer usually stayed under the radar for as long as possible. Attention drawn could result in suspicion and an arrest, cutting off his activities. Ronald didn't seem to have those qualms. If he was the killer, did he believe his role as a reporter gave him access to the investigators and their work without anyone questioning his motives?

"God is a construct made by people who wanted to control others." Creases appeared between his eyebrows. Ronald's gaze lifted to view over Charlotte's shoulder. "Your FBI friend appears concerned. How's the reunion going? A police detective and FBI agent make an attractive couple. Is love in the air along with murder?"

"Excuse me." Austin settled at her side. "We're needed back at the police station."

"Did you get a break in the case?" Ronald directed his voice recorder toward Austin. "Anything you'd like to share?"

"No." Charlotte swatted down the recorder like a pesky bee. "If you have any more questions, contact the police department's communication liaison."

"They're not telling the media anything." Placing the recorder into the back pocket of his jeans, Ronald frowned. Sweat appeared on his forehead, and he wiped it away with the back of his hand.

"Good," Charlotte muttered and walked away with Austin to her car. "I need to make sure it stays that way."

"Do you think it could be him?" Austin considered the idea. A harassing news reporter wasn't abnormal. Most performed their job with professionalism. Some used aggressive tactics to chase a story. He believed Ronald Rheault fell into the latter category. Could his motivations be more sinister?

"He's a weak suspect, given my suspicion is based on bad vibes. But he's still a suspect in my book." Charlotte wore a short-sleeve dress the color of the Louisiana sky overhead. The rainstorm last night had moved on, leaving a beautiful azure-colored sky with only a handful of puffy white clouds floating across.

"What's his personal connection to you?" Austin asked, pressing her for logic instead of feelings. An investigator had to rely on both. A good investigator always backed up opinions with facts.

With her eyes focused on the road, she came to a stop at a red light. "I went to school with him. I don't know which grades. He remembers me but I don't remember him. His news stories have always been hypercritical of me. I'm not a perfect cop but I don't feel I deserve being written about as a fumbling fool."

"Has Ronald ever contacted you outside of a professional interest, like to ask you out?" A rejected romantic proposal had pushed other unstable men to violence.

"No." The light turned green, and she stepped on the accelerator. "He's too busy trying to bury me in negative news stories." She checked her rearview mirror. "There's a white truck following us."

He turned in his seat to catch a view of what shadowed them. A white truck similar to the one he'd seen speeding away on Charlotte's street. "Didn't you say there's hundreds of those kinds of trucks in the area?"

"There are. Maybe I'm being too paranoid."

"A serial killer threatened your life. There's no such thing as too paranoid." Glancing back again, he watched the truck inch closer. The male driver's face was obscured by the lowered brim of a baseball hat. "Turn here."

She turned right at the next intersection. The truck copied their change in direction.

Adrenaline surged. Was this another method of intimidation?

At the next intersection, she turned right again.

The truck continued straight. Soon, he lost sight of it.

"That was probably some guy driving to meet his buddies for breakfast." Her hands trembled slightly as they gripped the steering wheel.

"You need to stay vigilant. And if that means overreacting on occasion, then overreact." He lowered the car window for fresh air. The AC was on in the car but he needed more. A pleasant fragrance drifted off the magnolia flowers that dotted the trees alongside the road. When he left town, he wouldn't miss the heat and humidity. But he would miss the sweetness that always floated in the air—Charlotte's peony perfume mingling with the scents of ever-prevalent flowers.

When they reached the police station, he breathed a sigh of relief. At least Charlotte was fairly protected inside its walls.

"I don't trust anyone anymore, present company excluded." She turned off the car and exited.

Austin got out and closed the door. He glanced at her over the roof of the silver sedan and hooked his thumb toward the brick building that housed the police station. "Even those you work with?"

"I don't want to suspect a member of law enforcement but how did Ronald know confidential information about the investigation?" She drummed her fingers on the hood of the car.

"There's a leak. Or Ronald could have spoken with Michael." Could an informant or killer be hiding under the cover of a badge?

Discovering an investigation had a leak, someone who spoke to the media without authorization, wasn't uncommon. In this instance, one of their own was under threat. What purpose did sharing the connection the serial killer had with Charlotte serve? To cause harm? "Request that Chief Gunther place a cone of silence over the entire investigation. No more press conferences. No comments on any questions going forward."

"I don't want residents to think we're keeping things from them." All the tension that had left Charlotte's body in church was reappearing. Her back was stiff, and her face tight with worry.

"We are keeping things from them for the integrity of the investigation." He rounded the rear of the car to stand next to her. Taking her by the shoulders, he turned her so she met his gaze. "We have four more days to catch this guy. After he's locked away, you can give the press conference of a lifetime."

"Are you confident he'll be captured in time?" Fear dilated her dark pupils.

"I'm confident in you…and in me." He paused. "And most importantly in God." Failure was not an option. Four more days. If the killer continued to elude them, Charlotte could lose her life. Four more days to track a madman and take him into custody. Clues remained hidden. What had they missed during the initial investigation that kept the killer concealed? All they needed was one big break. One piece of evidence that connected the dots and revealed the killer's identity. He had faith that a big break would come. But would it come in time to save Charlotte and the other kidnapping victim?

Chapter Twelve

The piercing ring of a cell phone startled Charlotte out of a restless sleep. She looked at the time—three o'clock. Nothing good came from a call in the middle of the night.

"Detective Reid." Her voice was husky from sleep.

"It's Chief Gunther. There's been another kidnapping. Officers are at the home of the potential victim, speaking with the family. I want you and Walsh down there now. Maybe we'll get lucky and find a witness."

While he was talking, she was slipping out of her pajama shorts and into jeans. "We'll be there right away."

Chief Gunther provided the address and some preliminary details. When she ended the call, she made another to Austin. He didn't sound nearly as groggy as she felt.

In the hotel's tiny bathroom, she washed her

face and brushed her hair, pulling it up in a ponytail. Taking a moment, she stared at her reflection in the mirror. Dark circles underlined
her eyes. Her skin looked sallow—possibly from
the yellowish bathroom light or possibly because she hadn't gotten a decent night's sleep
since the Presque killer had reemerged.

She exited her hotel room, closed the door
and locked it. Austin came out of his room at
the same time. They were noticeably acting
in sync these days. Must be due to the two of
them spending almost every waking minute
together. Strange to think he'd soon be out of
her life again—this time for good.

"Who's driving?" He asked. His dark hair
didn't have the same sheen as normal and not
every hair was in perfect order. In fact, short
bangs swooped on his forehead, and he brushed
them back off his face with his hand.

"You can. I want to be noticed." She walked
to his black SUV parked nearby. Given the lack
of faith from the community, their recogniz-
ing an FBI special agent was on scene, an active
participant in the investigation, would hopefully calm doubts. If the killer was to be caught,
law enforcement needed the cooperation of the
community. Someone could have witnessed the

kidnapping but kept quiet due to distrust. No solid tips had been received so far, even after the press conference.

They silently drove to the neighborhood where the victim was last seen. Her brain had fully awakened and was currently engaged in speculation. But until she knew the facts, she wouldn't get stuck on any one theory. This missing woman could be unrelated to the Presque Killer. People were jumpy and called the police for situations they normally wouldn't.

Austin parked behind a marked squad car. The street was dark beside the couple of streetlights that still worked and the flashing of red and blue from the light bars on top of police cars. A group of people were gathered in the front yard of a house, some wearing nightwear. The house they stood before was brightly lit from the inside. More people stood toward the back of the driveway, by a rickety garage.

Charlotte approached Officer Evans, who stood leaning with his back against his squad car. "What house was the missing person last seen in?"

He indicated the house where people had assembled. "Candace—better known as Candy—

Lyon attended a party at a home owned by
Rich Walker."

"He's the go-to if people want drugs," Charlotte added for Austin's benefit.

"True." Officer Evans nodded. "So it's no
surprise those in attendance aren't being very
chatty. We all know what kind of party Rich
throws."

"When was Ms. Lyon last seen?" During
these drug-and alcohol-fueled parties, people
stumbled off into the night all the time, making it home or onto a friend's sofa or a neighbor's front yard.

"Her dad came over to bring her home. Ms.
Lyon was attending addiction counseling and
had been clean for two months." Officer Evans
glanced over at the source of shouting coming
from the front lawn. "Her dad learned Candy
had left the party a little before midnight and no
one has seen her since. She didn't return home
and none of her friends know where she is.
Since she fits the victim profile of the Presque
Killer, her father made a call to the police."

"Is Mr. Lyon here?" She scanned the crowd,
which was appearing more restless by the second.

"We convinced him to go home by telling

him you and Special Agent Walsh would be over to speak with the family. It's too loud here to hear yourself think."

Two men began shoving one another. Charlotte, Austin and Officer Evans rushed over to intervene.

"Did anyone speak with Candy before she left?" Austin's voice rang over the buzzing of other conversations. "Did she say where she was going?"

"She had a drink and left." A skinny woman with short red hair pushed forward through the crowd. "Candy only came to the party to talk to her old boyfriend, Scooter. They fought and then she headed out the back door."

"Did she walk or drive here?" Charlotte ask.

"Walked." The redheaded woman pointed down the street to her right. "Candy lives with her folks and their house is only three blocks down that way."

"Where's Scooter?" Austin's rigid posture and wide-set feet warned anyone considering running. Even slightly disheveled, he looked the part of a man tasked with saving the day.

Charlotte too often forgot *not* to be attracted to him. His handsome charm frequently slipped past her defenses. While she was supposed to be one hundred percent focused on her mission here, she'd caught her gaze lingering on Austin for a second more than it should have. Dreams of romance were selfish considering similar flights of fancy had been one of the reasons the murdered women's cases had grown cold.

"That's Scooter," a different woman interjected. Charlotte's gaze landed on a tall, broad-shouldered man standing on the front porch of the house. "He's a mean one, so watch out. Don't know what Candy saw in him, except maybe a good time."

"Do you know why Candy wanted to speak with him tonight?" Charlotte inquired. Could be the former couple argued and Candy stormed off to find a quiet spot to think.

"He had some things that belonged to her and she wanted them back." The lady with the red hair offered. "Did the Presque Killer snatch Candy? Is that why y'all are here?"

"We don't want to speculate. Thanks for your help." Austin smiled at the two women before walking in the direction of the porch and Scooter.

Charlotte's intention to follow Austin was interrupted by the sight of a white truck rumbling down the street. Her alertness sharpened when she saw Michael Duncan. The man she unofficially considered a suspect. They were still waiting for the return of his DNA test to learn if it matched the sample taken from the first victim's sweater.

The truck stopped in the street and several people wandered over to speak with Michael.

She walked over and stood a few feet from the driver's-side door. "I'd like a word." The others dispersed when they saw her badge.

"What are you doing?" Folding her arms across her chest, she worked to not appear as tense as she felt.

"I live three houses down. Don't you remember paying me a visit the other day?" His scowl highlighted the lines on his face. Michael wasn't much older than Charlotte but hard living aged a person. "Had the night off and needed another six-pack of beer." A paper bag sat on the passenger seat.

She gazed down the street and found Michael's house, dark and dreary in the shadow of night. "A young woman went missing tonight. Candy Lyon. Do you know her?"

"Sure, I know Candy. Like all us know one another in the neighborhood." Michael stared at the party house and his scowl grew. "Was she at Rich Walker's place?"

Charlotte pondered if Michael had kidnapped Candy. If he were the Presque Killer, would he come back to the scene of the crime? Some perpetrators enjoyed witnessing the chaos their actions produced. She couldn't remember seeing Michael Duncan at any of the other crime scenes.

"Did you kidnap Candy?" She decided to push him to gauge his reaction. No time for a gentle approach.

"What?" His eyes widened. "You think I took her? The girl probably went to someone's place to crash." He rubbed his scruffy jaw. "I had nothing to do with it."

The denial seemed honest, on the surface. If she scratched a little harder, would she draw blood? "Do you remember this?" She lifted her arm to bring her bracelet into view. "Ruby and I had matching ones. You stole mine."

Michael snorted a laugh. "I stole a lot of stuff back then. Don't be offended. I don't remember swiping your bracelet, but you must have gotten it back."

"I did after you were removed from the home." She inhaled through her nose, trying to detect the aromas of alcohol or smoke coming from him. Nothing but a minty scent from the gum he smacked in his mouth. A person would need to be sober to pull off the types of crimes the Presque Killer had done. "You must like the crescent moon too? What is the meaning of your neck tattoo?" For Charlotte, the symbolism of the crescent moon linked back to her mom, who'd believed the small sliver of moon in the sky meant new beginnings.

He covered the inked spot on the side of his neck with the palm of his hand. "It's something I saw on TV. Are you done with the questions? I don't enjoy walking down memory lane. My time in foster care isn't something I like dwelling on."

She recognized the flash of pain that crossed his expression at the mention of foster care. Although the families she'd stayed with had been mostly kind and loving, they weren't her mom. They weren't her real home. At least she'd had Ruby. Caring for her sister had kept her mind off the loss of their mother. Ruby had needed her, and Charlotte hadn't had time for tears.

"If you learn anything about what happened to Candy, call the police station and you'll be put in touch with me." She took a step back, questioning whether she was allowing the killer to drive away.

"Girls like Candy go missing all the time, in these parts and elsewhere." He switched the transmission from Park to Drive. "No one cares. Why waste your time, Detective? Unless you're worried you might be next."

He pulled away, driving a couple dozen feet until he turned into his driveway. His taillights taunted her.

Charlotte considered chasing after him so she could press him on what he meant by *you might be next*. When she felt someone place a hand on her shoulder, she froze. Spinning around, she saw Austin. A breath of relief left her lungs, although her heart still pounded at a supersonic rate.

"Who was that?" Austin stared down the dark road.

"Michael Duncan. He denies being at the party or that he's involved at all with Candy's disappearance." The crowd around the house had mostly dispersed, whether by the direction of the cops or due to dwindling interest. She hoped the officers had taken the names and contact information of all. "I want to bring him in for questioning. He said he was coming from the store after getting beer. It's been almost four hours since Candy left the party and anyone has seen her."

"Order another officer to bring him in." Austin waved over a patrol officer who stood by the curb. "You and I can sit down with him but we don't have enough to arrest him. We'll need his cooperation. Unless we get the DNA results back and it's a match."

"And you don't think he'll cooperate with me." Not a question. Charlotte provided instructions to the officer, giving Michael's name, address and the command to take along another officer when making the house call. "We could be dealing with someone dangerous. Be on guard and if he acts or says anything threatening, slap cuffs on him and bring him in."

Shouting caught Austin's attention. A large man marched down the road, fists clenched at his side. "Where's my daughter?" His booming voice echoed on the otherwise quiet street. "Where's Candy?"

"Mr. Lyon." Austin strode up the street to meet a man visibly in distress. "Special Agent Walsh. We understand Candy was last seen at a house on this block. We have a large presence of law enforcement questioning those who were with your daughter before she went missing."

"Are you really searching or is this all for show?" Mr. Lyon glanced around, left to right. He wore tattered jeans and a wrinkled T-shirt. His bloodshot, puffy eyes left no doubt he'd been crying. "He has her, doesn't he? The Presque Killer. She'll end up just like those other girls, murdered with no justice."

Every reminder of his failure to catch the killer felt like an arrow piercing his heart. "We don't know if Candy is truly missing. Under normal circumstances, an adult will need to be missing for longer than twenty-four hours before law enforcement gets involved. The person could have gone somewhere else and not told others."

"But this isn't a normal circumstance," Mr. Lyon spit out. "There's someone hunting young women like my daughter. Last week, she applied at the local college to become a nursing assistant. She'd stopped doing drugs and wanted to make something of her life. I don't want to imagine all that being taken away." A gut-wrenching sob punctuated his last sentence.

Witnessing the raw grief of another human being ripped away a layer of the protective wall

Austin had placed around his emotions when he joined the FBI. To be a good agent, he'd learned to stay elevated above the personal feelings of those affected by the crime. He was taught to view his investigation like he was floating in a balloon, gazing down at the evidence and facts. Gaining a perspective often missed by those standing too close on the ground.

Caleb had trained Austin to use all his senses, including listening to his feelings. He had given everything to the investigation of his own daughter's murder, then dedicated his life to bringing justice to other victims of serial killers. But Austin had witnessed the toll that emotional investment had had on Caleb, especially at the end of a long career. His high level of personal dedication had drained his marriage and his health, and Austin believed it had cost Caleb his life.

Standing before a father fearing for his daughter's life, Austin felt the pull Caleb had not resisted. His connection with Charlotte already threatened to rock the steady course of his career. If he allowed himself to feel too deeply, would he ever find his way back to solid ground? Or would the internal turmoil upend him, sending him plunging into unfamiliar water?

He rested a hand on the father's shoulder. "We'll find your daughter, no matter where she is."

Mr. Lyon stumbled off in the direction of Rich Walker's house, likely having questions of his own that needed answering.

"Candy's father?" Charlotte, who'd been speaking with a party attendee, asked when she approached.

Austin nodded. "He's scared to death the Presque Killer took her." As was he.

"Does he have any idea where she may be?"

"He has no idea where she could have gone." He rubbed his eyes and yawned. The hour of sleep he'd grabbed while resting his head on the hotel room table felt inadequate. "We should call together the task force and then spread out. Once the sun comes up, a group can search this area in hopes of locating something that will point us to Candy's whereabouts."

Charlotte mirrored his yawn. She'd probably snuck in as much sleep as he had. "I'll take a look around." She removed a compact flashlight from her jacket pocket and clicked it on. A beam of light swept back and forth as she moved slowly along the street, head bent and gaze pointing to the ground.

He moved alongside her. A white folded piece of paper caught the light. After placing on gloves, he picked up the paper, already dreading what message it held. *Two.*

His optimism faded. There was no doubt Candy was a victim of the Presque Killer.

In the other direction, Michael Duncan's house had a few lights on, including the one on the front porch. Two officers stood on the porch before an open front door. Austin assumed Michael Duncan filled the doorway, although his view was partially obscured by the post supporting the porch's crooked roof.

He grabbed a flashlight from his SUV and began a search for more evidence. The Presque Killer had promised to cause turmoil and terror for a week. Seven days and then he'd take Charlotte, kill her and all his kidnapped victims. The leader of a cruel game where there'd be only one winner. The killer assumed he'd come out the victor. Then he'd slip back into anonymity without consequence. But the desire for another kill wouldn't leave. He'd want another life. More fame. His name to be whispered at gatherings and feared around the country. A serial killer did not stop until he was forced to.

But Austin would protect Charlotte from the madman even if he couldn't stay long-term.

Chapter Thirteen

The interview with Michael Duncan had gone as Austin expected. Michael had remained evasive, refusing to answer questions, and when he did, he'd given vague responses. His DNA results had come in as the interview ended—not a match to the sample collected off the first victim's sweater.

Austin now sat in Chief Gunther's office, having headed there from the interrogation room. Charlotte had gone to the restroom, likely needing a moment to calm her nerves after facing off against someone whose animosity bled through.

"He's not a DNA match." The chief reclined in his leather office chair, rocking slightly. "Do you believe this Michael Duncan is the Presque Killer?"

Austin considered the question he'd been asking himself since his initial interaction with the man. "We can't say definitively the DNA collected off Mary's sweater was left by the killer. That's been the theory, though. And the assumption has been that the Presque Killer worked alone but he could have had help. Now the helper has begun carrying out his own sick fantasies. There are too many loose ends to know for sure."

"Michael has been a suspect in a number of crimes but never charged. Mostly drug-related offenses." Chief Gunter straightened in his seat, then pushed up to stand. "Most of the issues we deal with around here are due to drugs, using or selling, or both. And overdoses and calls for medical attention. Having a drug problem is a far stretch to being a cold-blooded murderer."

"From what I sense after the interview, Michael is not a cold-blooded killer. He seems to be clever but not enough to get away with the Presque Killer's actions. He's proud of who he is and doesn't hide it." Michael's bluntness had rattled Charlotte more than once. "I'm worried about Charlotte. She's too close. The fact her sister was one of the murder victims makes working these cases tougher. Being a target herself while searching for a killer who's someone from her past is a strain. Do we send her out of the state until the killer is arrested?"

"I'm considering doing just that." Running his hand across his buzzed silver hair, the chief blew out a breath. "Charlotte would never agree."

"You can order her off the case." The loss of Charlotte as a partner was nothing compared to losing her permanently. But he knew this case was the most important thing in her life right now. She'd declare solving it was even more important *than* her life.

"You will do no such thing." The subject of their conversation charged into Chief Gunther's office. "You're not sending me away."

"Hear us out," the chief countered. "If you're in hiding, the killer may give up his plan and let those women go."

"Or he could kill them...and others." Hands on hips, Charlotte sent both men a piercing glare. "I can't take that chance. My life isn't any more valuable than Karen's or Candy's. Or the other women who could be next."

"While I agree with you on that, the killer is targeting you," Austin said. "You're emotionally and physically exhausted. I could see how Michael was affecting you while we questioned him."

She sank into one of the upholstered chairs in the chief's office. "I can handle Michael and any other suspects we need to question. I'm not stopping until we find him."

Austin had expected her to dig in her heels, though he'd had to try. In the end, they'd catch the killer but Charlotte would never be the same. Emotionally wrung out and possibly unable to continue in the police force due to trauma. Like Caleb had been at the end of his career in the FBI. Within a year of retirement, he'd been diagnosed with heart issues. Five years later, a heart attack stole his life.

"Charlotte, I know how committed you are to our mission. If you went into hiding for your own safety, you could trust me and the rest of the team to complete the job." Austin handed her a bottle of water that he'd taken earlier from the chief's mini-fridge.

She twisted off the top and took a drink. She appeared to consider his heartfelt plea and visibly relaxed. "I will not leave Presque while the killer I've been chasing for more than six years wanders our streets, creating mayhem. I don't care if I'm as emotionally damaged as a city after a category five hurricane. If I left now, I wouldn't be able to live with myself."

The shimmer of tears he saw in her eyes hit him hard. Austin understood passion and commitment to one's job. Charlotte had made it clear she was prepared to go to the cliff's edge to see this through. And he'd remain at her side. His job was to see the killer captured and the cases closed. More personally, he'd be a shelter for Charlotte during the storm they were combating.

"Okay." The chief stepped backward, hands up in a gesture of defeat. "But the offer remains on the table in case you change your mind."

A knock sounded on the doorframe. A state detective from the task force entered. "We received a match to the tire tracks found next to Karen's van." He placed a typed report with a color photograph on the chief's desk. "The tires are used in two different makes of medium-sized box trucks. We located the owners of matching trucks in a twenty-mile radius from town. And we found the driver of the one who'd been parked next to our victim's van. He's not who we're looking for. His name is Howard Meyer, and he drives trucks for an overnight delivery service. He stopped at the café that night with a coworker for pie and coffee, then they left ten minutes before midnight. The coworker corroborates his story. They were at their next stop a few minutes after midnight."

"There goes that lead." Austin scanned the report. Not likely he'd find a detail missed but he always verified. "The task force is meeting in ten minutes. We can cross off the box truck." Their list of leads had grown smaller instead of larger. What concerned him, besides the obvious lack of time until the killer's deadline, was how the killer's activity had increased but he continued to leave little to no evidence in his wake. Could he continue to stay that careful? Only one slipup—that was all they needed. One discarded item that helped make an ID. An oversight by the killer that they would pick up on.

The killer had gotten away with his crimes for so long he must be confident he'd never be caught. His actions supported the theory. Overconfident people made mistakes. Austin prayed the killer would make one soon.

By the time Charlotte left the police station, the sun had set and a half-moon hung low in the inky dark sky. Austin wanted to spend another hour reviewing case studies of other serial killers who'd been captured. He hoped something in those solved cases could shine light on a critical piece of the puzzle they were missing in the Presque Killer investigation.

Her eyelids were unwilling to stay up for much longer, so she'd packed up her notes and called it a day. If tonight was anything like the past four nights, she'd wake up with a start then find sleep evasive. After tossing and turning, she'd accept defeat, get out of bed to read and mull over her case notes.

The drive to the motel from the police station was thankfully brief. A pair of crime scene techs from the task force stood by the vending machine, trying to select a late-night snack. They waved to Charlotte as she walked by.

While she was grateful for the extra resources provided for the investigation, leading a task force meant dealing with administrative duties when she'd rather be out chasing the killer. But she couldn't be everywhere and do everything. Three victims, four including her, in less than a week meant multiple crime scenes needed perfect examinations. Nothing could be missed. Which was why she and Austin reviewed every report and photograph and statement. The killer wanted them drowning in police work.

She slipped the key into the lock on her room, unlocked the door and went inside. Humid, warm air struck her, and she noticed the absence of the hum of the air conditioner. After a brief check of the interior unit, she found it had been turned off. It had been on when she'd left in the morning. Why had housekeeping turned off her room's air conditioner when the temperature outside was topping eighty each day?

Pushing the button to turn it on, she eagerly waited for fresh cool air to blow. Soon, a steady stream of cold air filled the room. She kicked off her shoes, leaving them lying in the middle of the floor. For a second, she considered setting them inside the hotel closet, then chuckled. She'd been spending too much time around Austin. His tidiness was rubbing off.

Since she hadn't had a chance to shower this morning, sleep could wait for a few minutes while she cleaned off the day's sweat and grime. Inside the bathroom, she turned on the water, anticipating standing under the spray and feeling clean again.

She'd left the bathroom door open a crack, and while she took down her hair from out of the hair tie with her back toward the door, the lights went out and bathroom door closed. Someone else must be in her room.

Panic gripped her hard and fast. She clutched the handle to the bathroom door. It turned but when she pulled on the door, it wouldn't budge. Trying again, she was left with the same result. Charlotte pounded on the door in the blackness. "Help. I'm stuck." Had she locked the door behind her when she'd entered the hotel room? She assumed so, as the action was a force of habit after years as a cop.

"Help!" She banged on the door again. Nothing. Not even budging a fraction of an inch. Now what? Her cell phone sat on the bed where she'd tossed it. The compact bathroom had no windows.

She shut off the water in the shower. A faint sound coming from outside the bathroom made her press her ear to the door. *Tick, tick, tick.* The ticking of a clock. Realization produced a shot of fear. Was the Presque Killer inside her hotel room? Had he locked her in the bathroom? For what? To taunt her or to do her harm?

"Detective Reid." A familiar digitally altered voice came from the other side of the door. "Time is slipping away."

"You never said harassing me was part of your game." Anger was slowly replacing fear, though terror still held a tight grip.

His laughter in reply nauseated her.

"Are you afraid I'm getting close? Will you keep me locked away so I can't find you?" She could taunt as well.

"I enjoy our time together, that's all," he said.

"My FBI partner will be here any moment." A bluff. Worth a shot.

"Your FBI agent is an honorable man and not one to join a woman in her hotel room at night. I believe we're safe from interruption for a while."

Unfortunately, the killer was right. "Say what you need to say, then let me out." She pounded on the door again for emphasis.

"Three more days, Detective. Midnight is approaching, then you'll have seventy-two hours until time runs out." A ringing of bells replaced the ticktock of a clock.

She imagined a brass clock with a white face topped by a pair of bells. The hands of the clock read midnight and the bells rang out an alarm. The sound ended abruptly, replaced with an equally chilling silence. She gripped the door handle and pulled with all her strength. If she could get out, she'd have a chance to catch him. The darkness enveloping her made the small bathroom feel as tight as a casket. Panic rose. She pounded on the door and yelled. Someone had to hear and come in to get her out.

Finally, she sat on the closed lid of the toilet and concentrated on taking slow, steady breaths. Not even a sliver of light shone from underneath the door, meaning the power to her room must have been cut. The killer likely had been hiding inside her room when she'd arrived. With members of the task force staying nearby, the killer had taken a risk by sneaking into her room. Doubt swirled in her mind about the integrity of the team and other members of the Presque Police Department. Had the killer evaded capture because he had insight into the investigation?

She hated doubting others like herself who'd sworn to serve and protect. Outside the bathroom, her cell phone rang. The ringing ended, likely with the call going to voice mail. Then it rang again—and again. Someone was trying to reach her. Would they give up and try again in the morning? *I don't want to be stuck in here all night.*

A pounding noise started, seemingly coming

from the hotel room exterior door. She stood and struck her fists into the bathroom door. Then silence. Hope was fading she'd get out of the bathroom before sunrise.

The faraway echo of voices gave breath to optimism. She pressed her head against the bathroom door.

"Charlotte!" Austin shouted from the other side of the door. "Are you in here?"

"In the bathroom." She sagged in relief. "I've been locked in."

"I'll have the door opened soon." A thump heralded the opening of the bathroom door.

She rushed into Austin's open arms. "He was here. The Presque Killer must have been waiting in my room. I went into the bathroom to shower and he locked me in. He wanted to remind me of our dwindling time to stop him."

Austin's arms tightened around her. "You're safe. Did he hurt you?"

"No, besides giving me a fright." Resting her head on his chest, Charlotte listened to the steady beat of Austin's heart. In his embrace, she felt safe and protected. Being with him was like lying in bed on a cold morning underneath a comfy blanket, knowing the cocoon of warmth and security would dissipate as soon as she removed herself from under the covers. His was a temporary shelter. She'd be wise to remember that.

A length of red nylon rope rested on the ground. The killer must have tied it to the door handle and secured the other end to the heavy dresser set against the wall.

His hand cupped the back of her head, and he kissed her gently on the forehead. "Please reconsider leaving town. I couldn't bear it if something happened to you."

"I can't." Her words were spoken as fact, as if she'd reported her name or address. "It's my job to stop him."

"Don't let him drive the narrative. We keep pushing back. The press conference may not have flushed him out like we'd hoped but we're not giving up."

"He's messing with me." She raised her gaze to meet Austin's and almost became lost in the warmth of his brown eyes. "I won't let him win."

"But at what cost." He sighed and let his arms fall, releasing his hold.

The chill of loneliness returned. Charlotte thought of Ruby, who'd been her best friend. When Ruby had gone missing, Charlotte had found comfort in Austin's embrace. In his kiss. She'd believed Ruby would be found, the Presque Killer captured, and Charlotte's blossoming romance with Austin would bloom into love. How had she been so naive? Allowing ideas of falling in love again could not be allowed to take up space in her brain.

"At least agree to have someone posted outside your room at the hotel at all times to make sure this doesn't happen again." Austin's gaze moved around the dark room. "Is this your clock?" He pointed to a brass alarm clock placed on the table.

"No." It looked like the kind she'd imagined while trapped in the bathroom. "A gift from the Presque Killer." Her hotel room was a crime scene. Yet again, she needed to move. This time to a different motel room. "Did you see anyone lurking around outside when you arrived?"

"No one suspicious-looking." He pressed a hand to the small of her back and led her to the opened door of the room. Fluorescent light spilled in, bathing the room in an eerie, bluish glow. The power had been cut to Charlotte's room alone. "When you didn't answer my call, I became concerned."

"Lucky for me you checked in before heading off to your own room for the night." God had placed Austin in her life for a reason. A short-term gift she was grateful for.

She would call the chief and report the break in. Once again, she'd pack up a few belongings and settle someplace else for the short term. The crime scene investigator team would comb through the room, searching for anything that provided an identity of the man they hunted. A hair or fingerprint. Even a mark from his shoe. The most obscure thing could be the break they needed.

"Every time he does something in an attempt to gloat or intimidate or scare me, there's a chance he'll leave behind a clue. As deeply as I hate the events he orchestrates, they may be his undoing." Meaning she had to stay and keep him coming after her.

While standing outside her room to call the chief, she heard the phantom *tick, tick, tick* of the clock. The sound was only in her head. Likely the killer's intentions. She had three more days until the ticking ended and the alarm bells chimed. Her chest squeezed as the pressure to find the killer increased by the minute.

Tick, tick, tick. Each second pulled her closer into the killer's bull's-eye. But Charlotte had her sights set on him too. And she vowed to stop him before he had her in his crosshairs and took the shot.

Chapter Fourteen

Austin stood a dozen feet behind Charlotte. She'd wanted to visit the site where her sister had been found. After the being trapped in the bathroom by Presque Killer two nights ago and yesterday's frustration with their lack of progress on finding the killer or the two women he'd kidnapped, Charlotte had told him she was going where she felt her sister's presence. Austin wasn't letting her go anywhere alone.

He couldn't dispute her belief that the more the killer interacted with her, the more likely he'd leave behind evidence. Unfortunately, Charlotte's house and hotel room had been free of trace evidence. Austin didn't want her easily available to the killer in the rare hope of getting a piece of his identifying information.

He observed Charlotte, head bent in prayer. Little had changed here since Ruby's body had been dumped. The same thick gloom hung over the swampland trailing along the dirt road. Tall trees with limbs draped with Spanish moss gave the appearance of an old guard that kept out those who might travel into their lair.

Memories surfaced of the last time he'd visited here with Charlotte. Her scream at the sight of her lifeless sister had torn him apart. Ruby had been placed in a ditch between the road and the swampy area. He'd seen bodies of murder victims in worse shape but none had ever affected him like Ruby.

Nothing would bring Charlotte's sister back. Not even a life sentence for her murderer. Once the cases were solved, Charlotte would need to find a way back to a normal life. He allowed himself to imagine staying a part of her future. *No.* He'd never do that to someone he cared about. Not after witnessing other agents put their loved ones through lonely nights and worry-filled days. Some agents were professionals at shutting off their emotions while on the job and then flipping a switch to become a loving spouse once they came back home to their families. Austin, however, knew only how to repress his emotions. The fear of turning them back on and being washed away kept a tight rein on his feelings.

Charlotte turned around to face him and wiped her eyes. "Thanks for coming with me. I'd hoped for a vision or sign from God. I only heard the croaking of frogs."

"What if the frogs were trying to tell you something?" He took her hand and gave it a gentle squeeze. "God can work in mysterious ways."

Her fingers intertwined with his, as if holding hands with him was the most natural thing in the world. "I only studied frog language for a year in high school and don't remember a thing." She grinned. "No matter where we are or what's happening, you can always make me smile."

A tool for staying sane in the insanity of chasing serial killers. There weren't many tricks to make the work bearable. Humor definitely helped soften some of the hard blows. "You ready to go back to the station?"

"I'd like to visit the sites where we found the other victims' bodies." She spun back around to take one final look. A white cross painted with red roses marked the sacred spot. "If I follow the killer's path from start to finish, will I see something I missed before?"

"Do we have time for that?" He didn't need

to check his phone to know the date. Today was Wednesday and tomorrow at midnight would mark the end of the killer's countdown. "Visiting all the crime scenes will take the rest of the morning."

"I have to. If you want to head to the station and keep reviewing the case files, I'll drop you off." She walked down the center of the dirt road, swatting away a multitude of flying insects filling the air. "May be best to split up."

"No." With a slap to the face, he ended the life of a mosquito who probably left its remains on his cheek. The short whiskers he'd allowed to grow pricked his hand. He hadn't shaved in two days, not wanting to waste precious minutes.

Charlotte reached her car, pulled out her purse and removed a tissue. With a soft touch, she wiped his stubble-covered jaw. "Southern mosquitoes are a different breed. They grow as big as seagulls and are as bloodthirsty as alligators."

"I've only had one run-in with an alligator, which thank goodness was uneventful. I'll stick with mosquitoes." The sighting had been during his first work trip to Louisiana. The creature had floated up to the shoreline near where

Austin was taking a morning jog. It stared up at Austin with its reptile eyes before sinking into the murky water without making a ripple.

He took out a paper map from his bag and spread it over the hood of her car. "I'll visit each site with you." The locations where the Presque Killer's murder victims had been found were circled in red. The sites of the kidnappings were crossed with a blue *X*. Years ago, they'd sat for hours studying the map, trying to find a pattern or the home base of the killer. The red circles bordered the town of Presque with the two *X*'s placed inside the town limits. How did all these different crime scenes connect to a single killer? Or were they dealing with a partnership?

For the remainder of the morning, Austin and Charlotte visited each murder victim's final location. They studied the ground, the trees, the nearby buildings. Someone with no knowledge of the murders would think the rural spots held no significance. Even the crime scene where they'd found the latest victim, Ginny Gerard, had been released and no evidence remained of the woman who'd been disposed there.

By the time they returned to the station, pessimism had taken root. Charlotte headed into the station's kitchen to get a drink.

Austin went to the conference room and downed the remainder of the water in the stainless steel bottle he rarely was without. They were running out of time. He stared at the board filled with the victim's pictures. How could someone kill five women, kidnap two, and be walking free? Was the Presque Killer a phantom? Was he working alone?

Either no one had witnessed him with any of these women or, if they had, the killer didn't appear out of the ordinary enough to catch anyone's attention. Or were people too afraid to talk? The killer could be someone who produced fear in the community. Once more, Austin examined the color image of the last murder victim's dump site. Each murder victim had been placed beside rural roads of gravel or dirt. A person could stop, then drop something in the ditch before leaving without notice.

He opened the folder marked Ginny Gerard and pulled out more photographs. He studied the ground around the body and then the ground after she'd been removed. Those narrow row-like marks in the dirt continued to nag the back of his mind. He took out the magnifying glass he kept in his bag. Examining the area with the markings, he grew certain the victim's fingernails had made the drag marks. But her fingernails were relatively clean in the autopsy photos. He rubbed his eyes. *You're imagining things.* Desperation produced all sorts of wild theories.

Humor yourself. He removed photographs of each of the other four victims, one at the crime scene and one taken at the autopsy. He started back at the first victim, Mary Gury. Nothing jumped out regarding her hands. She was missing a fake nail on the ring finger of her left hand in both pictures. He reviewed the others, using the magnifying glass and slowly sweeping across the photos to check for any inconsistencies.

He'd begun examining Ruby's pictures when Charlotte entered the conference room. Glancing up, he saw the redness of her eyes. His instinct was to rush to her and hold her close. A kiss on the forehead for comfort. Another on the lips to show how deeply he cared. But that was how hearts were broken. Kissing her six years ago had been a mistake. He'd given in to temptation again. His willpower to avoid kissing her once more before he boarded the flight home needed to remain iron-strong. He returned his gaze to the photograph placed before him on the table.

"What are you doing?" She moved over to stand beside him and sucked in a breath. "I'll never get used to seeing my sister like this."

"A death like Ruby's is never something you'll get used to. She should be alive. She deserved better than what was done to her." Austin held the magnifying glass to Ruby's right hand at the crime scene. Her gold bracelet, the one that matched Charlotte's, glistened under the strong lights that had been placed around the scene.

He lowered the magnifying glass, hovering over her hands, fingers and nails. One of the fingernails on her right hand appeared broken. All of Ruby's nails were short, but this one had a slightly ragged edge. Could she have broken it during a struggle with the killer? Austin had found it strange that no evidence was found under any of the victims' nails while each had been strangled. Usually, the victim would fight back in an attempt to save their life. The Presque Killer had sedated the victims with the anesthetic Propofol. But had they been incapacitated the entire time of their captivity? Serial killers in general enjoyed the feeling of power they got when killing. How could the Presque

Killer feel powerful while taking away his victim's ability to struggle to stay alive?

Ruby's autopsy photo was set out beside one from the crime scene. He moved over to see if he could make out the ragged edge of her nail on the autopsy photo. Narrowing in on the nail on her right hand, he looked closely. The nail appeared smooth. He switched back and forth between the two photographs, comparing the condition of the nail. It wasn't the same.

"Take a look." He handed Charlotte the magnifying glass. "Ruby's nail is broken at the crime scene. It's hard to tell for sure since all her nails are short but it looks like it's been torn. Now, check out the same nail at the autopsy."

She switched to the other photo and leaned in. "Her nail is different. Like it's been filed smooth. Is that noted in the autopsy report?"

He found the report and set it on the table. A brief scan brought him to the section where the medical examiner gave a description of her nails and any evidence found in, under or around them. "There's nothing about a broken nail or that any part of the nail was removed for testing. No trace evidence was found in the area of her hands or nails."

His gut sounded an alarm. Had someone

tampered with the body between the crime scene and the medical examiner's office?

How could she have missed it? Studying Ruby's nail under the magnifying glass, Charlotte dropped her jaw in shock. She slid the magnifying glass to hover over the autopsy photograph. Austin was right. Ruby's nail on her right hand pointer finger was smooth instead of ragged. "Do you think someone tampered with Ruby's body?"

"It's a possibility. Unless the medical examiner has a good reason for the alteration." Austin rested his back against the wall, ankles and arms crossed. "I'd expect any change to the body would be included on the autopsy report."

And it wasn't. Charlotte had memorized Ruby's autopsy report. It was the photographs she'd had trouble viewing. "I should have caught the discrepancy."

"So should I. We had these photographs six years ago and I didn't notice until now." He pushed off the wall and strode to the table. "I closely examined the other victims, including Ginny, the latest, and didn't notice any other differences."

Charlotte stumbled back, too angry with herself to speak. The alteration to Ruby's nail had been there all along, and she'd missed it. Instead of using the information to dig further and possibly find the killer, she'd let the photographs rest in a folder in an evidence box. She'd spent thousands of hours reviewing the reports and evidence of the cases over the years but avoided the photographs of Ruby's lifeless body. "Seeing her like this is so hard." Her gaze dropped to a photo of Ruby lying on the ground. Ruby's dark hair was splayed out, almost blending in with the brown earth. Charlotte touched her bracelet while glancing at the one Ruby wore in death. She wished to reach back in time to when her sister was alive, to hold her close and tell Ruby how much she loved her.

"We used to do each other's hair and nails when we were kids." Charlotte floated a finger over Ruby's hair and face. "I remember the feeling of the brush on my scalp when she brushed my hair. Ruby did not work with a gentle hand." Her laugh blended with a sob. "I should have been there for her. I failed her."

"You didn't." As before, Austin pulled her into his embrace.

Austin's arms were the only things holding her together while her world fell apart. Her emotions hit in strong waves, and she pulled away. She couldn't rely on him to be her rock. Life had taught her not to find footing on another. Swim alone if needed and reach shore on your own.

"I'll call the medical examiner. He could have a logical reason for the change to her nail." She opened the contacts on her phone, pulled up the medical examiner's office number and dialed.

After three rings, the call was answered. "Baton Rouge Medical Examiner's office. How may I help you?"

Charlotte introduced herself and asked to speak with the medical examiner.

"Dr. Connor is performing an autopsy," the woman on the other end said. "He started not long ago, which means he won't be free to return your call until the end of the day or tomorrow."

Tick, tick, tick. They didn't have time to wait. "Is there anyone else, an assistant, who I could speak with?"

"One of our assistants is with Dr. Connor now. I'd have to check to see if the other is available."

She remembered her conversation with Robert

and his wife after church. He'd mentioned he'd be willing to help. "Is Robert Sinclair assisting?"

The clicking of a keyboard sounded. "No. He may be free to talk with you. I'll check."

"I have his number. I'll give him a call." She thanked the woman and disconnected.

"Dr. Connor is busy. Do you recall Robert Sinclair from church? We met him and his wife." They'd seemed like a nice couple, and were considering joining the church. She'd need to remember their names the next Sunday, when she'd run into them after the service.

"Do you think an assistant would have any idea what happened to Ruby's nail? He may not have worked there at the time of her autopsy."

"He's a start. We'll still need to speak with Dr. Connor but Robert will have insight into exam room procedures." She dialed the office number listed on his business card.

"Robert Sinclair," he answered with a distracted quality of voice.

"Mr. Sinclair, this is Detective Reid. We met at church on Sunday."

He coughed. "Excuse me. Summer cold. Let me take a drink of water." The line drew silent for about ten seconds. "Detective, yes, how may I help you?"

Keeping her statement of events as concise as possible, Charlotte explained the dissimilarity they'd discovered in Ruby's nail. "There was no reference to trimming the nail in the autopsy report and no trace evidence was found on her nails. Is there a reason someone would smooth her nail and not include it on the report?"

"I can't say for sure." The sound of his breathing punctuated the quiet after his sentence.

"Did you work in that office six years ago when Ruby Reid's autopsy was performed? If so, do you recall anything in the exam that stood out?"

"I've worked for the Baton Rouge Medical Examiner's office for eight years and assisted with hundreds of autopsies. I'm sorry, but the details of that particular one doesn't stand out." He paused again. "Normally, anything removed from the body, even pieces of fingernail for testing, would be cataloged and included in the report."

Her gut buzzed with hope. Had they finally found an obscure clue that would lead them to the killer? "When will Dr. Connor be free today?"

"He'll be working on the autopsy for hours, then elbow-deep in sending off reports and samples for testing," Robert said. "He has to-morrow off. A golf day, I think. You could try and catch him at the country club."

She had to speak with Dr. Connor today. If lives weren't in immediate danger, she could handle a day or two's wait. "Thank you for your insight. If you see Dr. Connor, please let him know I need to speak with him."

"Of course. Good day, Detective."

Detective. A title she'd recently been doubting she deserved. The killer called her detective to mock her. Soon, she'd no longer hear his digitally altered voice in her head.

"We're going to Baton Rouge." Her gaze met Austin's and held. "The answers we need are there and we need them now."

He grabbed his sunglasses and bag from off the table. "Are we taking the special-agent-mobile?"

"Why not? Put the miles on the federal government's tab." Gathering the photographs and paperwork from Ruby's autopsy, she cautiously placed everything inside the folders they'd previously been housed in. Taking one more glimpse of Ruby's pale face, she firmed her resolve. "Your death will be avenged. I promise you."

She climbed into Austin's black SUV and clipped the seat belt. A new clue pointed them to Baton Rouge. She'd follow its path no matter how many twists or turns it held.

Chapter Fifteen

Austin couldn't avoid taking his supervisor's call forever. He had three missed calls from his home office today. After arriving at the medical examiner's office in Baton Rouge, he checked his voice mail.

"I need to call my supervisor." He couldn't help but notice the grimace on her face at hearing the word *supervisor*. His obligation was to the FBI, first and foremost. If not for his job, he wouldn't be here. The FBI provided Austin with the means to use his skills to continue hunting killers, and therefore continuing Caleb's legacy.

"I'll go inside and let Dr. Connor's office know we aren't leaving until we speak with him." Instead of making quickly for the front door, she hesitated. "Will they reassign you when we may be closing in on the killer?"

"I'm not leaving. If my supervisor has other

plans, then I'll convince him that my only job is pursuing the Presque Killer." Tomorrow at midnight was the deadline. A deadline in every sense of the term.

She rested her hand on his forearm. "Don't abandon me." With that plea, she went inside the office.

Austin had learned the hard way not to make promises in his line of work. The good guys sometimes didn't find the bad guy. He occasionally left without providing the answers people desperately needed. Promises were too often broken, even with well-meaning intentions.

He called his supervisor's direct line. "It's Austin."

"Walsh, about time I heard from you. You still avoiding my calls?"

"Of course not, sir." Not on purpose. Or at least not mostly on purpose. He'd rather avoid hearing the word of his removal from this case than argue with his superior on why he had to stay. "We have a potential break in one of the cold cases. I'm at the ME's office with Detective Reid to dig a little deeper."

"Do you think this break will point in a direction of substance?" his supervisor asked.

Austin had been asking himself that same

question the entire drive to Baton Rouge with no confident answer. "We have reason to believe someone tampered with the victim's body postmortem."

"Keep tailing that for now," his supervisor said. "I sent you an email link with information about the three murdered hikers found in upstate New York. I'd like you up there—"

"I'm not leaving Louisiana." Disregarding orders could mean the end of his career or at least an end to further advancement.

"If you'd let me finish." His supervisor huffed out a breath. "Your skills are needed in New York. Be ready to head there soon."

"The Presque Killer will be behind bars before I leave." He prayed they'd get him locked away in time to save lives. "I'll read your email. Anything else, sir?"

"No, other than good luck."

When the call ended, Austin hurried into the office building. He exhaled a sigh of relief the moment the air-conditioning hit his face. He found Charlotte seated in a chair in the lobby.

She stood when she saw him enter. "Are you sticking around?"

He nodded. "Until the end." Taking her

hand, he squeezed it. He'd told her the same thing before. This time, he was certain.

"Dr. Connor is still performing an autopsy. I told the receptionist we must speak with him." She glanced over at the pleasant-looking woman seated behind the front desk. "We could be here awhile."

Austin checked the time. Almost noon. The pressure of minutes ticking away caused a wave of panic. "I'll work on compiling a list of everyone who had access to Ruby's body after it was photographed at the crime scene."

"Good idea. I'm sure her body passed through a few hands to get to the medical examiner's office. I want to review her photographs again as see if anything else jumps out." Her face scrunched in apparent pain. Seeing a loved one's lifeless body, especially after murder, was difficult.

"I can do that," he offered. "If you want to make the calls about the chain of custody of Ruby's body."

"No." Charlotte extracted file folders from her bag. "My avoidance at viewing her pictures may have led to the killer remaining free. I need to do this." She asked the receptionist for a private room where they could work while they waited.

Once they were settled, Austin went back out to speak with the receptionist about getting the names of the transport team who'd brought Ruby's body from Presque to Baton Rouge. Someone had smoothed out her nail. Had it been an innocent action that wasn't recorded or something more sinister, like covering up evidence? With any luck, he'd find out soon.

While Charlotte waited for Dr. Connor, she studied every inch of Ruby's crime scene and autopsy photos. The task was gut-wrenching and heartbreaking, and unfortunately it showed no additional inconsistencies.

She checked her phone and clicked on an email from Chief Gunther. He provided a link to a news article, which she opened. Her teeth clenched as she scanned the article's headline—*Detective Reid Spends Time in Worship*. The rest of the article conveyed Charlotte took an hour away from the investigation to attend church. Two women remained missing. Perhaps praying would lead her to the killer, because her work on the murder and kidnapping cases was getting them no closer to providing answers for the victim's families. Included in the article were several pictures of her and Austin standing outside of church. She didn't need to read the author's byline to know Ronald Rheault was responsible.

Not wanting to subject herself to more of his scrutiny, she closed the article and set her cell phone in her purse. If only she had evidence that supported putting Ronald in jail. He seemed to enjoy taunting her as much as the Presque Killer did.

After another hour's wait, Charlotte and Austin were called back. Just like on all her visits prior, she walked down the sterile hallway and through the double doors that opened into the autopsy exam room.

When she entered, a staff member was rolling out a metal table through a door on the other side of the room, taking along the recently autopsied body.

"I hear you need to speak with me." Dr. Connor removed his gloves and then his reading glasses. "What is so urgent?"

Charlotte moved forward. "In reviewing the photographs of Ruby Reid, Special Agent Walsh notice an alteration to one of her fingernails." She took out the two photos that best illustrated the difference in the nail and laid them out on the counter. "Her nail appears broken at the crime scene." Bringing Dr. Connor's attention to the autopsy photo, she indicated the nail of interest. "Do you see the difference?"

Dr. Connor returned his glasses to the bridge of his nose, then clipped on two small, round magnifying glasses, which he flipped down to cover each lens. Leaning in, he stared at one photo then the other, moving back and forth several times. Finally, he straightened and raised the magnifying glasses. "How peculiar. Did my report state a reason for the alteration? I will often clip off some of a damaged nail to send to the lab for testing."

Austin produced a copy of the autopsy report. "Nothing listed in your report and no nail sample was sent to the lab, or at least none that was documented. If the victim broke that nail while struggling with her killer, it held trace evidence."

"I agree. A broken nail on a murder victim, especially one who'd been strangled, would be of keen interest." Dr. Connor took the paperwork from Austin and read through it. "I can think of no reason her nail was trimmed other than someone tampered with it."

"Which is what we're speculating." Charlotte's pulse raced. "Who would have had access to a body—more specifically, Ruby's body—between the location she was found and when you performed your examination?"

"Well," Dr. Connor pondered. "I can't speak for the security at the crime scene. It's possible an officer or crime scene tech could have tampered with the nail after the photographs were taken. My transport team has possession of the body until it reaches my office. It is then transferred to my custody."

"Can you give me the names of the members of the transport team who handled Ruby's body?" Austin asked. "The woman at the front desk didn't have access to that information."

They needed names and they needed them now.

"Let me call in Cindy, who manages the office." He placed a call on the office phone set by his desktop computer.

Within a minute, a silver-haired woman rushed in. She powered up the computer, then placed her fingers on the keyboard. Dr. Connor asked her for the names of the transport team charged with Ruby's body. The office manager typed and clicked with efficiency. Soon, she pointed to two names on the computer screen.

Charlotte wrote them down. Neither sounded familiar. "Do these men still work here?"

"Yes," Cindy responded. "Here are their addresses." She printed out an information sheet on each. "Both are good workers."

Austin removed the printed papers from the nearby printer. "Who else had access to Ruby's body?"

Dr. Connor tapped his chin. "Well, myself, of course. No one else in the office besides my assistants have access to the bodies once they're in our custody."

She already knew one of the assistants. "We've met Robert Sinclair. Who is the other? And were both working here at the time of Ruby's murder?"

"Robert was." The office manager clicked through a few more screens to find the one she wanted. "The other assistant, Ken Murphy, started right before the murder. So yes, both those men worked here back then."

And both had access to Ruby's body. "Will you print out both these men's information?"

The office manager nodded.

"I don't like the insinuation that one of my

employees tampered with a body's fingernail without reporting it to me." The lines in Dr. Connor's forehead deepened. "My assistants transport a body to and from the storage area to the exam room, prepare the body for autopsy, assist in the exam, then return the body to storage. At no time are they charged with doing any of the examination or altering a body without permission from myself."

"We're assuming whoever cleaned off her nail wanted to hide something." Charlotte glanced at the work ID photo of both assistants. She studied Ken's before looking at Robert's. There was something familiar in Robert's boylike face but she couldn't put her finger on what it was. Likely, she'd seen Robert and his wife at church before their conversation on the steps last Sunday.

She scanned Robert's information, including his address, phone number and starting date of employment. "Are any of these men here? I'd like to speak with them."

"Ken assisted in the autopsy I recently completed." Dr. Connor lowered onto a round, rotating stool. "Robert went home sick a little while ago. None of the members of the transport team are at the office."

When she'd spoken to Robert earlier, he had mentioned a summer cold.

"Let me call Ken and ask him to join us." The office manager reached for the phone.

"Wait." Charlotte held her breath while gazing at the work ID picture of Robert. A faint scar on his neck caught her attention. "Can I see the color photo on the computer?"

"Sure." Within seconds, the office manager pulled up Robert's image.

Now the scar was more visible. It was crescent-shaped, appearing like a sliver of the moon. The scar ran from his Adam's apple up to his jawline. Where had she seen a similar scar before? Ruby had a crescent-shaped scar by her elbow. She'd gotten it falling off her tricycle when she was a toddler.

Charlotte pulled up her social media page on her phone and searched for Robert Sinclair's profile page. She studied the photographs on his page. Several included Robert and his wife, Vanessa. She zoomed in to Robert. There was the scar. While zooming back out, a glint of gold caught Charlotte's eye. She closed in on the image on Vanessa's wrist, and her heart stopped at the sight of a gold bracelet with a crescent moon charm. A match to Charlotte's.

"What is it?" Austin leaned in to view the screen on her phone.

"Look." She pointed to the bracelet on Vanessa's wrist then dangled hers. "Robert has a scar on his neck. I can't put my finger on it but I think he might be associated with the killings."

"Really?" Austin's eyes widened. "What connection does he have to you?"

"None that I know of." She pushed her brain to make a connection but nothing came. "Has Robert had any job performance issues or any behavior you'd consider odd?" Charlotte asked Dr. Connor and the office manager.

Both Dr. Connor and the office manager shook their heads in unison.

"He's a great assistant," Dr. Connor replied. "He's accurate and a good worker. It's hard to find people willing to do the work we do here. Some of the things we deal with are not for the faint of heart."

"Dealing with the dead is not for everyone," Austin agreed.

Viewing loss of life never got easier. And seeing the violence people were capable of often left her questioning God and humanity.

"We need to get back to Presque." Charlotte stuffed the papers they'd received from the office manager into her bag. "Thank you both for all your help." She hustled out of the exam room with Austin at her heels.

"What are you thinking?" he asked once they exited the building. He reached for his sunglasses and put them on. The sunlight reflected off the glass front of the building.

"Robert is involved, either directly or working with the killer. I just can't put the pieces together as to why?" She came to a halt, racking her mind for anything that made sense. Why would a nice man with a wife and steady job tamper with a murder victim's body? Why did his wife have an identical bracelet to Charlotte? When Charlotte and Ruby received them as gifts from their mom, about twenty-five years ago, the bracelets had been child-sized. Charlotte had taken both to the jeweler to get them resized to fit their adult wrists. But were those bracelets sold in a size suitable for a woman? Was Vanessa Sinclair owning the same bracelet as Charlotte a coincidence?

And the scar on his neck—so similar to the carvings on the victims' arms. If he hadn't had access to Ruby's body at the medical examiner's office, she might not have paid any attention.

"I think Robert Sinclair may be the Presque

Killer." Speaking the words caused her lips to tingle. They might have a real suspect after all these years. But an arrest needed evidence. All they had now was circumstantial. Regardless, they could get him off the streets for a short while. "Let's go talk to him. We can bring him into the station for questioning."

Austin gazed down at her through his dark sunglasses. "If Robert isn't involved, we could be wasting hours focused on the wrong person."

"I know." Doubt circled in her head. "We find him, talk to him, and see how he reacts. You've spent time with serial killers. Would you recognize if Robert is one?"

He combed his fingers through his hair. "Let's go to his house and find out."

Charlotte climbed up into the SUV. She took out her wallet from her bag and found the old photograph of herself and Ruby. They were standing hand in hand on the shore of the Gulf of Mexico. Her mom had taken the girls to Panama City Beach for a long weekend. That trip had gifted Charlotte with the best memories of her family before her mom was taken away.

She narrowed her gaze to the scar on Ruby's arm. Her killer had cut a similar shape into her other arm. A memory stirred in her brain, like the rumbling of a far-off thunderstorm. It grew louder but she couldn't make out what the voice in her head was trying to say. "Ruby's scar." Holding the photo, she touched her fingertip to Ruby's bare arm. "I remember," she whispered. Ruby holding up her arm to compare her scar to someone else's. Could it be? "Before we visit Robert's house, we need to stop at my place."

Austin glanced at her with a questioning expression.

The pieces of the puzzle were moving closer. A few had clicked together. Now she needed to find the box of old photos she'd kept safe all through her youth in foster care. Inside it could be the key to solving the mystery and catching a killer.

Chapter Sixteen

A man sat on the front porch of Charlotte's home, and the unexpected sight of him sent her pulse racing.

"That's Mr. Lyon. Candy's father." Austin parked the SUV next to the curb in front of her house.

"What is he doing here? I'm not even staying at my house." The sight of him, tired and ragged-looking, answered her question. The father of a kidnapping victim wanted to know the location of his little girl. Was she safe? Still alive? What were they doing to find her and bring her home?

"Mr. Lyon," she said, exiting the SUV.

The tall man remained seated on her front porch steps. Finally, he pushed to his feet at Charlotte's approach. "Have you found Candy?"

Her heart ached at the anguish in his eyes.

"We haven't yet, but we will. The task force is working around the clock."

"Candy is a gentle girl who never hurt no one." Mr. Lyon's voice cracked with grief. "Who would take an innocent girl? I need her back to me, safe, you hear? Bring her back."

"That's what we're working to do." Austin set a hand on one of the man's broad shoulders and squeezed. "Please go home and pray. An entire team is devoted to finding your daughter and bringing her home."

Tears filled Mr. Lyon's eyes. "I've been praying but I'll pray some more." He moved to the sidewalk then stopped. "People say the police don't care about these girls because they had trouble with drugs and drinking. Do you care about my Candy?"

"I do care, deeply." Charlotte wiped away her own tears. "We'll find your daughter and return her to you." The pressure continued to mount. She remembered the feeling of helplessness when Ruby went missing. No amount of platitudes made that horror go away.

Mr. Lyon nodded a wordless acknowledgment and shuffled away down the sidewalk.

She hurried to the back door, then tore down the crime scene tape crisscrossing the entryway.

The yellow plastic ribbon floated to the ground. She unlocked the door and went inside.

"What do you need here?" Austin glanced around the kitchen as if anticipating the killer would jump out from a dark corner.

During the ride home, she didn't give voice to her memories. They were so faded that she questioned whether she'd summoned a false recollection due to desperation. And she was desperate. Two frightened women were being held by the Presque Killer. If the killer weren't stopped by tomorrow at midnight, those women would die. And so would she.

"There's a box of old photographs I need to look through." She made for the stairs and bounded up two at a time.

"Does this have anything to do with Robert Sinclair?" Austin questioned from behind. He followed her up the stairs and into her office. "What are you looking for?"

She opened the closet door in the spare bedroom. "Can you get that down?" Pointing to a shoebox on the top shelf, she thanked God she'd kept all the photos from her youth. The ones with her mom were precious, and more than a few times the box had gone missing at a foster home.

Austin brought the box down and placed it in her outstretched hands.

She set it on the bed and lifted the lid with shaking hands. "When I saw the scar on Robert's neck, it shook loose a memory of my sister comparing the scar on her arm to another's similarly shaped scar. I see it in my mind's eye... Ruby holding up her arm and giggling that they matched."

"Do you think you knew Robert when you were children?" Austin watched Charlotte dump stacks of old color photographs on the bedspread. Most were partially faded. A few were spotted with water stains.

She examined every picture, looking for a boy who could be a young Robert. Most of her memories of her early years with her mom had been placed in a vault and locked away. Thinking of Mom and their chaotic lives together brought anxiety. Charlotte loved her mom, or at least the version of her she'd constructed in her mind. But she'd been afraid. Each move to a new house with a new man upended Charlotte and Ruby's lives.

She'd been eight years old when her mom was arrested and she and Ruby went into foster care. Charlotte hadn't decided which had been more traumatic—the years before the arrest or the ones after.

"My mom had a new boyfriend for what seemed like every month." She fanned through a stack of her grade school pictures. Her blond hair growing longer and wilder with every passing year. "I think she had a boyfriend with a kid. A son. They lived with us for a while." She strained her memory to fit the scattered mental images flashing in her brain. "The boyfriend was a real jerk, like most of Mom's boyfriends. But his son, I think he had a scar on his neck. He said his dad had cut him with a broken beer bottle."

Her search through the pictures intensified. It had to be in here. The recollection of standing in front of a rusty Chrysler remained too strong for it to be false.

"Is this what you're looking for?" Austin held the photo she'd been searching for.

She snatched it from his grip and held it close. Her gaze scanned over Mom, the mean boyfriend, Ruby, Charlotte and a boy about Charlotte's age. Bobby. That had been his name. She looked closely at the boy's neck, and her breath caught. There was the scar, identical to the one on Robert Sinclair. She matched it to the print-out of his work ID picture. "It's him. Here's the connection." To her and Ruby.

"What do you remember about him?" Austin stood.

With the floodgates of the recesses of her mind opened, the memories rushed back. She scrutinized the picture again, noting the uneasy look on each of the children's faces. "Bobby and his dad lived with us shortly before my mom was arrested. I think his dad may have convinced her to go along with some illegal way to make a quick buck and she took the fall. Ruby and I were scared whenever her boyfriend was around, and we usually hid in our bedroom, especially when he'd been drinking. If I remember correctly, Bobby would ask to come in and stay with us, most of the time falling asleep in our room."

"What's Robert's reason for targeting you? Not that a serial killer's actions are logical but the Presque Killer has picked you. He plans to kill you. Every one of the murder victims had your body type and hair color, except for Ruby." Austin halted his pacing to stare down at Charlotte and the photo still held tightly in her hand. "He's obsessed with you."

"I haven't seen him since I was a little girl."

She waved the picture. "Perhaps I've run into him at the medical examiner's office but I didn't make the connection and he never said anything. Even Sunday at church, he acted friendly but not familiar."

"We need to bring him in for questioning." Austin moved toward the doorway.

"He went home sick." Leaving the photographs spread across the bed other than the one that shifted the course of their investigation, Charlotte turned off the light to the bedroom. Could she finally be ready to take down the killer?

Austin stopped before a neatly kept rancher house. A row of bushes lined the front of the property, creating a boundary between the sidewalk and front yard. The Sinclair home appeared to be the residence of a happy, middle-class family. One car sat in the driveway. He touched his gun, which was secured in a holster at his hip.

Charlotte did the same. "Ready?" Her chest rose and lowered with large inhales and exhales.

His nerves hummed as well. A dog barked inside a neighboring house. They'd considered calling in backup and wearing bulletproof vests but decided against it. If Robert were the Presque Killer, he wouldn't be dangerous until cornered. And they might have already tipped him off that he was the killer they hunted.

The Presque Killer held two women. Somewhere. Austin was operating on the assumption they were alive. He held hope they'd be rescued before the killer followed through on his threat.

Charlotte knocked on the door then stepped back.

Within a minute, Vanessa answered. She wore athletic shorts and a blue concert T-shirt. "Hello, Detective Reid. How can I help you?"

"Is your husband home?" Charlotte asked in a calm voice.

"Robert, no. He's at work." Vanessa glanced at her watch. "I guess he's just getting off. He was planning to get together with some of his coworkers for drinks after work, so he won't be home until late. Probably not until after I leave for work."

That caught Austin's attention. He'd theorized the killer either lived alone or shared a house with someone who worked overnight, allowing him to engage in his crimes without anyone noticing he was gone.

"Can we have his cell phone number? I need

to speak with him about a case." Charlotte took out her cell phone, ready to enter his number in her contacts.

"Is this about the Presque Killer?" Vanessa gasped. "Robert said he assisted Dr. Connor with the autopsies. I don't know how he does it. I'm a nurse so sick people and death are part of my job but I couldn't handle examining a dead body."

She has no idea what her husband is capable of. Austin wasn't surprised. Psychopaths often were good at appearing normal. What better cover than a happily married, churchgoing man?

Vanessa rattled off Robert's number, which Charlotte entered into her phone.

"I'll see if I can reach him." Charlotte slipped her phone into the back pocket of her jeans. "You said you work nights at the hospital? How long have you been working those hours?"

"Since I started there about three years ago. I find it's quieter at night than the day shifts. When I met Robert and we got married last year, he was fine with me continuing to work overnights." An easy smile warmed her face. "He's good like that. Very supportive. I have to admit, though, since I got pregnant, it's grown harder to stay awake. It doesn't help I'm picking up extra shifts to save money for when the baby comes."

A baby on the way. Could that have been a stressor that tripped Robert into killing again?

"Congratulations," Austin offered. Though he feared for Vanessa's future if her husband was discovered to be a serial killer. "Hope you have a pleasant rest of your day."

Once the door closed, Austin glanced at Charlotte. More pieces fitting together. "We need to find Robert Sinclair. I don't believe for a second he's throwing back a beer with his work pals."

"Neither do I."

They returned to Austin's SUV, and he drove straight to the station. This update to the police chief should be given in person. An all-out manhunt for Robert Sinclair would commence. With good police work, he'd be found. If they could convince him to give up the location of the kidnapping victims, the community could put this nightmare behind them.

But first, they had to locate Robert. And Austin knew from experience that men like Robert, smart and cunning, were experts at remaining hidden in the shadows and were dangerous when cornered.

Chapter Seventeen

We need more time. A BOLO had been issued for Robert Sinclair, who'd disappeared like a bird in flight. Austin had lived through this before—a suspect going underground after being tipped off to the interest of law enforcement. He assumed Charlotte's phone call with Robert yesterday, asking about Ruby's nail, had been the catalyst for him going into hiding. Neither of them had suspected Robert at the time.

Now he was confident that they'd determined the identity of the Presque Killer. But if Robert wasn't found before midnight tonight, Charlotte and the other women he'd kidnapped might die.

Austin had begged Charlotte this morning to go into hiding for the duration of the manhunt, but true to her stubborn nature, she'd refused. So they'd spent a long night at the station along with some of the other members of the task force, taking calls and trying to track down Robert Sinclair's location.

He'd searched for properties held by Robert and his family. Nothing besides their places of residences. Robert's home was being watched. A warrant had been issued to search the house and property. Austin and Charlotte would be heading over shortly to assist in conducting the search.

Austin stood in the conference room, staring at the pictures of the kidnapping victims pinned to the board.

"Penny for your thoughts." Charlotte approached. She placed a cup of coffee in his hand.

The rich aroma steaming from the cup hinted at the caffeine hit to come. His exhaustion was bone-deep. He recognized the same drawn look on Charlotte's face. Austin vowed to get her through until tomorrow morning alive. Then, once Robert was locked up and the kidnapping victims were safe, they'd sleep for days.

He sipped his coffee with his focus glued to the board. "I want to believe Karen and Candy are still alive."

"My gut tells me they are," Charlotte said beside him. "I think he'll want me there to watch him murder them. Some sort of performance to punish me."

"For what, though? You were both children when he lived at your home." Austin hoped to be able to interrogate Robert soon. He might not offer many answers, at least at first, but in general, serial killers loved talking about themselves and spilled their life story.

"I still don't remember much about that time in my life but living with us must have made an impression on Robert." Charlotte touched the picture of Ruby and sniffled. "What did I do that made him hate me so much?"

"You did nothing. Could be an obsession or a twisted love." Austin turned as Chief Gunther entered the room.

"We have the warrant," the chief said. "You two ready to lead the search of the Sinclair house?"

Austin left the station along with a dozen other law enforcement personnel, with the sick feeling they were wasting time. Although searching Robert's home had to be done, Austin didn't believe he'd keep anything incriminating there. To hold hostages, the killer needed a private, out-of-the-way place. A building no one knew about other than himself. Somewhere close to Presque. A headquarters, so to speak. Once they discovered that location, they'd find him.

During the drive back to the station, Austin tamped down his disappointment. No evidence tying Robert to the murders had been found at the Sinclair home. Now the game was on. Robert knew without a doubt they hunted him while he hunted Charlotte.

Charlotte rode in the passenger seat, gazing out the window. "We have twelve more hours."

He glanced at the clock on the dash. "Robert is close, likely watching us search for him. We'll catch him soon." He approached the city park and was surprised by the number of people milling around.

"The city's jazz festival starts today." She pointed to the banner hung underneath the sign marking the entrance to the sprawling park. "Let's stop. I need to walk around and clear my head."

Once he found a parking spot, they exited the SUV and strolled in the direction of music.

"I need to remind myself why I do this job." She turned her head to take in the people filling the area. Despite the threat of a serial killer in their midst, the residents of Presque had decided to go forward with the town's annual music festival. It pulled in attendees from across the state and beyond.

"People shouldn't have to live in fear." But he could see it in some of the eyes of those he passed. Parents held tight to their children's hands. Women kept in groups. The presence of Presque Police Department and Kingston Parish officers couldn't be missed.

Austin wondered how he'd feel if he came to the city festival on a day in the future, when a dark cloud didn't hang over the event. The city put on a good show. Jazz music filled the air as well as laughter. The aromas drifting from a BBQ food truck made his stomach growl with hunger, reminding him that coffee was not food.

He longed to be part of a community. He hadn't felt a real sense of belonging to a town since his childhood. His army days then career in the FBI meant a life on the move. His work was important. He stopped killers and saved lives. But at what personal cost? There'd been moments when he considered leaving the FBI to pursue a different cause. He could find another line of work that offered a better balance and allowed him a normal life. But then he remembered Caleb and the vow he'd made to his mentor. If Caleb could see Austin struggling against the pull of falling in love, would he make the same request as he had before he died? Had Caleb known the choices Austin made to continue hunting serial killers, what advice would he offer now?

What if he came back to Presque next year to take Charlotte to the jazz festival? He'd hold her hand as they snuggled on a blanket, listening to a band play songs reminiscent of the past. Could he handle sneaking in moments of a normal life? In his line of work, daydreaming could get someone killed. His attention had to remain fixed on the target, not on his beautiful partner, who'd breathed life back into fantasies of love and home. A romanticized normal existence that reality had shattered.

The shouting of a name caught Charlotte's attention.

"Lisa Ann! Lisa Ann!"

Charlotte swung toward the direction of the voice. The jazz festival was in full swing, and packs of attendees sat on lawn chairs and blankets on the grassy area by the stage. Lining the perimeter of the park, food trucks churned out all sorts of delicious eats. But she blocked out everything else except the noise of a name being shouted through the crowd.

"Lisa Ann!" A young woman wearing white shorts and a pink tank top spun around, frantically scanning her surroundings.

Austin had stepped away to make a phone call to the FBI. The feds were sending additional resources to Presque. In addition, computer techs back East were combing databases and records for any clues on where Robert might be hiding.

Charlotte approached the frantic woman and showed her badge. "Detective Reid with the Presque Police Department. Is something wrong?"

The woman's eyes glistened with tears. "My friend Lisa Ann went to use the bathroom thirty minutes ago, and I can't find her."

Glancing to the side, Charlotte watched the flow of people going in and out of the restroom building. "Have you called her?"

"About twenty times." The woman choked back a sob. "I shouldn't have let her go alone, not with women being snatched by a serial killer. We shouldn't have come."

Charlotte set her hand on the woman's shoulder. "Take a deep breath. Let's try to locate her first before we panic. What's your friends full name? Give me a description of what she looks like and what she was wearing."

A few minutes later, Charlotte put a call over the police radio, asking officers to be on the lookout for Lisa Ann Benton, age twenty-four, approximately five feet six inches and weighing 120 pounds. She provided hair color, clothing and area last known to be at.

She took down the friend's phone number and name, praying they'd find Lisa Ann. Perhaps she'd found another group of friends to hang with for a while, or a food truck had grabbed her interest and she sat at a picnic table enjoying a paper tray full of BBQ. But what were the odds Lisa Ann was too transfixed on food to answer her friend's calls?

An hour later, Charlotte received a call on her police radio. She and Austin had spent the time patrolling the park in a desperate search for a woman fitting Lisa Ann's description. They hurried to where the officer had radioed from.

"I found a cell phone lying here on the ground." The officer directed their view to a cell phone with a pink case resting facedown on the grass. This space was set back from the main part of the jazz festival. A wooded section created a buffer between the park and an industrial area.

Austin put on gloves and turned the phone face up. He touched the screen and a photograph of the woman they'd been searching for appeared.

Charlotte's gaze concentrated on the space filled with trees and brush. She took measured steps, scanning for a footprint or anything else that might have dropped. About ten feet into the woods, she halted at a flash of light on metal. She bent over to find a silver ring partially buried under dead palm fronds. "Over here," she yelled.

The ring was identified as Lisa Ann's. Within minutes, the jazz music quieted and officers began questioning those at the park. With so many people around, someone had to have seen Lisa Ann escorted into the woods by a man.

"We have a witness." Austin ended a call. "A man with his daughter was over by the playground when he saw a woman matching Lisa Ann's description being held by the elbow by a man wearing a baseball cap and sunglasses. The witness commented that he thought they were a couple taking a break from the festival."

"He has her." Her stomach churned. The time on her cell phone glowed 4:00 p.m. "I'm next."

"No, you're not." Austin gripped her shoulders and stared straight into her eyes. "We're going to find him and the women he's captured."

Bile rose in her throat. She'd known all along the possibility of death hovered over her like an executioner's blade. Would her body be dumped in a mucky ditch like Ruby's had? Would she be found before animals got to her? She commanded herself to regain calm. She wasn't giving up. On the contrary, she planned to fight with everything she had.

Charlotte called all available members of law enforcement to the quickly established command center by the empty jazz festival stage. She directed teams to fan out and search the entire park and forest area.

Robert had likely parked his car by the industrial park then drove off with his prey. *Where have you taken them?* If he planned to come back for Charlotte, he couldn't have gone far.

"I want to take another look around the Sinclair property," she said to Austin. "Maybe we missed something." It was a long shot. His home and grounds had already been fully searched. But she wanted to walk through again. He was killing because of a sick connection to her. She might find a clue the others had missed.

"Let's go, then." Austin shot off a text while he walked along her side to the SUV. "So far, the FBI techs can't find any other property tied to Robert Sinclair or his family."

"He's hiding somewhere." She visualized the hundreds of acres of bayou surrounding Presque and nearby communities. An old fishing shack likely wouldn't have a property deed.

When she arrived at the Sinclair house, a pair of officers greeted them. After showing their credentials, she and Austin entered the house. The silence was unnerving. Vanessa had been escorted off the property and taken to her parents' house. She denied her husband was the Presque Killer, and without solid evidence, Charlotte wasn't in a position to convince her otherwise. Robert needed to be found first. A prosecutor wouldn't charge a person with the evidence she and Austin had pulled together so far.

But DNA didn't lie. Earlier, his toothbrush and hairbrush had been collected and taken to the lab for testing. A match wouldn't lead them to Robert's hideout. And they had to stop him by the end of the day. Only eight more hours.

Austin stood outside under a tall live oak that during the daytime provided shade to the Sinclair house. Now dusk fell, along with an evil darkness. He'd combed through every inch of Robert Sinclair's house and grounds and found nothing that hinted he wasn't an ordinary man living a boring life.

After studying the time line of Robert's life, Austin concluded Robert's childhood had been filled with abuse. He'd attended college and landed a job as a mortuary assistant before working at the medical examiner's office. Robert didn't seem to mind death. Actually, he'd made it his life's work. Austin calculated that Robert began dating Vanessa shortly after killing Ruby. Which explained the break. He'd tried to live a normal life. Something must have happened to trigger him back into killing, and escalating his activity. Could be the announcement of Vanessa's pregnancy. Or his path recently crossed with Charlotte. Perhaps he and Vanessa had gone to Charlotte's church before last Sunday. Likely a combination of factors.

Charlotte approached from the direction of

the house, ending a call. "Robert has vanished off the face of the earth. No sign of his car. No one has seen him since work earlier today when he left. He didn't come home." She blew out a long breath. "He's going to kill those girls if we don't stop him soon."

He checked the time. Only five more hours until midnight. They walked the property again. A small toolshed didn't provide any enlightenment. Vanessa hadn't offered any suggestions on where her husband could be. She'd closed up and hired a lawyer, who wouldn't let them near her for further questioning.

Austin tightened his hands into fists. He wouldn't allow anyone to stand in their way of finding Robert.

Tick, tick, tick. The sound in her head grew louder by the second. Charlotte knew what she had to do. They'd exhausted all other efforts. "I have a plan."

As they stood by the SUV at the front of the house, Austin's gaze snapped to focus on Charlotte. "Good, because I've run into a brick wall. What is it?"

The chorus of croaking bullfrogs seemed to keep time with her rapidly beating heart. "Robert wants me. I'm his ultimate prize. My death will satisfy his need to kill."

"I don't like where this is going." Austin scowled.

She held up her hands. "I give him what he wants."

"No," Austin barked. "We aren't sacrificing you."

"I don't plan on being killed." Though there was always the possibility. She wouldn't think about that right now. Fear of the unknown wouldn't stop her. "I'll be the bait you use to catch him."

His scowl deepened, as did the furrow lines between his eyebrows. "And what if we lose you? I'm not offering you up on the hopes he doesn't get away. Like he's had every other time, need I remind you."

The Presque Killer was smart. He'd evaded them for more than six years. "He's never taken a victim who's ready for him. I'll be ready. I will make it out alive with the women he's holding."

"No." Austin waved his hands in the air like a football referee calling a missed catch. "We're closing in on him, Charlotte."

"There's no more time." She stepped toward

him, putting only inches between them. "This is the only way."

He turned his head to look away. "I can't take the chance I'll lose you." His voice cracked.

"You've sent in people undercover before," she pleaded her case. Though she'd go forward with her plan alone if necessary.

Austin brushed his knuckles across her cheek, then held strands of her lose hair in between his fingertips. "You aren't just anyone. Not to me. I trust you're capable but I'm afraid Robert Sinclair is too large a risk to put your life in his hands."

Her heart raced at Austin's touch. As deeply as she valued his concern, Charlotte refused to back down. Using her as bait was likely the only way to get to him before he killed again.

Finally, Austin broke the stalemate. "Okay," he huffed. "I'll agree, but only if you wear a GPS tracker. Two even just in case. I have some back at the police station. You wear them and we'll track your movements the entire time. We'll be able to see where he's taking you then send in a rescue team."

"We make a dynamic duo." For the first time in a week, hope bubbled. She glanced around the dark front yard. "Do you think he's watching us?" she whispered.

"Possibly." He kept his gaze fixed on Charlotte. "You can change your mind at any time."

"I won't." Her resolution firmed to see this until the end, with Robert in handcuffs. Time to play offense. "We're going to take him down." She grinned. "I will win his game and make sure he never hurts another innocent person again."

He held open the passenger-side door of the SUV for Charlotte to climb in. "My money is on you, Reid. Always has been. Always will be."

Chapter Eighteen

"Are you sure?" Austin pressed a nickel-sized disk into the insole of Charlotte's sneaker. "There's no shame in backing out."

If she decided to pull the plug and abort the mission, Charlotte would live with the repercussions for the rest of her life. That was if they were able to catch the Presque Killer before he found, captured and murdered her.

"I'm sure." Her stomach fluttered with nerves. She wasn't concerned for her safety as much as she feared failing to lead the rescue team to the kidnapped women. It was all or nothing. Tonight had to be Robert's last hours as a free man.

Austin then handed the shoe to Charlotte. "Okay, then, everyone needs to follow the plan and make sure the operation goes perfectly." He faced a room filled with SWAT team officers who'd been called in for the important job of capturing Robert Sinclair and rescuing the women he was holding captive. "Detective Reid is wearing three GPS trackers. One in her coat pocket, one sewn inside the front pocket of her jeans, and the final one hidden inside her shoe. Her movements will be tracked. It's imperative that we don't give away our surveillance. Robert must lead us to his hideout. Three women are still missing and their families are counting on us to bring them home."

A murmur of voices filled the room before quieting.

"This is what we've been working for. We will bring the Presque Killer to justice." Charlotte slipped her hand into the pocket of her jacket and felt the bump of the GPS tracker. It was no bigger than a nickel, but Austin was confident that the GPS system inside was one of the most sophisticated available. Still, technology failed. And just because they hid three GPS tracking devices on her didn't mean Robert wouldn't find them or have a way to disable the signal.

She needed to have faith—in God, in Austin, and in the men and women assembled here, ready to risk their lives to catch a killer.

"Let's go." Austin dismissed the team to prepare. He turned to face Charlotte, and his eyes held a deep well of emotion. "I have your back." If he could, he'd hide her away someplace safe until the killer was found. But letting others be placed at risk while she stayed protected wasn't in Charlotte's nature, so he'd do anything necessary to ensure she came out of the mission unharmed. "The entire team has your back. He won't hurt you."

His words sounded reassuring to her ears but her head knew there were no guarantees during an undercover mission. Too many factors that quickly could spin out of control. *Don't think about that now.* Instead, she imagined Robert being hauled away in handcuffs.

She grabbed her bag and headed toward the door. Time to get to work.

Austin followed her out into the humid night air. "I'll see you soon." He paused as she continued walking to her car.

Before she could grab the door handle, he rushed up and pulled her into his arms. "Be safe," he whispered with his lips pressed to her ear. "God be with you."

"Until we're together again." Her fear calmed. God would be with her. He'd be right beside her every step of the way. And Austin wouldn't be far either. Her heart swelled with love for the man she'd tried so hard not to fall for again.

The next part of their conversation had been preplanned. Staged for the sake of Robert, who could be watching at this moment.

"Are you sure you should go back to the Sinclair house?" Austin asked. "If you wait for about thirty minutes, I'll go with you."

"I can't wait." She added urgency to her voice. "Two officers are still there to guard the property. I'll make sure to stay close by. I just need to walk through the house one more time. I feel I missed something." Charlotte got into her car and started the engine. After waving to Austin, who stood like a statue underneath the yellow glow of a parking lot light, she exited the lot.

Soon, she'd be back under the Presque Killer's control. Only this time, she was ready for him.

At the Sinclair house, she greeted the two officers who'd been assigned to stand guard over the home of a suspected serial killer. The officers had been let in on the plan, so they faded into the interior of the house while Charlotte headed toward the backyard. She turned on her flashlight and swept its beam over the grass. Trekking across the yard, she made her way to the storage shed. She was searching for something, desperate to find the one clue that would take her to the killer. Or at least that was what she wanted Robert to believe. She had no doubt he was close by, observing her. Creeping closer.

Her hand connected with the metal handle of the shed door at the same time she felt a familiar prick at the back of her neck. She cried out, partially for performance and partially due to real panic.

"I underestimated you, Detective." Robert's real voice hummed. "You figured me out. It's going to break Vanessa's heart that I have to disappear after tonight."

Charlotte tried to speak but her mouth felt dry and tasted of metal. "No," was all she managed to say.

"Don't worry. It will all be over soon." The sound of his words grew distant.

She blinked in a futile attempt to stay conscious. How could she see where he was taking her? Her foggy mind recalled the GPS trackers. "Austin." The last thought to cross her mind was the FBI special agent she'd grown to love, who was charged with saving her.

★ ★ ★

"They're on the move." Austin sat in the passenger seat with his laptop open, his eyes fixed on a blue dot moving slowly on the screen. A group of three vehicles was lined up on a street a block away from the Sinclair house. They were monitoring Charlotte from a distance. The last thing they wanted to do was spook Robert. He held three other women besides Charlotte, and Austin believed they were all still alive.

The tracker showed Charlotte moving through the wooded lot behind Sinclair's property. He'd wait until she reached the road and likely a car before his team would depart to follow.

Each flash of the dot tracking Charlotte felt like a heartbeat. His connection to her was stronger than a satellite signal. What would that mean for them after his assignment was complete? Charlotte might not feel the same. She could be happy for their work partnership to end, mission complete, and see him board a plane for home. But he wouldn't be satisfied leaving on those terms.

"Let me know when you want to go," the driver of the car said.

"Give them a little more time." Without

warning, the tracking dots disappeared from the computer screen. His breath caught in his throat. He held up his handheld radio to his mouth. "What's going on? I lost the GPS signal."

"So did the computers in the command room. Hold positions until we can bring the signals back on line."

Austin pounded the car window and shouted in frustration. The GPS trackers were his only link to Charlotte. "Go," he ordered the driver. "I'm not sitting here while they get away."

Fifteen minutes later, Austin's anger boiled over. The GPS signal hadn't been recovered. The street that bordered the woods of Charlotte's last-known location was empty of people and vehicles. Had Robert found the trackers on her and destroyed them? Austin had been foolish to think they could outsmart the Presque Killer. He pictured Charlotte, bound and afraid. Then another image appeared in his mind. Charlotte Reid was a fighter. Maybe Robert had outmaneuvered everyone else but Austin believed the killer wouldn't outsmart Charlotte.

Please God, stay with her and give her strength and wisdom. Austin continued to pray.

★ ★ ★

Charlotte's awareness slowly returned. Her mind felt foggy. It took almost a minute to remember what happened or where she was. Or more specifically, who she was with. A deafening roar drowned out all other noises. She blinked her eyes open and gazed up at the night sky moving quickly above. The smell of murky water and moss and the whirring noise of fan blades informed her that she was on an airboat, gliding through the bayou. High above in the heavens, stars twinkled and the waxing moon shone bright. *Guide Austin to me.*

She attempted to move. Her body was wrapped tight in some sort of blanket. With every effort to free herself, she produced a crinkling sound. She tipped her chin to try and view what bound her. The shine off the silver metallic blankets confused her initially. The air temperature remained warm all night, so why would he secure her in emergency warming blankets? She looked like a gas station burrito, which would have made her laugh under any other circumstance.

The reason for the blankets struck her so hard she gasped. The metal on the blankets wasn't to keep her warm. It was to block any GPS sig-

nals. The moment Robert wrapped her entire
body, from neck to shoes, in these blankets, the
trackers must've stopped providing Austin and
the rescue team with her location. She was left
on her own with a killer.

Charlotte struggled to free herself. The cord
wrapped around her body held tight. Robert
was taking her somewhere in the bayou. She
hoped he'd bring her to the place he was keeping the other women. Once they arrived, she
must free herself and his captives. No one was
coming to save them.

She glanced over at Robert, seated up by the
giant fan propeller in the back, smiling with his
success. He'd outsmarted everyone once again.
Or at least that was what he thought.

They'd placed three GPS trackers on her. The
one in her jacket pocket and jeans pocket were
stuck under the blanket. She had no freedom
of movement to get them out. But her shoe.
She might be able to slip it off her foot. Would
Robert question if she were shoeless when they
arrived at their destination?

The warming blanket around her feet was
wrapped loosely. Charlotte moved her feet back
and forth in small kicks to produce an opening in the folds of the blanket. The tracker was

inside the sole of her left shoe. And although she could stick out her shoe and leave it on, she worried Robert would wrap up her feet again or have another trick at their destination to block the signal.

Using the sole of her right shoe, she pushed down on the left heel. She had never been one to tie her laces tight, and after a short while, her left shoe slipped off her foot. She shoved it out from under the protection of the blanket through the opening she'd made earlier. With her heart racing, she slipped off the right shoe and then forced it out to join its mate. Now both feet were shoeless, and she prayed Robert would be too distracted to notice her stocking feet.

One GPS tracker now had an unobstructed line up into the sky. For how long? Hopefully long enough for the boat to reach its destination, providing Austin with her location.

The sound of the propellers quieted and the boat slowed. It passed underneath thick tree branches draped with Spanish moss. In the dark, they looked like skeletons wearing ragged clothing. The moonlight that had provided comfort had been replaced by spooky shadows. They traveled slowly, creeping along past bald cypresses standing majestically over their swampy dominion.

The boat glided to a stop, bumping into a solid surface.

"Welcome, Detective. I've been anticipating having you as a guest." Robert's voice blended with the deafening sounds of the croaking of bull frogs and droning insects. He hauled her up with surprising strength. Once she was upright, he climbed on the dock and pulled her up with him.

She could barely keep her balance. Her movement was so restricted by what she now saw as red nylon cording. Being pulled along by Robert, she waddled across the short dock then onto the front porch of a shack that had seen better days. These types of buildings had been built as fishing and hunting lodges, and for men to come out into the swamp and drink while escaping their families. Often the shacks, which were poorly built on wood pylons, fell into disrepair and were taken back by the bayou. The one that Robert had taken her to appeared to be on a similar route.

Robert stopped by the front door of the rundown stilt house. He pointed to the porch covering. "Metal roofing. If you got anything on you that's sending a tracking signal, it's not getting through the metal sheets covering the roof." His fingers worked to untie the cord. He unwrapped her, then tossed the balled-up emergency blankets on the porch. He reused the cord to tie Charlotte's wrists behind her back and then to secure her ankles.

Although she wanted to struggle, the drugs he'd given her hadn't fully left her system. Her muscles felt weak, and her brain remained foggy. She fought the urge to glance at the boat to make sure her shoe was still inside. The trees might weaken the GPS signal but it would have a better chance at reaching Austin than on her foot as she was led into the house.

Her gazed scanned the dark interior, searching for other signs of life. "Where are the others?" They had to be here. They had to still be alive.

"The reunion will commence shortly." Robert gripped her arm and guided her to a metal kitchen chair. "Take a seat and get comfortable." He made quick work of tying Charlotte to the chair.

She strained against her bonds but the cord wouldn't give. "I remember you, Bobby. I found a picture of us with our parents and

Ruby. How did you end up like this? A cold-blooded killer. You stole Ruby from me." Grief and rage blended together, creating a storm inside her. Looking into Robert's cold, emotionless eyes, Charlotte couldn't believe he was the same man she'd spoken with at church less than a week ago. Or that he was the same little boy who'd hidden from his father in her and Ruby's bedroom.

"I'm pleased your memory has been jogged. I can't begin to explain how distressing it is to see someone again, someone who you felt so close to at one time in your life, who does not recall your name." Robert pushed back the curtain covering a window and gazed outside. No light filtered through the dirty glass pane. He let the curtain fall back into place, then reached for a lantern hanging on a long nail set in the wall. After a few clicks, the room was illuminated by the glow of the propane lantern. Robert held the lantern up to his face. "Charlotte and Ruby, the inseparable sisters. You always looked out for each other."

"Until you killed Ruby," she hissed. "Why? Help me to understand why you kill? Why you wanted me to be the one to try to stop you?"

His sinister laugh bounced off the tight walls. "Your question only shows how little you understand of human nature. How little you cared about anyone else besides yourself and your sister. My days with you were a blip in your timeline. For me, they were the only bright spot of my childhood."

"Help me understand." A plea meant to buy time. She wasn't sure how long they'd been traveling before she woke up in the boat, but once Austin got a GPS signal of her location, it would take him a while to reach her.

Robert pulled out chair matching the one Charlotte was tied to, and dragged it over. The metal feet scraped across the raw plank flooring. He sat, feet spread, elbows on his knees, so his face was only inches away. "When I moved into your house, I thought I'd won the lottery. My mom had taken off before I was out of diapers. Your mom was so kind and loving. You look just like her, you know. She had a kind heart, unlike her daughters."

"Ruby and I didn't mean to exclude you. Our mom had people coming in and out of our lives all the time. We didn't grow attached to anyone." A manual clock hung on the wall. The ticking of the second hand boomed in Charlotte's ears. Ten minutes until midnight.

"I was only looking for a friend." His warm breath smelled foul.

She almost gagged. "I had a rough childhood too. Ruby and I went into foster care shortly after you and your dad moved out. Then our mom died in prison. I didn't grow up to be a serial killer."

"No. You became a police officer. Respected in the community. Unlike Ruby, who became a disgrace. But in actuality, I felt sympathy for her. She had to try and live up to a big sister who could do no wrong." He shook his head. "Ruby cried out for you to save her. How does that make you feel, Charlotte, to know your sister was looking for you and you never came?"

Charlotte burned with rage and stretched the cord around her wrists, trying to break free. All thought of the ongoing rescue operation had been replaced with the need to wipe that disgusting smile off Robert's face. Her bonds held no matter how she fought.

Rational thinking returned, and she stilled. Austin and his team needed more time. She had to keep Robert talking. Soon, the man known as the Presque Killer would prepare to take more lives, including her own. Would he strangle her like he did the others? What would her final thoughts be right at the end?

No. She had to fight. Good had to win.

Chapter Nineteen

"It's time for you to meet my other guests." Robert stood and kicked back his chair, sending it tumbling to the ground.

She instinctively recoiled, though her movement was restricted. At least he hadn't covered her mouth. "What brought you to this point, Robert? You've murdered five people, that we know of. And you want to add four more. There has to be a better way to deal with what you're feeling than killing."

"Somehow, I managed to survive childhood with only a few broken bones and emotional scars. For the most part I was able to blend in. No matter how hard I tried to be normal, dying and death continued to fascinate me. So I studied biology and pathology. Dealing with the dead during an autopsy satisfied my curiosity. Then, seven years ago, I traveled to Presque to attend the jazz festival." While he spoke, Robert wound and unwound a two foot section of red cord around his left hand.

Charlotte imagined the feeling of the cord around her neck. *Hurry, Austin.*

"Do you recall me coming up to you after the first band finished their set?" He stared down at her through narrowed eyes. "Of course you don't. I tried to talk with you but you barely looked at me."

"I'm sorry. I should have remembered you. To be honest, I blocked out much of that time with my mom. It's too painful for me to relive those years." Perhaps reminding him again that her childhood had left scars too.

"I saw you still wore that gold bracelet with the crescent moon." He continued talking as if she hadn't spoken. "A rage filled me. Ruby always had your love. Back when we were children and as adults. Not me. You acted like you cared about me but you never did. Not like you did Ruby. I thought if I snuff out the lives of women who looked like you, I'd feel at peace. Then I figured if I took away the one person you love, I'd be vindicated. And it worked, for a little while."

"You found a love of your own." The sick, twisted man standing before her wasn't worthy of love. He'd acted like a God-fearing man to trick a woman into marrying him. "Vanessa is pregnant. Robert, please don't hurt anyone else. Let us all go then turn yourself in. You're going to be a father."

"I never wanted that." His mouth twisted in a scowl. "Can you imagine me, responsible for raising another human being? I'm even worse than my own dad. I won't do to my kid what my dad did to me. No, Vanessa will be better off raising the kid alone." He lurched forward, untied Charlotte and dragged her to her feet. "It's finally midnight. You had more than enough time to stop me. I win. Let's go claim my prize."

She struggled against him as he yanked her toward a closed door at the back of the room. He swung open the door and shoved Charlotte inside. She landed hard on her knees, crying out in pain. An awful smell hit her, and she struggled to breathe the stale air. Then, she heard muffled cries.

When her eyes adjusted to the darkness of the room, Charlotte stilled at the sight of three women seated and bound in chairs—Karen Tremont, Candy Lyon and Lisa Ann Benton. At seeing Charlotte, their cries increased.

"Who's going first?" Robert strode before the three women, letting his gaze linger on each. "You'll be last, Detective Charlotte Reid. I'm sure after all the years of chasing me, you'd like a chance to observe my work."

"Stop, Robert!" Despite the volume of her cry, her voice didn't register with Robert, who was too fixated on his selection.

"Let's begin with the one who's been trapped here the longest." He grabbed Karen by the hair and yanked back her head. Robert stared down into her terrified eyes. "Put her out of her misery."

Charlotte struggled to get back up on her feet. Compelled by the will to protect, she lurched forward, ready to fight to her last breath.

"Go faster," Austin yelled at the airboat driver. "We're almost there." His gaze had barely left his laptop screen since the GPS signal had been restored. He'd almost kissed that flashing blue dot when it reappeared. Those with better knowledge of the area than Austin informed the team that Robert had taken Charlotte into a bayou approximately fifteen miles south of town.

Austin had never moved so fast or yelled

commands so loudly. Within minutes, they'd been speeding to the nearest landing. A group of airboats and drivers had been assembled on short notice, showing the resolve of the community to capture the man who'd terrorized them for too long.

The loss of the GPS signal had brought him to his knees. He'd raged they wouldn't be able to locate Charlotte or the kidnapping victims before it was too late. Now he was about a mile away from the source of the last remaining signal they tracked. He prayed it would lead him to Charlotte's location and not a spot where Robert had dumped a tracker. The number shown on the computer screen matched the number to the tracker he'd put inside her shoe. Robert might have found and disposed of the others but a tracker hidden inside the sole of a tennis shoe would be more difficult to find.

Without warning, all boat propellers were silenced. "We're close now," the driver of his airboat said. "Don't want to advertise we're coming. Grab an oar and quietly start rowing."

Austin, along with a member of the SWAT team, did as instructed. The boat glided over the water in the direction the driver indicated. Soon, they entered a forest growing out of the water. A bird cried overhead. Something splashed in the dark water nearby. A shadow of a large object hovering above the water's surface appeared. When the boat grew closer, he recognized the shape as a house built on stilts. It appeared to have been built many years ago and the next strong storm could blow it over.

Weak light spilled out the two windows at the front of the house. Besides the sounds of animals and insects, all was quiet and still.

Once his boat connected with the rickety dock attached to the house, Austin hopped up and out. He removed his gun from the holster and switched off the safety. Five members of the SWAT team joined Austin on the deck and unholstered their weapons. Three others remained behind a boat in case the suspect fled.

He gazed down into Robert's airboat and noticed Charlotte's shoes lying on the bottom. Smart. The metal roof of the house would block GPS signals coming from inside. Austin checked his emotions, which had bubbled up and spilled over like a pot of boiling water. Right now, he needed a clear head. After years of keeping a tight lid on his feelings, the possibility of losing Charlotte had turned up the heat. He couldn't bear the thought of facing a future without her. He loved her. She'd altered his life's goals. He needed Charlotte's light to escape the dark.

"There are four female victims being held inside," he whispered. "Only fire your weapon as a last resort."

After getting a visual confirmation each team member was ready, Austin crept to the door and gave the hand signal to breach. As they moved in, he prayed they weren't too late.

Charlotte had tried and failed. She'd been restrained again, tied up so tightly to a kitchen chair that she could barely breathe. Tears spilled down her face.

Robert, positioned behind Karen, wrapped a strand of red cord around her neck. "Quiet now. It will all be over soon."

A crash sounded from the front room, making them all jump.

"Robert Sinclair," a man shouted. "Surrender. You're under arrest."

"Austin," Charlotte cried out through the gag covering her mouth. He'd come. He'd found her.

Robert released the red cord and searched the

room for an escape. His eyes looked wild, like those of a trapped animal.

Austin burst into the room. He rushed to Charlotte and pulled down the gag on her mouth. "Are you all right?"

"He's getting away." While she appreciated his concern, capturing the Presque Killer was the priority.

An enraged scream sounded as Robert ran toward an open window.

"Stop!" Austin rushed forward, gun drawn.

Robert produced a gun of his own from the waist of his jeans, pointed and fired at Austin.

Fortunately, the bulled missed, striking the wall. All four women, including Charlotte, cried out.

In response, Austin took a shot, which struck Robert in the leg as he was fleeing through the window opening.

Robert fell and splashed into the water below.

Soon, a boat floated to the rear of the house and gave a brief chase. Robert, who was swimming, didn't stand a chance. "We got him," a SWAT team member yelled.

"Is he really captured?" Charlotte shook out her hands after one of the men who'd arrived with Austin untied the cord around her wrists.

Once her body was freed, she rushed to the window. Below, she saw an airboat with three men dressed in black with rifles strapped to their backs and headlamps glowing on their heads. The boat also carried the driver and one other passenger, who appeared to be treating Robert's nonlethal gunshot wound. A feral-looking Robert Sinclair lay surrounded on the bottom of the boat, soaking wet, with no chance of escape.

Charlotte removed her gaze from Robert to the three women in the room who were standing, free. Charlotte hugged each of them, then guided the women outside and into an airboat that would take them home. She watched the boat disappear into the darkness, and her legs began trembling. She grabbed a post to hold herself steady.

A strong arm wrapped around her waist and pulled her close. She leaned into Austin's strength. Every ounce of her own had been drained. She peered up at him. He looked uncharacteristically disheveled. His tousled dark hair complemented the stubble covering his lower face. Before heading out on the mission, he'd changed out of his usual dress clothes into black cargo pants and a black long-sleeved shirt covered with a bulletproof vest. Admittedly, she loved this rugged tactical look as much as his suave FBI special agent persona.

"It's over." He stared out into the distance. "Robert is being taken directly to jail."

"It's really over." The possibility seemed unreal. "He blames me for his need to murder. He killed Ruby as revenge for me loving my sister but not himself as a brother." Her chest tightened. Would she ever fully process the information Robert had provided? "He came up to me at the jazz festival seven years ago and I didn't remember him." Pain seared her heart. "If only I had remembered, all those he murdered would still be alive."

"Don't play that game." Austin held her upper arms and met her gaze. "A serial killer like Robert would have acted the same under different circumstances. It's not your fault he fixated on you."

She tried to shake out of his hold but his grip held firm. Charlotte wanted to run away and hide forever. How could she face the rest of her life haunted by Robert's actions? She'd jump in the water and swim away if she weren't so fearful of the murky water filled with alligators.

"Three women are alive today due to your

bravery, Charlotte." He gave her a little shake to regain her attention. "You saved those women. If you hadn't allowed yourself to be captured, he would have killed them."

His words sank in. Karen, Candy and Lisa Ann were free. They'd survived. Because Charlotte had faced a monster. "Well, you and your team saved the day."

One side of his mouth lifted. "You probably want your shoes back. How did he manage to block the GPS signal until you reached here?"

She pointed to the emergency blankets tossed in the corner of the porch. "He's smart, I'll give him that. But I'm smarter."

"Yes, you are." Austin kissed the top of her head.

Love for this wonderful man burst inside her. No use denying the obvious. No more fighting the pull. God had placed them together again for a purpose. She understood His purpose was greater than anything she could have imagined. A yawn as deep and wide as the Grand Canyon escaped her mouth. "As soon as I know Robert is locked up, securely behind bars, I'm taking a shower then sleeping for days."

"I can get behind that. Do you mind waiting until the crime scene techs and Chief Gunther arrive? Chief offered to be in charge of this crime scene so I can get you home."

Home. She pondered the reality of going home. With the killer caught, Austin would leave soon. On to his next assignment. And what about Charlotte? What came next for her life? Had the events surrounding the Presque Killer drained her to the level she had nothing left for law enforcement? Only time would tell.

She had a few more days with Austin. Then she'd once again say goodbye. Finally, she understood his commitment to his job didn't exclude him from a romantic relationship. Not when she was willing to sacrifice to make a relationship with him work. He'd need to fully let down his emotional guard, which she noticed had slipped more and more over their week working together.

The last time he'd left Presque, she'd allowed hurt to spill over into anger. She couldn't allow others to dictate her actions. To capture the Presque Killer, she'd stopped playing the killer's game and devised her own strategy. When facing her fears, she'd switched from defense to offense. Now she needed to take the initiative again in order to succeed at love.

Chapter Twenty

Two days later, Austin knocked on Charlotte's front door. His packed suitcase waited inside the SUV. He was leaving for Baton Rouge. His flight left in four hours. But he wasn't ready to say goodbye.

Since the night in the bayou when they'd arrested Robert Sinclair, he'd been caught in a whirlwind of activity. Statements were given. He'd traveled back to the bayou shack to walk through the scene for his report to the FBI. Charlotte had been busy as well, and he'd barely spent more than a few minutes alone with her.

He'd texted her, saying he was coming over. So she should be home. He knocked again. A moment later, the door swung open.

"I'm sorry." Charlotte stood at the screen door, waving him inside. "I was on the phone with Chief Gunther. He's extending my leave to six weeks."

"How do you feel about that?" He hoped she'd use the time to take a vacation. Rest and relax. Leave the trauma behind for a while.

She padded with bare feet through the front room and into the kitchen. "I'm not sure how I feel about being benched for six weeks. Part of me is relieved. I don't have a clear head for investigative work."

"Are you considering a career change?" He accepted a glass of lemonade from Charlotte. Last night, he'd typed his resignation letter to the FBI. While racing through the bayou to rescue Charlotte, not knowing if she was alive or dead, he'd concluded he couldn't continue keeping his heart separate from his work. When he let in all the suppressed emotions, Austin had been left with a clear vision of his future. He knew Caleb, who'd loved Austin like a son, would approve.

"I may decide to leave law enforcement. I'm not sure yet." She shrugged. "I guess that's what these six weeks are partially for." After setting her glass of lemonade down on the counter, she took a deep breath and strode toward him. When she reached him, Charlotte pressed her hand to her heart. "I do know that I don't want you to leave before I lose the nerve to do this." She lifted up on her tiptoes and brushed her lips against his.

The connection felt as light as a feather and struck him with the force of a hurricane.

"I didn't want you to leave before I told you that I love you, Special Agent Austin Walsh." She grinned. "You are a true partner in every sense of the world. Whatever comes next for me and for you, I want you in my life. Maybe with a little less logic and a little more room for love?"

She loved him. His body felt lighter than air. This farewell was an improvement over the last time he'd left. Austin swept her up in his arms. "I've made the decision to end my career chasing criminal and killers. By the time my mentor left the Bureau, he'd waited too long. Caleb was burned out to the point he never recovered. His daughter had been murdered and he'd made it his mission to hunt serial killers. Caleb's mission became mine." The image of Caleb lying in a hospital bed, hooked up to monitors and tubes often came to mind. Caleb had trusted Austin to take over the work of bringing serial killers to justice. But after years of doing just that, he felt his heart move in a different direction.

"Leave the FBI?" Charlotte's eyes widened. "Your work makes a real difference. You save lives."

"I still want to change the world, just go

about it a little differently." For the last two years, he'd been putting together a project that would identify youth with psychological tendencies corresponding with a potential serial killer and attempt to change their outcomes through intervention. "I need to go back to Virginia to collect my belongings, but I'm coming back to Presque."

"You're not needed to testify until the trial begins, which will be a while."

"You said you love me, right? Or did my ears play a trick on me?"

She nodded and wrapped her arms around his waist. "I did and I do."

"I love you too." He kissed the tip of her nose. "I'm returning soon because I don't want to be away from you any more than I have to. I want to take you out on a date, with good food and wine and no talk of murders or killers."

"I'd really like that," she said with a laugh. "So tell me about this different path you see yourself on. Is there room for me to travel alongside you? Another partnership, perhaps?"

"My darling Charlotte." He leaned in for another kiss. "I wouldn't want it any other way."

★ ★ ★ ★ ★

Romantic Suspense

Danger. Passion. Drama.

Available Next Month

Targeted With A Colton Beth Cornelison
A Spy's Secret Rachel Astor

....

Vanished In Texas Karen Whiddon
Christmas Bodyguard Katherine Garbera

....

LOVE INSPIRED

Trail Of Threats Jessica R. Patch
Unravelling Killer Secrets Shannon Redmon

Larger Print

....

LOVE INSPIRED

Fugitive Search Dana Mentink
Witness Escape Sami A. Abrams

Larger Print

....

LOVE INSPIRED

Sorority Cold Case Jacquelin Thomas
Hunted In The Mountains Addie Ellis

Larger Print

5 brand new stories each month

Romantic *Suspense*

Danger. Passion. Drama.

MILLS & BOON

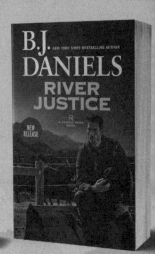

Subscribe and fall in love with a Mills & Boon series today!

You'll be among the first to read stories delivered to your door monthly and enjoy great savings.

WE SIMPLY LOVE ROMANCE